DAISY

ARCHERS CREEK #2

BY

GEMMA WEIR

Daisy

The Archer's Creek Series #2

Copyright © 2020 Gemma Weir

Published by Hudson Indie Ink

www.hudsonindieink.com

Daisy/Gemma Weir – 2nd ed.

ISBN-13 - 978-1-913769-94-9

For mom, it's okay you can read this one xx

ONE

Daisy

I don't see the point of weddings.

It's the 21st century; it's easier to get a divorce than it is to mail a letter. So what's the fucking point in bothering to get married?

Today is Echo and Liv's wedding day. Echo's been counting down the days until he gets to claim his woman in the eyes of the law. He owns her ass in every other way, but according to Echo, a wedding makes it official. That girl ran like the Devil himself was chasing her all the way back to England, and Echo chased right after her. Those two were meant to be together, and he brought her back home, to the Sinners where she belongs. Liv's a hell of a fucking old lady. Maybe if I found someone like her, I'd consider tying myself down permanently, but I doubt it.

I quietly chuckle to myself as I watch Echo fidget nervously at the front of the makeshift aisle. I don't understand why the fucker's worried, we all know Liv's coming. Pulling in a bored sigh, I lean back in my seat, stretching my legs out in front of me as far as I can.

Tipping my head back, I stare at the clouds slowly drifting across the sky. I rotate my neck to the side and that's when I see her. Long blonde hair, so white it's practically fucking glittering in the sunshine. A tight, round ass and perfect legs. I will her to turn around and beg the fucking gods that she's as gorgeous from the front as she is from the back. She steps slightly to the side, pushing her hair behind her ear and I glimpse absolute fucking perfection.

She's a walking wet dream. Her profile shows a hint of small perky tits, pouty lips, and a gorgeous face. Leaning forward, I peer around the people in front of me to try to get a better look at her. The flowery dress she's wearing covers her from her knees to her neck but even the loose fabric can't hide how stunning she is.

She's talking to some dude at the side of the makeshift altar, but I can't tear my eyes from her long enough to care who he is. Her head is bowed forward, and her hands are clasped together in front of her. Her body language screams at me and unthinking I rise from my chair.

Blade's hand on my arm grabs my attention and I slowly force myself to look at him. "Daisy, sit the fuck down; Liv's gonna be here any minute." I nod and lower myself back into my seat. Unable to help myself, I glance back to the girl. Her shoulders are slumped, she's withering into herself and she looks small and lonely. Her waterfall of white blonde hair shields her face completely and I watch her hands fidget nervously, bunching and releasing the fabric in the front of her skirt. She's a picture of sadness and sudden unexpected anger builds in my chest.

I force my eyes away from the girl and focus on the guy standing in front of her. Mayor fucking Jefferies, a pillar of the Archer's Creek community and a douchebag of the highest order. His piggy face is red and angry, and I try to read his lips, but he's speaking too quickly for me to make out any words.

My legs twitch, urging me to move. My mind's screaming at me to go to her, to cross the field and shelter her from whatever is making her cower. I move on autopilot and shuffle past the other guests sat in the row. As I walk toward her, I can hear Blade calling me, but I ignore him. He's not important right now.

A low buzz of excitement prickles across my skin, the feeling intensifying with every step closer to her I take. My mind blocks out everything around me and all I can see is her. My sole focus is getting to this girl.

When I'm only a few feet away from her, I hear Mayor douchebag's affected voice. I'm not sure if he's trying to pretend he's a big city politician, but someone needs to tell him the fake

Yankee accent makes him sound like a dick. "Young lady, you shouldn't be here," the mayor grunts.

I don't hear the girl's response, but I increase my pace reaching them a moment later. "Mayor, it's a beautiful day for a wedding, isn't it?" I say, smiling brightly.

Mayor douchebag lifts his head and scowls at me. "Can I help you?" he asks snootily.

I flash him my brightest smile, flicking my eyes to the girl next to me, then back to him. "Liv's gonna be here any minute, this might be a good time to take your seat," I say.

The girl's head slowly lifts, the waterfall of her hair parts, and I get a glimpse of pale, freckled skin. The mayor moves forward, but I sidestep, blocking his path. I turn to the girl and hold out my hand. "I'm sorry, it seems the mayor's forgotten his manners. We haven't been introduced. I'm Daisy."

Her head snaps up and her face comes fully into view. Huge copper-colored eyes stare back at me. Her high cheekbones lead to full pink lips, a slight smile twitching at the edges. She slowly reaches forward and takes my hand. When her skin connects with mine I wrap my fingers around hers and squeeze gently. Her eyes widen dramatically and her lips part as she starts to speak.

"Angelique, you need to leave right now. I won't tell you again," the mayor snaps.

She instantly reacts to his voice. I watch the spark in her eyes fade, her mouth closes, and her head falls forward. Her hair cascades around her face until she's hidden once again, and her hand becomes limp in mine. She silently pulls free, turns from me and walks away.

Like an idiot, I watch her go.

TWO

Angel

With my head down, I scurry past the rows of guests and rush toward my mama's Toyota Prius. Unlocking the door, I slide into the driver's seat and brace my hands against the steering wheel.

Daisy. A silly name for such a beautiful boy.

No, not a boy; a man—most definitely a man. Shamelessly, I'd allowed my eyes to rake over him. He was tall and slim; but with toned, muscular arms patterned with colorful tattoos. His scruffy blond hair and beard seemed to mask his age, but I'd guess at early twenties.

He was a biker and like nearly all the other men at the wedding, he was wearing one of the black leather vests all the Sinners wore. At first glance he'd looked too young to be a biker, but when our eyes met, there was a maturity and a hardness in his gaze I hadn't expected.

He was the first person, other than my parents, who had spoken to me in weeks. When he'd reached out to shake my hand, I was so surprised I'd reciprocated without even thinking about it. His grip had been gentle, and his thumb had rubbed circles on my skin.

I wanted to speak to him. I'd opened my mouth to tell him my name, but I missed my chance. Instead my father had interrupted, and I'd run away like a child.

Tears pool in my eyes and my father's voice rings in my ears. I start to replay what had happened with him before Daisy had arrived.

There were so many people there. Cautiously, I skirted the crowd and spotted my father talking to a group of people, at the side of the rows of wedding seating. Approaching him silently, I gently placed my hand on his suit jacket to let him know I was there. The moment his gaze landed on me, his cheerful face darkened and grabbing me around the wrist he dragged me away from the group, squeezing my wrist tightly. "Angelique, what the hell are you doing here?" he snapped angrily.

In the face of his anger I instantly dropped my head forward and stared at the ground. "Mama sent me; you forgot your cellphone."

He dropped my wrist, and I fought the urge to cradle my sore skin. "I don't want you around these types of people," he sneered, his eyes flitting from right to left.

"Why not? It's just a wedding," I asked, confusion clear in my tone.

My father scoffed and took a menacing step closer. "Exactly, Angelique. You don't see the problem because you're an idiot."

This wasn't the first time he'd told me I was an idiot. This wasn't even the first time he'd told me today. My father loved to remind me that I was stupid. His face was red now and his words had become an angry hiss. "These people are bikers—criminal scum. The Doomsday Sinners are bottom feeders who should be run out of Archer's Creek."

I spoke before I thought and instantly wished I could take back the words. "Mama says they're nice folk."

He laughed, a dry haughty sound that made me tense. "Nice. Nice. Well your mama's an idiot too, always has been and always will be. The Doomsday Sinners are dangerous, they'd chew up and spit out a little moron like you. I don't ever want to see you near any of them ever again."

There was no point arguing. Answering him back wouldn't end well, so instead I nodded. "Yes, Sir."

His voice dropped lower and his words seethed from him. "I'm serious, Angelique. Unless you want to end up like your sister, a biker whore. She got in with those bastards and look what happened to her. She's dead."

His daughter was dead. Why wasn't his voice cracking with emotion at the acknowledgment that his oldest child was no longer alive? He sounded like he enjoyed saying the words and I silently gritted my teeth together, forcing the angry accusation that was desperate to escape to stay on my tongue. I pushed the words down, squeezed the fabric of my dress between my clenched fists and stayed quiet.

I wanted to leave, to run away from my awful father and his nasty diatribe of insults. But I didn't. Instead, I stayed still and let him angrily dishonor the memory of my sister. "Your sister was a slut who couldn't keep her legs closed. She sullied our good name and made a fool of me. I refuse to allow you to behave like that too. Just look at you, all fancied up. Is that why you're here, to look for a biker to whore yourself out to?"

Overwhelmed with shame at his words, I dropped my chin until it nearly touched my chest. My hair fell around my face, hiding me from his anger and horrible insinuations. I clasped my hands together tightly and fought the urge to scream that I wasn't a whore and neither was Nicole.

My sister fell in love and then she died. I was never allowed to grieve for her. Instead I'd spent the last two years listening to him sully her memory and call her mean and nasty names. My sister was a good person. She sheltered me from him, but now she was gone.

His vicious words continued and like normal I stood quietly and took them. "I won't have another promiscuous daughter. I will correct the mistakes your sister made with you. You're too stupid to make sensible decisions by yourself, just like your mother. I don't know what I did to deserve such idiots in my life."

Silently I listened, never responding, ignoring his vindictive diatribe. Hidden behind my hair, I drifted away inside my head, humming the tune that had got me through his rants ever since I was a child. His voice rose until he was almost shouting. "Young lady, you shouldn't be here."

Black leather boots appeared next to my father's pretentious shiny loafers, and the smell of clean, woody aftershave wafted through the air. Lifting my head, I got my first glimpse of the man that smelled so delicious.

My father spoke, but we ignored him. The man reached out his hand and I took it. My skin tingled the moment it connected with his, and for one blissful moment I forgot who I was, and who my father was.

I was just a girl meeting a boy.

I snap back to reality. My fingers are clenched tightly around the steering wheel in front of me and I force my breathing to return to normal. Usually after dealing with my obnoxious father, I'm numb. I survive his behavior by zoning out and disconnecting from my emotions.

But today, despite my father I'm smiling.

Because I met a man—a beautiful man.

And I want to see him again.

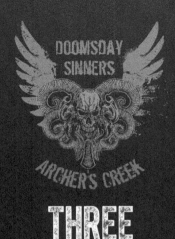

THREE

Daisy

I watch Angelique until she disappears out of sight. I'm a fucking Sinner and the club attracts a lot of beautiful women, but none of them compare to her.

"Stay the hell away from my daughter," Mayor douchebag's angry voice snarls.

I slowly turn and glare at him until he flinches. Turning my back on him, I continue to stare at the spot where Angelique went out of sight, hoping she'll reappear.

She dresses like she's Amish. In her shapeless dress, with her makeup free face, and that air of fragility that surrounds her, she should be forgettable. But instead, I have a feeling her eyes will be etched into my brain forever. The wide, doe-eyed look has never done anything for me in the past, only on her it's different. She's different.

Far too young, much too innocent, and the mayor's daughter!

Mayor Jefferies edges away from me and slinks back to his seat. I don't know why Echo and Liv invited the asshole, and after getting a glimpse at how he speaks to his daughter I want to punch him in the face more than normal.

Reluctantly, I walk back to my row, shuffle back to my spot and sit down. Blade raises his eyebrows, "What the fuck was that about?" he asks.

I smile cockily, "Did you know that Mayor douchebag has a daughter?"

Blade thinks for a minute. "Yeah, Nicole or Natalie, something like that."

I shake my head. "No, her name is Angelique. Young, blonde, fucking gorgeous."

Blade's expression blanks. "Sorry, Prospect, doesn't ring any bells."

I know the exact moment Liv's car pulls up because Echo tenses, then pulls back his shoulders ready for action. I watch him, watch her, and see the physical reaction Liv has on him. All it takes is a glimpse of a smile and he calms. His woman is here.

The wedding is quick and relatively painless. Liv looks hot in a bridal sort of way. Her white dress hugs her tits and it's not too puffball or flouncy. Echo growls through the vows, his face only breaking momentarily into a wide smile when Liv promises to honor and obey. The minute the service ends, Echo drags Liv into his arms and kisses her, only pulling back long enough to throw her over his shoulder and disappear into the clubhouse.

With the happy couple missing, the Old Ladies set to work organizing the BBQ and buffet. The smell of charcoal and steak wafts past me and my stomach growls. The cold bottle of beer in my hand drips icy water onto my fingers as I watch Mayor douchebag. Even from a distance I can see the sweat glistening on his forehead. His piggy face is bright red as he moves from group to group working the party crowd.

I've never liked the guy, but something about the way Angelique cowered from him has anger bubbling in my stomach and my eyes narrowing as I glare at him across the meadow. My view is suddenly blocked and Anders, the Sinners' President steps in front of me.

Anders is an intense guy. Honestly, he scares the fuck out of me. If he tells me to do something, I fucking do it. His heavy palm settles on my shoulder and he glances behind him at the partygoers before turning his attention back to me. I inwardly flinch when his fingers tighten around my shoulder, squeezing tightly. "Daisy, a word in my office please."

Fuck.

Cautiously, I follow him through the clubhouse, frantically wracking my brain to see what the fuck I could have done wrong. You don't get called into the Prez's office without good reason. I've either majorly fucked up and I'm gonna get the shit kicked out of me, or I'm fucking out. The Sinners are my life, if they kick me out I don't have anything else.

I've never wished so hard for a beating.

Anders holds open the door and gestures for me to walk ahead. I tentatively move through the room and stand behind the chairs in front of his desk, trying not to look like a nervous pussy. The door shuts and after circling the desk he lowers himself into his chair. Pulling in nervous breaths, I wait silently for what feels like hours until he gestures for me to sit. I lower myself into the seat and lean forward, bracing my elbows on my knees and clenching my hands into fists in my lap.

"Daisy, how long have you been a prospect for?" Anders asks brusquely.

Blowing out a shaky breath I respond. "About eighteen months, Prez."

Anders nods thoughtfully. "You spent a lot of time on security detail for Echo's old lady."

Echo nearly broke my neck the day Liv disappeared, but no one had mentioned that I let her slip away from me. I should have fucking known this was coming. I'm gonna get fucking kicked out of the Sinners over a fucking woman, and not even my fucking woman.

I sit up straighter in my seat and brace myself for the worst. "Yeah, I did."

Anders eyeballs me, but I force myself to meet his glare. *Never back down.* One of the only useful things my time in foster care taught me. "What else have you done, while you've been a prospect?" Anders asks.

"Whatever's been asked of me, Prez," I reply.

The silence is suffocating. "You enjoy being a prospect?" Anders asks.

Still holding his gaze, I respond. "I want to be a Sinner. I have to pay my dues."

Anders nods decisively and looks down, rummaging for something under his desk. He pulls out a cardboard box from somewhere by his feet and slides it across the desk. He motions for me to pick it up, then leans back in his chair, a relaxed smugness oozing from him. "Open it," he says.

Cautiously, I pull the box toward me and onto my lap. The box is light, and I fight the urge to shake it like a kid. The center seam is sealed with tape and I peel it from the edge, slowly lifting the flaps to reveal the contents.

The smell hits me first. Leather. My mouth drops open as I open the box further, revealing the Doomsday Sinners emblem, bold against the soft black leather. I rub my thumbs against my fingertips, then reach into the box and reverently lift the fabric out, turning it over in my hands. The patch on the front reads *Daisy*.

Choking back emotion, I close my eyes for a second before looking from the cut in my hands to Anders. My voice breaks as I try to speak. I cough and clear my throat. "You're patching me in?"

For the first time since we met, warmth and joy radiates

from the president's broad smile. "Welcome to the Doomsday Sinners, brother," Anders says.

My breath catches as I look back down at the cut in my hands. I'm a Sinner. The club is my family, and this is my home. Pride fills my chest and standing I slide the cut over my shoulders, pushing my arms through until it sits snugly against my chest. Gripping the edges, I lift my shoulders to straighten it, and smell the strong scent of the soft leather beneath my fingers. I stare down at the patch with my name on and pull in a deep emotion-filled breath.

Anders rises from his seat and moves toward me. Clapping me on the shoulder he pulls me into a quick hug. "Well, brother, I think it's time to celebrate."

Stepping ahead of me, he opens the door and leads a path through the clubhouse and into the meadow where Echo and Liv's reception is taking place. I silently follow behind him, still shocked at the unexpected twist the day has taken.

"Brothers, I give you our newest Sinner," Anders roars.

A crowd of people all break into whoops and hollers, and I'm pulled into the fray of congratulations. Echo and Liv push through the crowd until they're standing in front of me. "Congratulations, brother," Echo says, pulling me into an unexpected hug.

He steps back, releasing me and allowing Liv to launch herself into my arms. "Well done, Daisy," she cries.

I smile brightly and wink at Liv. "I thought I was getting

kicked out or a beating. I wasn't expecting my patch."

A heavy arm slaps down around my shoulders and I turn to see Blade. "We all voted on it last week, brother. You've worked hard, you deserve that patch."

Smoke and Puck join us. Both congratulate me. Smoke passes me a beer and raises his own into the air. "To Echo and Liv, well done on getting hitched; and to Daisy for earning his patch and becoming a fully-fledged Sinner," he shouts. We all raise our drinks and toast.

The day fades to night, and the party turns wild. Echo and Liv disappeared hours ago, and their wedding guests have all slowly started to drift away. Leaning against the bar my beer hangs from my fingers. I watch the guys move across the room, leisurely crowding around me until I'm surrounded. They're a motley group of bikers: big, small, fat, thin; these men are my brothers, my family.

Blade steps forward. "Daisy, when we patch in a new member we get them a gift. Here's yours."

His smile is huge and smug. The crowd parts and a brunette and a redhead step forward. "Ladies," I say with a smile. The women strut across the floor and don't stop until they're pressed one against either side of my chest. Laughing, I throw an arm around each of them and pull them in for a three-way kiss.

A roar of cheers explodes around us, but I concentrate on the girls, eventually pulling back to see the guys have lost interest in us and have gone back to partying.

The redhead giggles, leaning forward to whisper in my ear. "Congratulations, baby. I'm Bethy-Anne and this is Erica. We can't wait to be your gift. What do you want to do with us?"

The brunette's hand slides down my cut until she's cupping my dick beneath my jeans. Her fingers stroke along my length teasingly. I grab at her hand and stop her. She pouts sulkily, until I take hold of their hands and lead them away from the bar, toward my room at the back of the club.

Opening the door, I gesture for them to go ahead of me, then close and lock the door behind me. Both girls turn to face me. They glance at each other, then start to strip until they're both completely naked. A smile twitches at my lips as I let my gaze drop to their feet, slowly traveling upwards until I've looked my fill. Rubbing my thumb over my bottom lip, I raise my eyebrow expectantly. The girls giggle then step closer to one another and kiss.

Red told me their names, but I don't care enough to remember. She smiles at me, then reaches out to cup the brunette's breasts, tugging at her nipples. The brunette's head falls back, and she moans loudly. I clear my throat; the girls pause and turn toward me. "Girls, I'm feeling left out over here."

Red rushes over and reaches for my cut, but I grab hold of her arm to stop her. Sliding off my cut, I place it carefully over the back of a chair and then turn back to the naked women. At twenty-one I'm young, but I'm hardly a fucking virgin; hell, this isn't even my first threesome. I know what I want and apparently so do these girls.

I pull my T-shirt over my head and drop it to the floor. "Ladies, this isn't a spectator sport, at least one of you should be on your knees sucking my cock." Both girls drop to their knees and my dick twitches at the sight of their plump wet mouths, just desperate for a taste of me. Stepping out of my shoes, I unbutton my jeans, and push them and my boxers to the floor, kicking them to the side.

Both girl's eyes widen dramatically when their gazes drop to my semi-hard cock. I smile smugly. I know I've got a big dick, but the look a woman gets when she sees the size always amuses me. Wrapping my hand around my thick girth, I stroke my fingers up and down the length.

I step toward Red and stop in front of her. Releasing my cock, I touch her cheek with the tips of my fingers. "Do you want to suck me, Red?" I ask. She licks her lips and nods. Smiling salaciously, I grab my dick and move until my tip is level with her mouth. "Open up, baby, take me as deep as you can; I wanna feel the back of your throat."

Red opens wide and I feed my length into her mouth. She immediately sucks in her cheeks, swallowing me, until her mouth is so full of my dick she chokes. My eyes roll back in pleasure as she goes to work on my cock, sucking and licking my length. "That's it, baby, suck me. That's so good, so fucking good," I murmur.

I close my eyes and enjoy the feeling of Red's warm, hot

tongue swiping up and down my cock. But instead of focusing on the gorgeous and very willing redhead sucking on me, a vision of Angelique pops into my mind. The beautiful, ethereal blonde, with those huge doe eyes and an innocence that makes her the perfect kind of untouchable.

Fuck.

My dick hardens and Red groans. I feel the vibrations along the length of my cock and my eyes crash open. The fantasy dissolves and instead of seeing an angel, I'm looking down at the two women at my feet.

What the fuck is wrong with me? I'm about to have a threesome and all I can think about is the fucking blonde angel that screams untouched virgin.

I flex my fingers and force myself to forget about Angelique and concentrate on the brunette who has moved until she's behind Red. Her hand is between Red's legs and her arm pumps up and down as she fingers Red's pussy.

Still working my cock with her mouth, Red's eyes are closed. Her legs are spread wide enough for me to see the brunette's fingers as they thrust in and out of her wet pussy. The brunette lifts her head until our eyes lock. She flashes me a teasing smile and pulls her fingers from Red's pussy and sucks them into her mouth.

Grabbing a handful of Red's hair, I pull her mouth off my dick. "Ladies, I think it's time to really get this celebration started. Red, go lie on the bed, I want your legs spread wide, so I can watch your pussy get licked and finger-fucked by your friend. Hang your head off the end, so I can fuck your face until I come down your throat," I say with a grin.

Red jumps up from the floor and giggles excitedly as she rushes across the room. She hurries into position, her mouth open and waiting for me. The brunette crawls between Red's legs, wrapping her fingers around Red's thighs and pushing them wider. The brunette looks up at me and winks before dramatically licking a long, wet line from Red's pussy to her clit. I saunter across the room toward Red's waiting mouth, and she watches me, waiting for me to get close. As soon as I'm close enough, her hands reach out and grab my cock.

Eager to get back inside her hot, wet mouth, I take a step closer until her lips are wrapped around me and she starts to suck. Biting down on my lip, I groan in pleasure. Any blowjob's a good blowjob, but Red's a pro and the free porn show I'm getting courtesy of the brunette, makes this a fucking awesome blowjob. The brunette is enthusiastically lapping at Red's pussy like it's the sweetest fucking ice-cream and her hands are between her own legs playing with herself.

My balls are heavy, and my cock twitches with my impending release. Red arches her back and moans as the brunette pushes her fingers deep into Red's pussy and starts to fuck her with them.

The muscles in my stomach tighten and my thighs tense. I'm gonna come soon, but this is a party, not a solo act and I need Red to come too. "Lick her clit and fuck her hard with your fingers. I'm gonna come in a minute and I want you to make her come before I do." I say to the brunette. She nods and her head dips back down to lick at Red's clit whilst her fingers plunge in and out of her wet pussy. Red tenses, her mouth tightening around my dick as her orgasm pulses through her. Her moans tip me over the edge and I thrust forward, spilling my seed down her throat.

With a groan I pull out of Red's mouth, and she smiles, licking her lips like my cum is the best thing she's ever tasted. "On your hands and knees, Red. I wanna fuck that ass of yours, you good with that?" I say.

She rolls over and nods. "Baby, you can put that massive cock wherever you want," she purrs.

God, club girls are easy. They just wanna be fucked by as many bikers, in as many ways, as possible. I almost want to tell her to get some self-respect, but who the fuck am I to talk? I've got two beautiful women who want to engage in a little dirty partying. I'll keep my opinions to myself.

I grab my length and shout. "Hell yes, ladies! Red, your friend over here is gonna get that ass of yours ready for me while I fuck her wet, patient pussy."

I fucking love being twenty-one. I emptied my balls a minute ago, but as Red turns onto her hands and knees, and the brunette spreads her wide, licking at Red's tight asshole, my cock twitches and starts to harden again.

Walking over to my dresser, I grab a bottle of lube and a condom. I rip open the foil wrapper and slide it over my now fully hard cock. The brunette's working away at Red's asshole but sensing my presence behind her, she pauses and looks over her shoulder. Swaying her ass, she slowly spreads her legs and displays her dripping pussy for me. "Fuck, baby, licking Red's pussy and ass has got you all wet, hasn't it?" I say.

She smiles and nods. "You want me to fuck you, baby?" I ask. I know what her answers gonna be, but I ask anyway.

She nods quickly. "Hard."

I raise my eyebrows and smile. "You work her ass, get it nice and ready for me to fuck and I'll fuck your pussy hard, I promise, baby." She grabs the bottle of lube and squeezes it between Red's ass cheeks. Stepping closer to the brunette, I line my cock up with her pussy and grabbing her hips I plunge forward into her slick sex. Fast and hard, I plough into her, as she pushes back onto me with every thrust.

Still bouncing on my cock, the brunette coats her fingers in lube and works them into Red's asshole. Red moans and wiggles toward her friend, while one, then two fingers disappear deep into her ass. The three of us get into a rhythm: I plunge into the brunette's pussy, and she pushes into Red's ass, then I pull back and she pulls her fingers almost out of Red's ass. In and out my cock slides as I fuck her pussy while she finger-fucks Red.

My eyes drift shut and Angelique flashes in my mind again. I'm literally balls deep in another woman, but my thoughts keep going back to the angel with her waterfall of hair, and the hollow, lost look in her eyes. Red screams, orgasming loudly and I'm forced back to reality. She collapses forward onto the bed with her ass still in the air.

The brunette rests her head on the bed, pushing me deeper inside her. Her pussy immediately tightens, strangling my cock. Reaching between her legs, I find her clit and rub circles over the sensitive bundle of nerves until her muscles tense and she comes with a shout. I thrust twice more and groan, spilling my cum into the condom.

Two hours later, both girls are asleep in my bed. I pull on my jeans and sink down into a chair, resting my bare feet on the bedside dresser. Grabbing my beer from the side, I take a deep pull on the bottle. The warm liquid flows down my throat and I grimace.

I should be on cloud nine. I'm a fully patched-in member of The Doomsday Sinners and I just had a threesome with two beautiful women. I fucked every hole on both of them and they loved every fucking minute. But I feel unsatisfied. How that's possible when I've come four times in three hours, I don't know.

My mind should be clear, peaceful. But instead it's full. My head falls back until it's resting on the back of the chair. I close my eyes and all I can see is those pools of sadness.

Angelique. She looks like a perfect, fucking angel, and when I should be focused on the two naked women in my bed, all I can think about is her.

FOUR

Angel

My dad's voice drones on, but with my head bowed, I pretend to be submissive and hide in the safety of my mind. Almost every day since Nicole left, I've coped by retreating inside myself, to a place where my dad's words don't hurt me; where my mama's weakness doesn't devastate me; and where my sister's death doesn't feel like the worst kind of betrayal.

This is the first time in over a year where instead of withdrawing to the blissful blackness of my mind, I see a technicolor picture of *him*.

Daisy.

I remember every detail: the blond hair, the scruffy beard, the strong arms covered in colorful tattoos. I don't even know him, but somehow, he's become my safe place—my escape.

Strong hands pinch my shoulders, painfully dragging me back to reality.

"Angelique, you idiot. Are you even listening?" my father screams at me.

Years of silence, of constantly forcing myself to hold in my words has conditioned me to change the tone of my voice when I speak to my father. He'll take any hint of confidence as disobedience—speak too loudly and I'm aggressive; too quietly and I'm an imbecile. So instead, I use the monotone drawl of the role I'm forced to play. "Yes, Sir. I'm listening."

Without even looking at him, I can picture his face. Red and angry, he always looks the same; like just being around me is unpleasant. If I were braver, I'd tell him I hate being around him too. But instead, like too many times before, I stand silently and take the insults and abuse.

"I don't know what I did to be punished so badly. God must really hate me to lumber me with you and your stupid mother for the rest of my life. Where the hell am I going to find a husband who's prepared to take on someone like you? At least you're not plain, I suppose that's something you've got going for you. I'm sure your husband can train you to stand silently at his side and look pretty. That's all your mother's ever been good for, at least until she lost her looks," he sneers.

Husband? For a moment I forget to zone him out, years of practice shattered in the blink of an eye. I do the unthinkable, I lift my head and words spill from me before I consider them.

"I'm eighteen. I'm not getting married, I'm going to college."

His eyes bulge in his head, a frown forces his lips down at the sides and then he laughs. The coarse sound is mean, a fake laugh intended to belittle me. I brace myself for his reaction. I'd almost prefer violence than the biting sting of words that bury themselves into my soul, still festering years later, rotting me from the inside out.

Bruise's fade, but years of emotional torture tattoos itself onto your soul.

"College. You? Ha, they don't let morons into college," he snarls. Stepping closer, he grabs my chin between his fingers, squeezing painfully. He forces my face up until I have to either look at him or close my eyes.

I might be silent, but I refuse to be defeated by him. I listen to his insults and mentally store them all.

"You're a stupid little moron who will never amount to anything. You're too ignorant to go to college; they'd laugh you out of the place on the first day when they realized how much of an idiot you are," he shouts.

I pull in a silent breath and brace myself for his onslaught. He's on a roll, a glint of excitement in his eyes.

"The only thing you're good for is making someone a pretty little doll that does exactly as she's told. Just like your mother, and your sister if she hadn't turned into a desperate slut who whored herself out to anyone who smiled at her."

He drops my chin, but I steel my shoulders. He hasn't

finished yet. He's enjoying himself. Abusing me and my mama is one of his favorite things.

"Now, if you're a good little idiot, I'll find you a nice husband who'll be happy with a dimwit for a wife. But if I ever hear any of this college nonsense again I won't be so particular over who I let marry you. Maybe that's what you need, someone to beat some sense into you?"

He leans in closer, so he can whisper into my ear. I force myself not to cower even as revulsion eats away at my flesh. I want to push him away, but I refuse to give him the satisfaction of knowing he's got to me.

"That's what I had to do. I had to take a belt to your stupid mother over and over again until she learned how to be quiet and pretty."

I force my body to stay rigid, but on the inside, I'm shaking from head to toe from a mixture of rage and fear. His coarse laugh and smug smile taunt me as he steps back. I dig my nails into the palms of my hands and force myself not to speak. Squeezing my fists tightly, I feel the skin break, the pain a balm for the emotion pulsing through me. My hands burn, the familiar feeling is the only reason I don't reach for the closest thing I can use as a weapon and attack him with it.

His eyes roam over me and obviously finding me wanting he walks away; his disgusting smile is the last thing I see before he turns his back to me. I wait until he leaves the room and the door to his office clicks shut, then I grab a cushion from the sofa, hold it against my face and scream into it.

Tears fall down my cheeks, but I'm not upset, I'm angry. No, I'm furious.

Turning on the spot, I stare at the front door. The verbal attack I've just endured will be nothing to what I'll get if I sneak out, but I can't stay in his house for another moment. I check over my shoulder, just in case he's sneaking up behind me, but the room's still empty. Rushing for the door I throw it open and step outside, carefully pulling it closed behind me.

Fresh air surrounds me, and I pull in a deep cleansing breath. Thoughts of returning to the house makes my shoulders tense. I back away in jerky steps and then I'm running, away from my home and toward the freedom of our tiny town of Archer's Creek.

Head down, I run down the sidewalk, desperate to get as far away from our house and my father as possible. My heart pounds in my chest and realizing running is conspicuous, I slow down to a walk, but still move as fast as I can. I barely take notice of my surroundings and let my feet guide me along the familiar streets. I don't know where I'm running too. It doesn't matter. Anywhere is better than at home, with that monster. I hurry around a corner just off Main Street and run straight into someone.

I bounce off a hard chest and land on my butt on the sidewalk. Disoriented, I sit on the floor with my hair falling over my eyes and hiding my face. Gentle fingers part my hair, tucking the strands behind my ears. I lift my eyes and my breath catches. It's him.

"Hello, Angel," Daisy says.

DOOMSDAY SINNERS

ARCHER'S CREEK

FIVE

Daisy

Her eyes are just as I remember them, a deep copper color that should be full of life, but hers are dull and listless. As we stare at each other, I watch her pupils dilate, a spark of something glinting enticingly. Reaching out, I take hold of her hand and lift her to her feet. Once she's standing, I keep hold of her, enjoying her small, warm palm, resting in mine. Her eyes are wide, her expression shocked, and she drops her gaze to where our hands are joined before silently looking back up at me.

I didn't notice how small she was the first time we met; her head barely reaches my shoulder. Her hand tenses and she starts to pull her fingers from mine, but I don't want her to run away, so I tighten my grip. She flinches. I drop my eyes to her hand and slowly slide my fingers underneath hers until her palm rests on top of mine. Dried blood coats four small cuts on her soft skin. "What happened, Angel? Did you cut yourself?" I ask, concern lacing my voice.

Her copper gaze moves to look at her palms. Seeing the cuts and blood she tilts her head to the side in wonderment. I prompt her again, "What happened?" She pulls her bottom lip between her teeth and worries the skin as if she's unsure how to speak.

"I don't know." Her voice is quiet, but strong, almost melodic.

"You're bleeding, Angel. How didn't you notice?"

She shrugs and looks down again, turning both of her hands over. The other palm has matching cuts and her skin is stained red with blood.

Carefully, I reach out and wrap my fingers around her wrists. She stiffens beneath my touch and I feel her shake. I bend my knees and lower myself until we're level, eye to eye. "You need to clean these cuts, Angel." I say, keeping my voice quiet and unthreatening.

This girl is throwing warning signs left, right and center. She's the mayor's fucking daughter, she's dressed like she's from the fifties, and she's fucking scared silent. Why the fuck I'm not dusting her off and sending her on her way I honestly don't know.

Her eyes are full of complete desolation and I can't seem to look away. She's tiny and fragile, and young—so fucking young my jailbait alarm should be screaming in my head. But I don't even care if I never get to lay a single hand on her, I just can't leave her.

We stand frozen in the middle of the street and just stare at each other. She doesn't speak, and I don't release her. We're both lost in a silent standoff, but at least for me this isn't war, it's the ultimate peace. Just touching her soothes me, the feeling of distance I get from my normal life has dissolved and heat pulses through me from the spot where my skin touches hers.

"You should probably let me go," she says, smiling quickly before it fades, and nonchalance replaces it.

I nod in agreement, but my grip doesn't falter. "I probably should. But I don't want to," I say frankly.

When she smiles this time, her whole face comes to life. I watch as every feature becomes animated: her nose twitches and her eyebrows lift. Her smile changes her entire being. She stands straighter and for a second, I watch her blossom, a glimpse at the happiness that should glow constantly from her.

"You have a beautiful smile, Angel." I say.

I see the moment she starts to retreat back inside herself, and panic-stricken I search my brain for something, anything, to do to prolong her happiness. Fear fills me, fear of seeing the desolately stricken sadness that I'm sure will engulf her eyes once the glow fades.

I drop her wrist and slide my hand around her waist, pulling her into my chest. With my other hand I reach out and tuck a strand of her hair behind her ear. Running my finger tip along her jaw I lift her chin and gently lead her to my waiting lips.

SIX

Angel

Captured against his chest, he kisses me.

His lips coax mine in a gentle caress, urging me to respond but not demanding. He never forces my compliance and when my eyelids flutter closed, I melt into him.

He's a complete stranger, but in the space of a mere moment he's forced me out the blackness and given me light. Fireworks explode behind my eyes and I sink deeper into his embrace, my lips begging for more. His tongue strokes against my lower lip, asking for admission and I eagerly allow him entrance.

He plunges his tongue into my mouth and tingles start in my fingers, gradually moving along my skin, until I feel alive for the first time in years. Lifting my arms, I wrap them around his shoulders and tangle my tongue with his, pushing closer into his hard chest.

Far too quickly I feel him start to pull away. The kiss slows, finally ending when he leans back, separating his lips from mine. Dropping my arms to my sides, I still, unsure if I should turn and run, or stay and hope he'll kiss me again.

His hands lift to cup my cheeks, and I force my eyes to focus on him. "Angel, what the hell are you doing to me?" he asks. His lips dip again, barely brushing over mine before he pulls back. "Come on, let's go get those hands cleaned up."

Confused, I reach for his arm. "Why did you kiss me?"

Stepping close to me, he touches my lips with his thumb and when he speaks, his voice is rough. "I don't know. You've been all I can see when I close my eyes since that day at the wedding. I've never kissed an angel before."

His strong fingers wrap around my wrist and I let him lead me down the street for a few steps before I pause. My shoulders slump as reality rushes back. "I can't go with you."

Daisy stops and turns to face me. "Why?"

"My father. He hates you guys. He'd kill me if he found out I was talking to you."

Daisy flashes me a confident smile. "Who's gonna tell him, Angel?"

I want to go with him, but it's too much of a risk. If my father found out, it could ruin everything I've worked so hard for. My escape, my chance to get away from my father's prison and take my mama with me could be shattered to pieces. I can't risk it.

"I'm sorry," I say as I pull my wrist from his fingers and walk away.

SEVEN

Daisy

As I watch her walk away, I question if I should chase after her. Is this all a game? Does she want me to chase her? She seems guileless but surely nobody's that innocent?

Staring at her back, I take in her outfit. Another ugly dress, plain and shapeless. But despite her clothes, her sadness, and her innate ability to seem constantly terrified, she exudes a sensuality I've never seen in a woman before. It's natural; there's no primping or artificial sexiness. Angel's just graceful and poised, quietly sexy, so that you can't help but notice her, even when she's hiding.

My feet move without my consent and I follow behind her, quickly striding until I'm walking at her side. I throw my arm over her shoulders and she squeals and turns to look at me. She stumbles over her own feet and I tighten my grip to stop her from falling. "Careful," I say.

Her arms shoot out as she tries to regain her balance and I hold her close, until she tries to shrug out from under my arm. "Daisy, you need to let me go. You don't understand what will happen if my father finds out we've been talking," she says, her eyes wide and imploring.

Everything about her body language tells me to pull her closer and keep her in the shelter of my arms. But instead I lift my arm from her shoulders, clenching my hands into fists as they hang at my sides.

She turns her head toward me and her eyes try to convey something, but all I see in their depths is conflict. Her head lowers, blonde hair falling across her face as she walks and seconds later she's completely shielded from me.

"Angel." Unable to leave her and unwilling to allow her to withdraw within herself, I pull in a deep breath and try to think of somewhere we could go that would be inconspicuous and away from her father's prying eyes.

Walking beside her, I reach out and tuck her hair behind one tiny ear, stopping myself from pulling her into my arms again. "What if we could go somewhere that no one could see us? Where the mayor would have no idea that we were together."

She pauses and slowly turns to face me. "Daisy, I'm not going to sleep with you."

Her cheeks tinge pink and I puff out a quick laugh, lifting

my hands in front of me. "Whoa, have I ever mentioned fucking you?"

Embarrassment makes her cheeks turn bright red, and her gaze lowers again. I stop her chin with my finger and lift her head back up. I bend my knees until we're eye-to-eye. "Angel, I just want to spend some time with you, get to know you. That's all, no expectations. Okay?"

I see the conflict in her eyes. "Why?" she asks.

With that single word she pleads for me to explain, like she's got no idea why I'd want to spend time with her. I touch her lips lightly with mine, hardly a kiss but even that minute touch calms me. "Because you make me feel something," I say honestly.

Her brow wrinkles. "I don't understand," she whispers.

Desperate to feel her close, I pull her into my chest again. Her heart races and mine beats faster in response. I lift her chin up so I can see her eyes and then I speak. "I know you don't understand it, Angel, but I've been numb and distant my entire life. Being around you makes me feel alive. You're a tunnel of light in a lifetime of darkness."

Gemma Weir

EIGHT

Angel

My mouth drops open. I make him feel alive. I feel like he stole those words straight out of my thoughts and I'm so shocked that I struggle to speak. I want to tell him that he makes me feel that way too, but my tongue feels heavy in my mouth. So instead I reach for his hand and entwine my fingers with his.

"Meet me at the playground behind the elementary school in fifteen minutes." Daisy says.

I nod. I don't even try to argue with him. He flashes me a glorious smile and drops my hand, then he turns and walks away. I watch him go until he turns a corner and disappears from view.

Stood alone in the street, I glance around me, searching for anyone who could tell my father what just happened. Life continues, but no one seems to pay me any attention. Why would they? Most people have no idea I even exist. My heart pounds and I pull in a shaky breath, smiling, while my skin tingles and every nerve ending pulses with both terror and excitement.

Meeting him is silly and reckless. I should turn around and go home before my father realizes I've gone. But being around Daisy is the first time in years that I don't feel stupid, or useless. It's the first time in forever I forgot my mama is a doormat and my sister is dead, and I want more of that. For whatever reason, Daisy treats me like I'm someone worth spending time with. Is it wrong to crave that?

His lips on mine woke something inside of me. It wasn't my first kiss, but when he looked at me I felt like he was seeing straight past the image I show to the rest of the world. He wasn't seeing the fearful shell of a person that I feel like most days, he was seeing the real me. The one I keep hidden—the brave, worthy person I know I am deep inside.

Full of confidence, I pull back my shoulders and start to walk. I weave a path through side streets and alleys until I reach the elementary school. It's lunchtime and hordes of children are playing, running and laughing. Envy overwhelms me, and the feeling burns in my chest. I'm almost an adult and yet I'm jealous of the freedom afforded to children less than half my age. My life has always been one of expectation and obligation and sometimes I almost envy Nicole. At least before her death she got a glimpse at life; she laughed and smiled and fell in love. She might only have gotten a few short months, but better a moment of happiness than a lifetime of misery.

With my head down, I cross the street and walk past the school. I reach the playground and quickly look around scanning the area, but it's empty. The park is old and shabby, usurped by a new one in the center of town, which opened a year or so ago. The swing-set and jungle gym sit unused and abandoned waiting to be torn down.

He's not here.

Disappointment hits my stomach and wandering over to the single remaining swing I sit on the wooden slats, my hands grasping the cold chain between my fingers. Scraping my shoes along the gravel beneath my feet, I slowly walk my feet backwards a couple of steps. When I lift my feet off the ground the swing sways forward slowly. Hot sun beams down on me as I sit in the empty playground and I tip my head back letting the warmth of the sun coat my skin.

Walking backwards again, this time until my legs are straight, I push up onto my toes and jump up, so the swing rushes forward. Cool air flows past me and I hold my legs out in front of me, leaning back until the swing peaks and I pull my legs beneath me and fly backwards, the momentum propelling me effortlessly through the air.

I don't remember the last time I sat on a swing, but the push and pull becomes second nature and I fly higher and higher. Closing my eyes, I tip my head back and indulge in the freedom of the wind in my hair and the joy of merely swinging back and forth.

I throw my legs in front of me and the swing flies so high that my stomach seems to drop from my body as I cascade backwards. Squeezing my eyes tightly shut, I tip my face to the sky and enjoy the sensation of weightlessness.

The swing starts to slow, and I sway gently to an almost stop and gradually open my eyes. Sitting on top of a picnic table, in front of the swing-set is Daisy. His watchful eyes are focused solely on me as he waits patiently with his elbows rested on his knees.

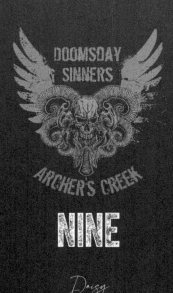

NINE

Daisy

I'd almost convinced myself that getting involved with the mayor's daughter was a really stupid idea and then I stepped into the park and saw her flying through the air on a swing. Her sack dress had ridden up revealing shapely legs. Her skin was pale and porcelain like, her head tipped back, and her hair flowed behind her with the swing's motion. She looked so fucking free.

I'm so drawn to her that before I even know what I'm doing, I'm sitting on a bench just watching. I'm not even touching her but being this close to Angel makes me feel like I've done a couple of lines of coke. Who am I kidding? This girl makes me feel more alive than all the drugs I've ever tried.

Her swinging gradually slows, and she opens her eyes and sees me.

"Hi, Angel."

She visibly swallows and nervously smiles at me. "Hi," she whispers.

I stand from the bench and reach for her. Wrapping my hands around her hips, I lift her from the swing and place her on her feet in front of me. Reaching for her hands, I turn them over, so I can see the cuts. The blood has dried around the small wounds, but I can still see the remains of red blood beneath her fingernails. She must have done this to herself.

Pulling a sealed alcohol wipe from my pocket, I clean the cuts. With the blood cleaned away I can see three perfect nail marks on each palm. I take the tube of antiseptic ointment from my other pocket and gently rub the cream into each cut. Angel stands, silently watching me look after her. Her expression is unreadable, and I lean down and drop a kiss to each of her palms before I straighten and tuck her hair behind her ears.

"Why do you keep doing that?" she asks.

"Doing what?"

Her fingers bunch in her skirt and she agitatedly twists the fabric. When her eyes drop to the floor, I lift her chin, forcing her gaze up to mine. "Doing what, Angel?" I say again.

"Y- you keep, err… You keep moving my hair," she finally stutters out.

Smiling, I dip my head and kiss the corner of her mouth. "I don't like it when you hide, Angel. I want to see your face."

She takes a step back and pulls in a deep breath. "Why do

you keep calling me Angel?" she asks, her voice barely above a whisper.

"Would you rather I call you Angelique?"

She shakes her head with disgust. "No. I hate my name," she says, anger flashing in her expressive eyes.

There's a thousand things I want to ask, but she looks like a scared rabbit and one wrong word could make her run from me. "Do you hate me calling you Angel, too?" I ask warily.

She shakes her head. "No, but no one's ever called me that before."

"That's good," I say. "That means you're only my Angel, nobody else's."

Her eyes widen, then narrow slightly. She doesn't understand what I'm saying, but that's ok for now.

"What do your parents call you?" I ask, taking a small step closer to her. Angel's expression shutters at the mention of her parents and I silently curse myself for bringing them up.

"I should go," she says.

My heart drops. I close the distance between us and pull her into my arms. "Don't go yet."

"What do you want from me, Daisy?"

Her beautiful, musical voice is small and full of insecurity, so I lift her up and carry her over to the bench. Sitting down, I place her in my lap and she instantly tries to get up, but I hold her still. "I don't know what I want, Angel, but just know that I want to be near you. I know that you wake something up in me, something I haven't felt in a really long time. Don't go yet. I just want to sit here with you in my lap and talk to you. Please?"

Self-consciously she pulls down the hem of her dress and I brace myself for her rebuttal. Instead she twists her fingers together in her lap and offers me a small nod.

"Okay," she whispers, so quietly I barely hear her.

I fight the urge to fist pump the air and quickly kiss the top of her head, tucking her hair behind her ears again so I can see her whole face.

Time passes as we sit on the bench in the abandoned park. She doesn't try to move again, but her body is stiff in my lap. I wrap my arms around her and she slowly relaxes in my embrace. "How old are you?" I ask.

I pray to every god out there that she's at least seventeen. I'd still be too old for her but at least she'd be legal. I hold my breath waiting for her to speak.

"Eighteen," she says.

I physically relax.

"How old did you think I was?" She asks, amusement evident in her voice.

"I was praying for at least seventeen," I say. She laughs and light flashes in her eyes.

"Can I kiss you again?" I ask.

She stills and seems to be thinking. "It's only a kiss, Angel," I say.

She nods, and I lean in and take her lips with mine. I kiss

her gently to begin, sweet caresses and light touches. Angel lets out a small moan and I start to lose control; I push my tongue between her lips and dominate her mouth. I half expect her to push me off, but instead she fists her tiny hands into my hair and pulls me closer, her tongue dueling with mine.

Forcing my hands to stay on either side of her face, I cup her cheeks. I don't want to send her running or frighten her by exploring her beautiful body, so I'll go as slow as she needs me to.

She's *my* Angel now and I plan to keep her.

Finally pulling away from her, I rest my forehead on hers, panting heavily. My cock is like steel and pressing against my jeans so hard it fucking hurts. But he definitely isn't coming out to play today, so I pull in a deep breath and attempt to calm the fuck down.

Angel looks shell-shocked. Her lips are pink and swollen from our kisses and her eyes are wide and lust-filled. If I didn't know how innocent she was, I'd think she wanted to jump me.

"I need to go before my father realizes I'm not there," she says breathlessly.

I nod, but my arms stay wrapped around her, holding her close while I breathe in her light, fruity scent. "Where's your phone?" I ask.

Her cheeks tinge pink and she pushes against my hold and moves out of my lap. "I don't have one," she says quietly.

"You don't have a phone?" I say, confused. "What, you

don't have it with you, or you don't have one at all?" I ask.

I can't take my eyes off her as I wait for her to reply. She looks too young and so fucking innocent. Her fingers twist together, and her head begins to drop.

"Angel," I say. She doesn't look at me. Jumping off the bench, I close the distance between us and cup her face, tilting her head back so I can look into her eyes. "Please don't hide from me," I whisper.

Her eyes slowly rise until our gazes lock. Relief fills me. Her eyes are filled with an emotion that I don't immediately recognize. I don't know if she's horny, sad, or pissed off, but I'll take anything over the lost, vacant look I'd seen at the wedding.

"You don't have a phone," I say, not asking anymore.

She slowly shakes her head.

It's 2017, who doesn't have a phone? The mayor's a douchebag and a wealthy one at that, he can absolutely afford to get his daughter a cell phone.

"Why not?" I ask, then instantly wish I hadn't.

"My father won't let me have one," she replies quickly, obviously embarrassed.

"When can I see you again?"

Angel shrugs. "I don't know. My father would kill me if he found out I was here with you."

The stirrings of anxiety claw at my chest. I need to see her again. Now I know she exists, that my Angel is out there, I need to be around her.

Leaning in, I steal a kiss from her perfect lips. "So don't tell him you're coming to see me. Tell him you're going to a friend's instead."

Her eyes drop from mine. She pushes against my chest and takes a step away from me. "I can't."

Anger starts to bubble within me. "Why not?" I snarl.

Angel visibly shrinks at my fury. Her shoulders hunch and her head drops forward until her hair falls across her face, shielding her from me.

"Fuck," I curse and step closer to her, wrapping my hand around her hip.

She flinches.

Clenching my free hand into a fist, I pull in a deep, calming breath. I fight to still the anger flowing through my body and force my muscles to relax. "Angel," I say gently.

She doesn't move a muscle. Her fingers are twisted together, but she's frozen. Dropping to my haunches, I squat at her feet. "Angel, look at me please?" I beg and reach up to tuck her hair behind her ears. Her eyes are closed tightly, so I tentatively stroke her cheek with the pad of one of my fingers. "I'm sorry, Angel. I've never lifted my hand to a woman ever. It doesn't matter if I'm angry or if I'm shouting. I would never hurt you. Ever"

Her eyes flutter open and our gazes lock again. "I'm sorry," I whisper.

She doesn't nod, but her chin lifts slightly. "I don't have any friends."

How could this beautiful woman have no friends? "How's that possible?" I say.

Angel twists her lips into a wry smile. "We moved here when I was thirteen. I've been home schooled ever since."

"Everyone needs friends, Angel," I say.

"My father's strict. He doesn't let me go out very often," she admits.

I inwardly curse, mayor douchebag just became mayor asshat. How could he keep my Angel hidden away? She's eighteen and has no friends, no cell phone. She's jumpy and scared. What the fuck is he doing to her?

"Does he know you're out today?" I ask.

Angel shakes her head. "No, I snuck out," she says with a small rebellious smile.

"You gonna be in trouble when he figures out you're gone?" I ask.

The smile drops from her face. She steps back from me and starts to twist her fingers agitatedly together. "I need to go," she gasps.

"Angel." I grab her arm and pull her toward me. "Is he gonna hurt you?" I pray to God that she laughs, that she says no and assures me I'm jumping to conclusions, but instead her eyes drop to the floor again.

"No, of course not," she says robotically, her entire body rigid in my arms.

Fuck.

I scream the word in my head because I don't want to scare her again by shouting it out loud. I want to pull her on the back of my bike and run away with her; take her to the Sinners and tell them she's mine. We protect what's ours. But she's so young and as much as I want to claim her and own her, I think I'd probably scare the shit out of her if I suggested it.

"Angel, if he's hurting you, just tell me and I'll protect you." I try to keep the anger out of my voice and nearly succeed.

Angel pulls back her shoulders and lifts her head to look me right in the face. "I'm not your problem, Daisy. We just met. I don't need you, or anyone else, to look after me because I'm not a child. I can take care of myself."

Her eyes are filled with anger and righteous indignation and I feel proud. It's a ridiculous feeling because she's right, we only just met, but I'm already thinking of her as *my Angel* and I love the attitude she's throwing at me right now.

With a smirk I prowl toward her and pull her into my chest, lowering my head and kissing her thoroughly. When I pull away from her lips, I wait until she looks up at me. "You're right, Angel. We only just met. But I like you and I want to get to know you better. I want you to be safe. So when can I see you again?"

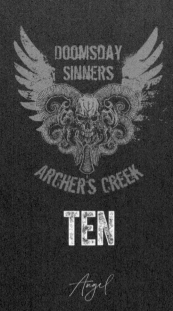

DOOMSDAY SINNERS

ARCHER'S CREEK

TEN

Angel

I fight the blush that threatens to bloom in my cheeks. Daisy wants to see me again. He's kissed me too many times to mention today, and now he wants to know when he can see me again. I rarely wish for a cell phone—most of the time I don't really care that I don't have one because I don't have anyone to call. But today I could have given Daisy my number and behaved like a normal teenager and God, I haven't felt normal in so long. Most days I long for the insipid trivialities that people my age face—normal angst ridden teenage drama would be a welcome relief. I'm not a normal teenager and I haven't been since Nicole died and the full force of my father's wrath fell onto my shoulders.

"Angel." Daisy's voice prompts me.

I falter. If my father finds out I snuck out today it'll be bad, very bad. My father's rules are absolute; if he catches me, I won't be given the opportunity to sneak out again.

"I don't know when I'll be able to sneak away again," I say.

Daisy frowns. "I only just found you, Angel, I can't give you up now. How are we gonna do this? You don't have a cell, so how can I speak to you?"

I could give him the phone number for our house, but my father doesn't allow me answer it. "I have a computer."

He smiles brightly. "Are you on Facebook? I'll send you a friend request."

My shoulders slump and I shake my head. "No, my father doesn't allow me to have a Facebook profile." Daisy scowls and I feel myself tense. "Email," I shout. Daisy turns to me "I have email. He doesn't know about it."

"I wanna see you though, Angel. I wanna touch you and hold you in my arms. But I suppose email will do until you can sneak out again."

I smile shyly and type my email address into his phone when he hands it to me. "I need to go home," I say.

He sighs but nods in agreement. "I'll give you a ride," he says as he entwines his fingers with mine.

I shake my head. "I can't. My father or one of his friends might see."

Daisy growls. "I don't give a fuck. I'm gonna give you a ride home. Look, I'll park around the corner if that makes you feel better, but honestly I'd rather walk you to the door and tell your dad that I'm your guy and that he can go fuck himself if he doesn't like it."

My guy.

I shouldn't be doing this now. My number one priority should be on getting myself and my mama away from my father. But it's been so long since I've felt anything but anger, fear, and sadness. Daisy makes me feel hopeful, I don't want to lose that.

"You can drop me around the corner," I say.

Daisy smiles and pulls me along behind him to where his motorcycle is parked around the corner from the playground. He climbs on, then holds my hand while I timidly climb on behind him. I tell him where I live, and he drives away, the motorcycle's engine roaring loudly.

I don't admit that this is the first time I've ever been on a motorcycle. The wind blows through my hair and exhilaration tingles through every single one of my nerves. Is this how my sister felt when she left with her biker boyfriend? Was this why she chose him over me? I've never really understood or experienced actual freedom, until I climbed onto the back of this bike and we rode away. But this feeling, this overwhelming sense of opportunity is intoxicating; we could drive into the sunset and go anywhere we wanted. We could be free.

The ride is over far too quickly, and Daisy pulls to the side of the road around the corner from my house. I slide off the bike on shaky legs and run my fingers through my windswept hair. I don't want my time with him to be over, but reality hits me and I turn to face Daisy. "Goodbye," I say, reluctant to leave in case this is the last time I ever see him.

"Where do you think you're going, Angel?" Daisy says smiling. His arms reach for me and he pulls me toward him and kisses me deeply. "I'll email you tonight, okay?"

I nod, a slither of hope building in my chest. Daisy releases me, and I slowly walk away from him. I can't resist glancing at him over my shoulder once more, before I drop my head and rush toward my home. My heart's pounding in my chest as I scurry around the side of the house and into the yard. A trellis, covered in wisteria climbs up the wall and ends just beneath my bedroom window.

I watched my sister climb up and down this trellis a hundred times over the years, so I know it'll hold my weight. Reaching up I hold onto the wooden slats and climb toward my window. It only takes a minute to reach the window ledge and I grip it tightly, thankful that I left my window open this morning.

I throw my leg through the space and try to silently lower myself to the carpet, holding my breath until my feet hit the floor. Quietly, I kick off my shoes and brush down my dress and then I turn around.

My father is seated on the edge of my bed staring at me. His face is twisted in rage when he stands up and silently stalks toward me. I know I should lower my head and try to make myself invisible, but the glimpse at freedom Daisy has given me, refuses to allow me to cower. Instead, I stand tall, my shoulders back and I stare back at him. I know the exact moment he sees the look of defiance on my face.

I watch in slow motion as he raises his hand and swings it toward me. His knuckles backhand me across the cheek and fire explodes across my skin. He hits me with so much force, my head snaps to the side and I crash to the floor. Cowered in a heap, I lift my hands to cradle my face. When his feet step into my line of sight, I pull in a terrified breath. His hand grips the neck of my dress and he lifts me up only to backhand me again.

I feel the skin split on my lip and taste the blood in my mouth. Tears run down my face, but I refuse to let him hear me sob. His hand tangles into my hair and he drags me from the floor and flings me over the bottom of my bed. I hear the clack of his belt unbuckling and feel the cold air cover my exposed skin as he rips my dress over my butt.

The belt makes a thwack noise when it crashes down against the backs of my legs. I shudder at the sound because I know in mere moments the pain will start to burn through my skin. Closing my eyes tightly, I block out the pain. The belt thrashes down again and again but I zone out and pretend this isn't happening. Later the pain will overwhelm me, but for right now I hum a familiar comforting tune in my head and drift away into my subconscious.

I don't know how long my father's punishment lasts, but the next thing I'm aware of is my mama tiptoeing into my room and helping me to crawl up my comforter until my head is on the pillow. She leaves, only to return moments later with a bowl of warm water. In a practiced art she carefully bathes the welts I know must cover my legs and butt. I watch the cotton balls that start off white, turn bright red with blood. She discards them only to grab another white one and start all over again.

Once the blood is removed she covers the injured skin with an antiseptic ointment. I don't have to watch to know what she'll do next; this isn't the first time she'd tended to the injuries my father's belt can dish out. I had no idea that all the times my sister would stay in her room for days on end and I wasn't allowed to visit her, were because she was recovering from one of my father's punishments.

I never realized while I was growing up, that when I'd done something to anger my father, Nicole had always stepped in to divert his attention from me. She'd protected me for years before it finally became too much, and she had to escape.

How ironic that she only got a few short months of freedom before death claimed her. She'd survived years of abuse at my father's hands and then her chance of happiness had been ripped away from her far too soon.

My mama works silently, wiping the blood from my face and holding an icepack against my swollen cheek and lip. She quietly hums the tune to a song I've never known the words to; the tune that allows me to hide inside my mind when my father releases his rage against me. She places two painkillers on my tongue and holds the bottle of water to my lips as I swallow the tablets. Her hands gently stroke my hair and tears run down both of our cheeks. This might be our lot in life right now, but I'll get us away from him. I'll find us freedom.

I remain in my room for the next three days. I don't see my father at all in those days and I'm grateful that he chooses to stay away. My mama bathes my wounds daily, helps me to the bathroom, and brings me food. We never talk about the fact that my father beat me so badly that even three days later I'm still struggling to move. It's the eternal elephant in the room. My father—her husband—is an abusive asshole.

I've tried to talk to her about it many times since my sister's death. I've begged her to pack up and run away, but she always refuses. I think he's beaten her into submission. Over the years I've heard every excuse and listened as she's defended him. She told me that it was his right as my father and her husband, to punish us as he saw fit. That we need to do better, to be better, so he wouldn't need to punish us in the future.

I cry myself to sleep only to have nightmares of my mama. Once lively and animated, my dreams show her as beautiful and kind, and I watch as he slowly, relentlessly abuses her until she loses every facet of herself that made her alive. I cry for myself and the life that's been thrust upon me and the only thing that makes nights like these bearable is knowing that we won't live like this forever.

Four days after my father's punishment, I wake up as the

sun is rising. My skin is stiff and sore as I tentatively move to the edge of the bed and carefully roll into an upright position. Lowering my feet to the floor my legs feel weak, but I manage to stand up and make my way to the bathroom to relieve myself.

I wash my hands and walk slowly over to my wardrobe where a full-length mirror hangs from the back. I gasp when I glance at my reflection. My cheek is still slightly swollen, and a yellowing bruise circles my eye, another at the side of my mouth. He doesn't often hit my face, preferring to keep his marks to places that are not easily visible. Lifting my nightdress, I turn around and look over my shoulder at the reflection of my legs and buttocks. The backs of my thighs are black with deep bruises. Thick lines crisscross back and forth across my skin from each hit of his belt, and angry scabs have formed over the patches where he hit me so hard he broke the skin.

Saliva fills my mouth and I silently rush to the bathroom and vomit into the toilet. Acid burns my throat as I expel everything held in my stomach. I finally stop retching and clinging onto the sink I flush the toilet and wash my face and hands. It doesn't matter how many 'punishments' he inflicts, it still shocks me to see the aftermath in the mirror.

I turn on my shower and after stripping off, I step into the torrent of warm water, wincing when it hits my battered skin. Once I'm clean, I carefully dry off and pad back into my bedroom. Opening my wardrobe, I avoid my reflection, knowing if I see the damage he did I'll be running back into the bathroom to vomit again. I choose a light maxi dress with capped sleeves from my closet and pull it over my head. My breasts are so small I don't need to wear a bra and I can't face the idea of pulling panties over my tender legs.

Grabbing my hairbrush from the dresser, I start to carefully remove the tangles from my long hair. My scalp is still sensitive from my father trying to pull my hair out at the roots, so I gently plait it and push it over my shoulder.

I spot my ancient laptop hidden on the shelf under my dressing table and my mind instantly turns to Daisy. I know he won't have actually emailed me. Why would he bother when I'm sure he can have any women he wants. Why would he want me? I think of a hundred reasons why he won't have contacted me, but I still grab my laptop and power it up.

My father for all his high and mighty superiority is barely computer literate. He believes and repeatedly tells me that I'm an idiot and he thinks I don't know how to use a computer either. He's wrong. I'm not a computer genius, but I know enough to get onto the internet and finish my GED without him having any idea. I know enough to have set up an email address, so I could try to speak to my sister even after she ran away. Also, I know enough to have been able to set up online banking for both myself and my father, and to have been secretly stealing money from him for the last six months.

For all my father's appearance of the Richie Rich lifestyle, I've realized that he's actually very cash poor. I don't understand how he's paying for the big house and new cars because his bank accounts show that he barely has two pennies to rub together. The small amount of money he does have I'm slowly and very carefully siphoning into my own bank account.

My father has no idea. He has so many bills coming out each month, the small amounts I take are barely noticeable. He owes us a hell of a lot more than the measly few thousand I will have taken from him, but at least when me and Mama finally run away from him we'll have enough money to rent an apartment and tide us over until we can get jobs.

The internet server finally pops up on the screen and I quickly log into the banking website and move another ten dollars over to my account. Even though I've done this many times before, I still panic and check over my shoulder every few seconds just to make sure no one's coming into my room. My father has no idea I even have a laptop, I stole it from my sister's room after she left, and I've kept it hidden from him for two years. My fingers hover over the keyboard, my mouse clicked into the search bar to enter the website for my email. I know deep down that Daisy won't have contacted me, but actually finding out that he hasn't feels like it'll be worse than just thinking he hasn't. I sigh and my hand starts to close the lid on the laptop, but I can't force myself to do it. Instead I type in the web server address and open my email inbox.

I steel myself for it to be empty, but it's not. Four unread emails all from the same address sit waiting to be read with the first one dated four days ago. My hands shake as I move the cursor and click on read.

> From: Daisy@tddsmc.com
> Sent: 09/27/17 19:38
> To: Angelique@webservertx.com
> Subject: When can I see you again?
>
> Hi Angel,
> This is so fucking weird. I don't remember the last time I sent an email.
> We need to get you a cell phone soon 'cause I wanna actually speak to you.
> When can I see you again? I miss those perfect fucking lips of yours.
> Daisy.

My heart's beating so hard in my chest I actually have to remember to breathe. He emailed me! He wants to see me again. I can't help the smile that spreads across my face, even though I wince when the movement pulls at my split lip. I don't stop. I let the smile come because I'm happy and I refuse to let my father invade this moment.

I quickly click on the next email.

> From: Daisy@tddsmc.com
> Sent: 09/28/17 20:15
> To: Angelique@webservertx.com
> Subject: Playing hard to get?
>
> Hi Angel,
> You don't strike me as the type who plays hard to get. You

don't seem like you play games at all. But maybe I'm wrong.

Why didn't you reply?

Come meet me. Name the time and place and I'll be there.

Daisy.

I giggle inwardly. He thinks I'm playing games by not replying. He couldn't be more wrong. I don't know the games girls play and I sure as hell wouldn't try to play them with a guy like Daisy. He's older, and I'd be stupid to think that he's an inexperienced virgin like me. Maybe I'm a game to him.

The thought makes me feel sick again. I barely know him, but he seemed to be genuinely interested in me. I want him to be interested.

I click onto the third email.

From: Daisy@tddsmc.com
Sent: 09/29/17 16:55
To: Angelique@webservertx.com
Subject: Don't ignore me.

Angel,

I'm starting to feel like a bit of a pussy now. I've emailed you twice and you haven't replied.

I don't chase girls. But I'm fucking chasing you.

If you don't want me to, then just tell me. I can't promise I'll take any notice but at least I'll know you're okay.

Did you get in trouble with your dad when you got home?

Let me know you're okay.

Please.

Daisy.

I know nothing about Daisy—hell, I don't even know his real name—but I saw the way he looked at me when he asked if my father hurt me. I saw the darkness in his eyes and the shadows that followed him. He's seen the evil that lurks in life, maybe he's even experienced it. He said I made him feel, and that's exactly what he did for me too. Even the short time I spent with him and in his arms, made my father and even the punishment I received for sneaking out, easier to endure.

I click on the last email and hope to God that this isn't the one where he tells me I'm not worth the effort.

> From: Daisy@tddsmc.com
> Sent: 09/30/17 11:00
> To: Angelique@webservertx.com
> Subject: Freaking out.
>
> Angel,
> I'm freaking the fuck out.
> Maybe I'm overreacting, I really fucking hope I am.
> But I'm worried about you.
> You need a cell phone!
> You can come to me any time day or night. I live at the Sinners clubhouse on Deer Lake Road. Just ask whoever's on the gate for me. If they question it, just tell them you're mine.
> If I haven't heard from you soon I'm coming over to your house to check on you. Fuck your dad.
> Daisy.

I sit on my bed, my laptop on my knees and I stare at the screen. He can't come here. My father would actually kill me. If Daisy came to my door and asked for me I'd have to run away.

I'd never be able to come back here, because my father would make the beating I got for sneaking out look like child's play in comparison to what he would do to me if he found out I was involved with a Sinner.

I quickly hit reply and start to type.

From: Angelique@webservertx.com
Sent: 10/01/17 05:57
To: Daisy@tddsmc.com
Subject: I'm fine.

Daisy,
I'm fine, don't come here!!!!!!!!!!
Sorry it's taken me a few days to reply. I've been sick and haven't been well enough to check my emails.
Also, I'm sorry if I've made you worry.
I don't know when I'll be able to sneak out to see you.
My father definitely won't let me get a cell phone and if he did, he would want to know who I was calling.
I know I'm not worth all this sneaking around. I wish I could stand up to my father and I will eventually.
I'll understand if you stop writing.
Angel.

I hit send just as a tear falls from my chin and drops onto the laptop's keyboard. Lifting my hand to my cheek I wipe the skin—it's wet. Tears are streaming from my eyes and I'm crying over the loss of a man I never really had. I'm pathetic.

The laptop dings and confused, I look down. A new email has popped up in my Inbox and I quickly click on it.

From: Daisy@tddsmc.com
Sent: 10/02/17 06:00
To: Angelique@webservertx.com
Subject: Thank Fuck!

Angel,
Thank fuck you're okay! You had me worried, and I didn't fucking like it.
Why the fuck would I stop writing??

Daisy.

Air catches in my throat. He makes it seem so simple. '*Why the fuck would I stop writing*'. I want to laugh, but I daren't make a noise in case I wake up my father. Daisy shouldn't be interested in me, and I shouldn't be interested in him. My sole focus should be on getting me and my mama away from my father, but Daisy is the first thing I've ever wanted just for me.

Should I reply? Emailing Daisy is the most selfish thing I've done in years, but for once I push my responsibilities to the back of my mind and quickly type out a response.

From: Angelique@webservertx.com
Sent: 10/02/17 06:05
To: Daisy@tddsmc.com
Subject: I'm fine.

Daisy,
This isn't normal. Normal people see each other and talk on the phone.
Plus, we literally met four days ago.
We don't know anything about each other!
How old are you?

I can't believe I don't know this yet. You asked me the other day, but I never asked you.

Angel.

Hitting send, I place my laptop down on the floor and start to strip the sheets from my bed. The pale purple bedsheets are stained with streaks of browny-red blood and I quickly stuff them into my laundry hamper, along with my bloodstained nightdress, and the dress I was wearing when my father decided to punish me. Blood is such an awful stain to get out, but my mama and I have become accustomed to it over the last few years.

My laptop pings and I rush to pick it up, freezing in my tracks when pain surges through my legs. I smile through the discomfort realizing that my excitement over Daisy's emails had made me forget how tight my skin was feeling. As I try to move again, a fresh surge of pain hits me and with trepidation I lift my dress up. Fresh blood has pooled on my skin where one of the newly formed scabs has split open, and I have to physically press my hand to my chest to stem the pain that overwhelms me when I remember that my father did this. It doesn't matter how many times he hits me or punishes me; it still hurts to know my own flesh and blood is capable of doing this.

Wiping away the blood from my legs, I drop my dress and carefully lower myself onto the edge of the bed. Picking up my laptop from the floor, I block out the pain and hurt I feel and eagerly click on the new email that's waiting for me.

From: Daisy@tddsmc.com
Sent: 10/02/17 06:15
To: Angelique@webservertx.com
Subject: Who wants to be normal.

Angel,
Who gives a fuck about normal?

I want to speak to YOU. I don't care how I have to do that as long as you don't disappear on me. I only just found you Angel, and I have no intention of giving you up now.

I don't wanna hear the 'we don't know each other' bullshit, so I'm gonna give you the cliff notes on me.

My birthday is April 10th. I'm twenty-one.

I just got my full patch at the Doomsday Sinners.

I ride a Harley Davidson Heritage Softtail. She's my baby and my pride and joy.

I live at the Sinner's clubhouse, but I plan to get an apartment in town soon.

I've lived every minute of my twenty-one years. I've done a lot of shit and I won't apologize for any of it.

I like you.

Your turn...

Daisy.

As I read the words, my heart pounds in my chest and a huge smile erupts from me. He likes me. It's such a childish thing to say, but it's perfect. I may be young, but I'm not foolish enough to believe in love at first sight. We've only spent a very short amount of time together, but I like him too.

I hit reply and start to type.

From: Angelique@webservertx.com
Sent: 10/02/17 06:23
To: Daisy@tddsmc.com
Subject: Get to know me 101

Daisy,
My turn…
My birthday is July 25th. I'm eighteen.
I want to get to know you better too.
I just finished my GED.
Since we moved to Archer's Creek, my life has stood still, and
I wish I was truly living it instead of just existing.
My sister died two years ago, and I miss her every single day.
I want to leave home and go to college.
No one has ever called me Angel before, but I love that you do.
I like you too.
Angel

The door to my parents' bedroom creaks and I hit send on the email and quickly close the laptop, sliding it back into place underneath my dresser. I'm busy scooping up my laundry hamper when my father enters my room—as usual he doesn't bother to knock. It's the first time I've seen him in four days and I'm shocked when a wave of hatred pulses through me. I don't remember a time when I haven't hated him, but today my hands are clenched into tight fists and I imagine swinging the hamper at him and hitting him as hard as I can. I don't know how much damage I can do, but maybe I could smother him with my bedsheets, suffocate him with the fabric that's covered in my blood? The blood he made run when he decided I needed to be punished.

I give him a sidelong glance. There's no point offering him full eye contact, he doesn't want that. He enjoys my fear. I always thought parents felt love and affection for their offspring, but my father has never looked at me with anything but indifference and annoyance.

"Get yourself cleaned up, Angelique. I have a visitor coming to the house today and I expect you to be presentable," he snaps.

I swallow down the sardonic laugh that threatens to escape. By presentable, he means I need to put on enough makeup to cover the bruises that are still evident on my face. The bruises that he caused but that can never be seen by anyone else. Because if the outside world saw what my father did, then they'd see the monster lurking behind the fake smiles and cordial personality, and that can never, ever happen.

I offer him a small nod and hate myself for being so weak. I wish I was brave enough to look him right in the eyes and tell him how much I hate him. Instead, I flinch in fear when his fingers pinch my chin viciously.

"When my guests get here, you will wait in your bedroom until I send for you. Then you will come downstairs and remain silent unless you are asked a question directly. You will not say a word, nor offer an opinion. No one is interested in anything you have to say. You will dress appropriately and behave appropriately. Do. You. Understand?"

I nod, and he releases me, stalking out of my room.

ELEVEN

Daisy

My phone pings telling me I've got a new email and I grab for it like a little bitch. I seriously never thought I'd be this fucking excited to get an email. I quickly devour her words and when I see the last line, '*I like you too*', I smile like I just found a winning lottery ticket.

Flopping back down onto my pillow, I think about what to write her back. It's not even 7am, and with my blinds closed, my room is dark and quiet. I live at the Sinners clubhouse and have done since I started prospecting eighteen months ago. I fucking love the Sinners, they're my family, and this is the first place I've ever actually called home.

I'll be a Sinner until the day I die. We look after each other and until I joined the club, I'd never felt the lifelong camaraderie of family before. Honestly, until I met my Sinner brothers, I'd never given a fuck about anyone else. I grew up in foster care and that doesn't exactly promote healthy relationships.

For four fucking days, Angel has been all I can think about. I care about her. I've been worried about her. Fuck I've been going out of my mind for the last few days waiting for her to email me back. I was so close to driving over to her house yesterday just to check she was okay. I probably would have, if Anders' hadn't sent me over to work security at Beavers, the titty bar a few towns over.

Normally a day surrounded by strippers would end with my cock buried deep inside one of them, but yesterday my dick never even twitched in the direction of their bouncing tits. I'd probably be freaking the fuck out that my dick was broken, if it didn't stand to attention every time I pictured Angel's petite body with those perky breasts and gorgeous legs.

Immediately, images of her flash into my mind and I drop my cell onto my bedside table and push the sheets down my legs. I always sleep naked, so my cock is already hard as a rock and resting against my stomach. Fisting it, I start to stroke up and down, pre-cum already leaking from the swollen head. I close my eyes and picture Angel. I try to imagine her naked, but my mind always goes back to the way she looked and felt sitting in my lap.

My hand moves quicker, and I groan. Fuck this feels good. Her soft curves nestled against my chest, her hair pushed behind her ears, so her face is fully on display. Angel's huge eyes full of desire and her chest panting after I kissed her. I imagine the feel of her full lips and try to visualize what they would look like wrapped around my cock. My hips start to twitch, and I jerk, hot streams of cum spurting over my hand onto my stomach.

Panting, I open my eyes to stare at the ceiling above my head. My cock's still twitching in my hand and I reluctantly release it and reach for the towel I dropped onto the floor the night before, cleaning my hands and wiping the cum off my skin.

What the fuck is wrong with me? Angel's got me jacking off to the feel of her sitting, fully dressed in my lap. I feel like a fucking teenager with his first boner.

My breathing evens out and I grab my phone and type out a quick reply to her email. I want to wait for her reply but instead I force myself out of bed and into the bathroom. Turning on the shower, I wait for the water to heat up and then step under the warm spray. My cock's hard again and I jack off again, Angel's face my inspiration for a second time this morning.

I dry myself off and get dressed in jeans and a T-shirt, pulling my cut on over the top. Grabbing my phone, I check for a new email and feel myself scowl when there isn't one. At least I know she's okay, and as much as I want to storm over to her house to see her, I know I can't. I don't know what's going on with her dad, but something isn't right there. I hope the mayor's just a fucking douchebag, but I have a gut feeling that he's worse than that.

A couple of the club girls live in the clubhouse. They cook and clean and are always up for a fuck if any of the guys are feeling horny. The moment I walk into the main room, Ali stops what she's doing and makes a beeline straight for me.

"Daisy," she purrs as she plasters her barely contained tits against my chest.

"Ali," I say and move her off me while I continue toward the bar where a pot of coffee is bubbling away enticingly. I pour myself a cup and carry it across the room, sinking down into a sofa opposite the silently playing TV.

Ali crawls into my lap and kisses up my neck.

"Daisy, I need you to fuck me with that big cock of yours. You're the only one who stretches me out so good I can feel it for days afterwards."

I bring my cup to my lips and take a sip of my coffee. "Ali, I know you got fucked more than once yesterday. In fact, didn't you have a cock in every one of your wet holes all at the same time last night? You put on quite a show on the pool table with Flip in your pussy, Erickson in your ass, and K.C. fucking your face. Bitch, you must still have cum leaking out of you with the amount of cock you took, you damn sure don't need my dick in you this morning."

"I always want your dick in me, Daisy. I only put on a show, so you'd watch me. You like to watch, baby. If you made me your old lady, I wouldn't let anyone else touch me again; my pussy would be just for you. I know how much you like my pussy, it always gets so wet, just for you."

I take another sip of my coffee and spread my legs, so Ali falls to the ground.

"What the fuck?" She screams.

I laugh dryly. "Listen up, Ali. I am never gonna make you my old lady. Ever. I fucked you once when I was so drunk I was impressed I could even get it up. Your used-up pussy is of no interest to me at all and never has been. If I ever make someone my old lady, she definitely won't be a whore whose pussy's been used as a cum bucket by every biker in the club. Now get your fucking skanky ass away from me, it's too fucking early to deal with you."

Ali scrambles up off the floor and stomps away. She looks back over her shoulder and shouts, "Asshole," at me before she disappears into the kitchen.

I sigh and take another sip of my coffee. My phone buzzes and I quickly pull it out of my pocket, hopeful that it will be an email from Angel. It isn't. I dismiss the stupid Facebook notification and force my phone back into my pocket.

Blade slumps down next to me on the sofa, his eyes barely open. Harper, the other live-in club girl places a steaming cup of coffee on the table in front of Blade.

"Here you go, honey," she says sweetly and taps Blade's leg before she walks away.

"Thank you," Blade groans, as he sits up and blindly gropes

with his hands until he finds the coffee and brings the cup up to his mouth. We sit in companionable silence, both drinking our coffees for a few moments. Blade's voice breaks the silence. "Fuck, I was on it last night. God knows how many whiskeys I had, but my mouth feels as dry as a nun's cunt this morning."

I chuckle lightly. "Happens to the best of us, brother."

Blade gradually blinks his eyes open and turns to face me. "What happened to you last night, you disappeared pretty early?"

I shrug. "I wasn't feeling it. A day dealing with all those fucking, shrieking strippers at Beavers wore me out. I crashed."

Blade sniggers. "Haven't you figured out the best way to shut those women up is to put something in their mouths?"

I deadpan, "Yeah, but then I end up with a sparkly dick. Those bitches wear so much fucking glitter."

Echo and Sleaze drop down onto the sofa to the left of us and both Blade and I nod acknowledgments at them.

"Prez called church in thirty minutes. Blade, you got any idea what's up? I hope it's not this shit about running guns again," Echo growls, obviously annoyed.

Blade shakes his head and scowls. "What's crawled up your ass, Echo? I only woke up thirty minutes ago. I didn't even know there was church."

Echo grunts and runs his hand through his hair. "I just got dragged out of bed, where my wife is lying naked as the day she was born. My balls are fucking hurting. I wanna know there's a damn good reason why I'm here with you ugly bastards and not at home reminding my old lady who she belongs to."

A quick laugh bursts from me, and Echo instantly turns pissed off eyes in my direction. I hold up my hands in an 'I surrender' gesture and sit back in my seat, grabbing my coffee cup and lifting it to my lips.

I grab my cell from my pocket and check my email again, but there's still nothing from Angel. The clubhouse gradually starts to fill as my brothers enter and wait for Prez to appear. Park, Puck, and Slow, drop down into the sofa in front of us. Park and Puck nod greetings, but Slow glowers at me. Until recently we had both been prospects together, but I'd earned my top rocker and was now a fully patched in member of the Sinners. Slow hadn't and the fact that he still remained a prospect had seriously pissed him off.

For the past couple of weeks, he'd stomped around the clubhouse, grumbling to anyone that would listen that he deserved his patch more than I did because he had been a prospect longer than me. Honestly, I couldn't give a fuck what he thinks, the kid was slow in name and fucking nature. He was a lazy, entitled bastard, who thought he should have been an automatic full member because his daddy and granddaddy were Sinners.

That isn't how the club works. It doesn't matter if you're sixth generation legacy, everyone prospects. It's a rite of passage that teaches you the hierarchy of the club and how to respect the traditions that the Sinners value. Sure, being a prospect is shitty—you're the lowest of the low and generally have to do all the crap none of the other members want to do. But when you finally earn your full patch, it's all worth it.

I eyeball Slow and dare him to say something. I'll fucking kick his ass if he tries it and we both know it. His narrowed eyes shine with barely held anger and I really want to fucking smirk at him, but I hold it in. Barely.

"Brothers." Anders deep voice booms through the room and a respectful silence falls through the group of guys. "Time for church, we got business to discuss."

Pushing off the sofa, I stand up and join the other guys slowly walking toward the meeting room. Prospects aren't allowed into church, and as I glance over my shoulder, I see Slow's angry face glaring at me. I can't fucking help myself, I wink, then follow my brothers into church, and find my chair at the end of the room.

There are about thirty-five active members of the Sinners, with a couple of brothers in lock up and a few retired guys who don't often make it to the club. Shuffling around the huge table that sits at the center of the room, I make my way to my seat at the end of the worn wooden slab that proudly displays the Doomsday Sinner's emblem painted across the middle. The walls are covered in photos of club members from all the way back in the sixties, when the Archer's Creek Chapter started, right through to present day.

The longstanding members move around the room at ease, but I'm still awed by the way it feels to finally be allowed entry into the hallowed room. The Sinners church is sacred and only ever seen by the men that have created the legacy I look up to. It makes my breath catch in my throat every fucking time.

Anders slams the gavel down onto the table and the loud noise silences the chatter. We all turn, giving our president our full attention.

"Brothers, it's been brought to my attention that Eric Carduccio is coming to Archer's Creek today. As you all know, the illustrious Senator Carduccio is as dirty as they come. Normally he stays in New Mexico and runs his drugs through his own state, so I want to know exactly what the fuck has brought him to our town."

A murmur of chatter rumbles through the men surrounding the table until the bang of Prez's gavel pulls our attention again.

"Echo and Puck, I want you to do your thing and see what you can find out. Park, go lock down the weed grows and take enough guys with you to keep them secure. Sleaze, get word out to the Arizona and New Mexico Chapters and see if they know what Carduccio's up to. Blade, take some guys and get eyes on him the moment he gets to town. I wanna know where he goes and who he sees," Anders orders.

Nods of agreement and murmurs of discontent pass through the group. We all know Carduccio's reputation. He runs all the distribution of heroin and cocaine along the south coast of America and his links to the cartels are well known. Fuck knows how he got into office, but he's seriously influential and a dangerous fucking bastard.

"We don't have class A running through this town and that's not going to change. I don't know what the fuck Carduccio's doing here but until he's gone, everyone stay alert and let's find out what this fucker is up to. Any questions?" Anders asks.

The room falls quiet, so I quickly scan my eyes across my brothers focused, determined faces. Anders bangs the gavel again and then stands from the table and moves to speak to Blade, our vice president. Dismissed I rise from my chair and follow the guys as we file out of church and head toward the bar.

The club owns several businesses in Archer's Creek and the surrounding towns, including several bars, a tattoo shop, a garage, and a few shops. The club is one hundred percent self-supporting and the profit from the businesses is split between the members in a monthly stipend so we all work hard and are happy to do so. I'm a big guy so I tend to work security, but as a prospect, you kind of just do as you're told. The bar slowly empties as some guys leave for their regular jobs and others to start the recon Anders ordered.

A heavy hand slaps down on my shoulder. "You're with me, brother," Blade says, and I nod and follow him to the exit doors.

Smoke, Flip, Erickson, and K.C., leave with us and we all walk to our bikes, stored on the right-hand side of the compound. Smoke is a few years older than me and at least six feet six with a skinhead and pretty boy features that make the ladies fall at his feet. Flip is in his thirties; blond, clean shaven, and rocking a fifties-inspired slicked back hairstyle. Erickson is mid-forties; pot-bellied with greasy hair and beady eyes—he looks like a fucking perv, but he's harmless and funny as hell.

K.C. is huge—as wide as he is tall—with shocking ginger hair that stands straight up in angry carrot-colored spikes. I'm not sure how old he is, but I'd say thirties, maybe older. K.C. stands for King Carrot, but in my time with the Sinners I've only ever heard one person call him that. K.C. broke three of his ribs and one of his legs. I've never heard of anyone stupid enough to try calling him anything but K.C. since.

Blade, our V.P., is only in his forties, but his hair is almost completely gray and lines pull at his eyes. His silver beard is cut short to his face and meets the tattoos that cover his neck. "Smoke and K.C., you guys head out to the Iron Tire and watch for Carduccio. He'll be easy to spot, we don't get many senators in these parts. Call in once you see him, then follow at a distance. Flip, Erickson, you guys head to the other side of town and make sure that he doesn't come in from Creek side. Daisy, you're with me," Blade says, throwing his leg over his bike and turning the key.

The engine bursts to life and one by one we all jump onto our bikes and start them. As a unit, we ride through the gates of the compound and onto the road. We convoy in three groups of two, until we reach an intersection and the others split off, headed for their respective destinations. When it's just me and Blade left, we cruise through the town and stop at Al's diner. Parking our bikes out front, I follow him into the diner and slide into a booth opposite him.

The waitress comes straight over. "Good mornin', my name is Christie and I'll be your waitress today. Can I get you some drinks to start you off?"

"Coffee," Blade groans.

Christie turns to me and I nod. She flips over the cups in front of us and grabs the coffee pot from the counter, filling them with steaming, black coffee.

"Eggs over easy, bacon, and toast please," Blade says with his head in a menu.

I don't even bother looking at my menu before I turn to Christie. "I'll have the same please." She nods, takes our menus and leaves to get our food.

Blade groans and I laugh. "You suffering, brother?"

He pulls some Tylenol from his pocket and pops out two tablets, washing them down with his coffee. "I feel like ass." The waitress places our food in front of us and Blade grabs for the toast, biting it then moaning in pleasure.

My phone buzzes. Pulling it from my pocket, I'm filled with hope that it's an email from Angel, but it's just a text from a random girl I fucked a few weeks back. I delete the message without reading it and slam my phone down onto the table in frustration.

"What the fuck's up with you?" Blade asks, his hungover eyes slightly more open than before.

"I'm waiting for someone to message me."

Blade pauses with his fork halfway to his mouth. "Who?"

I shrug and pick up my fork, spearing a piece of bacon from my plate. "No one, don't worry about it."

"Bullshit," Blade says. "It's a woman, isn't it?"

I scowl at him, ignoring his question and shoving bacon into my mouth and chewing.

Blade barks out an obnoxious laugh. "Well fuck. I never thought I'd see the day when you were waiting for a woman to message you. Hell, there's normally a line of bitches waiting to drop their panties for you. So, who is she?"

My cell beeps again and I drop my fork and snatch it up off the table. It's another stupid, fucking Facebook notification and snarling, I jam my cell back into my pocket. I look up at Blade, his eyebrow is raised in question and his mouth is twisted into a smirk. "You don't know her," I say and grab my fork again.

"She must be one hell of a fuck, if she's got you strung this tight."

My fingers clench into fists. "It's not like that," I say through gritted teeth.

"It's always like that with you, Daisy. You're a walking hard on, fucking every bit of pussy that takes your fancy. You've had more threesomes in the last six months than I've had in my entire life and those girls come out of your room purring and wrung dry 'cause you've given them so many orgasms."

"Well, this time it's different," I say quietly, shifting uncomfortably in my seat.

Blade looks at me, his eyebrows furrowed together, then he carries on eating. We finish our breakfast in silence, pay the bill and leave. "Where to?" I ask.

The shrill ring of Blade's cell phone interrupts him before he can speak. "Smoke," Blade says brusquely.

I can't hear what Smoke's saying, so I walk over to my bike and climb on, ready to go if we need to.

"No worries, brother. Yep," Blade says and ends the call. He moves to his bike and swings his leg across the saddle. "Carduccio and his goons just drove into town. They're in two black Range Rovers and heading onto Elm Street. Let's go head them off on 2nd and see where they're going."

I nod to Blade and start my bike, pushing it off the kick stand and following him onto the road. Archer's Creek has been an MC town for decades, so the sight of bikers isn't unusual, and no one notices when we drive through town and meet up with Smoke and K.C. We all ride together for a few blocks, then Blade signals to Smoke, and he and K.C. drift off down a side street.

The shiny black paintwork on Carduccio's car glistens in the Texas sun and we follow at a discreet distance, occasionally diverting down side roads only to catch up with them again a block later. The two SUV's take a right off Maple and a prickle of unease pulses through me.

We follow the cars along the suburban streets until they slow to a stop outside a familiar house. My heart starts to pound in my chest. Blade and I ride straight past the cars, not slowing or showing any indication that we aren't simply heading in the same direction. We park around the corner and Blade turns to me, confusion etched across his face. "Whose house is that?"

I scrub my hand over my face before I reply. "The Mayor's."

TWELVE

Angel

They say silence is golden, but sometimes it's the quiet moments that cause the most pain.

After my father visited my room, he insisted that I cook breakfast and then sent me upstairs to 'clean myself up'. Standing in my bathroom, I watch my mama's reflection in the mirror as she applies enough makeup to disguise the bruises on my face. "Mama, do you know who these guests are? Why would I need to be there? He doesn't normally introduce me to anyone."

My mama pointedly looks down at the makeup sponge in her hands and avoids making eye contact with me. "Mama?"

She finally looks up, a sad smile on her face. "I don't know who they are, just that they're important people."

My mama is not a good liar, and I know she's not telling me everything. She finishes my makeup and I look into the mirror. My skin looks flawless; the bruises are hidden, and I look fresh and beautiful. Appalled, I turn away from my reflection. It's a lie, a façade, and I can't stand to look at it for another minute.

My eyes drift to my mama. From a distance she still looks the part of the perfect mayor's wife. Blonde hair cut into a sleek bob, perfect makeup, and an omnipresent beauty queen smile. It isn't until you look closely that you can see the cracks in her mask. She's still a beautiful woman, but her eyes are dull and not even the artfully applied makeup can hide what the years of sadness and abuse have done to her. Her tiny frame is elegantly dressed in a silk dress and matching shoes, and she never looks less than perfect. But beneath the hair, clothes, and makeup, is a frightened, beaten-down shell created by my asshole of a father.

Her hands shake as she undoes the braid in my hair and brushes it until it falls across my shoulders in soft waves. I turn to face her and grasp her frail fingers in my hands. "Mama, I don't want this life for us. I don't want to spend years covering up the bruises *that* man gives me. Let's run away and find a new happy life, where we don't have to be scared of being hurt or punished. Nicole got away from him and so can we. We can start over somewhere no one knows who we are. Let me take care of you, Mama. I want to see you smile a real smile for once. I want to see happiness in your eyes, not the emptiness that's in there now. Please? We can go tonight. I can pack a bag now and by tomorrow we could be free. Please, Mama."

She weakly squeezes my fingers back for a second and then pulls her hands free from mine. "Angelique, I'm sure I don't know where you get your imagination from. Your daddy loves us, why on earth would we want to leave him? It's his job to look after us and he does; look at this beautiful house we live in and all the wonderful things we have. Soon you'll find a husband of your own and all this silliness will be forgotten. You'll start a family and have daughters of your own. My life is perfect. I couldn't want anything more."

I stare at my mama in shock. I don't honestly know if she believes the words that had just fallen from her lips. Fear, stark and real, builds in my chest until I struggle to pull in oxygen and my vision starts to go black at the corners. Tears spill from my eyes and I shake my head from side to side. "I don't want to live like this. I don't want you to live like this. Look at me, Mama. Look what he did to me."

Angrily, I pull at the skirt of my dress, lifting it high enough to expose the inflamed red marks that cover the backs of my thighs. "He did this to me. It's not the first time. He hit me again and again and he enjoyed it." My voice cracks and I pull in a shaky breath, my fists clenched in the fabric of my dress, my legs still exposed.

Mama reaches out and pries my fingers loose. The dress falls, and my raw skin is hidden again. My eyes bore into hers and I search for something—anything—to say that she knows this isn't right. Desperate, I try to find an emotion in her that says she doesn't want this life, but instead her features remain blank and only her eyes betray her resigned sadness.

A sob escapes me, and I turn away from her. She's gone, buried so deep in the bullshit my father has fed her for the last thirty years, that she doesn't realize that this life is wrong. I've lost her. She's beyond my reach and even though glimpses of my loving, caring mother still exist in her, they're hidden so deep, I don't know if I can help her anymore.

But I can help myself before it's too late.

My mother leaves my room without another word. There's nothing left to say, so I fix my makeup and then sit on my bed and wait. I want to get my laptop out and message Daisy. We've only exchanged a handful of emails, but I know that talking to him—even if it's only through written words—would make me feel better. He makes me feel like there's a world out there and that maybe I can escape this prison of a life. But I can't risk my father walking in on me, so instead I sit quietly and plan my escape.

The doorbell rings a few minutes later and I hear voices and footsteps moving through the foyer and into the family room. A sense of dread pools in my stomach—my father never introduces me to people; honestly, I think a lot of the folk in this town don't even know I exist. So why does he want me to meet these visitors?

Several minutes later, my mama pushes open my bedroom

door. Her face is taut, and her perfect smile has slipped slightly. "Your daddy would like you to meet some people, so come on downstairs."

I silently follow her, trepidation building with every step. When we enter the family room, the conversation halts and all eyes turn to me. I scan the guests. An older man is sat on one side of my father and a petite woman is next to him; on the other side of my father is a younger man who's openly assessing me. Several large men are standing sentry around the room and the urge to turn and flee is so strong I actually start to move.

"Angelique, sweetheart," my father calls, rising from his seat and walking over to me. His meaty arms wrap around my waist and pull me into his chest. I stiffen. He leans down and kisses my forehead and I know my eyes must be comically large.

"Gentlemen, let me introduce you to my daughter, Angelique. She just turned eighteen and I'm sure you'll agree she's the most beautiful young lady you've ever seen."

My mouth drops open in shock and my father looks down and notices. His hand tightens around my hip and squeezes to the point of pain. I close my mouth and hold my breath to stop the wince of pain escaping me.

My father releases me but remains standing beside me and I turn my eyes back to the visitors. The older man has risen and is making his way over to me. He's not that tall, maybe five feet ten, with a lean build. His hair is short and although he was obviously once dark, gray covers the sides, and peppers through the top. I'm unsure of his age, but I'd guess at mid-to-late fifties; his face is lined, and his dark assessing eyes don't hold any youthfulness.

When he reaches me, he lifts my hand to his lips and kisses it. "Miss Angelique, it's a pleasure to meet you. My name is Eric Carduccio, you might have heard of me before? I'm one of the Senators for the great state of New Mexico."

Something about this man makes me uneasy. He's being cordial and polite, but his eyes hold a hardness that suggests that he isn't always this nice.

"It's a pleasure to meet you, Senator Carduccio."

He releases me, moving his hand to the base of my spine and guiding me forward a step. I instinctively flinch at his touch. Mr. Carduccio looks down at me and a grin twitches at the edge of his lips.

"Angelique, let me introduce my wife, Marissa," he points to the woman sat on the sofa.

She rises and steps toward me, holding her hand out. I take it but instead of shaking it she wraps the other hand across mine and greets me. "Hello, Angelique. It's lovely to meet you. You are absolutely stunning and so young."

Unsure what else to do, I smile. "Nice to meet you, Mrs. Carduccio."

She squeezes my hand and then releases me and returns to her seat. The hand on the base of my spine pushes and turns me slightly. "And lastly, this is my son, Jeremy," Mr. Carduccio says.

Jeremy rises from his seat. Taller than his father, he's at least six feet tall. His shoulders are broad, and his pitch-black hair is styled back from his face. His thin mouth is twisted into a scowl and his dark eyes start at my feet and assess every inch of me. I feel his gaze move over my body and linger on my breasts before slowly looking at my face. Where his father exudes charm, Jeremy is all anger and disapproval. When our eyes meet, his lips lift into a sneer. "It's a pleasure, Angelique." His voice doesn't make it sound like it's a pleasure, in fact he sounds bored and annoyed.

Once the introductions are made, Senator Carduccio steers me to a seat and then returns to my father's side. My mother delivers drinks and I sit silently, watching the others interact. No one speaks to me again and bemused, I try to understand why my presence was required.

Ten minutes later, Senator Carduccio stands and glances between his wife, my mother, and me. "If you ladies will excuse us for a few minutes, we have a little business to discuss."

My father and Jeremy both stand, and my father leads the men out of the room and toward the patio overlooking the garden. Two of the huge men that I'm now assuming are security, follow the Senator and his son, while the other two remain in the family room.

Mrs. Carduccio's cell phone rings, and she looks regretfully at me and my mother. "I apologize, I've been expecting a call from a charity I'm involved in. It is a time-sensitive matter so

I'm going to have to take the call."

My mother nods. "Of course, Marissa. It was so nice to see you again."

Marissa turns to me and smiles sweetly. "It was lovely to meet you, honey." I smile, and she takes her phone from her purse and answers the call. One of the security guys opens the door and my mother and Marissa file into the foyer with the last security guy following behind. The front door opens and shuts and moments later my mama returns to the family room.

I wait expectantly, hoping she'll explain what's going on, but she doesn't. She walks past me and heads for the kitchen, but I jump to my feet and reach out to stop her. "Mama, what's going on? Why is a Senator coming to visit?"

Mama reaches out, placing her hand on my cheek and smiles. "Your daddy thinks that Senator Carduccio's son Jeremy would be a good match for you."

My mouth falls open. "Mama, what are you talking about?"

"Your father and the Senator have known each other for a while now. They both feel that Jeremy would make you a great husband and connecting our two families would be an unbelievable asset to your daddy. You know that he hopes to run for senate someday."

She starts to move, and I grab her frantically. "Mama, I'm eighteen. I'm not getting married to anyone and definitely not a stranger."

Lifting her arms up, she places her hands on my shoulders.

"Baby girl, I got married at your age. Your daddy knows what's best for you. Now, why don't you run on back upstairs before the men folk come back inside?"

Leaning forward, she kisses my cheek and then walks toward the kitchen. Dumbstruck, I make my way back upstairs into my bedroom and drop onto the bed. I let my head fall forward into my hands and try not to cry.

My father's voice disturbs my misery. My bedroom window is open and the patio they're sitting on is directly underneath. I slowly move closer to the window. Normally, I could care less what my father does, but now that he's trying to plan my marriage to a complete stranger, I need to know what the hell is going on.

"Eric, it's the perfect solution." My father's voice booms out.

"This isn't the way we normally conduct business, Jefferies," the Senator replies curtly.

My father laughs dryly. "I know, but you've seen her. She's worth way more than I owe you."

"You're a sick motherfucker, Jefferies, selling your daughter to cover your debts. I don't deal in girls, too much hassle. What if Jeremy doesn't want her for a wife? What if I decide to put her out to work?"

There's a pause and I wait with baited breath to see what my father says.

"Then she'll make you a hell of a lot of money," he says

smugly.

I feel sick. Slumping onto the floor, I pull in gasps of air. I can hardly believe what I'm hearing. My father owes Senator Carduccio money, and he's offering me up as payment.

Fighting to pull myself together, I ignore the tears that are streaming down my face. I roll to my knees and listen to the conversation. This isn't the time to fall apart.

"Gentlemen, I'll go and grab us some more whiskeys," my father says.

The hatred I feel when I hear his voice overwhelms me. He's negotiating with my life, giving me a price value and offering me up to settle his debt. I've always thought he was a horrible father, but this right here has confirmed that he's also a despicable human being.

It's silent for a moment and then I hear Jeremy speak. "For fuck's sake, dad. What are you doing? We don't take people as payment. This asshole owes us money. I don't want to marry this girl, she's a mouse."

"She's fucking gorgeous though. I'm almost tempted to keep her for myself. Virgin eighteen- year-old pussy that doesn't speak or make demands. She's the holy grail of fuck toys. I only agreed to meet with Jefferies to see if he was actually serious about this. I can't stand the asshole, and who really offers up their daughter to cover their debt? But now I've seen her, she's the perfect politician's wife, the voters would love her," The Senator says.

"She's a fucking virgin?" Jeremy says, outraged.

The Senator laughs dryly. "So Jefferies assures me. Says she's been home schooled for the last five years. He told me her sister was a wild one, so he kept this one on a tight leash. She's pure as the driven fucking snow."

"Maybe I should marry her. Train her up just the way I like." Jeremy's voice is a low growl.

"I know how you like it. This one has to be seen in public, Jeremy." The Senator's voice is stern and Jeremy grumbles in response.

I pinch myself. This is actually happening. This kind of thing only happens in films and books, not in real life. My father can't actually sell me, can he?

"I got us the good stuff, gentlemen. So, tell me do we have a deal?" My father says, his voice jovial.

I want to scream at him through the window. How could he do this, offer me up as collateral to settle a debt? I'm his child—his only child since Nicole died. Why would he do this?

The clinking of glasses pulls me from my inner turmoil. "Yes, Jefferies, you've got a deal. One week from now, bring the girl or the hundred grand you owe us to the warehouse. Juan will deal with the exchange. You're a cold son of a bitch, but we'll take her, that virgin pussy is just too tempting."

He isn't a good person, but this. This is beyond inhumane. This is my life. I'm a person, not property to be sold. But this is actually happening. My father's selling me, and a Senator—a

United States Senator—is taking me as payment for a debt.

"Excellent, she'll make you a great wife, Jeremy. I assure you she's untouched, and she knows her place and what happens if she forgets it," my father says cheerfully.

The blood in my veins turns to ice. The men laugh and chat, but I stop listening. I've bided my time and planned my escape for a year, but I can't wait anymore. I didn't want to run until I'd convinced my mama to run with me, but it's too late now. I'm not experienced with the ways of the world; my father has made sure of that. But I do know that if I allow him to deliver me to the Senator and his son, I'll never be free again.

I have to run, and I have to go tonight.

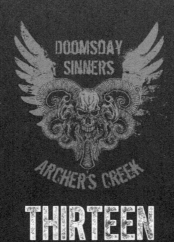

THIRTEEN

Daisy

Hidden around the corner from the mayor's house I pace agitatedly back and forth on the sidewalk. Carduccio is in there with the mayor and my Angel. I don't have a fucking clue why he's here, but I do know he's one dangerous son of a bitch and I don't want him within a hundred fucking miles of my girl.

My fingers clench and unclench into fists, my chest is heaving, and my teeth are gritted together so hard my jaw throbs with pain. I want to stomp across the street, beat down the door and get my girl out of there.

"What the fuck's up with you?" Blade asks.

I glare at him. "Nothing."

"Bullshit. You're pacing like a fucking wild animal. I've never seen you this wound up before. What you got against the mayor, you fucking his wife or something?"

I pull in a steadying breath and force my fists to unclench. "The mayor is a fucking dick, that's all."

Blade laughs. "Yes he is. You still didn't answer my question though. What's got you so riled up?"

Pointedly ignoring Blade, I pull my cell from my pocket and check my email, still nothing. It's the fifth time I've checked since Carduccio, a woman, and five other men, trailed into Angel's home forty-five minutes ago.

The cell phone is yanked from my hands and I swing round ready to attack Blade. "You might be my V.P., Blade, but I swear to fucking God you need to back off, right now. Now give me my fucking cell."

Blade ignores me, his eyes focused on the screen of my cell. "Who's Angel?"

I growl. "That's none of your goddamn business."

"She the girl? The one that's different."

I nod begrudgingly. "Yes."

Blade's face darkens. He looks over his shoulder to the mayor's house, back to me, then down to my cell that's still gripped in his hand. Slowly he raises his head until his eyes lock on mine. "You meet her at the wedding?"

I nod.

Blade's eyes fall closed for a moment and his shoulders sag. "That's why you were asking about Jefferies having a daughter. Angel is the fucking mayor's daughter."

I straighten my spine and keep my gaze locked on his, refusing to break the stare. "Yes."

Blade lifts his hand and rubs at his eyes. "So, you're telling me, that your girl is in that house over there with Eric fucking Carduccio?"

I nod.

"Well, fuck. How close to breaking down that door are you?"

"Pretty fucking close. It's new, me and her. But she's different, she's important. I don't know what the mayor's doing to her, but something's not right, all the warning signs are flashing."

Blade's eyes soften. "She got you all wrapped up in her, brother?"

"She looks like she needs saving. I wanna be the one to save her," I admit

Blade hisses air through his front teeth. "I hear you, brother, but if she's mixed up with Carduccio she might already be beyond saving."

The front door to the house opens and the woman and two of the security guys exit. They quickly climb into one of the Range Rovers and drive away. Thirty minutes later the door opens again and Carduccio and the other three men exit. Carduccio and the younger guy shake the mayor's hand and Mayor fucking Jefferies smiles and waves them off.

"Let's follow them, make sure they're not planning on

paying anyone else a visit before they leave town," Blade orders.

Reluctantly, I throw one last look at the mayor's house before I start my bike and ride away. A sick feeling pools at the bottom of my stomach. What the hell is a small-town mayor doing getting involved with a US Senator who's as dirty as they come?

We discreetly follow Carduccio straight out of town until he hits the freeway that will take him away from Texas and back toward New Mexico. Blade makes a U-turn and heads back to the clubhouse and I follow behind, even though all I want to do is ride straight to Angel and make sure she's okay.

When we enter the club, Blade disappears, and I head to the bar and take a seat. Billy, one of the retired brothers, is stood behind the worn wood and after taking one look at me, he drops a shot glass onto the bar and fills it to the top with whiskey. He fills another for himself and lifting his, he gestures for me to do the same. I pick up the glass and lift it to my lips; the whiskey burns as the liquid coats my throat and I slam the glass back to the bar. Pulling out my cell I scowl when there's still no email from Angel, so I write her instead.

From: Daisy@tddsmc.com
Sent: 10/02/17 14:24
To: Angelique@webservertx.com
Subject: I'm Worried

Angel,
Something fucked-up happened today. I ended up following a really dangerous guy straight to your house.

What the fuck is going on?

Eric Carduccio is bad news on an epic fucking scale. You need to stay the hell away from him.

I have a really bad feeling, Angel.

Remember what I said—you can come to me anytime and I'll keep you safe. This is an offer without any expectations. I'll keep you safe as your friend, or your guy; I just need you to be safe.

The Sinners clubhouse is on Deer Lake Road. Day or night there's always someone here. Ask for me, tell them you're mine.

Daisy.

I click send and blow out a hard breath. I literally just met this girl. How the fuck did I go from single and carefree, screwing as much pussy as I could handle, to completely hung up on an eighteen- year-old that I've only kissed a handful of times? This isn't how I operate. I don't get emotionally involved. I just like sex and lots of it.

I'd lay money on the fact that Angel's a virgin; she exudes innocence. Her huge desolate eyes say she's lived a hard life, but she's a sea of contradictions and I want her more than any other woman I've ever met.

"Daisy, get in here," Anders voice bellows from his office and I blow out a resigned breath. I knew this conversation was coming. Standing from the stool, I tap the wood of the bar before I make my way through the clubhouse to Prez's office.

Anders is standing in the doorway when I get there, and he moves to the side, signaling for me to enter. I walk past him and into the smaller room. Blade is sat in a chair to the right-hand side and I slide into the empty one next to him.

Anders slowly walks around his desk, lowering himself into the large chair behind it. He steeples his fingers and rests his chin on top of them. "Son, want to tell me what's goin' on with you and the mayor's daughter? Normally I wouldn't give a fuck where you're sticking your dick, but Carduccio drove all the way in from New Mexico to see our illustrious mayor and I need to know what the fuck's going on."

I scowl. "You're right, Prez, it isn't any of your goddamn business."

Anders lifts his head and clenches his hands into fists, banging one down onto the desk. His face darkens and his lips twist into an angry line. "Watch your mouth, son. Carduccio is a fucking viper, he's into everything: drugs, guns, human trafficking. I don't want him in this fucking town. So I'm not asking you, I'm ordering you, as your president, to tell me what the hell you're doing with the mayor's daughter."

Gripping the arms of the chair tightly, I force my anger down so I don't launch myself at him. "Her name is Angelique. I met her at Echo's wedding and then again in town four days ago. She's eighteen," I say begrudgingly.

Anders stares at me expectantly. "And…"

"And that's it. I haven't seen her since. She doesn't have a cell phone and the only way I can contact her is through email. She replied for the first time in four days today. I can't prove it, but I think the mayor's abusive. She flinches and cowers, I've seen the signs before. She had a sister that died a couple years back. That's all I know," I say.

"So no way she's using you to get intel for Carduccio?" Blade asks.

"No," I roar. "She's not like that; she's innocent, practically scared of her own shadow."

"Calm the fuck down," Anders says, his voice cutting through the red haze that's started to descend upon me. "You barely know this girl."

"She's different," I say, my voice quiet but laced with warning.

"Well, fuck, let's hope she's not mixed up with Carduccio, else this one's gonna want us to start a war because *she's different*," Blade says snidely.

I stand from my chair and angrily turn to face Blade. "Fuck you, Blade. She's not mixed up with Carduccio. Mayor asshat might be, but Angel isn't. She's never asked a single question about the club, not one."

"Shut up the pair of you," Anders shouts. "Sit your ass back down," he points at me and I slump back down into my seat.

"Why doesn't this girl have a cell phone?" Anders asks.

"Her dad won't let her have one. Apparently, she's been home schooled since she was thirteen. She doesn't have any friends. She's hardly ever allowed out the house. The mayor has her on lockdown. When I met her at the wedding, asshat was ripping into her for being there, then sent her home before she could even speak to me. She told me he'd kill her if he found out she was talking to me, that he hates the bikers," I say.

Anders looks at me and blows out a breath. "Email her and see what you can find out about Carduccio. If Jefferies has got into bed with him, we need to know why, and she might know something."

I scowl. "I already emailed her, but I'm not using her for information, Prez, and honestly I don't think she'll know anything anyway."

"Well, I hope for your sake that she's not already involved with them. Let me know when she replies," Anders says and dismisses us.

I follow Blade from the office and into the main room of the clubhouse. I head straight for the bar and seat myself back on a stool.

Blade sits next to me. "You need to keep your head straight, brother. I know you like this girl, but you don't know what games she's playing. This innocent thing could just be an act."

I shake my head. "I thought it was; fuck no one is that innocent. But she is. I'm telling you Blade, if her dad and Carduccio are planning something she hasn't got a clue."

Blade looks skeptical but his hand slaps down on my shoulder and he squeezes lightly. "Billy, we're gonna need some shots."

Two shot glasses full of whiskey appear in front of us and I lift mine to my lips and down it. I signal to Billy for another and he fills the glass again. I throw that one back too. The whiskey calms my fraught nerves, but I still pull my cell out and check for an email. Yet again there isn't one.

FOURTEEN

Angel

Two hours ago, my father negotiated using me as payment for the hundred thousand dollars he owes to Senator Carduccio. I keep replaying the conversation over and over in my head, but it doesn't make any more sense to me now, than it did at the time.

People are not property to be sold or bartered with, or at least that was my understanding. Until today I genuinely believed that. I know that my father is a bad man. I know that the violence he expresses toward me and my mother is wrong and completely unacceptable. But I think deep down I thought he loved me, the child he had helped to create.

I was wrong.

My ass and legs are numb, but I force myself to move from the spot I collapsed onto hours ago. Hearing my father clink glasses and celebrate selling me, rendered my limbs useless. It's ironic really, my father has told me again and again that I'm worthless, but apparently he was wrong. I laugh dryly to myself; apparently my value is a cool one hundred thousand dollars.

I know exactly what the balance of my father's bank account has been for the last year and never at any point has he that kind of money. So where did he put it and what did he spend it on?

I don't know the answers to those questions, but I do know that I need to get away from this house. I no longer have the luxury of time to plan my escape. I need to go as soon as possible and get as far away as I can to somewhere my father will never find me.

Padding across my room I silently click the door shut and slide the lock across. My father has never allowed me to lock the door, but right now I don't care about his rules and I need to make sure no one comes in. Rummaging at the back of my wardrobe I pull out the rucksack I used when I was in elementary school; it's ancient and childish but it's all I have.

Adrenaline courses through me and my hands shake as I grab my laptop and power cord and shove them into the bag. Dragging a couple of dresses and some underwear from my closet I push them on top of the laptop and quickly make my way to my bathroom. I grab some basic toiletries and throw them haphazardly into the bag along with my driver's license and the small amount of cash I have hidden beneath my mattress.

Panicking, I spin around and scan the room, trying to decide what else I should take. My eyes fall to my dresser and a gasp escapes me. Rushing across the room I drop to my knees and quickly slide open the bottom drawer. Pushing my hand inside the dresser I pull out a framed photo of me, my mama, and Nicole, that was taken years ago. We're smiling and laughing. I don't remember where we were, or what we were doing, but we look carefree and even though that's not the life we've actually lived, at least for the moment the picture captured we were happy.

I place the photo in the bag and pull the zip closed. Stepping back, I stare at the small bag. I can't risk taking more than I can comfortably carry, but when it really comes down to it, this small bag is all I want to keep, a handful of things that I don't want to leave behind.

Placing the rucksack back in my closet, I unlock the door and crawl onto my bed. I lie with my head on my pillow for five minutes, pulling in deep, controlled breaths and then exhaling slowly. A wordless tune plays in my head, constantly on loop and the familiar lullaby soothes me and allows me to force my tumultuous thoughts into a box. Falling apart is not a luxury I can afford right now. Once I'm away from Archer's Creek and beyond my father's reach, I'll allow myself to break down and grieve the loss of my family, but for now I need to be strong.

An hour later I roll into a sitting position and brace my hands against my knees, my feet flat on the floor. The damaged skin on my legs pulls and the pain is a constant throb, but I ignore it. I stand up and make my way into my bathroom. I touch up my makeup, making sure all of the bruises on my face are still hidden and then make my way downstairs.

The smell of tomato and herbs hits me when I enter the family room. My mama is cooking. Where I hide inside my mind, Mama hides in the kitchen, and the more elaborate the meals, the more anguished she really is.

Several pans sit atop the huge range stove and Mama is busily stirring a wooden spoon into a mixing bowl. She looks up and smiles. "Angelique, grab me the cinnamon please."

I nod and turn to the spice rack, finding the cinnamon and passing it to her. She takes it and spoons out a measure, adding it to the bowl. Moving to the stove, I start to stir the pan full of tomato sauce and the rich smell of oregano wafts upwards making my stomach growl. Mama chuckles. "The pasta should be about ready, drain it then make yourself a plate."

Mechanically, I move around the kitchen, fetching a sieve and draining the pasta. "How many plates?" I ask.

"Just you, honey. Your father has gone out and I'll have something later."

I spoon some of the pasta into a bowl and pour the rich sauce on top. Mama hands me a fork and I eagerly dig in. Lifting a forkful to my mouth I groan appreciatively when the first piece hits my tongue and I continue to eat, watching Mama flit around the kitchen. The first tear takes me by surprise, the second hits the bowl of pasta and I blink rapidly hoping to prevent any more from falling. I'm leaving my home tonight and I don't know when I'll get to see her again.

A low sob escapes me, and Mama spins around. "Baby, what's the matter?"

I can't tell her. She'll either think I'm making it up, or worse she already knows what my father has planned for me and is so brainwashed by him that she doesn't understand how wrong it is. I'm so scared that it's the latter that I just throw myself at her and let her hug me.

Her weak, thin arms hold me tightly against her and she hugs me like she used to when I was a child. We hold each other for a long time and when we break apart tears are running down her face too. Our gazes lock and without saying a word we say goodbye. I haven't told her I'm leaving, but the peace that settles in her gray eyes tells me that somehow, she knows.

Her frail fingers cup my cheeks and she smiles weakly at me, then her hands fall from my face and she walks to the other side of the kitchen. Opening the cupboard that holds the first aid kit and medicines, she pulls down a brown pill bottle and opens it, taking out five tablets. I watch as she drops them into her pestle and mortar and grinds them into a fine powder.

My mouth falls open when she crosses to the stove and sprinkles the power into the red tomato sauce. With a small smile on her face she walks past the counter I'm sitting at and places the medicine bottle in front of me.

I lift the bottle and read the label. "Benzodiazpine, one tablet to be taken at night time." Sleeping tablets, my mama just laced the food she plans to feed my father with sleeping tablets. She lifts the bottle from my hands and takes it back to the cupboard. Returning to me she pushes my bowl of pasta toward me and gently squeezes my shoulder.

"I'll tell your Daddy you're sick and that you won't be joining us for dinner," she whispers, a sad smile on her face.

I want to beg her to come with me, to run away too, but I don't. Instead I eat my pasta then place my dish in the dishwasher and pull her into another tight hug.

"Be free," she whispers into my ear, then pulls away and continues to cook.

I spend the rest of the afternoon in my room. I hear when my father comes home and wait patiently as the sun sets and day turns to night. Hours later I hear my parents climb the stairs and go to their room; it's only 10pm but minutes later I hear my father's snores echoing through the walls.

I wait silent and on edge until the clock hits 11pm and then I remove the bag from my closet and pull on my jacket. Taking a last look around my room I realize I have very few fond memories from this house and I'm not sad to leave. Despite the reason for my escape, this is a chance at a new life and excitement hums through me.

I don't look back as I sneak down the stairs and out of the front door. Looping my arms through both straps of my backpack, I quickly walk down the street and away from my home. I anxiously check over my shoulder, my heart pounding with fear that my father might wake up and come after me. Archer's Creek isn't a big town, so I easily make it to the bus station ten minutes later. A small schedule is taped on the wall and my heart falls when I see that the last bus left at 10:30 pm and there isn't another one until 7am tomorrow.

Panic starts to churn in my stomach. I can't wait until the morning to get out of town. I don't know how long the sleeping pills will last and I can't risk still being in Archer's Creek when my father wakes up and finds me missing. Next to the bus schedule is a business card for the town's only taxi. I pull the card from the wall and try to remember if there's still a payphone in town.

I think I remember seeing one at the convenience store a few blocks away, so with my head down I start the walk across town. It's late and most of the streets are empty; the people I do see don't give me a second glance and I sigh in relief when the store's neon sign comes into view. I walk through the door and it beeps to inform the cashier of my entrance. Making my way to the back of the store I spot the payphone and quickly rush toward it.

I pull a small pile of change from my bag and lift the phone's receiver. Silence. There's no dial tone and nothing happens when I press the buttons.

"Phone hasn't worked for about a year now," the cashier says from his spot at the counter.

Closing my eyes, I will back the tears that are threatening to escape and slowly replace the receiver. I make my way back to the front of the store, where the cashier—an overweight man, with greasy hair and stains down the front of his gray sweater—is sat, his hand inside a huge bag of Cheetos.

"Is there another payphone anywhere in town?" I ask.

The cashier thinks about this for a minute. He lifts his finger to his ear, twists it inside the hole and then inspects the orange wax that's now visible on his nail. "No, I can't think of any," he eventually says.

Disgusted, I nod and quickly leave the store. Hurrying around the corner, I eventually collapse onto a street bench. "What am I going to do now?" I say aloud. I should have considered that buses don't run this late at night, but the last time I got a bus was the one that took me to school more than five years ago. I could go back and ask the cashier if he has a cell phone I could use, but I really don't want to go back into the store with him.

Sitting on the bench, I try to decide how long it would take me to walk to the next town. They might have a working payphone, or at least I could wait there until the bus came along in the morning. A motorcycle engine roars loudly in the quiet night and I sit up straighter in my seat.

Daisy.

I could go to Daisy and use his cell phone to call a cab, or maybe I could ask him to take me to Houston. Daisy would help me, I'm absolutely certain of that. Even though we've only known each other for a very short space of time I know he would help me.

I'm up and walking in the direction of the Doomsday Sinners clubhouse before I even fully make the decision to go. Daisy had told me where it was in one of his emails, but he hadn't needed to. Everyone in town knows where the clubhouse is, even me.

The club is only about two miles out of town, but the quiet country lanes don't have any streetlamps and walking in the pitch black takes longer than I expect. It's close to midnight by the time the lights of the clubhouse first come into view and I spot the high fence that circles the bikers' compound. Huge security lights are hung on high poles, illuminating the metal gates that mark the entrance and my steps slow to an apprehensive crawl as I approach.

What if I was wrong about Daisy? What if he turns me away, or if I can't get to see him at all? My heart races and nerves pulse through me as I step into the arc of light and toward the gates.

A small hut is situated to the left of the entrance and as I reach out to push the gate, a figure moves in the darkness from the direction of the hut. "Think you're in the wrong place, darlin'. There's no party here tonight."

I jump at the voice and strain my eyes to make out what the figure looks like in the darkness. My voice is small and full of fear. "Excuse me, I'm looking for Daisy."

A man steps into the light and openly appraises me. He's

maybe a few years older than me, tall and slim, but his eyes glint menacingly and I instinctively step back. "Get out of here, bitch. There's no party tonight and we wouldn't let you in dressed like that anyway."

He starts to turn away, so I panic and shout, "I'm not here for a party. I need to see Daisy. Could you tell him I'm here please?"

The man smiles and laughs dryly. "Daisy isn't here, darlin', but you can come visit with me. I'll audition you, see if you have something under that nasty dress the boys might like." The look on his face is lascivious and his lips are twisted into a sneer.

Taking another step backward, I start to turn away, but my eyes are drawn to another figure moving in the darkness. When he moves into the light, this man is older and wearing a leather vest with colored patches on it. His eyes move from me to the young guy and back again. "What you got here, Slow?" He says to the young guy.

"This one wants in. I've offered to see if she's got anything the guys might want." The young guy says as he slides the lock across and starts to push open the gates.

My heart races and the urge to run builds in my chest. I take another step back and turn to the older man. "I'm looking for Daisy; he told me to come here."

The older man's face changes from leering to confused. "Daisy told you to come here?" he says stepping toward me.

"Yes," I nod. My mind flashes back to Daisy's emails and

his offer for me to come to him. The words run through my head; he said if I had any trouble to tell them I was his. "I'm his," I blurt loudly.

Both men stop and turn to look at me. "You're Daisy's?" the older guy says looking unconvinced.

"Yes," I say with as much conviction as I can muster in my voice. "I'm Daisy's. Could someone tell him I'm here please?"

The older guy pulls opens the gate and reaches for me. I flinch, but his hand wraps around my wrist and holds me tightly. "Let's go find your man then, honey," he says with a smirk and walks away, pulling me along behind him.

I stumble but manage to stay upright and hurry to keep up with the fast pace as he leads me across the dark courtyard and toward the main building. The windows are all lit up and I can hear music coming from inside. The guy pulls open a door and drags me through it and into a room filled with rowdy men and a few women.

I try not to stare, but my eyes dart from person to person, unsure where to look next. People are watching the guy pull me into the room and I see the curious stares and amused laughs. I search the faces for Daisy, but I don't see him, and I question if coming here was a really stupid idea.

"Daisy," the guy shouts. "Daisy, does this belong to you?" he coos.

Glancing around me I watch as more people stop what they're doing and turn to stare at us. I look over my shoulder and toward the door we just entered through. Maybe I should try to break free and run for the exit? My eyes fall on the younger guy from the gatehouse. He's standing behind me, his arms crossed and a salacious smirk on his face. I shudder. I hadn't realized he had followed us.

"Daisy," the older guy calls again in a singsong voice. "Daisy." He turns back to me and drops my wrist. "Sorry, honey, doesn't look like Daisy wants to claim you."

Arms wrap around me from behind and the young guy's voice speaks into my neck. "I'll have her. Reckon this dress is hiding something wet and willing beneath it."

I freeze. Coming here was a mistake.

"Let go of her, Slow. She don't look like that kind of a girl. She's practically still a child," the older guy says, and I release a slow breath of air.

"Nah, she's legal aren't you, darlin'?" The younger guy says, amusement filling his tone.

"Let me go please and I'll leave. I thought Daisy would be here, he told me to come," I say, my voice trembling with fear.

"Get your fucking hands off her," Daisy's voice roars and I sag in relief.

DOOMSDAY
SINNERS

ARCHER'S CREEK

FIFTEEN

Daisy

ost nights I hang out at the bar with the guys. I play pool or indulge in the whores that like to party at the club. Tonight, I'm pissed and not in the mood to be social with anyone. I've lost count of how many times I've checked my email since I left Angel's house earlier today, but she still hasn't replied.

I want to drive over and see her, but I know I can't, so instead I check my email again. My TV is playing quietly in the background, but I'm too agitated to watch it. Images of Angel are running on a loop through my mind and my cock is rock hard and begging me to go find her. I pull off my T-shirt and punch my pillows to try to get comfortable, but my balls are aching and nothing I do is going to make me feel better unless I find a woman or my hand to take care of it.

I'm undoing the buttons on my jeans when a fist bangs against my door. "Yeah?" I shout.

The door opens and a smiling K.C. leans into my room. "Brother, you need to get out here. Erickson's dragged some Amish looking girl into the club and he's shouting about her being yours."

I jump off the bed and push past K.C., running toward the bar.

Angel. Her eyes are wide and full of fear and my body goes on full alert. I quickly take in the situation. Erickson is standing next to her, but Slow, the fucking bastard, has his hands on her, talking into her ear. "Get your fucking hands off her," I roar. Angel visibly sags in relief when she hears my voice and I push people out of the way until I'm in front of her.

Slow lifts his head and smirks at me. "What's the matter, Daisy? She doesn't seem like your type."

A deep feral growl escapes from my throat, "Let her go. NOW. Before I break both of your arms."

Slow's eyebrows snap up, but his arms don't loosen from around Angel.

"Slow," Erickson warns.

I take a step toward Angel, and Slow releases her, lifting his arms into the air and sneering at me. "Fuck this, you can have her. Jailbait Amish pussy isn't worth the effort."

Angel rushes over to me and I pull her into my arms, her

tiny body is shaking and her face is pale. I quickly kiss the top of her head and hold her away from me, so I can look at her. "Are you ok?" I whisper.

Her nod is barely perceptible, but I see it and carefully guide her behind me. Stepping into Slow's chest, I twist my fists into his shirt. "Don't ever touch what's mine again," I snarl, my voice full of hatred. Slamming my head down onto his face, his nose explodes with the force and as I release my grip on his shirt, he drops to the floor.

I hear his cries of pain and outrage as I turn my back on him, but all my focus is now on Angel. Wrapping her in my arms I silently walk her through the crowd of my brothers who quickly clear a path for us.

Angel's body has stopped trembling by the time we reach my room, and opening the door, I guide her inside and quietly close it behind us. She pauses a few steps ahead of me, her spine ramrod straight and her hands clenched into tight fists. I step closer to her and place my hand on her arm. She flinches.

Anger burns in my chest. Why the fuck would this beautiful, innocent woman flinch at my touch? I want to scream and demand to know who has hurt her, but I don't want to scare her any more than she already is. Taking a deep calming breath, I swallow my rage and then as gently as I can, I slide my hand between her fingers and un-pry her fists.

"I'm so sorry, Daisy. I shouldn't have come here. I never even considered that it would cause trouble for you. I just needed to use a phone and the only payphone in town wasn't working and you said I could come to you. I'm just, I'm so sorry."

The words rush from her, while her eyes stay glued to the floor beneath her feet. Using my free hand, I lift her chin and force her eyes to meet mine. I don't say a word, just lean forward and capture her lips with my own.

The moment my mouth touches hers, tingles start to move through my nerve endings and my mind quiets. Her flowery smell surrounds me, and I lose myself in her. My body relaxes and I drop her face to wrap my arms around her back and pull her closer into my chest.

She comes willingly; her tiny hand tentatively moves up my arm and grips onto my bicep, until she's holding me as tightly as I'm holding her. The kiss is slow, our lips massaging each other in a loving caress. I nip at her lower lip and she gasps, opening her mouth wide enough for me to slide my tongue inside and slowly tangle with hers. Her response surprises me. Her tongue moves against mine and a low and sensual moan escapes from her.

My cock pushes against my jeans as her breasts press against my bare chest. I want to throw her onto my bed and rip away that ugly dress. I want to make her moan and scream and pant. To touch and lick and stroke every perfect fucking inch of her and I want to do it now. But this is Angel, and I can't—won't— treat her like a club whore looking for a quick fuck.

Pulling my lips away from hers, I physically move her a

step back from me and hold her at arm's length. "What are you doing to me, Angel?" I pant.

"I'm sorry," she whispers, her eyes half-lidded and full of desire.

Her voice is breathy, and I close my eyes and groan, searching for some self-control. I pull in a deep breath and slowly release it before I open my eyes again and look at her.

Her head is still raised, and her eyes stare back at me unsure. "I'm sorry, I just needed to use your cell or maybe get a ride into Houston. I had no idea coming here would cause this much trouble."

I blink at her words and tilt my head to the side. "Wait, what? Why would you need to go to Houston?"

She drops her eyes to the floor, but I lift her chin up so she's looking at me. "I like those pretty eyes, Angel. Keep them on me, not the floor, okay?"

She nods.

"So, explain to me why you would need to use my cell phone or have me give you a ride to Houston at midnight." I watch her closely; she swallows and her eyes flit from me to the door, then back to me again. I see the moment she decides to explain and wait silently for her to speak.

"I need to get out of Archer's Creek before my father realizes I've gone."

That wasn't what I was expecting. It shouldn't surprise me. I knew something was going on with her dad and I'd told her to come to me. But why is she running and what, if anything, does Carduccio showing up today have to do with it? "Where are you going?"

"As far away as possible," she says.

I hear the steel in her voice and see the emotion swirling in her eyes. She means it; my Angel is running away. "Wait, what's happened to make you run?" I ask. I can hear the panic in my own voice. If she runs I might never see her again, and that is not okay.

Fuck, I'm in deep with this girl already. I didn't know how deep until I saw her standing in my club, looking terrified. I only just found her and now she wants to run away—to run as far away as possible from Archer's Creek and me.

"I completely understand if you can't take me to Houston, Daisy. We barely know each other. But would it be okay if I used your cell to call a cab please?"

"Whoa, whoa, whoa, slow down. Now what the fuck's happened? Did he hurt you?" Dropping my hold on her arms, I lift my hands to my hair and twist at the strands agitatedly. Without my touch, she drops her gaze back down to the floor and tangles her fingers together in front of her.

"Angel," I call. Her gaze stays locked at her feet, so instead of demanding her eyes I crouch down in front of her. "Angel, it's late. Stay here tonight, explain what's happened to me and if you still want to go I'll take you to Houston in the morning."

She starts to shake her head. "No, no. I need to get out of

Archer's Creek now. If my father finds me he'll hand me over and I'll never get away."

Fear laces her voice and I quickly stand and pull her against my chest, rubbing my hand soothingly up and down her back. "It's okay, Angel, you're safe here. I promise he can't get to you here."

Tiny hands push against my chest and I reluctantly release her. Angel steps back and looks up at me, tears pooling at the corners of her eyes but not spilling over the edge. "You don't understand," she cries.

"So explain it to me, Angel."

Her eyes have tormented my dreams since the very first time we met, but I've never seen them look like they do today. Her huge amber depths are swirling with so many emotions they almost seem to glow.

Her teeth pull at her bottom lip and her eyes move from me to her hands and back again. She laughs humorlessly. "You wouldn't believe me if I told you."

All the air in my lungs seems to disappear and fear trickles up the back of my neck. "Try me," I say, my voice lower than I intended.

Angel stiffens at the tone of my voice and I silently curse myself. Stepping closer to her, I slowly reach up and slide the straps of her backpack down her shoulders and place it on the floor. She turns her head to watch me as I move behind her and place a kiss on the back of her neck. I guide her jacket down her arms allowing one of my fingers to caress a path along her skin, before I step away and fold the jacket over the back of a chair.

Her eyes follow me as I step in front of her again and slide my hand down the silky skin of her arm, entwining my fingers with hers. Angel lets me lead her toward the bed and when I sink against the pillows she moves next to me. I don't release her hand, instead I turn to face her and rub my thumb back and forth across her palm.

"Tell me what's happened, Angel. It doesn't matter how crazy it sounds, I promise I'll believe you and I'll help you."

As she stares at me, her pupils dilate and her head tilts to the side assessing. I recognize the look in her eyes, she's deciding if she can trust me or not. When her face softens, the breath I hadn't realized I'd been holding exhales in a relieved hiss.

"Some people came to visit my father today and he told me that they would want to meet me. That's never happened before, my father doesn't introduce me to people—he pretends I don't exist most of the time. After I met them, I went back up to my room and my father went out onto the patio with some of the men to talk. I could hear them from my window."

I stiffen, her father introduced her to Carduccio. I want to scream and rage, but I need to know what else happened, so I silently wait for her to continue speaking.

"I don't really know how to say it. I almost don't believe it's true and I heard it all," she says, laughing weakly.

Pulling in a deep breath, her eyes lock with mine. "My

father apparently owes these men a lot of money and he offered me up as payment. My father sold me to settle his debt. He's supposed to deliver me or the money in a few days time."

A single tear falls from Angel's eyes and I lose it. Jumping from the bed I pick up a chair and fling it across the room. The wood hits the brick wall with a loud bang and then drops to the floor.

I don't process Angel's scream of fear until I turn to face her. All the life has disappeared from her face and an expressionless mask has replaced the myriad of emotions she had shown me tonight. Remorse hits me like a freight train.

Rushing across the room I sink to my knees at her feet and grasp her hands. "I'm sorry, I'm so sorry. Please look at me. I would never hurt you, I promise you. I'm angry at what you just told me, I'm angry that your father would do that and that he put you in danger. Please, Angel, please."

I'm literally on my knees begging, but I'd do it forever rather than have her retreat into herself. She flinches when I reach up to touch her face and I quickly drop my hand and move away from her. "Angel," I beg, my voice broken.

It feels like forever before she finally lifts her eyes to look at me again. The huge copper orbs are lifeless and only a tiny spark of something gives me hope that I haven't frightened away the fire I'd seen earlier.

I curve my hand around her cheek and look deep into her eyes, imploring her to see me. "I'm sorry, Angel. I might get angry, but you need to know that I will never turn that anger on you. Ever. Scream at me, Angel. Scream, shout, but please, please, don't shut down."

Long arduous moments pass, then she nods and her eyes start to warm with life again. Carefully, I pull her into my arms and hold her until she relaxes into my chest.

After a few minutes I pull back from our embrace. "Did they mention how much money your father owes?" I ask.

"One hundred thousand dollars," she says quietly.

I whistle through my teeth. "Fuck."

"I need to get away from Archer's Creek, Daisy. My father was celebrating, he was happy to work out this deal to sell me. Senator Carduccio is a powerful man and they talked about me marrying his son, but I'm not for sale. I'm not going to let him do this to me, so I need to run."

"Fuck, Angel, once Carduccio owns you he'll track you down. He won't let you run. He's a really fucking dangerous man. He's got ties to more than one cartel and enough dirty cops in his pocket to find you no matter where you hide. When's your dad supposed to deliver you to him?"

"He's supposed to take me to a warehouse a week from today. Senator Carduccio said to bring me or the money."

I blow out the lungful of air I'd unknowingly been holding onto. "That's good, Angel, that gives us a week to decide what to do."

"No," Angel shouts, standing from the bed. "We don't

need to decide on anything, Daisy. I need to get as far away as possible from my father and then he can't hand me over. I just need to get to Houston."

I stand up and Angel tips her head back to look at me.

"Let me help you, Angel. I can keep you safe. What happens when your dad starts to search for you? What happens if he finds you? You'll be on your own. Stay here, the club will protect you. I will protect you."

I watch as Angel processes my words. She has no idea how much danger she's in. She doesn't understand that unless we do something to make sure she becomes off limits to Carduccio, this might not end once the payment deadline passes.

Angel opens her mouth to speak, but I interrupt her. "I like you, Angel. Let me protect you." Then I kiss her. I pull her into my arms and hold her against my chest. My lips devour hers and our tongues entwine. She matches my intensity move for move. Wrapping her hand around my neck she digs her nails into my skin, holding me to her. Soft moans keen from her throat and unconsciously she rubs her hot pussy against my rock-hard cock.

I force myself to pull away from her. I need to convince her to let me help and I don't know if fucking her would persuade her to stay or make her even more convinced to run. "Stay here with me, let me help you, Angel." I murmur against her lips.

"I'll stay for tonight," she whispers.

I let out a sigh of relief and crush her to my chest. Dropping a quick kiss against her lips I release her and move to pick up her bag from the floor. "You got any sleep stuff in here?"

She takes the bag from my hand and opens it. I watch as she roots through her stuff and then turns to me and shakes her head, biting her lip nervously. "I didn't pack any. I just have a couple of dresses and some underwear. I can just sleep in my clothes, it's fine."

Walking across the room to my dresser, I open a drawer and I pull out a T-shirt and a pair of my boxers. I hand them to her. "They're gonna be huge on you, but it's better than sleeping in a dress. Do you wanna have a shower before bed? I gotta go speak to Prez for a minute."

She nods silently and steps toward me to take the clothes from my outstretched hand. The moment she gets close enough I pull her to me and kiss her quickly. "Shower's just through there, clean towels are on the shelves. Use anything of mine you need, okay?"

Angel looks up at me shyly. "Okay, thank you."

I kiss her again and smile. "I won't be long, but just stay in here and click the lock on the door behind me." She nods and watches as I open the door and leave the room.

Leaning against the wall outside my room I wait to hear the lock click into place. My heartbeat starts to slow once I hear the reassuring clunk of the lock and I slowly walk down the corridor and into the main room of the clubhouse. Scanning the faces of my brothers, I find Blade within a group of guys sitting around the pool table. "Blade," I call.

He turns to face me with a wide smile on his face. "Fucking hell,

Daisy, that was quick! I heard you had a pretty little piece of jailbait turn up asking for you. I figured you'd be balls deep by now."

Ignoring his jibes, I signal off to the side with my fingers. "I need a word."

Blade's eyebrows rise in question, but he stands and follows me to the side of the room where it's quieter. "What's going on," he asks.

"Is Anders here? I need to talk to both of you."

Blade nods. "Yeah, he's in his office I think. I saw him heading that way a while back."

Blade walks toward Anders' office and I follow behind him. The door is open and Anders waves us in when he sees us. I close the door behind us and both men stare at me expectantly.

"What's up, Daisy?" Anders asks.

Aggravated, I pace the small space between the chairs and the door. "Prez, the girl that turned up asking for me is Angelique, the mayor's daughter. I don't know all the details, but the reason Carduccio went to visit Jefferies today was because our fine mayor owes the Senator a hundred grand. It doesn't look like he's got the money because he negotiated a trade of property instead of cash." Fisting my hands into my hair I pull at the strands. "The fucking asshole agreed to give them his daughter to cover his debt." I say, my voice a deadly snarl.

"Daisy, calm down." Anders growls.

"He tried to sell her. I can't fucking calm down!" I shout. Stopping my pacing I stand behind a chair, my fingers gripping the black fabric tightly.

"Where's the girl now?" Blade asks.

"She's in my room. She wants to run. The only reason she came to me is because she needs to get to Houston. I'm not gonna let Carduccio have her, Prez, no fucking way."

"Of course we're not gonna let her go to Carduccio. For fuck's sake we don't condone human trafficking, we've never touched that shit. But right now, we need to stay calm and think about how we're gonna handle this. She's not part of the club. I don't know if the rest of the brothers are gonna be up for a stand-off with Carduccio for a girl you just met. Plus, this could all be an act; the girl could be working with Carduccio to infiltrate the club."

A growl escapes me, and I squeeze the chair between my tense fingers. "She's not playing a part, Prez. She's scared and running. She overheard her dad and Carduccio talking about it. Apparently the mayor wants to marry her off to Carduccio's son, but either way he's supposed to hand over her or the cash in a week's time."

Anders taps the top of his desk with a finger, staring thoughtfully at me. "Go fetch her. I want to talk to her."

I nod and turn to leave, then pause and turn back to him "She scares easy, so don't be a dick to her." I don't wait for a response before I open the door and start walking back to my room and my Angel.

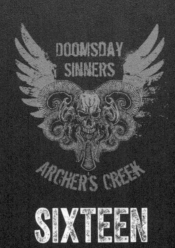

SIXTEEN

Angel

Daisy leaves the room and I quickly lock the door behind him and sink onto his bed with his clothes clutched in my hands. A ragged breath escapes me, and I pull my knees up to my chest and rest my chin on them.

What the hell am I doing here? I'm so out of my depth. The guy from the gate scared the hell out of me and now Daisy's overwhelming me too. His kisses scramble my brain and somehow instead of running away from Archer's Creek as fast as I can, I've agreed to stay, at least for tonight.

Daisy is so potent that I can't help being drawn to him, but I don't want to pull him into the mess that is my life. The man is a whirlwind and even though the violence of his anger scares me, the peace and calm I feel in his arms is so tempting that I'm struggling to say no.

It's the first time since my sister died that anyone in my life has offered to protect me and the idea is so unbelievably enticing, that I want to agree and stay shielded in his safe, warm arms. But this isn't his mess, it's mine, and I won't put him or his friends in the middle of it.

Resolved, I drop my feet to the floor and stand up. Daisy's offer of a shower sounds wonderful and I cross the room to his bathroom and close the door behind me. The small room is surprisingly clean. Reaching into the shower, I twist the lever that brings it to life and steam quickly fills the small space.

Stripping out of my clothes, I place them neatly on top of the counter and then step into the shower. The torrent of scolding hot water hits my naked skin and I shriek, jumping out of the water's reach. Fumbling with the lever I try to turn down the heat, but the water changes from scolding hot to freezing cold. I twist the lever the other way, testing the water with my hand until finally, I tentatively move my entire body back under the shower spray.

I moan in pleasure when the warm water hits me and the knotted muscles between my shoulders gradually start to relax. My eyes fall closed and I tip my head back under the water. All I can hear is the noise of the shower and the racing of my own heart. Breathing becomes hard and my sinuses sting with the onslaught of tears. I've held myself together all day, but here, naked in the shower of a virtual stranger, I fall apart. Grief, fear, and anger consume me and sinking to the floor of the shower I sob uncontrollably.

The hot tears that run down my cheeks are immediately washed away by the deluge of water that's pouring over my body. I allow my despair to engulf me for a few minutes, and then I force all of the emotion into a box in my brain and lock it tightly. I can process my father's betrayal another day when I'm far from his grasp and no longer under his control.

Pulling myself together, I rise from the floor and turn my face under the water to wash away the remnants of my tears. I sigh as I remember that my shower things are still in my backpack. There are bottles stacked neatly on a shelf to the side of the shower, so I reach out and grab his shampoo. Squeezing some into my hands, I lather up my hair, breathing in the clean soapy smell that is masculine but not unpleasant. Returning the bottle to the shelf I find a shower gel and wash my body quickly as the water starts to cool.

Turning off the water, I reach for a clean towel and wrap it around my wet body. The mirror above the counter is covered in a layer of condensation and I lift my hand to wipe it away then pause. I don't want to see the fear and uncertainty that I'm sure will be obvious in my eyes, so I lower my hand and leave the glass hidden.

Quickly drying my body, I wrap the towel around my wet hair and pull Daisy's T-shirt over my head. It falls almost to my knees. The fabric smells delicious and I lift the cotton to my face and inhale deeply. I pull on his boxers, but they immediately fall to the ground. The waist is far too big for me and I try rolling the fabric of the waistband to make them tighter, but as soon as I release them they fall straight down again. Giving up, I grab them from the floor and add them to the pile of clothes in my arms as I re-enter the bedroom.

My eyes fall to Daisy who is sat on the end of his bed. I'm barefoot and only wearing his T-shirt. Feeling uncomfortable, I pull at the hem of the shirt hoping to somehow make it magically longer.

He looks up and his eyes narrow. "What the fuck happened to your face?"

For a split second I just stare at him. What's wrong with my face? Realization dawns on me, he can see the remnants of my father's punishment. My face is a mess of bruises and I just washed away all of the makeup that was hiding them. The after effects of my father's temper are never talked about. Mama was so good at her makeup that I only ever suspected what it hid and whenever he hit my face we never talked about it. His abuse was the eternal elephant in the room, constantly present but never acknowledged.

"Angel." His voice is a low growl and I instinctively drop my eyes to the floor and stay quiet. I flinch when his fingers lift my chin, and I force my eyes to meet his. The anger in his gaze is palpable but as his soft fingers trace the bruises on my cheekbones and around my eye it turns to sorrow. Each emotion flares so vividly across his beautiful face that I stop breathing for a moment.

"Angel, who did this to you?"

Telling him the truth will only pull him even deeper into my life and I can't allow that. Instead I reach up and lift his fingers from my face. Taking a step back I turn and walk away from him.

"What the fuck happened to your legs?" He roars.

I spin around, clutching the clothes to my chest and hiding my bruised and battered legs from his eyes. Daisy strides toward me and I back away. "Daisy, no," I cry.

Ignoring me he pries the clothes from my fists and drops them to the floor. Firm hands wrap around my waist and lift me to stand on the bed. "Daisy," I shout and try to move, but his unrelenting grip on my waist stops me.

Careful fingers lift the hem of his T-shirt, exposing more of my abused skin. "How far up do they go?" his voice is quiet, barely above a whisper.

I sigh. "To the base of my spine."

"Belt?"

I nod.

"Your dad?"

I nod again.

I feel, rather than see him drop the hem of the shirt and walk away from me. Shame fills me, and I want to curl in a ball and hide from the mortification of admitting that my father did this to me.

Holding the hem of the shirt I silently step down from the bed and hurry to my backpack. Pulling out a pair of clean panties I glance at Daisy, his prone figure is facing the door with his hands braced on either side of his head.

I step back into the bathroom, remove the towel from around my head and pull on my panties. The wounds on my legs are sore, but until Daisy saw them I'd forced the discomfort to the back of my mind. The first time my father punished me this way I had allowed the pain and agony to show. That had only angered my father further and I quickly learnt to pretend I was fine.

Reluctantly, I open the bathroom door, expecting to find the bedroom empty. Instead Daisy stands a few feet away, waiting for me. His eyes blaze with fury and sorrow and some emotion that I can't quite identify. I wish I could ask what it was. I don't want his sympathy and my stomach churns at the thought that he might feel sorry for me.

Stepping into the room, I fight the urge to lower my eyes. Ignoring my years of conditioning I strive to accept his gaze and offer him mine in return. My insides quiver; I should cower from him, to submit to his anger and protect myself. But despite the fury that's so evident in him, I don't fear him.

My father shows the world his mask of cordiality and affability, but the real Mayor Jefferies is cruel and heinous with no regard for right and wrong. I wonder how many of his friends and constituents would believe he beats and abuses his wife and daughter?

We all wear a mask; mine hides both the crumbled ruins my father's abuse has created and the strength and resolve I've had to suppress to survive. I want to see beneath Daisy's mask. He told me I make him feel and even though he tries to hide his emotions, right now I can see them all too clearly.

"Come here." His words are softly spoken but resolute, and I cautiously step closer to him.

"When did he do that to you?" he asks.

My voice is barely above a whisper. "Four days ago."

Daisy audibly pulls in a ragged breath. "Because you sneaked out?"

I nod.

"Motherfucker," he cries.

My insides quiver in the face of his anger. My mind starts to retreat to my safe place, but I shake my head and pull back my shoulders. Steeling myself, I lock my chin in place and force my eyes to stay focused on his.

"Is this the first time he's done that to you?"

I maintain my eye contact and silently shake my head. I'm not looking for his pity; this is my life and though I may cower, I'm not broken.

The roar that escapes from his throat is animalistic and grabbing the chair he threw earlier, he swings it against the wall, hitting it over and over against the brick.

My resolve to be brave lasts until the wood cracks. The noise splinters something inside my mind and without realizing

I'm moving, I back into the corner of the room and sink to the floor. I fold my head against my knees and close my eyes tight, silently humming the melody that allows me to separate my mind from my body.

Some part of my brain registers when the noise stops. It registers the gentle hands that wrap around my waist and the cool air that brushes across my skin as I'm lifted from the floor and held tightly in warm arms.

"Angel."

I fight to stay hidden in the safe place my mind has created to deal with the darker side of my life. A voice begins to entice me back to the present, but I don't want to live in the present. I want to stay safe and cocooned in my warm and fuzzy subconscious.

"Angel, please?"

The voice calls to me and the blackness starts to recede. I hum the tune louder in my head. I squeeze my eyes shut tighter and I hold my knees even harder to my chest. No. I'm not ready to go back yet. I want to stay here, safe and protected.

"God. Fuck. Angel, I don't know what to do."

The voice is low and so full of pain that I stop humming. The blackness recedes, and I start to feel my body again. I examine my fingers first, mentally checking them for sensation. I move up to my wrists and into my arms, waiting for the pain to hit me.

I tense and un-tense my shoulders and neck. No pain. I pull in a silent, shallow breath. No pain. I start again at my toes and move to my ankles. No pain. The pain hits me when I get to my knees, but it isn't the usual searing agony that I expect; instead it's a dull burn.

I assess my entire body and when I realize that I'm not hurt, my mental barrier drops, and the world rushes back in. I'm filled with an explosion of emotion and with a gasp I pull in a ragged breath and snap my eyes open.

"Angel, oh thank fuck. I'm sorry, I'm so sorry," Daisy cries.

His voice is close and his warm breath whispers across my neck. His arms tighten around me and he pulls me closer to him. My arms are still banded around my knees but as my muscles relax, I melt into him and let my head rest against his warm chest.

The memory of his anger flashes into my mind and I stiffen and push at his chest. "Let me go," I mumble. Daisy hears me and releases his hold. I scramble off the bed and back away until my legs hit the dresser on the other side of the room.

I look from him to the door and back again. His eyes are wide, and his chest is rising and falling almost as wildly as mine.

"I'm sorry, Angel," he says, his voice full of anguish. "I would never hurt you, Angel. Fuck, not just you. I mean I'd never hurt any woman ever. I'm only angry at myself. I thought maybe he was hurting you and I just let you go back there." Dropping his chin to his chest, he blows out a labored breath.

"You had no way of knowing what he would do. We've only known each other a few days and I'm not your responsibility," I say.

"I knew something wasn't right," he argues.

I sigh. "My father's been hurting me for years, Daisy. I don't need you to protect me. I need to be strong enough to protect myself. I don't want to live in fear anymore. But it's fine. I'm fine"

"You're not fucking fine. What the fuck was that, Angel? You were catatonic. Did I do that to you?" he asks, fear and pain so vivid in his eyes that tears start to pool in my own.

"You started hitting the chair off the wall and you scared me. I reacted."

Should I be scared of him? He's had two violent reactions already tonight, but neither of them were directed at me. As I watch him react to my words, something in my gut tells me that he won't hurt me, at least not the way my father does anyway.

"I don't ever fucking want you to be scared of me, Angel. I'm so fucking sorry. It's no excuse but I just reacted to my anger. He hurt you. He marked your skin and made you bleed and that is so fucking far from okay. I hate that this happened to you. I hate the fact I can see the scars from where he's done it before. I want to kill him. But I never want to make you afraid of me and I'm sorrier than I've ever been, that I made you react that way. Seeing you huddled into the corner, curled into a ball and completely unresponsive. God. I'm just so fucking sorry."

His voice breaks and his eyes are begging me to believe him, to forgive him, and as stupid as it might be, I do. I nod, a single acceptance of his apology, and his shoulders sag in relief.

"Can I touch you? Is that okay?" His voice is shaky, and I stare at him unsure what he wants.

"I just want to hold you again, just for a minute. Wait. No. I'm sorry, that's stupid. I just scared you into a catatonic state, of course I can't fucking touch you." His fingers bury themselves into his hair and he pulls at the strands in aggravation. He turns to face the opposite wall and I watch the muscles in his shoulders contract as he drops his face and cradles his head in his hands.

"You can hold me," I speak the words without thought and then watch as he slowly turns to face me again. His hands fall from his head and his arms hang loosely at his sides.

"What?" he says.

"Y- You can hold me. I- If you want," I stutter out nervously.

Daisy takes a tentative step nearer to me, and then another. Between each step he pauses and looks at me. Two more steps bring him directly in front of me and I pull in a shaky breath and tip my head back to look at him.

"I don't want to scare you again, Angel. So how bout I just lift my arms up a little and then if you want to, maybe you could come to me?"

His voice is cautious, and I feel tears pool in my eyes. Nibbling on my bottom lip nervously I nod my head. My eyes scan his face for a second. I like this boy. If my life was different right now, I could fall hard for him.

He isn't moving, and his arms lift from his side in a non-threatening stance. I step into him and wrap my arms around his waist, burying my face into his chest. Who am I kidding, I'm already falling for Daisy.

His chest hitches when our skin touches, but his arms don't wrap around me in return. A single tear escapes from my eye and rolls down my cheek and onto his chest. I hold him tighter and close my eyes. I don't understand why I feel safe in his arms; he's violent and unpredictable. But even though he scared me in the moment, I'm not frightened of him. "You can hug me back," I say, my voice muffled in his chest.

He audibly sighs and his arms wrap around me, holding me tightly. His head drops to rest on top of mine and his lips whisper. "I'm sorry, I'm so fucking sorry," over and over against my hair.

Daisy falls silent and we just stand, holding each other. I pull away first, reluctantly stepping out of his embrace. His arms fall to his sides and he closes his eyes for the briefest of moments before coughing to clear his throat. Daisy's gaze locks with mine again, the emotions that had been so obvious in his eyes have disappeared. His mask is firmly in place.

"Prez wants to talk to you."

"Why?" I ask.

"Cause he's the president of the club and you're mixed up in a whole heap of mess."

I nod and then glance down at myself. I can't wander around in just a T-shirt in a building full of bikers. "I need to get dressed," I say, heat pooling in my cheeks.

Daisy's eyes drop to my bare legs and then move back up to

my face. "I'll grab you a pair of my sweats to put on," he says with a wry smile.

I open my mouth to tell him they won't fit but he's already opening a drawer and pulling out a pair. I wait for him to hand them to me but instead he kneels at my feet and holds the pants open for me to step into. I falter for just a second and then rest my hand on his shoulder and carefully step into the fabric.

Daisy's eyes purposely lift to my face, as he works the pants up my bare legs. He never touches my skin and his gaze never leaves my face. Rising from the floor he works the sweats over my butt, carefully making sure nothing touches the raw skin on my legs. Once the waistband is in place, he pulls the drawstring as tight as it will go and ties it into a bow.

He carefully pulls my T-shirt from inside the sweats and then drops back to his knees to roll up the legs where they sit on the floor. By the time he rises from the floor again, my heart is racing. He leans forward and places a gentle kiss on the corner of my mouth. "Better," he whispers against my cheek.

I nod. The sweatpants are still far too big, but they're secured on my hips and the bottoms are rolled up enough so I can walk in them. My eyes and throat burn with the need to cry. His touch and the way he dressed me was so reverent and so careful. I try to remember the last time anyone cared for me in that way.

My mama loves me, and I love her, but her constant justification of my father's actions has forced a distance between us that neither of us can find a way to lessen. She always takes care of me after an incident with my father, but other than that I take care of myself.

I want to ask him why he's behaving like this, why he's being so kind to me, but I don't get the chance. His hand lifts, palm up and he smiles at me. "Come on, Angel. Let's go see Prez then you can get some sleep."

I stare at his offered palm for a second, then place my hand in his and let him lead me out of the room.

SEVENTEEN

Daisy

Holding her hand tightly in mine as we leave my room is the only thing that's keeping my anger and rage simmering just below the surface. She has a black eye, marks on her cheek, and a cut on her lip. How had I missed them before?

My thoughts flash back to earlier when I'd first seen her legs. Her fucking legs and her ass, and God knows how far up the damage actually goes. Fresh red welts and newly scabbed cuts mixed with older scars, so many fucking scars. Her beautiful skin is marked, a permanent reminder of the pain her fucking father has caused her. I want to hunt him down and hurt him just like he's hurt her.

When I'd grabbed that chair my vision had been red. I'd seen the signs, I knew that something wasn't right, and I'd let her go home. Smashing that fucking chair against the wall was the only thing that had stopped me from leaving her in my room and going to kill the fucking bastard. My mind had been so consumed by my anger that I'd almost forgotten she was there.

She'd screamed. I'll never forget that sound. While I was losing my mind and smashing up furniture, she'd curled her tiny body into a ball and had huddled into the corner of the room. The moment I'd seen her like that my anger had drained away. Her asshole of a father might be the one who causes her physical pain, but I'd hurt her today.

I feel sick as I remember the fear I'd felt at seeing her in that corner. Her head had been buried against her knees and her hair had shielded her face from view. She was so still and so small and I'd thought she was unconscious until I heard the quiet humming sound she was making. I don't know what song it was, but it was the same tune over and over again.

I'd lifted her into my arms and talked to her, begged her to come back to me. Fifteen fucking minutes I'd held her close, waiting for her to come around. I never want to see her like that again. I never want to be the cause of that again.

I force my mind back to the present and look down at her. She seems to have forgiven me, but I haven't forgiven myself. I want to be selfish with Angel. She wants to run away, but I want to keep her here with me. I thought I could keep her safe, but maybe getting her away from Archer's Creek, her father, and me, might be the best thing for her.

Her tiny hand in mine keeps me grounded and I silently lead her down the dimly lit corridors until we get to Prez's office. I knock and Anders' voice immediately calls for us to come in.

Opening the door, I guide her inside. Prez is sat behind his desk with his old lady, Grits, perched to his left and Blade in one of the chairs in front of the desk. Angel cautiously lowers herself into the seat next to Blade. Her bruises look darker in the harsh office light and I sit down next to her, angling my body in front of hers protectively.

She looks terrified; her hands are clasped together in her lap and her chin is lowered submissively. Her waterfall of hair has escaped from behind her ears and is hiding her face. Moving unconsciously, I lift her chin up with my finger and turn her face to mine. I smile at her and hope it reassures her slightly. She offers me a silent nod and then I watch as she pulls in a deep breath and turns to face Prez.

Prez, Grits, and Blade, are openly assessing us and I fight the urge to squirm in my seat. Prez turns his attention to focus on Angel and I watch his eyes narrow when he sees the bruises on her face. Standing, he reaches across the desk and holds out his hand. "Hello, my name is Anders and I'm president of the Doomsday Sinners."

Angel turns to look at me for a moment before she stands and tentatively places her hand in his. "Hi, I'm Angelique Jefferies." Her voice is quiet but strong and my chest fills with pride.

Prez points to Blade and then to Grits. "This is Blade, the

club's vice president, and this is Grits, my old lady." They both nod at Angel in acknowledgment. Prez sits back down and Angel follows suit. "Well, young lady, you seem to have got yourself mixed up in a heap of trouble," Prez says matter of factly.

"Sir, I didn't come here to get Daisy or any of you mixed up in my life. In fact, that's the last thing I want. All I need is a ride to the bus station, or for someone to call me a cab. I just want to get as far away from Archer's Creek as possible, as quickly as I can. I wouldn't be here at all if I hadn't missed the last bus of the day and I apologize if I've inconvenienced y'all."

Angel's cheeks are tinged with pink and her fingers are restlessly plucking at the fabric of the sweatpants she's wearing. I don't know her that well, but I can tell that she's uncomfortable, so I drop one of my hands over both of hers and squeeze reassuringly. She glances to where my hand covers hers and pulls in a deep, calming breath. When she looks back to Prez her chin is raised a little higher, and she patiently waits for him to speak.

"What happened to your face, Little Dove?" Anders asks, his voice gentle and coaxing.

She stiffens. "Nothing, it was an accident," she replies robotically.

A growl escapes my throat and I lift my hand from hers. "Her father beat the shit out of her for sneaking out the other day."

"Daisy," Angel cries but I ignore her.

"Not the first time it's happened and it's not just her face," I grit out between clenched teeth.

"What else did he do to you?" Anders asks Angel, but her eyes are focused solely on her hands in her lap and she ignores him.

Prez turns his question to me with a raised eyebrow. "What else did he do?"

I won't let her lie to protect her jackass of a father, but this isn't my story to tell. Angel needs to be the one to explain so I move from my chair and drop to my knees in front of her. Covering her hand with one of mine, I lift her chin with the other. She reluctantly makes eye contact with me and I smile at the annoyance that's so obvious in her expression.

"Do you trust that I want to help and keep you safe?"

She thinks about it for a few moments and then nods. I release the breath I didn't realize I'd been holding and nod in return. "Then tell him what happened. I want to help and he wants to help you, but we can't do that unless you tell him everything. If we can't help, then I'll get you as far away from here as you want. I promise."

Angel stares at me and then nods. Getting up from the floor I move back into my seat, then reach over and entwine my fingers with hers.

She lifts her head to look at Prez and then speaks. "Since my sister died two years ago, my father has chosen to punish me when he thinks I've done something wrong. He enjoys using his belt."

There's an audible gasp from Grits, and Prez places a

reassuring hand on his old lady's leg. "When was the last time this happened?" Prez asks.

"Four days ago," Angel says quietly.

Prez nods thoughtfully then turns to Grits. "Go grab a drink, baby. Blade will come get you in a minute." Grits nods and immediately gets up and leaves the room. Prez waits for the door to close and then turns back to Angel. "A man came to visit with your father today."

Angel nods. "Yes, Senator Carduccio."

"Did he come on his own or were there other people with him?"

"He came with his son, his wife, and four other men that I think were security guards."

"Why were they there?" Anders asks.

"My father told me that important people were coming and that he wanted them to meet me. We had sweet tea, and I was introduced to them all. My father, the senator, and his son, all went to talk on the patio and shortly after that Mrs. Carduccio was called away on a phone call. I went upstairs to my bedroom and overheard the men talking. I heard my father negotiate using me as payment for money he owed."

"Did they say how much money your father owed?" Prez asks.

"One hundred thousand dollars," Angel answers.

Prez pauses for a second, staring intently at Angel. "Why would your father offer you up to pay a debt?"

Angel wipes away a tear that has streaked down her cheek. "Because he's a monster. He talked about me marrying the senator's son. But the senator said they might put me out to work instead. My father told them that I'd make them a lot of money if they did." Her voice breaks and more tears roll down her cheeks.

"Why should we help you, Angelique?" Prez asks, his voice hard as steel.

Angel angrily wipes the tears from her face. "I don't want your help. I just want to get to the bus station in Houston."

"Carduccio is a very powerful man, Angelique. How far do you think you'll get before he finds you? If you belong to him, he'll hunt you down. He likes to keep a tight leash on his possessions."

Angel suddenly stands, dropping my hand. "I don't belong to him. I'm a person not a possession. I cannot be bought and sold."

Prez nods, a small smile twitching at his lips. "That's better, Little Dove. You stand tall, you don't cower. Ever. Why didn't Carduccio take you with him today?"

"He told my father to bring me or the money to a warehouse in five days time," Angel says.

Prez's smile gets bigger, and he nods. "Good, that's good. As long as they don't find you and hand you over before the payment date, your dad will have no choice but to pay what he owes. We're gonna keep you safe, Little Dove, but I'm sorry, running isn't an option."

"What?" Angel shouts. "No! I need to get out of Archer's Creek. My father will find me here. I need to get away, I need to run. He'll know I'm gone by the morning and start looking for me."

"Little Dove, if you run, your father and Carduccio will have you found and back home in less than two days. No one will ever think to look for you here. The compound is a fortress; no one gets in without coming through the guard on the gatehouse. I promise you, this is the safest place for you until the exchange date has passed."

"No, no, no," Angel exclaims shaking her head. "This isn't your problem. I don't need to be saved, I just want to get away and start again."

Prez stands and walks around to the front of his desk. Perching against the wood in front of Angel he reaches to take her hand. She flinches. His eyes harden, and he slowly moves his hands behind him to rest on the desk. "We're not saving you, Angelique. We're just keeping you safe while you save yourself."

"You really think it'll be easier to find me on the other side of the country than five miles from our house?" Angel asks sardonically.

Prez laughs. "Yes, Little Dove, I do. You said yourself that by the morning your dad will know you're gone and start to look for you. He'll report you missing and have every police department in the state on the lookout for you. But no one will ever think to look for you here. It's the perfect hiding place."

Angel falls back into her seat and seems to be lost in thought. After a few moments she lifts her head up to look at Prez and slowly nods. "Okay. Thank you. But once the exchange date has passed then I leave."

Prez looks from Angel to me and back again, smiling widely. "Of course, Little Dove. Now Blade is gonna go fetch my old lady. She's gonna take you back to Daisy's room and have a look at your legs to make sure they're not infected. She'll stay with you until he comes back. You're safe here, but don't wander around on your own. Do you understand?"

Angel nods and Blade leaves without a word, returning a few moments later with Grits following behind him. The Prez's old lady smiles kindly at Angel. "Come on then, sweetie."

Angel looks at me and when I nod reassuringly, she stands up and follows Grits out of the office. When the door closes behind her, I pull in a deep breath and wait. Prez is silently assessing me, but I can feel Blade's gaze on me as well. His intense eyes lock with mine and he stares at me for a moment, then nods and turns his attention to Prez.

"Do you believe her?" Blade says gruffly.

"Yes," Prez replies.

I let out a ragged breath. I'd hoped that Prez wouldn't question Angel's sincerity, but I'd feared he might. Because women like Angel aren't real—she's too beautiful, too innocent and too sweet. It's almost easier to believe she's fake because in this life no one is that guileless. Except her.

"She could have cried and whined about the hand life has dealt her, but she hasn't; she's still fighting. I genuinely think she'd be happy if we dropped her off at the bus station. She doesn't want our help. She might be starting to see that she needs it, but she'd be just as happy with a ride. Plus, she's not an actress. I've met a lot of manipulative women in my life and Dove isn't one of them. She's just a frightened teenager," Prez says, his voice impassioned.

"I agree. She's got nothing to gain from coming here. I thought she might be working with Carduccio, but now I've met her it just doesn't ring true," Blade says.

"What are we gonna do Prez?" I ask.

Prez blows out a breath and rests his chin on his steepled fingers. "Way I see it, we've got a couple of options. We can lie low and wait for the exchange date to pass, or we can make her club property and let Carduccio know that she's not for sale."

"Does Jefferies have the money to pay what he owes without her?" Blade questions.

Both Blade and Prez turn to look at me and I shrug my shoulders. "I don't know. I don't know if Angel knows either. My guess is that if he's trying to sell his fucking daughter, he doesn't, and he's fucking desperate. Either that or he's a heartless bastard who really couldn't give a fuck about his own flesh and blood." My fingers clench into fists just thinking about Angel's father. I want to hunt him down and kill him for hurting her. He deserves to get everything he's ever done to her delivered back to him three-fold. Karma's a massive bitch and I want to be the one who delivers her retribution.

Prez nods thoughtfully. "Ask her, see if she knows what the money situation is. I think we should lie low and see how the mayor reacts to his daughter not being in her bed in the morning. She's pretty adamant about leaving once this shit storm is over, so we don't wanna get her too ingrained in the club unless we absolutely have to."

A growl escapes from me at the idea that she'd leave, but I've got no claim on her. If what happened earlier is any indication of what having me in her life would do to her, then for her sake I need to let her run when the time comes.

"You laying claim to her son?" Prez asks.

I silently shake my head, but never make eye contact. I hear his low chuckle at my response. "I'll ask you again in a few days time. That pretty little dove has got you all torn up already."

My eyes shoot up to Prez's and his are full of knowing amusement. He turns to Blade. "Blade, go spread the word that the girl in Daisy's bed is his new plaything. See if anyone recognized her as the mayor's daughter and shut that shit down if they did. Daisy, go keep your eye on her; get her some clothes, something that won't make her stand out. Tomorrow, we'll keep our ears to the ground and see what Jefferies does."

Both Blade and I nod and rise from our seats, I open the

door and leave Prez's office with Blade following behind. I turn to head toward my room, eager to get back to Angel, but Blade's hand on my shoulder stops me. "That's the girl," he says.

I nod. "Yep."

He nods back, a smile twitching at the edges of his lips. "I can see why."

A wave of anger pulses through me and I react, grabbing a handful of my V.P.'s shirt in my fist. "What the fuck are you talking about? She's mine."

Blade laughs loudly, prying my fingers from the fabric of his shirt. "I know, brother. I know. I was just wondering if you knew yet. She's a beautiful girl, but she comes with a hell of a lot of baggage, make sure you're ready for that before you claim her." He pats my shoulder and then heads for the bar.

Spinning on my heel I hurry to my room and my Angel.

EIGHTEEN

Angel

With one last look at Daisy, I follow the woman from Anders' office. She glances at me over her shoulder and offers me a reassuring smile. "That's a hell of a shiner, baby girl. Let's go get you checked over."

We walk straight back to Daisy's room and pulling out a key she opens the door and motions for me to go in first. I don't know what to make of her; at first glance she looks angry and kind of mean. I'm not sure how old she is, definitely in her forties but maybe older. Her hair is midnight black and pulled back into a severe high ponytail on top of her head. Her makeup is beautifully applied, and her skin looks youthful and flawless, but her eyes betray her age. She's wearing a tight black tank that says 'Beavers' in bold white print with a silhouette of a women hanging from a pole beneath. Her arms are slim and toned and one is covered in tattoos from her wrist right up to her shoulder. She's wearing leather pants and sky high black pointy stilettoes. She's beautiful but terrifying at the same time.

Walking past her, I stand in front of the bed and fidget. I don't know what to do, or what to say, so I just stare at her uncertainly.

She smiles at me again and holds out her hand. "I know Anders sort of introduced me but let's do it properly. My name is Eve, but everyone calls me Grits. Anders is my old man."

I take her hand and shake it. "I'm Angelique, it's nice to meet you."

Grits smiles ruefully and reaches out to cup my cheek. I try not to flinch, but it happens anyway. She pauses at my reaction then slowly and carefully touches her warm fingers to my face. "I'm sorry this happened to you, Angelique."

Dropping my eyes to the floor I nod, embarrassed that anyone has to see the damage my father did to me. "It is what it is."

Firm fingers lift my chin and the anger on her face surprises me. "No, Angelique, it isn't. What he did to you isn't okay. A man should never raise his fist to a woman, ever. You don't accept it and you don't grin and bear it—ever. You're a beautiful young woman and you should never have been treated like this. Do you understand me? I'm sorry that your father did this to you. It isn't your fault. But from this day onwards you don't accept this kind of shit from anyone, okay? Tell me you understand, Angelique."

My chest is rising and falling so rapidly that I'm struggling to get enough air into my lungs. There's a huge lump in my throat and I'm trembling so hard that my legs feel like they're going to give way. This is the first time in my entire life that anyone has told me what my father does to me is not okay. I've always known it was wrong, but my mother has spent years making excuses for him and telling me it was our own fault.

I look straight into Grits' eyes and I can see my pain reflected back in hers. She doesn't have to tell me that she knows exactly what I'm feeling, because in this moment I know that she does. I nod. "I know that it's not okay. I've always known that, but I had no idea how much I needed someone to tell me. Thank you."

Pulling me into her arms she hugs me tightly. "You're gonna be okay. But if you need anything, you tell Daisy or Anders to come get me. I mean it, Angelique. The other girls will tell you I'm a mean old bitch and they'd be right, but that's because I've got no time for club whores. I have a feeling you and I are gonna be friends. I know this is scary as hell for you, but you're not alone anymore."

Tears pool in my eyes but I blink them back. I don't want to cry in front of this woman. She's so strong and self-assured and I want to be like her. She doesn't strike me as the type who would cry often so I pull in a deep fortifying breath and smile.

"Thank you. I'd really like to be your friend."

Grits smiles back and then takes my hand. "Come on, sweetie. Let's go take a look at your legs. How bad are they? You been taking care of the wounds?"

I follow her into the bathroom. "My mama cleaned them up and put antiseptic lotion on them, they're not too bad."

"Your mom knows what he does to you?" she asks, surprised. I nod.

Grits closes her eyes for a second and her lips twist into an angry grimace. When she opens them again her face is full of sympathy. "Come on then, Angelique. You okay to show me? I know it's creepy as fuck to get practically naked with a stranger, but I spend all day with strippers. You haven't got anything I've not seen a hundred times already this week.

She barks out a laugh and I laugh too. She's right, this is creepy, but Grits has been nothing but sweet and caring so I undo the drawstring on Daisy's sweatpants and let them fall to the floor. I can't watch as Grits inspects the raw skin, cuts, and welts. I'm going to lose hold of the fragile strings that are keeping me together if I see any more sympathy in her face right now. She gasps as she lifts the hem of the shirt I'm wearing and sees the new wounds and the older scars that cover the skin from my thighs to the base of my spine.

I hold my breath as she assesses the damage, then I feel her lift the sweats back up and I tie the drawstring tight again. When I turn to face her, she's discreetly wiping a tear from the corner of her eye, but it's anger, not pity, I see in her expression. "That's never gonna happen to you again. I promise you that. If the club doesn't sort this for you, I'll help you run. On my life I will never allow you to be hurt like that ever again."

I don't know what to say, so I stay silent. Grits audibly exhales and then she forces her face into a half smile. "Angelique is a real pretty name, but it's a bit of a mouthful. Do you shorten it? Maybe Angie or something?"

She opens the bathroom door and I follow her out of the room. Flopping down onto Daisy's bed she pats the cover, so I climb onto the mattress and sit cross-legged next to her. "Honestly, I've always hated my name. Daisy calls me Angel, but it's never been shortened before."

Grits smiles widely. "Angel, huh? I've never seen that boy behave like he does with you before. He's always been a cocky little bastard with the girls but he's different with you. How long have you known each other?"

I shake my head shyly. "Only a few days."

"Huh," Grits says with a smirk.

"What?" I ask.

"Nothin', sweetie. How bout I just call you Dove like Anders did? It's probably better if no one here knows your real name anyway, and I doubt Daisy would be happy with everyone calling you Angel."

I nod. "Dove's fine, but I'm sure Daisy wouldn't care. We've only known each other for a handful of days. I never planned to drag you all into my mess, but when I missed the bus I just didn't have anywhere else to go."

Grits laughs. "I can guarantee that he'd care, Dove. I don't know what you're caught up in, except that you're running from something, and I don't need to know unless you want to tell me. But I can guarantee that if Anders didn't want to help, he wouldn't. If he didn't see something in you worth helping, he'd have had your pretty little ass out of the club and on the sidewalk in the blink of an eye."

Ashamed, I let my eyes fall on my fingers in my lap. "My life is such a mess."

Grits reaches over and squeezes my knee. "It's okay, honey. I'm here if you need to talk about it."

Lifting my head, I nod. "Thank you."

Grits smiles, then tilts her head to the side. "How old are you, Dove? You look about fifteen, but I figure Anders wouldn't have you here unless you were at least legal."

"I'm eighteen."

"Hell, eighteen. You're still a baby. You gonna be okay staying here with Daisy? If you want, you can come stay with me and Anders. It won't be as easy to keep you hidden at ours, but we can make it work if you'd feel more comfortable."

"No!" I shout. The vehemence in my voice shocks me, but I don't want to leave Daisy. He frightened me earlier, but he's been so sweet with me and he said he liked me and I like him. "No, I'm fine here with Daisy. Plus, like Anders said this is the last place my father would ever think to look for me, and I'm only going to be here for a few days and then I'm leaving town."

Grits smile is so big it's practically splitting her face in two. She opens her mouth to speak when the door opens and Daisy walks in.

My mouth goes instantly dry. His naked, chiseled chest is perfection. Tan skin stretches over toned muscles and defined abs. Tattoos cover one side of his pectoral muscle and flow over his shoulder and down his whole arm ending at his knuckles. I stare at him, unable to tear my eyes away. His tattoo is a colorful bouquet of flowers: poppies, peonies, daisies, and roses, cascading through an angry black skull. The contrast between the beautiful flowers and the gruesome skull is harsh but stunning and I try to examine the artwork from my seat on the bed. Had he been shirtless this whole time? How had I not noticed?

Grits clears her throat and I snap back to attention and turn to look at her. A knowing smirk is etched on her face. "I'll see you in the morning, Dove. I'll bring you some clothes, cause I'm guessing yours aren't gonna blend in real well. Remember what I said, you need me, just tell Daisy or Anders and I'm here. Okay?"

"Thank you," I say earnestly.

She smiles and squeezes my cheek before dropping her hand and walking up to Daisy. "You look after my Little Dove. She's special and you treat her that way, okay?"

Daisy nods. "I will."

Grits smiles then leaves the room, pulling the door closed behind her. Daisy turns the lock and walks toward me, sinking to his knees in front of me. "You okay, Angel? You did real well with Prez."

"I'm fine. Look, I just want to say thank you and I'm sorry. I didn't come here thinking you would get involved with my problems; I just didn't know where else to go. I still feel like I should be running, but Anders is right, this is the last place my father would ever think to look for me. I promise in a few days time I'll leave and take all my drama with me."

Daisy's face hardens for a minute but then his expression clears and he offers me a small smile. Reaching for my hand he entwines his fingers with mine. "Come on, Angel, it's late. You need to get some sleep. Are you in pain? Do you need me to get you some meds or anything?"

I shake my head. "No, I'm fine. I am tired though," I say, as a yawn escapes me.

Daisy smiles and standing he lifts me into his arms and places me at the top of the bed. Pulling the covers over me he leans down and places a kiss on the corner of my mouth. His lips are soft and warm and when they touch me I want more. He pulls away and our gazes lock. I watch his pupils dilate and my heart beats harder in response. I lift up at the same time that he leans forward and our lips meet in the middle.

The kiss is slow and sweet. His lips are a drug and I close

my eyes and fall into the sensation. His strong arms are braced on either side of me and I cling to him, desperately enjoying every moment of his lips on mine.

The kiss ends too soon, and he pulls back, resting his forehead against mine. Breathless, I stare into his eyes, hoping he'll kiss me again.

"Sweet dreams, my Angel," he whispers and pulls away from me.

I let my head fall back against the pillow and watch as he rummages in the closet. Pulling out a pillow and a handful of blankets he makes a pallet on the floor next to the bed and then slips off his shoes. He watches me, watch him undress, with a shadow of a smirk flickering across his beautiful lips.

He lies down on his makeshift bed and I roll to my side, so we lie facing each other. I fall asleep staring at him as he stares at me.

***

I wake up still facing him. Stretching my legs under the covers, I gasp as burning pain pulses through my skin.

"What's the matter, Angel?" Daisy says immediately, jumping from the floor and hovering over me, his face full of concern.

"Nothing, it's nothing. I'm fine. My legs just sting after not moving all night."

"Do you need to see a doctor? Do you want pain meds? Tell me what I can do, Angel."

I carefully sit up, reach for his hand and squeeze it gently. "I'm fine, I promise."

He nods but looks dubious. "Do you want to eat breakfast in here or out in the clubhouse with everyone else? It might be best to let everyone see you and then they'll forget you're here. The longer you stay hidden, the more curious they'll be."

I fumble with the fabric of the T-shirt I'm wearing trying to decide if I'm ready to face the rest of the bikers and whoever else is still here this morning.

"It's okay, baby, we can just stay in here," Daisy says.

I force my fingers to still and then look up at him. "No, you're right. It'll be better to go eat with everyone else. Grits said I needed different clothes, but I only have a couple of my dresses from home with me."

Grabbing his cell from the dresser he quickly dials someone. "Hi, yeah, it's Daisy. You mentioned sorting a few clothes for Angel. Yeah, okay. See you in a few. Bye."

I listen to the one-sided conversation and wait. Daisy ends the call and then smiles triumphantly. "I'm gonna grab a quick shower. Grits will be here in ten with some clothes for you. I don't know what you said to her last night—she's normally mean as a snake—but she sure seems to like you."

I smile. "She was really nice. I like her a lot."

Daisy grins and shakes his head in amusement. "Fucking

hell, baby, you cracked Grits. I don't think that's ever happened before." Chuckling to himself he crosses the room and disappears into the bathroom.

Sitting up in bed I stare at the half-closed bathroom door. I hear the shower start, quickly followed by Daisy's awful, off-key singing and I have to cover my mouth with my hand to muffle the sound of my laughter. The shower stops, and he emerges from the bathroom naked, except for a towel that sits low on his hips.

I watch slack-jawed as he pads half naked and barefoot over to the dresser and pulls out some clothes. His back is to me and I admire the rippling muscles that tense and pull as he moves, almost swallowing my tongue when he loosens the towel and it falls to the floor.

He's completely naked. His tight, round ass is perfect, and I want to shout out in protest when he slides on a pair of boxer briefs. Pulling on jeans and a T-shirt, he turns to face me with a knowing smirk on his lips and I feel the heat bloom across my cheeks. I fight the urge to curl up into a ball, my face is on fire and I'm so embarrassed at being caught ogling him.

Striding across the room he lifts a black leather vest from the back of a chair and pulls it on over his T-shirt, then he crawls onto the bed and flops down next to me. He doesn't touch me, just sits propped up with his head leaning back against the wall. His legs are crossed at the ankles and his T-shirt has ridden up, so his stomach is on display. He's so masculine but beautiful at the same time. His fingers edge across the space between us and he lifts my hand to his lips, kissing my skin gently. "Go take a shower, Angel. I'll stay until Grits gets here."

He doesn't release my hand immediately and I look from his face to where he holds my fingers in his and back again. Deliberately, he turns my hand over and lifts my palm to his mouth, dropping a kiss to the very center. He folds my fingers over the spot his lips just touched and then releases me. I pull my hand into my chest, keeping my fingers folded protectively across the kiss in my palm. Something about the way he just touched me feels so incredibly intimate and I panic, scrambling from the bed and hurrying into the bathroom.

Closing the door firmly behind me, I rest against the wood and pull in a deep breath. I lift up my arm and slowly uncurl my fingers from my palm. I half expect his kiss to be branded into my skin, but my palm is empty and only the lingering feeling of his lips on my skin is left behind. Showering quickly, I wrap myself in a towel and half open the bathroom door, peeking through the gap. Grits is sitting on the bed messing with her cell phone and when she spots me she jumps up, a bright smile on her face. "Morning, Dove, how you doin' today? I brought you some clothes. I wasn't sure what size you were, so I got a selection."

Opening the door fully, I step into the bedroom with the towel wrapped around me tightly and hurry to grab a pair of panties and a bra from my backpack. Grits is busy sorting through a pile of bags on the floor next to the bed, so I walk back into the bathroom and slide on my underwear and Daisy's T-shirt. When I return, the bed is covered in clothes and Grits is busy organizing them into outfits. I hope that whatever she's chosen for me has more fabric than hers. She's wearing a short, tight black dress; knee high boots; and a leather vest that says 'Property of Anders' on the front. She looks fantastic, but I've never had that much flesh on display and I'm not convinced today is the day I want to start.

Grits smiles wide, takes two steps forward and pulls me into a tight hug. "Wow, Dove, you're gorgeous even with that mean black eye." Releasing me she points at the bed. "Okay, so I got you a few choices. You need something that will cover the backs of your thighs and not rub against the cuts, so bootie shorts and jeans are out. I know it's probably not what you're used to wearing but I have plenty of dresses and skirts for you to choose from."

I start to reply but she cuts me off by thrusting three outfits into my arms. "Go try these on, come on out once you're dressed so I can see."

I obey and turn back into the bathroom; all three outfits are so unlike my normal clothes I barely recognize myself when I look in the mirror. Grits decides on the third outfit. A leather skirt that's short enough to hit me mid-thigh but covers up the raw cuts and welts, a white shirt with the Doomsday Sinners logo on it that's cut at the side and tied in a knot so a sliver of my stomach can be seen, and chunky black heeled boots with a bow at the back of each ankle. She braids back the front section of my hair but leaves the back loose and flowing over my shoulders. Lastly, she adds a quick coat of mascara and some shiny lip gloss.

She turns me to look in the mirror and stands to my side, a proud smile on her face. "You look beautiful, Dove."

I stare at my reflection, hardly recognizing myself in the fitted clothes, and with my hair pinned back from my face. The heels are uncomfortable, and I want to tug at the hem of my skirt to make it longer. But I don't; instead I just look at myself. My black eye and the bruises on my cheek glare back at me and I turn to Grits. "Shouldn't I cover up the bruises?"

Grits shakes her head. "No, baby girl. It happened to you and no matter how much makeup you put over it, it still happened. Better to just put it out there and then let them fade. In a few days they'll be gone, but you don't hide from the bruises, you own them, then you watch them fade, knowing you won't ever let them happen again."

I nod, then turn back to the mirror and stare at my face. A knock at the door pulls me from my introspection.

"Come on in, she's all ready," Grits shouts.

The door swings open and Daisy walks in. Grits hangs her arm around my shoulders and turns me to face him.

His mouth falls open.

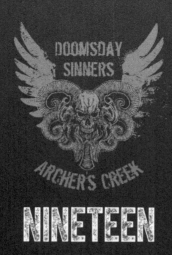

DOOMSDAY SINNERS

ARCHER'S CREEK

NINETEEN

Daisy

Holy fucking shit.

My mouth drops open and I try to speak, but the noise is more of a surprised splutter than actual words. My Angel looks like a different fucking person. Her gorgeous white hair is pinned off her face, her shirt is fitted and that skirt, fuck, that skirt is so short I can see her perfect legs. She's wearing heels, but she's still absolutely tiny, and even with the extra height she only just comes up to my shoulder.

"You're not leaving this fucking room looking like that," I shout indignantly.

Grits laughs, she fucking laughs, and I turn and glare at her. "What the hell did you do to her?"

She throws back her head and guffaws. Her arm is still

around Angel's shoulders but now she's leaning heavily on her because she's laughing so much she's struggling to stay upright.

I ignore the Prez's old lady and turn what I'm hoping look like imploring eyes to Angel. "Baby, you can't go out there looking like that."

Angel's shoulders sag into herself and I instantly know I've fucked up. Grits stops laughing and pulls Angel closer to her. "Daisy, I don't know what the fuck is wrong with you, but Dove looks fucking gorgeous," she growls.

Angel tugs awkwardly at the clothes and I lift my hands to my hair and pull at the strands. I watch the life dull in Angel's eyes and I drop my hands and march forward until I'm right in front of her. "Angel, you look fucking beautiful, but I think you look beautiful in my sweats or in your ugly sack dresses."

Her eyes lift from the floor and lock with mine. "You do?" She asks, shocked.

"Of course I do. You're perfect. The clothes you're wearing don't make any difference," I say, my hands moving to cup her jaw. Grits silently backs away and fusses with the sea of clothes spread out across my bed.

"I look stupid, don't I?" Angel asks, turning to look at herself in the mirror behind us.

"No, baby, you look absolutely amazing. That's the problem. I'm gonna be fighting the guys off you the moment they see you dressed like that."

Her eyes jump to mine in the mirror and her mouth makes

an 'O' shape at her surprise. I chuckle and then carefully curve my arm around her waist and turn her to face me again. "Can I kiss you, my pretty little angel?"

She pulls her bottom lip between her teeth and then nods. I don't give her chance to change her mind. Dipping my head, I kiss her and she immediately parts her lips. I slide my tongue into her mouth and hold her close, devouring her. Her body molds against mine and every nerve ending in me sparks to life. Emotions I haven't felt in years, and don't truly understand, force their way to the surface and an overwhelming sense of comfort and happiness radiates through me.

Only Angel makes me feel this way.

I rub my fingers along the slither of skin that's on display between the end of her shirt and the start of that leather skirt. God that skirt—my Angel in leather is the most tempting kind of perfection. Sliding my hand down from her waist I cup her ass and pull her tighter against me, so she can feel how hard I am.

She freezes and I remember that she's not just another plaything. She's my Angel and as much as I want to lift that fucking skirt up and feel the heat between her legs I can't. Angel hasn't told me that she's a virgin, but I'd be surprised if she wasn't. I'm desperate to be the first to see and feel all of her untouched sweetness, but I can't—not unless she's mine to keep and definitely not while she's scared and hiding from her dad's bullshit.

Loosening my hold on her ass, I bury my face into the curve of her neck and pull in deep steady breaths while I try to calm down. Grits clears her throat loudly. I'd forgotten she was even in the room. Reluctantly, I lift my head from Angel's neck, and she turns to Grits.

Grits lifts her eyebrows and smirks. "Dove, you look gorgeous, sweetie." Turning to me she points her finger menacingly. "Daisy, don't be a dick." Walking to the door she waves over her shoulder. "I gotta work today, baby girl, but I'll be back to see you later."

Angel laughs. "Okay. Thank you for the clothes."

Grits waves her off and leaves, closing the door behind her.

I turn Angel to face me again. "Dove?" I question.

"Yeah, Grits said I shouldn't tell people my real name and Anders called me Dove last night, so she said I should use that. I told her that you call me Angel, but she said that she didn't think you'd be happy if everyone started calling me that. I told her you wouldn't care, but she laughed and then just carried on calling me Dove."

I scowl. "She's right. No one else gets to call you Angel but me. You're my Angel, nobody else's."

Angel's huge doe eyes look up at me and I can see the confusion in them. "You make me feel all kinds of crazy possessive, Angel. Hell, you make me feel all kinds of things I haven't felt in a really long fucking time. You're my Angel and I don't want anyone to think they get a share."

Her eyes widen as my words register. I don't think she really understands what I'm saying. I don't fully understand what I'm saying, but her body is relaxed in my arms so at least she's not freaking out. "You ready to go eat?"

She glances down at herself and her new clothes and then pulls in a deep breath and nods. "As I'll ever be."

I laugh. "Come on, it'll be fine. If you start to feel uncomfortable just tell me and we'll come straight back in here, okay?" She nods and I drape my arm over her shoulders and guide her out of my room.

The bar is quieter than normal, the breakfast buffet is laid out on tables to one side of the room and my brothers are dotted around, eating in small groups. I spot Echo and Liv at a table in a corner, so after taking Angel to grab a plate and encouraging her to add more than a cinnamon bun to hers, I guide her over to the table.

As usual Liv is sat in Echo's lap, but she jumps up when she sees me, and I give her a quick one-armed hug. Echo growls and drags Liv back into his lap, and both Liv and I laugh at his caveman behavior. I drop my plate on the table and then pull out a chair for Angel. Moving my chair closer to hers, I sit beside her, draping my arm along the back of her chair and absentmindedly playing with the strands of her hair.

I look up to find Echo and Liv openly staring at me. "Guys, this is Dove. Angel, this is Echo, and his old lady, Liv."

Liv's face breaks into a huge smile and she waves excitedly.

"Hi, Dove, I'm Olivia, but most people call me Liv. I've never seen you here before."

Angel freezes for a second but then relaxes and forces a taut smile. "It's nice to meet you, Liv. Are you British?"

Liv laughs loudly. "I swear that's the first question anyone ever asks me. Yes, I'm from England originally but now I live here. What happened to your face, it looks sore?"

Angel's back goes ramrod straight. "Liv," I snap.

Liv winces and looks apologetically at Angel. "I'm sorry, apparently I forgot my brain to mouth filter today."

Echo's watchful eyes move between me and Angel and I angle my body in front of hers protectively. He smiles widely, as if he just discovered something fascinating and then addresses Angel. "Nice to meet you, Dove."

Angel smiles but doesn't respond. "Eat," I whisper into her neck and she slowly starts to pick at the food on her plate.

Blade flops down into the chair next to me and he nods to each of us in greeting. When his eyes get to Angel, he does a double take. "Little Dove," he says shocked. His assessing eyes roam over her body and I growl and lean forward to block her from his view.

Blade laughs and holds his hands up in a gesture of surrender. "Just looking, brother."

"Well don't," I snarl.

I run the tips of my fingers up and down the bare skin on Angel's arm, and she gradually relaxes, ripping small chunks off her cinnamon bun and eating slowly and silently.

Across the table Echo is whispering into Liv's ear and every now and then she giggles. Blade's eyes are downcast, and he looks tired and hungover as he nurses a cup of steaming black coffee. I focus on my Angel sitting next to me.

"Eat," she whispers, and I smile and fork up a rasher of bacon from my plate.

A hand with bright-red painted nails tiptoes down my chest and Ali slides in between me and Blade, sitting on the edge of the table. She parts her legs slightly and her short denim skirt rides up enough to show that she's not wearing any panties, her shaved cunt fully on display. "Good morning, baby," she purrs at me.

"What do you want, Ali?" I ask, annoyance clear in my tone.

"You know what I want, Daisy. When are you gonna make me your old lady? I'd make you so happy, baby," Ali drawls seductively.

"For fucks sake, Ali. I'm sitting here with my girl. Look at her. Why the fuck would I be interested in you when I have her?" I snap and lean down to drop a gentle kiss on Angel's shoulder. Her muscles are tense, but she shudders when my lips touch her skin and she leans in to my kiss. Smiling, I move her hair away from her neck so I can run my fingers over the beating pulse point.

"Eughhh, her. Seriously Daisy, she looks about fifteen. Why would you want a child like her when you could have a real woman like me? God, she's ugly and skinny, and she's got no tits. Is it the virgin look that's doing it for you baby cause I'll play virgin for you? You can break me in good and then I'll play the dirty little slut for you as well."

My chair scrapes back when I stand up. "Ali, to start off with you were just annoying and desperate, but you just insulted my girl and that doesn't fucking sit with me. Apologize right fucking now and then get your skanky ass away from her."

"I'm not apologizing to her, she's not your old lady. She's just a whore looking for a biker to ride." Ali shouts. She peers around me to yell at Angel. "You hear that, bitch? You're no better than me. We've got enough club whores, we don't need no more, so why don't you get your ugly virgin ass back to wherever you came from?"

"Ali." Anders voice booms and the entire room goes silent. The prez walks the few steps until he reaches our table, with Grits held at his side possessively. Ali pales and steps back nervously.

Grits steps over to Angel and pulls her from the table. She keeps hold of her hand and leads her to stand next to Anders. He looks at my Angel with a gentle expression on his face. "You okay, Little Dove?" he asks her.

Angel nods but her eyes drop to the floor. Instinctively, I move to her side and Grits releases her hand when Angel easily curls into my chest.

"Ali, what's your role here at the club?" Prez asks her.

Ali brightens and smiles seductively. "I look after the Sinners and make sure all of the boys have what they need."

Prez nods. "Do you belong to anyone, Ali?"

Her cheeks redden and she shakes her head.

"And who decides when we add a new girl?" he asks.

"You do," Ali says sheepishly.

Prez smiles brightly. "Exactly. I do. You don't have any say in that decision. But you see this girl over here." He points to Angel and smiles at her. "This is Dove. She's Daisy's girl, and you were rude and insulting. That's not how we treat visitors to our club. You will apologize, sincerely, right fucking now, or you will get your ass out of my club and never come back."

Ali's face turns pale, and she looks to Angel. "I'm sorry." She's not exactly contrite but all of her bluster has gone.

"That's better. Now, Ali, there's cleaning up to be done from breakfast," Anders says dismissing her.

I turn my head to watch Ali scurry away. Her normal strut is more of an angry stomp and when she pauses and looks back over her shoulder her eyes focus on Angel and she glares furiously. Quickly, the room fills with chatter again and Anders and Grits wave their goodbyes and leave. Pulling out my chair, I sit, leading Angel down into my lap and wrapping my arms around her. "You okay?" I whisper into her shoulder.

She twists in my lap until we're facing each other. "Is that girl your girlfriend?"

Her eyes are bright and her mouth is twisted into a tight

line. She's either pissed or jealous and I fight the smile that's threatening to overtake my face. "No, baby, she's not my girlfriend. She's a club girl that I fucked once. She wants it to be more than it is, but I'm not interested."

"You had sex with her," Angel says almost like she's speaking to herself.

"I fucked her once when I was drunk as hell, it was nothing."

Angel doesn't speak and instead turns back to her plate and starts to pick at her cinnamon bun again. Wrapping my hands around her hips I lift her up and turn her to face me. Gently cupping her chin, I hold her so she's looking at me. "She was a drunken fuck that's all. I've fucked a lot of women and I won't apologize for stuff that happened in the past. But it was just sex, Angel. They never made me feel, not like you do. I only have to hold your tiny hand or kiss your perfect lips and you make me feel more in those brief moments when you let me touch you than any of those mindless fucks did."

"It's none of my business. I'm sorry. I shouldn't have asked," Angel whispers, trying to pull her chin from my fingers.

Instead of letting her go, I slide my hand under her hair and palm the back of her neck. "You've got every right to ask, Angel. I thought we got this fixed. I like you, I want to get to know you better. I told you this before all the shit happened with your dad. Fuck, the only good thing about the shit storm rolling around us, is that now I get to be with you, and I don't have to wait for you to sneak out."

Angel's eyes drop from mine and her cheeks tinge with a pale pink blush. "You hearing what I'm saying, Angel? The circumstances that brought you to me are shitty, but despite that I'm glad you're here. In fact, I love that you're here with me."

She nods. The movement is so small I wonder if I imagined it. "Don't hide from me," I say, my voice sterner than I intended, but if I can't see her eyes I have no fucking clue what going on in her head. Her eyes tip up to meet mine and I smile at how bright they are. "You gotta tell me what you're thinking, Angel."

Her lips part and when she speaks it's barely a whisper. "I hate why I'm here. I hate that I had to drag you into my mess. But I'm glad I'm with you too."

My shoulders relax, and I release the breath I'd been holding. "You want me to kiss you, Angel?"

I watch her mouth part and her tongue dip out to moisten her lips, then she swallows and looks away from me for a second. When her gaze moves back to lock with mine, she pauses and then slowly lifts her head and drops it again in a decisive nod.

"Come here," I say, and she leans into me, lifting her hands to rest on my shoulders. I take over and with the hand that's still wrapped around her neck, I pull her the last few inches toward me and take her mouth.

Our lips clash in a consuming kiss. When our tongues meet, I pull her flush with my chest, so I can feel her heart pounding against mine. I love that I make her feel this way. Slowing the kiss, I worship her, tasting her lips and tongue, trying to memorize every inch of her. Her hands move up to my hair and I groan when her nails scratch against my scalp.

"Dove, put him down, Prez wants a word." Blade's words pull me from my Angel induced bubble and I reluctantly pull away from her. Angel's cheeks are bright red, and she buries her face in my shoulder in embarrassment.

I stand, lifting Angel and placing her next to me. Taking hold of her hand, I entwine my fingers with hers needing to stay connected to her. I wave to Echo and Liv who are too consumed with each other to even notice that we're leaving and then follow Blade through the bar to Prez's office.

Angel's cheeks are still stained red and Blade chuckles when he looks at her. "Don't be embarrassed, Little Dove. No one cares that you and your man were dry humping at breakfast. A little making out over the bacon and eggs is nothing, to the orgies and strip shows at lunch and dinner."

Angel's gasp is loud, and Blade cracks up with laughter. I chuckle and pull Angel into my chest, dropping her hand and throwing my arm over her shoulder. Leaning down, I kiss the top of her head. "Come on, baby. Let's go see what Prez has to say."

Blade knocks on Prez's door. "Come in," Prez shouts. We file into the office and take the same seats we'd all used last night. Prez is sat behind his desk looking pensive; his eyebrows are drawn and his eyes look tired. "Little Dove, I think it's safe to say that your absence has been noticed. Your father reported you missing at 7:30 am this morning and he's been tearing the town apart looking for you. He's got the whole sheriff's department searching for you, as well as the police department in Houston on alert."

"I didn't think they could even class her as missing until she'd been gone for twenty-four hours," Blade queries.

"Apparently the rules don't apply when it's the mayor's daughter that's disappeared. He's saying that you're mentally ill and a danger to yourself, Little Dove," Prez says, wincing slightly.

"What?" Angel gasps. "I'm not mentally ill. There's nothing wrong with me," she cries.

Prez lifts his hand to silence her. "You got any history we should know about?"

Angel shakes her head. "I haven't seen a doctor since I was thirteen when I fell and hit my head at recess. A month or so after that we moved here, and I started home schooling. I wasn't even allowed to go to the hospital when my sister died."

Prez nods. "Okay. Obviously, your father is using the idea that you're ill as a ploy to find you. You're eighteen, Dove; he can't class you as a runaway and you're well within your legal rights to leave your parents' home and never return."

"Has the club had any heat?" Blade asks.

Prez shakes his head. "No. Dove has no links to the club. No one here apart from us and Grits knows who she really is, so they haven't got any reason to look for her here. My leads say that the mayor's planning a TV interview this afternoon to appeal for help in locating her."

"Fuck," I say.

"Dove, what do you know about your parents' financial situation? Can they pay this debt without using you as payment?" Prez asks Angel.

Angel shakes her head. "Mama doesn't have access to any of the bank accounts and as far as I know my father has about six hundred dollars in his account."

Prez stares at Angel assessing. "How do you know how much money is in your father's bank account?"

Angel glances at me for a second and then turns back to Prez. "Because even though my father thinks I'm an idiot, I'm not."

"Explain," Prez demands.

Angel's back goes rigid and her fingers wrap around the arms of her chair. "My sister died two years ago. A few months before this happened she met a guy and ran away with him. My father lost his mind when she left. He's always been an angry person—we just got used to him shouting and belittling us—but I had no idea that my sister had spent years shielding me from him and dealing with his abuse. Once she was gone, he turned his anger and punishments on me. I've been home schooled for the last five years, not allowed friends or a cell phone. I don't get to pick my own clothes and God forbid I argue or talk back to him. He didn't allow me to finish high school or get a decent education. I only learnt to drive because my sister taught me. My father truly believes I'm stupid. But I'm not. My sister had a laptop and when she left I took it hoping that I could find a way to speak to her. We have internet at the house, even though my father doesn't let me, or Mama use it. So I set up access to online banking without him having any idea. I refuse to be used as a human punch bag, I didn't deserve to be punished or beaten with a belt. I needed to escape, so I set up a bank account and for the last six months I've been slowly syphoning money from my father's account into my own. I was biding my time until I had enough money to get me and my mama far enough away from Archer's Creek that my father couldn't find us."

A smile that's full of pride is etched across Prez's face. "How much did you take?" he asks.

"Not enough. I needed a few more months, but I ran out of time." Angel says sadly.

"If you were saving for you and your mom to get away why isn't she here with you?" Blade asks.

Angel turns to look at Blade and I can no longer see her face, but I can hear the sadness in her voice. "She's too far gone to know that what he does is wrong."

"So, she didn't know you were going to run?" Prez asks.

Angel turns her attention back to Prez. "Actually, she helped me."

"Explain," Prez asks, more gently this time.

"Mama knew that my father was doing something. We

didn't talk about what she knew or what I knew, but yesterday she cooked a big batch of spaghetti, gave me some and then ground up a load of sleeping tablets into the rest and told me she loved me." Angel says.

Prez stands up from behind his desk and slowly walks around until he's in front of Angel. He leans forward and places his hand gently on her shoulder. She flinches, but Prez just bends and kisses the top of her head. "You're strong, Little Dove. You'll get through this and I promise you we'll do everything in our power to keep you safe. When this shit with Carduccio is over, if she wants to leave, we will help your mama too."

Prez lifts his hand and steps back from Angel, then he looks at me. "Take your girl and keep her safe in your room. Lay low for the rest of the day and we'll clear out anyone who isn't part of the club."

I nod and then taking Angel's hand, I lead her back to my room.

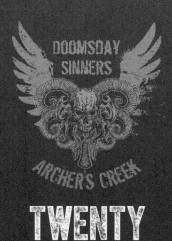

DOOMSDAY
SINNERS

ARCHER'S CREEK

TWENTY

Angel

Daisy's hand is wrapped around mine. I silently follow him down the corridors that are becoming more familiar and into his room. He shuts and locks the door behind us and for a minute we just stand and stare at each other.

"You okay, Angel?"

I release a drawn-out sigh and shake my head. "No, not really."

"That's understandable, you've had a shitty few days."

I scoff loudly, the sound bubbles up from my stomach and I start to laugh hysterically. I don't know when the laughs turn to sobs, but Daisy folds me into his arms and holds me. My body wracks with the emotions I've managed to keep under wraps since I heard my father sell me to cover his debts.

"Shh, it's gonna be okay, Angel, it's all gonna be okay."

I want to tell Daisy that it's not going to be okay, how could it possibly be okay, but I don't. Instead, I let him hold me and soothe me and I try to believe his words even though deep down I'm not sure things will ever be okay again.

My sobs subside, and Daisy eventually pulls back to wipe the tears from my cheeks. "Don't cry, Angel. Come on, let's watch some TV. I'll even let you pick the show."

I nod shakily and climb onto the bed resting my back against the wall. Daisy climbs on and sits beside me—we aren't touching, just simply sitting next to one another. He flicks through the channels and then moves to the series boxsets. "What do you want to watch?" he asks.

I shrug. "I don't mind. I don't really watch a lot of TV. The only one in our house was in the family room and watching that meant sitting with my father. It was easier to sit in my room on my own."

Daisy looks at me, his head tilted to the side, his teeth worrying his lower lip, like he's deciding what to say, then he hands me the remote. "Your dad's a fucking dick. Pick whatever you want. I'll watch anything except reality dating shows, those things make me want to throw up."

I smile at him then turn to the TV and flick through the boxsets. I settle on a supernatural drama series and start the first episode. Dropping the remote onto the quilt between us I wiggle into the pillows to get comfy and watch as girl meets boy and realizes he isn't exactly human.

I try to force my eyes to remain on the screen and not wander to Daisy lying stretched out beside me, but I fail. His body is huge and after the first ten minutes of episode one he shuffles down the bed, so his head is on the pillows and his long, lean body is stretched out along the quilt. My eyes keep glancing at him, quietly watching the screen with one of his arms rested behind his head and the other laid across his stomach.

"You like what you see, Angel?"

My cheeks instantly redden, and I quickly dart my eyes back to the TV. Daisy chuckles at my side and the bed dips as he moves. I jump when his arms stretch across my stomach and I squeal when his grip tightens, and he pulls me down the bed so my head rests next to his on the pillow.

"That's better, now I can look at you too, Angel."

I lift my hands to cover my face. I want to deny that I was staring at him, but I can't and instead try to hide my embarrassment.

"Don't hide, baby. I love that you're staring at me. I'm pretty awesome and honestly I was starting to think you hadn't noticed."

Pulling my hands from my cheeks, he rolls, so he's half leaning over me. "You're too beautiful to hide, Angel, and those big doe eyes of yours tell me everything you don't say."

"What are they telling you now?" I say breathlessly.

"That you want me to kiss you, but you don't want to ask."

I lick my lips and nod. His lips immediately dip down to mine and I eagerly open my mouth. The kiss is lazy and wonderful. He's not devouring me, but more like exploring every inch of my mouth and claiming it as his. Gently framing my face with his fingers, he strokes at my cheek reverently and when his lips finally release mine, I feel worshipped and cherished.

"If you want me to kiss you, Angel, you ask. I always want my lips on yours, always. Okay?"

"Okay," I whisper.

Moving from above me he lies back down on the bed and lifts his arm into the air. "Come here, Angel."

I don't know what he wants me to do. Does he expect me to lie on top of him like he did to me? I'm not sure I can do that, I'm not sure I'm ready for that.

I must take too much time thinking because he curls his arm beneath me and pulls me next to him. "I just want you to lay closer to me, Angel, that's all."

He moves his arm until I'm nestled against him, my head on his shoulder. Lifting one of my legs he repositions it so that it's resting over the top of his and I'm essentially draped across the side of his body. I'm uncomfortable and tense and he must know because he tenses too.

"Do what you need to do to relax again, Angel. If that means you move back to the other side of the bed that's okay. I don't want you to be here with me if it's making you uncomfortable. Just do what you need to do, baby."

His voice is open and reassuring and my muscles begin to relax. I lift my head off his arm and move it to rest on his chest, over his heart. I tentatively place my hand on his chest and stretch out my leg, so it rests alongside his.

"It's not that I don't want to lie here with you, it's just I've never done this before," I say quietly.

I feel him drop a quick kiss to the top of my head. "Fucking hell, Angel. You really are as innocent as you look, aren't you?"

I don't know what to say so I shrug.

"You're hiding from me again," Daisy says.

"No, I'm not. I just don't know what to say."

"Would it be easier if I asked questions, and you just said yes or no?" he asks playfully.

I giggle. "Yes."

"Okay." He sounds dubious and I half expect him to just stay quiet and watch the TV show.

"Was I your first kiss?"

"No."

"But I'm the first guy you've ever snuggled with?" he says as his arms pull me closer to his chest.

"Yes."

"Do you like lying here with me?"

"Yes."

"Have you ever done anything else with a guy, besides kiss?"

I pause for a minute, embarrassed to admit that I'm eighteen and so inexperienced. The sum total of my history with boys is a chaste kiss when I was thirteen at Kristie Manors' birthday party. I'd spent seven minutes in heaven with her brother's friend. In truth it was seven minutes with a spotty fourteen-year-old who'd kissed me closed mouth for a minute and then spent the remaining six minutes asking me if my friend Georgie liked him.

"No." I finally say quietly.

"Fuck, Angel. You're a virgin."

"Yes," I whisper and then bury my face into his chest.

Daisy rips his arm from beneath me and jumps away so quickly the bed bounces. My mouth opens, and I sit up in bed and stare at him, as he stomps to the other side of the room.

"You're a fucking virgin, Angel, and you're curled up in bed with me. What the hell, baby? You shouldn't be in here alone with me."

I watch him pull at the strands of his hair in frustration and I fill with anger. I want to shout at him, but I can't. My survival instincts tell me to tamp down my fury and annoyance, to become placid and inoffensive. It's safer to stay hidden.

"I don't know what's going on, but I know that you're a fucking virgin, pure and untouched. I haven't been a virgin since I was thirteen. If your asshole of a father was any kind of a man, he would be protecting you from men like me. I'm the guy your mama warned you to stay away from," he rants, almost to himself.

"Grits said I could go stay with her and Anders. Can I stay here until she gets here?"

Daisy stops pulling at his hair and looks at me. "What?"

"Grits said she was coming to see me tonight. Is it okay for me to stay until she gets here and then I'll ask to go stay with them? It's only a few days, so I don't think she'll mind."

"What's wrong with you, why are you talking like that?"

I stand from the bed and circle around it to the other side where my backpack is leaning against the wall. "I'm fine. I'll go speak to Anders and see if I can wait with him until Grits gets here."

"What the hell are you talking about, Angel? Of course you can stay here."

"Okay, thanks," I say and then sit down on the edge of the bed with my feet on the floor and turn to face the TV again.

"I don't know what the hell's happening here. Have you been taken over by aliens because you're talking, but it's like I've never met you before?"

Turning my head to look at Daisy, I keep my face deliberately emotionless. "You just said that I shouldn't be in here with you. I can't just leave, but when Grits gets here, I'll go." My voice is monotone and passionless and Daisy gapes at me like he doesn't recognize me. I hum the tune that helps me hide my emotions over and over in my head, the familiarity of the act calms me, and I sink into my mask. Hiding, always hiding.

I stare at the TV. I don't want to hear what he's saying

because I can read between the lines. He's used to women who know what they're doing and I'm a virgin who doesn't even know how to snuggle with him. A pathetic eighteen-year-old that's been frozen in time for the last five years. "I understand you don't want me here. I'll go find Anders."

Standing up, I reach for my backpack, slinging it over my shoulders. I take one step forward and Daisy blocks my path. I don't make eye contact. Never make eye contact, it only makes it worse.

"Angel, I never said I didn't want you here."

"You said I shouldn't be here. That's okay, I understand."

"Angel."

I stare at a spot on his neck and try to sidestep him, but as I move, he moves with me blocking my escape.

"Angel?"

I ignore him.

"Angelique."

The use of my real name jolts me, and my eyes shoot up to his face. My mask splinters. "Don't call me that. You don't call me that."

"That's your name. Angelique."

My eyes narrow. "It might be my name, but you don't call me that, you never call me that."

"What do I call you then?"

"You call me Angel, you always call me Angel."

Daisy steps closer and his hand slowly rises and cups my

cheek. "I do call you Angel. But the person you've been for the last few minutes, that wasn't my Angel. That person wasn't you—it wasn't your face, or your eyes, or your voice. I don't know who that was, but that robotic version of you scares me almost as much as when you went catatonic last night."

I close my eyes. "Look, Daisy, I think I just need to leave."

"Fuck, Angel, I freaked out, okay? You told me you're a virgin, and I freaked out."

My eyes snap open and all the emotion I'd buried surges to the surface. "You're freaked out I haven't had sex?" I say acidly.

"Yes. I'm not the type of guy any virgin should be messing around with."

"Okay, so you don't want me here because I still have a hymen," I say my voice raising as I start to step around him.

"That's not what I said," Daisy snaps and steps to block me again.

I desperately try to force down my emotions. "You said I shouldn't be here with you, so I'm trying to leave," I say as calmly as I can muster.

"I don't want you to leave. I want to know what the hell happened a few minutes ago."

"Nothing happened. Can you move please? I want to leave."

"No."

"No?" I repeat shocked.

"No, Angel, I won't move. I want to know how your eyes went from dead a few moments ago to bright and sparkling with anger right now. I want to know what I did to make you turn into robot Angelique because I never want to do it again. Then once you've told me I'm gonna apologize for being a dick and freaking out."

He takes a step closer, and I let him. His fingers curl around my chin and lift it up. "I'm sorry," he whispers.

I'm so weak—one small touch from him and I soften. "I thought I had to tell you what you did before you apologized?"

Daisy chuckles softly. "I'm probably gonna need to apologize more than once, so I was getting started early."

The anger starts to melt from me and when Daisy pulls me down to the bed and into his lap, I go willingly.

"What happened, baby?"

I shake my head. "I don't know."

"Yes you do, Angel."

"I hide, Daisy; it's how I cope," I say quietly.

"So robot Angelique is you hiding?"

I nod.

"I don't want you to leave, that's the last thing I want. I just. Fuck, I'm bad for you. I'm older and I'm not a fucking virgin and I don't deserve someone as innocent as you. You're too good for me, and if your parents weren't dicks they wouldn't let me within ten feet of you. I don't want you to think I'm taking advantage of you, so when you told me you were a virgin I freaked out." Daisy's eyes are imploring me to believe him.

Pulling in a deep breath, I offer him a small nod. "I started to get angry with you and I'm not allowed to get angry, so I hid. I shut down. That's how I cope. My life, well, err, it was better if I didn't show too much real emotion. The other stuff, well yeah, I'm a virgin. I'm only eighteen that's not really that unusual. I don't feel unsafe with you, but I'd rather leave than have you be weird just because I haven't had sex yet."

Daisy slides the straps of my backpack down my arms and once it's free, he drops it onto the floor by his feet. "This club isn't a place for innocent virgins, but I'm selfish enough to want you to stay. I hate that your life has been so hard and that you've known anything other than love and protection. I'm glad you're here and that I'll have a chance to prove that I'm not bad for you. I like you, Angel, I really like you. You've woke something up in me, something that I'd buried a long time ago. I don't really know how to do this, us, but I want to try. So, get angry at me. You know no one here is gonna hurt you if you lose your shit and start shouting. Please don't go robot on me again. I'm gonna fuck up and you're gonna be pissed at me. That's okay, we can be mad as long as we're honest."

"I'm only here for a few days," I say in confusion.

"But what if you stayed longer than that?"

I shake my head. "I won't ever be safe here. My father thinks I'm property that can be sold. I need to get away from Archer's Creek and figure out who I am when I'm not scared all the time."

He sighs. "Do you like me, Angel, or am I in this on my

own? What do you feel when I kiss you? Do you feel anything? This might make me sound like a pussy, but every time I touch you I feel like I'm lighting up like a fucking roman candle. I won't lie, I've kissed a lot of fucking women and the only thing that's ever sparked to life is my cock. Everything's different with you, but you need to tell me right now if this thing I'm feeling is all me or if you feel it too," Daisy asks raggedly.

My eyes burn with the need to look away from him, his intense gaze heats my skin and makes my heart pound faster and harder. "I like you too. This feels like it could be something more, but I have nothing to compare it to. I've only ever kissed one person before and it didn't feel anything like when I kiss you. I still have to leave, but you could come with me, when I go? We could start over somewhere new," I whisper hopefully.

"This is my home," Daisy says.

"It was my home too, but we could make some new place home."

"This is my family, Angel," Daisy says, his eyes sad.

"I didn't realize your parents live in Archer's Creek," I say wondering who they are and if I've ever met them.

"No, no, I don't have parents or siblings. The club is my family, the guys are my brothers. The Sinners are my home and I couldn't ever leave that."

"You don't have parents?" I ask cautiously.

"Nope, I grew up in the foster system. Group homes mainly with the occasional foster parents. The only family I've ever known is the club—they took me in and gave me a home. I won't ever turn my back on that, Angel. I owe them everything."

My stomach churns with disappointment. For a moment I'd hoped that this man I hardly knew—who had become so entangled with what I think happiness feels like—might be part of my future. But obviously he wouldn't leave his life behind to run away with me. "How did you end up in foster care?" I ask wanting to change the subject.

Daisy sighs. "Usual story. Mom was a drug addict, Dad was a blank space on my birth certificate. Apparently, my mom overdosed when I was two and I've been in the system ever since. They spent about a year tracking down my mom's parents hoping they'd take me, but they weren't interested, so I bounced from home to home until I hit eighteen and got booted."

"I'm so sorry, Daisy."

He laughs dryly. "You didn't exactly win the parent lottery, Angel. The system wasn't great, but I survived just like you did. We only get dealt as much as we can handle. I found the Sinners and then I found you. I'm feeling pretty lucky with my lot right now."

"How did you find the Sinners?" I ask, eagerly taking advantage of this opportunity to learn more about him.

"The group home I lived in until I turned eighteen was in Houston. I was a punk thinking I was badass, stealing cars and motorbikes. One day I was walking past this bar and this sweet Harley was parked up outside, so I tried to steal it. Turns out it was Billy's bike—he's a Sinner but he's retired now. Well, he took one look at me trying to boost his bike and before I got a chance to run he'd got me by the back of my shirt and he kicked the crap out of me. Then he took me into the bar and bought me a drink. He told me I scratched his bike and that I need to work off the cost of the re-spray. He gave me an address and told me to meet him there the next day. I don't know why I did it, but the next day I went to the address and it was one of the Sinners' garages. I worked every day for three months, sweeping up and running errands to cover the cost of the repairs. At the end of the three months, Billy told me that the scratch on his bike had been there for ten years, but the day I'd tried to steal his bike I'd reminded him of himself at eighteen. I was so mad, but then he brought me here and introduced me around and when I was old enough, I asked if I could prospect and the rest is history. The Sinners saved me from my stupid eighteen-year-old self, they gave me a home and a family. I'm a Doomsday Sinner to my very soul. I couldn't turn my back on them if I tried."

I smile warmly at Daisy. "You were lucky it was Billy's bike you tried to steal that day."

He laughs. "Yeah it could have been a very different story."

"What's your real name? Oh and I'm dying to know where Daisy came from," I ask with a raise of my eyebrows.

He licks his lips and smiles. "I don't use my real name and haven't in fucking years, so don't get thinking you can use it once I tell you, okay?"

I nod earnestly.

"Oh God, right. My real name is Marion," Daisy says, a pink blush covering his cheeks.

"Marion," I say swallowing a giggle.

"Yep, sure helped me get into a shit ton of fights when I was a kid. I started going by Rin when I was eleven and got sick of punching people for making fun of me. When I started to prospect for the club, the guys didn't believe that my full name was Rin so they got me really fucking drunk and got me to admit what my real name was. The bastards laughed their fucking asses off—didn't help that I was in the middle of having my sleeve done and I'd just had all of the color added on the flowers on my arms. Then the fuckers decided that with a name like Marion and a load of flowers tattooed onto my skin I should get the nickname Daisy. Unfortunately, it stuck and I've been Daisy ever since. From one stupid name to another," he says with a smile full of fondness for the memory he just shared.

"You definitely don't look like a Marion," I say with a smirk as a giggle bubbles up from my chest and escapes. I slap my hand over my mouth to try to stifle the sound, but Daisy hears it and gasps in mock outrage.

His arms wrap around me and I shriek when he lifts me into the air and then carefully drops me down flat onto the bed. He crawls over me, caging me against the quilt with his arms on either side of my head. His body isn't touching mine, but my heart starts to pound, and my breath comes in frightened, excited gasps. I look up at him and silently will him to kiss me. He smiles, then he freezes and looks down at my body stretched out beneath him. "Fuck, Angel, you're like the sweetest temptation. So fucking beautiful and hell, knowing that no one has ever touched you before, makes me want to beat my chest like a fucking caveman. I don't want to push my luck or do something that's gonna make you uncomfortable and I promise I won't let this go too far but I really want to kiss you like this. You okay with that?"

I nod and his head immediately drops to mine. Our lips meet and we kiss. This kiss is sweet but measured like he's holding back. This is a kiss you give to a virgin and nothing like the passionate kisses he's given me before. Frustrated, I push at his chest and he immediately lifts his head and sits up. I push myself up and rest on my elbows. "Daisy, I don't want you to kiss me like that."

He looks at me confused. "Like what?"

"Have I ever seemed like I was used to kissing men I only just met?"

He smiles and seems embarrassed. "No, Angel, you didn't. Why?"

"Is it, err, is it a surprise that I haven't had sex yet?" I ask him, my eyes unable to make contact with his.

"No, it's not a surprise. I've thought you were innocent from the moment I saw you at the wedding."

"So why are you treating me differently now I've confirmed

what you already assumed? I don't know how many times I'll get to kiss you, so I want to make them count. Don't kiss me like you think you should kiss a virgin. Kiss me like time is running out," I say, my voice laced with desperation.

My words hit home because Daisy scoops me into his arms and kisses me like this is the last kiss either of us will ever have. It's sweet and powerful; he consumes me but gives me part of himself at the same time. His tongue is in my mouth searching for more and I respond giving him everything I have. Daisy slows the kiss to a torturous pace; his lips explore mine, nipping at the skin on my lower lip then soothing it with his tongue. Small moans of pleasure escape from my throat, as his hands move into my hair and he wraps himself around me, plastered against my chest.

Daisy pulls back, panting. I can feel his heart beating a staccato thump in his chest, his pupils are dilated and an excited twinkle sparkles within his beautiful depths. "Was that better my Angel?"

TWENTY-ONE

Daisy

"**Y**es," she sighs breathlessly.

I laugh. "I aim to please."

Rolling onto my back, I pull her against my side and hold her close. My cock is rock hard, and I need to calm down enough to get it back under control.

She's a fucking virgin. It's really not a surprise, but still, hearing it come from her lips makes it real. A fucking virgin. Untouched. Far too good for me to sully, but fuck if I don't want her. I want to peel that tiny skirt from her and pull down the white cotton panties that I know are underneath. I want to stroke and lick and touch her perfect virgin pussy knowing that I'm the first person to do it.

I'm getting in too deep with her. When she'd asked me to

run with her, for a minute I wanted to say yes. I still want to say yes. But I won't turn my back on the only people I've ever called family for a woman, not even a woman like Angel.

My breathing slowly starts to return to normal and I slide my hand up to tangle in Angel's hair. I turn my head toward her and watch as her fingers absentmindedly play with the fabric of my shirt. "I like you here with me. In my arms and in my bed. Stay with me, for however long you're in Archer's Creek I want you here with me. Promise me you'll stay with me."

Her fingers stop moving and she stretches her arm across my stomach and turns closer into my body. "I want that too."

"Then no matter what, you stay with me. I want you to feel safe, I know what it's like to be scared and I fucking hate you've lived like that," I say, forcing my body to stay relaxed and not react to the anger that's starting to swell within me.

"What made you scared?" she whispers.

"I've lived in a lot of places, Angel. Not all of them were nice. In an ideal world, the foster care system would be full of caring people, but sometimes it's just a place for sick and twisted fuckers to hide in plain sight."

Neither of us speaks. Sometimes there's nothing to say and talking about it doesn't always make it better. The TV murmurs in the background, but I don't watch it. Instead I drop my chin on top of Angel's head and close my eyes. The feeling of her chest rising and falling as she silently breathes lulls me to sleep and I dream of a beautiful Angel that changes everything.

A quiet knock at the door wakes me. Lifting my head I take in the sleeping figure of Angel. She's lying on top of me. Her head is in the middle of my chest and her legs are entangled between mine. She's so tiny she fits perfectly, and my arms are wrapped around her holding her close to me.

There's another knock at the door, so I carefully move Angel off my chest and onto the quilt beside me. She immediately curls into a ball, her face twisting into a disgruntled scowl. Smiling, I lift myself off the bed and pad over to my door. I open it just wide enough to see who's on the other side. "Blade, what's up?" I say rubbing the sleep from my eyes.

"There's news. Prez wants you and Dove in his office."

"She's sleeping," I say turning to look at her still curled up in my bed.

"You wear her out?" Blade says with a laugh.

"Fuck you, Blade."

Blade holds his hands up in a consolatory gesture, then smirks. "My bad, brother. I just figured you'd been busy tapping that fine ass of hers and fucked her unconscious."

Seeing red I launch myself at him. "Don't ever talk about her like that, ever," I hiss at him, holding him up against the wall by his shirt. "She's not some club whore you can talk shit about, she's mine, and she deserves some fucking respect."

Blade's face sets in a firm scowl. "I disrespected your woman and for that I'm sorry, but I suggest you get your fucking hands off me right now, before I put you on your ass."

I eyeball my V.P. for a second and then drop my hands from his shirt and take a step back.

"Five minutes, see you in Prez's office," Blade says, turning and walking away.

Pulling the door closed, I pause for a moment with my fingers on the handle. "What was that?" Angel says, her voice small and unsure.

I turn to face her. She's sitting up, her hair deliciously rumpled and her back nestled against the pillows. "Nothing, baby, just Prez has got news."

"What did Blade say to you?" she pushes.

"Something he knows not to say again. Don't worry about it," I say and cross the room to sit beside her on the bed. I reach out my hand to her, palm up, and she places her hand in mine. Entwining our fingers, I stand and she shuffles across the bed on her knees, cautiously sliding her feet to the floor. Without the heels Grits gave her she's tiny; her eyes look tired and the bruises on her face seem darker illuminated by the afternoon sunshine that's peeking through my blinds.

Leaning forward, I drop a kiss to the corner of her mouth and then to her cheek and eye. "You didn't flinch," I blurt.

Her lids close for the smallest of moments and then her doe eyes look up at me. "You won't hurt me."

Those four words ricochet off my heart and without thought I scoop her off the floor and into my arms. Holding her against me tightly she instinctively wraps her arms and legs around me.

"Never," I whisper into her neck.

Angel loosens her legs and I slowly lower her to the floor. Grabbing her boots, she slides them on and runs her fingers through her hair smoothing it. "What do you think my father's done now?" she asks quietly.

"Let's go find out," I say and reach for her hand leading her from the room.

I knock, then enter the office when Prez shouts. Angel and I take what I'm starting to think of as our usual seats and wait.

Prez turns to look at Angel. "How you doing, Little Dove, you holding up okay?"

"I'm fine, thank you. I really appreciate you letting me hide out here. I know this must be causing you some hassle," she says politely.

Prez looks at me then back to Angel. "Don't you worry about it, little one. You're one of us now and we take care of our own."

"What's happening, Prez?" I ask.

He sighs and rubs at his temples. "Dove, your face is on every TV station in the state. Blade's been monitoring the sheriff's department, and the mayor has lost his shit. He's been down there all day demanding that they put out an amber alert. He's not taking it well that because you're eighteen, in the eyes of the law you're an adult and there's no evidence to suggest you were kidnapped. This afternoon he held a press conference. He begged for you to come home and appealed for help in finding you. He's offering a reward for information that leads to your whereabouts."

"Fuck," I hiss under my breath. "Any word from Carduccio?"

"No," Blade says.

"That's the only good news so far. Hopefully the fact that Carduccio hasn't commented on Dove's disappearance, means that as far as he's concerned she's irrelevant. We put out feelers to people we know in Carduccio's circle to see if he's looking for her, but so far her name's not been mentioned," Prez says, his elbows resting on the surface of his desk.

"I should leave," Angel suddenly says.

"No," both Prez and I say in unison.

"This isn't your problem, it's mine. I have enough money to buy a cheap car and then I'll leave. I'll drive to the other side of the country where no one will have heard of me and my father won't have any influence. I can change my name and start over. My father might find me eventually, but it won't be before he has to pay the money he owes," she says decisively.

"Little Dove, as much as I admire your courage, you need to be smart about this. At some point you'd have to stop to pump gas or buy food and you'd be spotted before you even got out of Texas. People are greedy and the moment you were seen they'd be trying to claim that reward your dad's spouting on about," Prez says.

"But…" Angel starts to speak but Prez interrupts her, holding up a hand and cautioning her to let him finish.

"Now the way I see it we've got two options, we can sit tight and see what happens, or we can cut them off at the pass," he says thoughtfully.

"What you thinking, Boss?" Blade asks.

Prez turns his attention to me. "How deep are you, brother?"

I glance at Angel and our entwined hands. "Bout as deep as it gets."

Prez smiles and chuckles lightly. "That's what I figured, so what I'm suggesting is that we make it official. Nothing the sheriff or state police can do about it, cause she's an adult and if Carduccio knows she's club, I doubt he'll be interested anymore. She won't look so shiny and new wrapped around a Sinner wearing a property cut."

"I don't understand," Angel says, her head swinging between me and Prez.

I start to speak but Prez gets there before me. "Daisy's your man, right?" he asks Angel.

She turns to me wide eyed, then back to Prez. "Err."

Prez tilts his head to the side. "Little Dove, you're sleepin' in his bed, wearin' his clothes, holdin' his hand, kissin' him, and doin' whatever else you're doin, right?"

Angel flushes bright red, looks at me then quickly turns back to Prez and nods at him without making eye contact.

"You doing any of those things with anyone else?" Prez asks.

"No," she answers as her head snaps up and she glares at

Prez.

"Exactly. So like I said, Daisy's your man. What I'm suggesting is that we let your father and anyone else that might be interested know that Daisy's your man and that he's a Sinner, and as his woman so are you. You're no longer a missing person, you're just a teenage girl who left home to be with her boyfriend. Your father might think he's a big man around town, but he's got no ties to the club and as long as you stay put he's got no way of getting near you. Carduccio might have been interested in your value as a sheltered teenage beauty, but I doubt he'd be as interested once he finds out you're living as a biker's old lady," Prez says.

Blade barks out a booming laugh. "That ought to work. It'll piss the mayor off, but he hates the club anyway and maybe his daughter joining the dark side will mean he gets booted out of office at election time."

"He'll kill me," Angel says quietly.

I turn to stare at her. "What?"

"He'll kill me; this will push him over the edge and he'll kill me," she says, her eyes wide with fear.

"We won't let him, Dove. He'll never get close enough to hurt a hair on your head, I promise," Prez assures her.

Angel starts to curl into herself, her shoulders slump and her chin drops onto her chest. Her body's trembling, and she shakes her head rapidly from side to side mumbling. "He'll kill me, he'll find me, and he'll kill me."

Jumping up, I lift Angel from her seat and pull her into my lap. I can see the concern on Prez and Blade's faces, but I ignore them, wrapping my arms tightly around her and gently rocking her against my chest, stroking her hair to soothe her. "We won't let him near you, you don't need to be scared anymore. You're mine and I'll keep you safe, I promise I'll keep you safe."

I know we're not alone, but I don't care. I promise her over and over that she's mine and I'll protect her. When Prez asked how deep I was, it all clicked into place for me. I've fallen for her doe eyes and beautiful face, but more than that I've fallen for her incomparable strength. Since the first time I set eyes on her, I knew she was something special; one touch from her gathers all of my broken pieces and bonds them back together again. I want to do the same for her.

I'm grateful for the club, I'm grateful for the family and home they've given me, and I never thought that anything would be more important than that. I've been adrift and unwanted since I was two years old, I didn't know that I was craving roots until I was given the opportunity to plant some.

Meeting Angel has made me rethink everything. The Sinners ground me, they're my safe haven, but I've only been taking from them. I took a home, a family and a band of brothers but I hardly gave anything of myself except my loyalty. With Angel I want to give her everything. I want to be her safety, her roots, and her strength when she can't find her own.

"I'm your man, Angel, let me keep you safe," I whisper into

her neck.

When she lifts her head, a single tear rolls down her cheek and I lean forward and catch it with my lips. "He doesn't get any more of your tears, baby. Let's show him that you aren't alone anymore, that you're a Sinner and that he'll never touch you again."

She turns her big doe eyes on me. "He won't accept this without a fight; he'll cause trouble for you all."

Blade laughs a hard laugh. "Your father is an asshole, Dove. I'm gonna enjoy telling him to go fuck himself. He can't do shit to us and he knows it. He's been trying to get rid of us since he first stepped foot into town. Whatever shit he tries to pull on us after he finds out you belong to the Sinners is more of a pain in the ass than something to worry about."

"Belong to the club?" Angel asks Blade warily.

"Figuratively, Little Dove. Your old man is a Sinner, you're a Sinner," Prez assures her.

She turns back to look at me and my heart starts to race "Do you want to do this?" She asks me.

"Yes," I say immediately.

Angel stares at me for a moment then a small smile twitches at the side of her lips. "Okay."

I know she's thinking that if this doesn't work she can still run, but this is my home and she's my woman, running is no longer an option. I don't fucking know what love feels like, but I do know that I need her, she's become the center of everything for me and I'm gonna fight like hell to keep her.

Prez slaps the desk and smiles brightly. "Excellent. Right, lay low for tonight, then in the morning I'll make the call to the sheriff and let him know that Dove is safe and happy and living here in the clubhouse with us. Then we'll wait for the bombs to drop."

Blade laughs, and I fight a smirk. I know that Prez has developed a soft spot for my Angel, but he seems to be enjoying this whole situation a little too much.

There's a knock at the door. "Come in," Prez shouts.

Opening the door, Grits enters the room and walks behind Prez's desk. His hands reach for her, pulling her by the back of the neck straight into his waiting arms. He kisses her thoroughly for a second, then leans back, turning her in his arms so her back is to his front.

"Dove, how you doing, baby girl?" Grits cries happily.

"I'm okay, I think," Angel says.

"Why don't you take Dove with you and see what the girls have got cooking for dinner? I'm starved, and I need to have a quick word with Daisy," Prez says to Grits.

With a smile, she quickly walks to Angel and pulls her from my lap. Angel goes willingly with a soft smile on her face, happily chatting with Grits as they leave the office.

The door closes behind them with a click and Prez immediately turns to me. "You sure you know what you're doing here, brother?"

"I'm sure," I reply.

"I thought you weren't fucking her," Blade asks.

Growling, I turn to Blade. "Not that it's any of your fucking business, but I'm not fucking her."

"Then what the fuck's going on here, Daisy? You're gonna claim a woman you're not even screwing? Is this some kind of messed up hero complex or what?" Blade asks, obvious confusion clear on his face.

"Fuck you, Blade. She's mine and I'm gonna claim her. You don't need to know any more than that," I reply tersely.

"You don't actually have to put her in a property patch," Prez says. "Jefferies doesn't know how the club works, he won't know the difference. You can play the part of being her old man and the only ones who will know it wasn't real would be us."

I shake my head. "No."

Prez smiles knowingly. "No?"

"No. I want her wearing my patch," I say staring at him intently.

Prez stands from his chair and leans across the desk, bracing his arms against the wooden surface. "You falling in love with her, or is this your dick talking? I like the kid, Grits likes her, and I don't want you messing her about if it's just your hard cock taking control of your brain. Make sure you're not confusing a need to get into her virgin pussy with something else."

Anger pulses through me and I stand, shoving my chair behind me. "Mention her pussy again and I'll forget that you're my prez and knock you the fuck out. I have no fucking clue if I'm in love with her, but I know she's mine and I'll do whatever I have to do to keep her here and safe from her asshole of a father. I want her wearing my property patch and that's got absolutely nothing to do with sex and if I'm getting it or not."

As I turn to look at Blade, I realize he's on his feet as well, tense and ready to intervene if I lose my shit. "I'm fine," I say, pulling my chair back from behind me. Slumping down into it I start to rub at my temples with my fingers.

"Okay then. She's a good kid and once she figures her shit out, she'll make you a good old lady," Prez says simply.

"She doesn't understand the rules, Daisy. You gotta tell her. Don't do to her what Echo did to Liv and send her out there blind wearing your property patch. That shit didn't fly with Liv and Dove might be a timid little thing, but I doubt it'll sit well with her either," Blade offers.

I nod. "I won't. I'll explain the basics and we can deal with the rest later, once we get her dad, and hopefully Carduccio, off her back."

Blade pushes up from his seat. "Right, I'm gonna go find a wet pussy and lose myself in it for a few hours. Might as well enjoy myself tonight in case the shit really hits the fan in the morning."

Watching Blade disappear through the door I stand, planning to follow him. Prez steps in front of me, blocking my path. "The day I met Grits she was hiding in the corner of a room. She was covered in bruises and only wearing a pair of blood stained panties. I was only a couple of years older than you and I was prospecting with the Atlanta chapter. They were into some deep shit: guns, prostitutes, you name it. We'd got intel that a new pimp was trying to muscle in on the club's girls. So one day we get orders from the prez to go and bust into this rundown house. There must have been thirty working girls all happily fucking their marks every which way.

Then there was Grits. She was so young and so fucking scared. I don't know how long she'd been there, but it was too long. She was so skinny, just skin and bone. That fucking bastard had been starving her, beating the shit out of her again and again and raping her. She watched as we killed that sadist monster. We rounded up the girls, offering them work with the club or the chance to leave and the whole time Grits just hid in the corner watching me. There was this look in her eyes and I just couldn't leave her, so I pulled off my shirt and covered her with it. He'd beaten her so bad her eye was almost swollen shut, and he'd fractured her cheek and broken her jaw. She'd been raped so many times and so brutally it was months before she healed. I took her to the hospital, visited her every day until she was better. She never told me what happened in that house, but I know she wasn't there willingly and that it was bad. I've asked, and over the years she's told me some stuff, but never everything. Until the day I die I'll never forget the look in her eyes that day, I didn't realize it at the time, but looking back, that was the moment that changed everything. I fell in love with her the first time she spoke to me and I asked her to be my old lady the first time she let me kiss her. She was mine for two years before we fucked. Sometimes you find someone and just know, it doesn't have to make sense."

Prez falls silent and I stare at him, not knowing what to say.

"What I just told you stays between us, no one here knows Grits history and they don't need to; we got out of Atlanta and made a home here in Archer's Creek. My woman has more grit and strength to survive inside of her than the ten biggest men you'll ever meet combined. Dove's got the same look in her eyes as Grits did, she's a fighter. Like I said sometimes you just know. Dove's yours and I'll do everything I can to help keep her safe."

A lump forms in my throat and I try to swallow past it. "Thank you," I say.

Prez nods and his hand on my shoulder pulls me forward into a quick hug. He slaps my back once and then releases me. "Go look after your Old Lady."

I leave his office, closing the door behind me. Blowing out a heavy breath, I back up to the wall and fall against it. I always thought Grits was a bitch, but fuck, what Prez just told me has given me a whole new level of respect for her. She's a survivor. No, she's more than a survivor, she fucking won. Life dealt her a horrific hand, and she stuck her middle finger up at it and she won anyway.

Angel's a survivor too. I could see it in her from day one and Prez is right, she has got that look in her eyes. I glimpsed it at the wedding, it sparkled that day at the park. But it wasn't until she turned up here looking for me that I realized what it was. It's the look that says she refuses to cower any more. The look that says she's ready to fight back. The look that says she's ready to win.

She's changed everything for me and I want her to be mine.

TWENTY-TWO

Angel

Grits slings her arm around me and we silently walk away from Anders' office and toward the bar. The room is littered with people, but the atmosphere feels relaxed and jovial. A TV is quietly playing in the corner and I glance at it as we walk past.

My feet root to the spot and I stare at the screen. Grits turns to face me, noticing that I've stopped. Her eyes move to see what I'm staring at and then back to me. "My picture's on the TV," I say quietly.

"I know, honey. Didn't Anders' tell you that your dad's been plastering your face on every local station since lunchtime?"

"No, he told me, but it's right there," I say pointing at the TV sitting in the corner of the room.

Grits nervously glances around us to the men that are

lounging throughout the room, but no one seems to be paying us any attention. "Come on, Dove, let's get you some dinner and take it back to your room, okay? No point drawing too much attention to yourself tonight."

I let her pull me across the room and follow her through a door into a huge industrial kitchen set-up. Gleaming aluminum counters edge two walls, with huge stoves, fridges and dishwashers built underneath. Scanning the room, my eyebrows lift in surprise. "Wow, this kitchen is like something out of a restaurant."

"If the club's full there are a lot of hungry men to feed and we need a big kitchen to be able to cater for everyone." She walks over to the huge crock pots that are sitting on one of the counters and lifts the lid. "You like chili?" she asks with a smile.

The rich, spicy flavor hits my nose and my stomach growls in response. "That smells amazing," I say and move closer to look into the pots.

"Go grab bowls for you and Daisy, they're just over there." She points at a rack in the corner of the room stacked high with bowls, plates, and serving dishes.

"Are you eating too?" I ask.

"No, I'll eat with Anders a little later."

Grabbing two bowls, I walk back over to the food and hold them out while Grits spoons the steaming chili into them, then places huge chunks of corn bread on the sides. Grits leans over and starts to rummage under the counter, finally pulling out a large black plastic tray. I place the bowls on the tray and then grab cutlery from the baskets by the china.

Opening one of the fridges, she pulls out bottles of beer and water, adding them to the tray, just as the door swings open and Ali saunters into the room.

"Oh my God, are you still here?" Ali says to me, rolling her eyes and sighing dramatically.

I want to speak, but I don't know what to say. I don't know if Ali knows who I really am and if she doesn't, I don't want to be the one to let it slip. So I ignore her and instead pick up the tray and walk to the door, ready to escape.

"Give it a rest, Ali. She's Daisy's, so get used to her," Grits snaps at Ali.

Ali looks me up and down, fully assessing every inch of me. Her mouth twists into a sneer and she raises her eyebrows dismissively. "How old are you? You look about ten. Are you his sister or something?"

I wait for Grits to say something, but she just looks at me expectantly. "No, I'm not his sister, and I don't really think my age is any of your business," I say politely.

"Daisy's my business. I don't know what the hell he's doing with you, jailbait, but don't get comfortable. He'll get sick of you soon enough and I'll be in his bed again," Ali says acidly.

"Jesus, Ali, take the fucking hint. Daisy isn't interested in you. You're the club whore, honey, you take more cock a week than a hooker. There's nothing wrong with that, you always seem to be enjoying it and God knows I walk in on it enough. But really, stop trying to force your way into the guy's bed, it makes you look desperate," Grits says with a smirk, holding open the door for me as I gratefully escape the kitchen.

Grits doesn't walk, she struts, and I can't help admiring the confidence that exudes from her with every step. I have no idea how she does it. I've been wearing these heeled boots for less than an hour and my feet are already pulsing. She opens the door for me and I cross the room and place the tray on the dresser.

Kicking off the boots, I groan in pleasure when my bare feet hit the cold wooden floor.

"How are your legs feeling?" Grits asks.

"Fine. Apart from where the skin was broken I can hardly feel it."

"Are you sure, honey? They looked sore yesterday," she says sympathetically.

"I'm sure. It wasn't that bad this time."

Flopping down onto the bed, I sit against the pillows and Grits perches on the edge. "How long has it been since your sister passed?"

"It was two years a few months ago," I say, picking at the sides of my nails.

"How long after she died did he start hurting you?"

Sighing, I scan the room, looking for something, anything, that will mean I don't have to talk about this. When my gaze reaches Grits', she raises an eyebrow at me and just waits expectantly. "Pretty much straight away. He was so angry that she'd left. She'd been gone about two months and he came back from work one day with his tie loosened and his hair all messy. He told us that the police had visited him at his office and that Nicole had been in an accident. He had to identify the body. Mama broke down, she was hysterical—so full of grief—but my father was cold. I remember being confused that he wasn't upset, his daughter was dead, and he'd had to see her body, but it was like he didn't care. It didn't sink in straightaway; I didn't believe that she was really gone and I asked if I could see her at the funeral home, to say goodbye. He got real mad and slapped me across the face. I couldn't believe he'd hit me, he was always mean, and he shouted at me all the time, but he'd never hit me before. My mama didn't leave her room for a week, she just lay in the dark and cried. My father went back to work, he carried on like nothing had happened. When I asked him when the funeral would be he completely lost it."

I pause and look up at Grits. She reaches out and takes my hand, squeezing it. "You don't have to tell me, Dove, but it might help to talk about it."

Gripping her hand tightly, I blink back the tears that try to escape. "He started to yell. He told me that I was stupid and that I shouldn't ever say her name again. He said she didn't deserve a funeral, that she was a dirty whore who'd disgraced our family. When he punched me in the face, I was so shocked that he'd punched me, and it hurt so much. He stood over me and said I was just like her and that I needed to be taught a lesson. Grabbing me by my hair he hit me in the face again and I remember crying and begging him to stop, that he was hurting me. He was ranting about Nicole being a whore and me being stupid and useless, that she deserved to die, and he was glad she was dead. My father said he wished they'd had an abortion, that her dying was just God's way of rectifying their mistake.

He kept hitting me and I fell to the floor, cowering with my hands in front of my face. I thought he would stop, but he didn't. He dragged me up off the floor and threw me onto the bed. He pulled off his belt and just started hitting me with it. I was screaming, begging him to stop. I tried to get up, to get away, but he pushed me back down and told me he'd kill me if I didn't stay put and accept my punishment. After that he turned the belt around, pulled down my panties and started to hit me with the buckle end; the pain was so bad that I just lay there. I don't know how long it lasted, I passed out. My mama found me the next morning. She did the best she could to take care of me, but some of the cuts got infected and my father wouldn't let her call a doctor or take me to the hospital. Most of the scars are from that day.

We never got to go to the funeral; my father arranged it for two days after he attacked me. He had her cremated, came home and handed Mama a wooden box with her ashes in. Mama begged him to buy a headstone, so we could at least bury her ashes with some dignity, but he refused. Neither me, nor Mama ever got to say goodbye to her."

My voice cracks, tears stream down my face and I want to curl in a ball and force the memories of that night back into the box in my mind. I'm clinging to her hand, and sensing I need it she pulls me into her arms and holds me tightly.

Silent minutes pass and I force myself to move out of her embrace. Wiping my cheeks, I pull in a deep breath and look up at Grits tear-streaked face.

"I'm sorry. I'm so sorry this happened to you, baby girl. Did he, did he rape you?" Grits asks, her face pale and haunted.

My vision blurs from the tears that refuse to stop. I shake my head and she exhales an audible breath of relief.

"Never again, Dove. You have to say it to yourself and believe it. Never again, will someone hurt you like that. Never again will someone make you feel like that. Being helpless is the most soul- destroying feeling, but never again," Grits says, her voice strong and firm.

Blinking away my tears, I look at her and her eyes echo an understanding that only someone else who has experienced this can offer.

"Never again," I say squeezing her hand tightly.

"Never again," she replies.

Something passes between us in this moment. I don't know what Grits has suffered but I know that she has. She pulls me into a hug and I go willingly, holding her tightly as she strokes my hair.

We pull away from each other and I can see more tears shimmering in her eyes. Shaking her head, she blinks the emotion away with a smile. "I went shopping for you again today. I'll bring the new stuff over in the morning and we can pick out another outfit for you."

Wiping the tears from my cheeks, I nod. "Thank you, Grits. You didn't need to do any of this, but I really appreciate it."

She waves off my thanks. "You don't need to thank me, baby girl. I love to shop. Maybe once all this is over we could go together? Fill that closet up with clothes for the newest addition to the Sinners' Old Ladies."

I smile shyly and blush. "I'd love to go shopping with you; it's been years since I've been. But I still don't think I'm going to be able to stay here, not in the same town as my father. He's gonna lose his mind once he finds out I'm here. I'm being lulled into a false sense of security hiding out with you guys, but I'm not safe, not once he knows where I am."

"The guys will figure it all out for you, baby girl. This place is a fortress and no one's getting in here unless they're let in. You're Daisy's old lady now, we protect our own. I promise you, this is the safest place in the world for you."

I sigh, slide off the bed, pick up the bowl of chili, and then sink back down against the pillows. I eat a spoonful and moan. "Wow that's good chili. Who made it?"

Grits smiles ruefully. "Ali did. She might be a pain in the ass but that girl can really cook."

"Ali? Wow. She doesn't strike me as the type of girl that spends time in the kitchen."

"Most of the time she's harmless, but she's got a real lady boner for Daisy. She lives here with one of the other girls; they cook and keep the place clean and the Sinners take care of them. The guys love her because the girl loves sex, and she's not shy about it. She stays away from the guys that are taken, so the old ladies don't mind her. I've never known her push so hard for a guy before," Grits admits.

"Daisy said he, err, had sex with her," I say, my eyes firmly fixed on my bowl.

"Doesn't surprise me, that girl's spread her legs for pretty much every member of the club. But he wants you as his old lady not her."

"I don't really understand the Old Lady title. I'm only eighteen," I say.

Grits bursts into laughter. "Oh, baby girl, I forget how sheltred you really are. Old Lady is the official title given to a biker's woman. Some guys still get married but for most, the title's enough."

My hand refuses to move and my spoon wavers in mid-air between the bowl and my mouth. "What?"

Grits looks at me quizzically.

"I only met Daisy a few days ago," I whisper.

"Yeah, I know, baby girl, but he's your man and given the circumstances it makes sense."

"I don't understand," I say.

"I think it might be best if you let me explain," Daisy says from the doorway.

My eyes jump to look at him, I hadn't realized he was there. Grits stands from the bed and makes her way to the door. "See you in the morning, Dove," she says over her shoulder as she leaves. She pats Daisy on the shoulder as they pass in the doorway and he closes and locks the door before slowly padding across the room to the bed.

"You get me any?" he asks pointing to the bowl.

I nod and gesture to the tray sitting on the dresser. He steps over to it and twists the top off one of the bottles of beer, putting it to his lips and drinking deeply. After a moment he lowers the bottle to the dresser again and then lifts a beer in one hand and a bottle of water in the other and gestures to me. "Beer or water?"

"Water please," I say and take the bottle when he hands it to me. I watch as he grabs his beer and his bowl and walks around the room to climb on the bed next to me. He starts to eat, and I do the same. He finishes quickly and places the bowl on the floor. When he turns to face me, my appetite vanishes and I place my bowl on the dresser next to me and copy his body language.

He stares at me for a minute and then reaches for my hand and pulls me into his chest. His lips drop to mine and he kisses me. My mind scatters, all rational thought lost and replaced with the sensation of his mouth covering mine. The kiss is soft and sweet, his tongue gently tangles with mine and I moan in pleasure when one of his hands slides down my ribs and around to caress my butt.

I tangle my hands in his hair and push myself closer to him, wanting to sit in his lap but unsure how to tell him. His lips still and firm hands move me carefully away from his chest. My eyelids flutter open and I stare at him in confusion. I don't want to stop kissing him. I love kissing him. I love being close to him and feeling his body pressed against mine.

"Why did you stop?" I ask breathily.

"Because we need to talk."

My shoulders tense and I pull my hands into my lap, absentmindedly picking at my nails. "Is this about my father? I'll understand if you decide you don't want to tell him I'm here. This is my problem not yours and I still think maybe running is the best option."

"You're not running," Daisy says sternly.

I lift my eyes to look at him, his face is twisted into a frustrated scowl. "How many times do I have to tell you, Angel, you're not running anywhere? I want you here with me where we can keep you safe. Where I can keep you safe. What I need to talk to you about is something different."

"Okay," I say drawing the word out in confusion.

Daisy sighs and scrubs at his face with his hands. "I like you, Angel, a lot."

"I like you too."

Daisy smirks, then his face clears, and the smile falls away. "Fuck. Okay, I don't really know how to explain this. From the age of two to eighteen I lived in thirty-five different homes. The first few times I had to move I got really upset. I was just a kid, and I didn't know why every time I got settled with a new family, they'd make me pack up and move somewhere new. By the tenth home I decided to stop caring, it was easier that way. I couldn't keep making friends and then have them taken away from me every single time I moved, it was too hard. So instead of trying to be nice, I blocked out all the other kids crying because they missed their families or the siblings they'd been split up from. I got real good at not caring and until I met Billy and got involved in the club, there wasn't a single person in my life that I gave a fuck about. When I patched into this club, I gave them my loyalty and they gave me a home and a family and, Angel, I really fucking like my life."

"I understand," I say interrupting him. "These people are your family, I understand that you don't want to drag them into my mess."

"No, no, that's not what I'm saying. The guys are my family, but you, you are everything."

"I don't... what?" I say, shocked.

"I know we haven't known each other for that long, but from the very first time I saw you I've felt everything. Lust and want, fear, anger, hope and adoration. You make me feel everything, every emotion that I've tamped down and buried for years. Angel, I have no idea what love is, but I know that I want you here with me, in my room, my bed, in my life. I promise I'll take care of you and keep you safe. Baby, I want you to be my old lady and wear my property patch. I'm in so fucking deep with you, and I have been since that day at the park. Your dad doesn't scare me but the idea of you leaving fucking terrifies me. I'm doing a shitty job of explaining this, but I need you. Sometimes you just know, and I know, that you're it for me."

Shell-shocked, I stare at him. I think of everything that's happened since I first met him. He's taken care of me and kissed me. He's held my hand and told me he likes me. More than that, he's made me feel safe and worthy. He makes me want to risk staying in Archer's Creek, when all I've thought about for the last two years is running away.

"Okay," I whisper.

"Okay?" he says.

"Yes."

"Be more specific, Angel. What are you saying okay to?"

My heart's pounding and my chest feels tight, but I force myself to speak. "I've spent the last two years hiding and I can't promise I won't do that anymore, but I want to show you the version of me that's not scared. You make me feel safe and even with everything that's happened you've made me smile and feel happy. I don't want to leave you either, Daisy, you make me want to risk staying."

He moves closer and reaches out to cup my cheek with his

palm. "Angel, will you be my old lady?"

Smiling shyly at him I nod. "I'm too young to be your old lady, so how about I just be yours?"

Daisy laughs lightly and leans his head down until our foreheads are touching. "Mine. I like the sound of that."

Our lips touch and we kiss. Slowly our mouths move together in a tender sensual caress. This kiss is a promise, and it's perfect.

Eventually we pull apart and Daisy lies back against the pillows, tugging me down next to him. "I want you to wear my property patch."

"What does it mean?" I ask, my fingers drawing patterns on his T-shirt.

"It just means that you're mine, my old lady. It's a smaller version of the cut I wear, with a patch that says 'Property of Daisy' on it.

I stiffen. "I'm not property, Daisy."

"I know that. It just means that you're my woman. The Sinners aren't metrosexual pansies, baby, when we claim a woman they belong to us. You're mine, but I'm yours too."

I frown and push myself up onto my elbows. "So, you belong to me?"

"Angel, you've owned my ass since that day at the park."

Laughing, I settle back down onto Daisy's chest. Reaching for the remote he turns the TV back on and we carry on watching the boxset we started earlier.

A couple of hours later the heroes of the show are on the verge of defeating the bad guy when I start to yawn. "You want to shower tonight or in the morning?" Daisy asks

"Tonight," I say yawning again.

Lifting me up he walks us to the bathroom door and gently lowers me to the floor. "Go shower, then we can get some sleep."

Nodding, I pad into the bathroom and turn on the shower. "Do you need another one of my shirts to sleep in?" Daisy shouts from the bedroom.

"Yes please, and could you pass me my backpack." A few moments later Daisy's arm pushes through the door with my bag and a shirt clutched in his fist. Reaching up, I take my things from him and his hand disappears back through the gap. "Thank you," I say, stripping out of my clothes and stepping into the hot shower.

I wash quickly, then dry myself and re-dress in his shirt and a pair of my cotton panties. Wiping the mirror free of condensation, I look at my reflection—the bruises are still visible and my cheek is still a little puffy, but I've looked much worse in the past. Pulling the hair brush from my bag I quickly run it through my wet hair then plait it into a long braid that falls over my shoulder. I look so young. Daisy says he wants me, but when he could have women like Ali, how long can I hold his interest?

Shaking my head, I ignore the insecurities that are trying to push their way into my thoughts. Daisy asked me to be his, he told me I was everything. If he wanted Ali he wouldn't have said those things to me. I walk back into the bedroom. Daisy is lazily sprawled on the bed watching the TV so I make my way to the other side and climb in, lifting the cover up so I can crawl underneath.

Daisy leans over and kisses me quickly then rolls off the bed. "I'm gonna take a shower, baby."

"Okay," I say, watching his retreating back as he pulls his shirt over his head. The shower turns back on and steam billows from the open bathroom door. Tilting my head to the side I stare into the steamy room hoping for a glance at him. Before I get a chance to see anything the shower turns off and a wet Daisy walks out, wearing a towel wrapped around his hips and another slung over his shoulders.

I blatantly watch as he drops the towel and slides on briefs. It's the same routine that he did last night and just like before he starts to set up a pallet on the floor next to the bed. "Daisy."

"Yeah, baby," he replies, not looking up.

"You don't need to do that."

He pauses and looks up at me. "Do what, Angel?"

My cheeks flush red and I fidget with the edge of the quilt. "Sleep on the floor."

"That's okay, I don't mind."

"This is your bed, Daisy," I say hoping he'll understand what I'm making a mess of trying to tell him.

"I know. My woman, in my bed," he says grabbing a pillow

and dropping it to the floor.

"Daisy."

He stops and looks at me again.

"I don't want you to sleep on the floor. I want you to sleep in here, with me," I say, forcing my eyes to stay locked with his.

"What?"

"Please don't make me say it again," I whisper, embarrassment coloring my cheeks.

Daisy stares at me for a second and then sits down on the bed and pulls me into his lap. "Angel, you being my old lady now doesn't change anything. I have no expectations. We'll get to that side of things when you're ready and whenever that is I'm okay with that. So much has happened in your life in the last few days and I don't want you to do anything you're not ready for."

"Daisy, I want you to sleep in the bed with me. I'm not saying it because I think you expect it, I'm saying it because I like lying in your arms."

Grabbing my chin, he lifts my face up so our eyes lock. "Are you sure?"

"Yes," I say, slowly leaning in to kiss him. He cradles me to his chest as I explore his lips and tentatively push my tongue into his mouth. Warm hands move up the length of my spine and one wraps around the back of my neck while the other tangles into my hair. Wiggling restlessly in his lap, my heart races and the steady ache between my legs becomes desperate for more.

Pushing myself closer to him I freeze when my butt rubs against what I think is a very large, very hard erection.

"Angel," Daisy whispers pulling back from our kiss.

I force open my eyes and look up at him. "That's what you do to me, Angel, you're the most beautiful woman I've ever fucking laid eyes on. I want you baby, I'm not gonna lie, but only when you're ready, okay?"

I bite my lip, I want him too. But I have no idea what to do with him. I want to run my fingers across his tattooed skin and into the defined peaks and valleys of his muscled stomach. I want to follow the line of hair that disappears beneath his briefs, but I've never even seen a penis, apart from on TV and the internet. Right now, I really wish I wasn't this clueless idiot who has no idea what she's doing. Ali wouldn't be unsure, she'd be naked and confidently having wild monkey sex with him right now. "I'm sorry," I say and cover my face with my hands.

"What the hell are you sorry for, Angel?" he asks, pulling my hands down and forcing me to look at him.

"For being so clueless. You could have any woman you want, who would know how to do this. You shouldn't be stuck in this PG-13 hell."

"What the fuck are you talking about, Angel?" he snaps at me. "I want you and only you. Do you have any idea how fucking sexy it is, knowing that no one else has ever touched you? You've turned me into a fucking caveman, baby. I'm beating my chest and celebrating that you're untouched. I'm gonna be the first and only man that gets to sink into your perfect pussy. God, I'm rock hard just thinking about it and I don't care how long I have to wait for it. I get to teach you how to ride me and suck me and I can't wait to explore every inch of you. You're the holy fucking grail, Angel, and when you're ready to give yourself to me, I already know you'll be utter perfection."

My breathing has turned ragged and the ache between my legs has morphed into a pulsing heat. "I want that now," I say, my voice barely audible.

Daisy chuckles. "No baby, not tonight."

"I need…"

"What do you need, Angel?" Daisy drawls, his voice smoky and low.

"I don't know," I admit, ashamed and frustrated.

"I think I know what you need. Do you ever touch yourself, Angel?"

My cheeks burn red. Mortified, I focus on my hands and shake my head.

"You're telling me you've never pushed your hand inside your panties and stroked that virgin pussy, Angel?"

"No," I force out of my dry throat.

"I don't believe you. I think late at night you lie in your bed and stroke your hot clit until you come. Show me baby, touch yourself."

"I don't. I've never," I stutter.

Daisy's eyes widen for a second, then wordlessly he lifts

me up and turns me so my back is to his chest and I'm sitting between his legs. He leans back against the wall and pulls me with him.

His fingers tangle with mine and he holds one of my hands against my stomach and then guides my other down my torso toward my panties. "Tell me if you want to stop," he whispers against my ear.

"Don't stop," I gasp as I watch his hand guide mine slowly beneath the waist of my white cotton panties.

"This is what I was talking about, Angel. Lying in bed and pushing your fingers into your panties. Moving through your wet heat and moaning quietly when your finger slides over your needy clit."

As he whispers the words into my ear, he mimics the actions with our fingers, moving us over my skin until we meet the hot, wet folds between my legs. A tingling sensation pulses through me as he glides our fingers through the wetness that's coated my sex and drags upwards until he pauses and circles. I moan when a glorious spasm of pleasure hits.

"That's it, baby. Circle your clit, tease yourself, so it doesn't end too quickly."

His fingers move mine as he speaks, glancing over the sensitive peak then moving down to my center, only to drag more wetness back up and circle again. Heat pools in my stomach and butterflies dance as the sensations consume me.

"Fuck, Angel, once you're hot and ready then you slide a

single finger into your wet pussy and push at the needy spot deep inside."

He pushes us back down to my center, untangling our fingers so that mine still while his moves further between my legs. My fingers rest on top of his hand and I grip him tightly as he pushes a finger slowly inside my hot sex. The feeling of fullness is blissful, and I moan through my ragged panting breaths. My head falls back against Daisy's shoulder and I watch as he oh-so-slowly, pumps his finger into me.

I gasp as he withdraws and then fills me again. His thumb lifts and he slowly starts to circle my clit. My back arches and the muscles in my thighs tense, a heaviness building in my sex as heat starts at my toes and slowly burns upwards.

"Beautiful, Angel, so fucking perfect. Your pussy is so tight and you're gripping my finger so hard. Focus on how it feels, baby, my finger deep inside of you, my thumb on your clit. I can feel you tightening around me. Come for me, Angel. Let it happen, let me see."

His words leave me breathless, the heat builds and builds and I pant. My sex burns, a painful bliss that I don't understand, but never want to stop. His thumb pushes on my clit and I explode. My shoulders clench and I feel my body fold into itself; the tension releases and a wave of tingling floats over me. I groan with the sheer feeling of pleasure and gasp when the tension takes me again and another wave of tingling cascades through me.

Gemma Weir

My head flops against Daisy and a desperate sigh escapes from me. My eyelids flutter open and I look down to where both mine and Daisy's hands are still nestled inside my panties.

"That was so fucking sexy, Angel. Watching you come is one of the most beautiful things I've ever seen," Daisy rasps.

He slowly withdraws his hand, taking mine with it. Firm fingers grip my hips and I'm lifted into the air and turned so we're face to face. His eyes are hooded, and his chest is rising and falling in ragged breaths. He stares at me for a moment, then slowly lifts the hand he used to pleasure me up to his mouth and sucks his fingers clean.

I gasp.

"You taste so fucking sweet, Angel," he says and leans forward and kisses me. He releases me a moment later and then settles back against the pillows and pulls me to lie on his chest.

"Sleep," he whispers into my hair, and I fall asleep sated and listening to his heart beating beneath my ear.

TWENTY-THREE

Daisy

I fall asleep with a raging hard-on and wake up fucking rock hard again. Glancing at Angel, I plan to sneak out of bed and jerk off before she wakes up, but her gorgeous doe eyes are open and trained on the massive morning wood I'm sporting.

"Morning, baby," I croak out.

"Morning," she replies, never taking her eyes off my dick.

"It's my dick, Angel, it's not gonna bite you. It's morning and I've been lying in bed with you all night. I'd be worried if I didn't wake up hard."

Her cheeks flush red and I immediately feel like a jackass for teasing her. "Come here," I say and open my arms. She crawls against me and nestles into my chest.

"I fucking love waking up next to you, baby," I coo into her ear. My mind flicks back to last night and touching her for the first time. Fuck she was so perfect. I almost blew my load just watching her come.

I never thought that something as simple as finger-fucking her would drive me so crazy, but her reactions were so honest and raw. I'll wait as long as it takes for her to be ready, but God I want to fuck her so bad. I've gone without before, so it's not just about the sex; it's about her, everything is heightened with Angel.

Her small body fits perfectly next to mine and I sigh contentedly. Her hand is resting on my chest and her fingers are drawing patterns along my skin. Her fingers slowly start to work their way from my chest and down over my abs. I smile to myself, watching as my girl tries to discreetly cop a feel of my toned muscles. I'm not ripped but I work out and my six pack is fairly defined.

Angel's fingertips hit the first set of muscles and a tiny tremor vibrates through her arm. She strokes across the peak of the muscle and into the valley, then back up again. Stifling a laugh, I watch her. She pauses for a moment and then breathes deep and continues her exploration. "What you doin', baby?" I ask in amusement.

"Nothing," she says quickly and her hand freezes, immediately returning to my chest.

Gently, I reach for her hand and place it back against my stomach. "You can touch, Angel."

"No, that's, that's errr, not what I was doing," she stutters.

"Bullshit. You were trying to cop a feel, baby. No need to lie about it. I like your hands on me, so have at it," I say, smirking.

I half expect her to pull away, embarrassed, but instead her hands tentatively move across my stomach. She lifts her head slightly from my chest and watches as she curves her fingers across my skin. Her hands are warm and her nails scrape gently up and over my abs.

My cock twitches in my boxers and her movements falter. Her fingers gradually move lower and lower until her nails scrape along the waistband of my boxers. One finger pushes under the elastic and I reach up, placing my hand on top of hers, stopping her. "Baby, what's the end game here?"

"I don't know. You're, well you're like that and I thought maybe, err, maybe I could do to you what you did to me last night."

I don't need to see her face to know that it's bright red with embarrassment. "I fucking love that you want to do that, baby, but I didn't give you an orgasm last night hoping you'd return the favor."

"I know, I just wanted to, you know," she mutters quietly.

"Say it, baby. What do you want to do? If you want to touch my cock, all you got to do is ask. Hell, there's no way I'll ever say no. But I want you to tell me."

I feel her pull in a deep breath and then exhale the warm air against my ribs. "I want to touch you."

"I'm all yours, baby, but if you're gonna touch me then I want to watch," I say, lifting my hand from hers to push my boxers down my hips. My cock springs free and Angel gasps. I know I've got a big dick and honestly, I usually get a similar reaction from most women when they first lay eyes on me. But my chest swells and my cock jerks again at the sweet sound coming from her.

Wrapping my arm around her, I lift her up, shuffling further up the bed so I can get the best possible view when she finally plucks up the courage to touch me. Her hand lifts into the air and then freezes. I hold my breath. The idea that she might stop before her fingers make it to my cock is unthinkable, so I stay quiet and try not to spook her. I don't know if this is the first time she's gotten this close to a cock; I kind of hope it is. Either way, now she's offered it I'm fucking desperate for her to touch me.

I watch as she tries to decide what to do. Her face either shows every thought she has or closes off so tightly she's unreadable. I see the exact moment she decides to reach for me and when a single fingertip strokes across the head of my cock I almost come then and there.

Silently, I watch her movements gain momentum. She strokes from the tip of my cock straight down the length of me to the trimmed patch of hair at my base. Her fingers tentatively wrap around my girth, not quite able to touch and then she stops.

"What do I do? I want to make you feel good," she whispers.

"Are you sure? You don't have to do anything, Angel. I don't want to push you." The words come out of my mouth, but my thoughts are begging her not to stop, begging her to wrap her hand around my cock and stroke me until I come.

"I want to do this, but I need you to tell me what to do. I don't... I've never..." Her words trail off.

Her fingers are still around my dick, so covering her hand with mine, I close her palm tighter around my hard shaft. "Just like this, baby," I say moving her hand up and down my length slowly. I let my hand drop to my side and she continues the movement. A bead of pre-cum pools at the top of my cock and her thumb slides over it as she reaches the top of my dick and slowly slides back down again.

"That's it, fuck, yeah just like that," I say, letting my head fall back against the wall. Her face is fascinated and completely focused on her hand and my hard cock. Watching her jerk me off is driving me crazy and the first stirrings of my orgasm pool in my balls.

"Hold me tighter," I groan, my voice ragged and strained. She does as I ask, and her hand squeezes my cock and starts to move quicker, sliding confidently up and down my hard length. "Oh fuck, Angel that feels so fucking good."

More pre-cum seeps from the tip of my cock and I watch as she collects it with her fingers and spreads it down the length of me. Heat pools in my stomach and my balls feel heavy. All of the blood in my body rushes into my cock and lifting my head up I reach for Angel and pull her above me. Dragging up the shirt she's wearing, I groan when her hand grips me tighter and I explode. Long lines of cum spray onto the perfect pale skin of her stomach. I tense again and another wave of cum hits her.

A deep sigh escapes from my throat and my head falls back against the wall with a thump. Wrapping my arm around her back I pull her to lie on top of me and breathe heavily into the top of her head. "Fuck."

Angel chuckles softly. "Did I do okay?"

"Perfect baby, that was fucking perfect," I force out, as lethargy fills my body and my muscles relax into the pillows.

I feel her arms flex and she starts to pull away from me, but I clamp my arm around her back and hold her tightly. "I need to get up," she protests.

"Why? Stay here."

"Because I'm sticky," she says shyly.

Releasing my hold on her she immediately sits up and I catch a glimpse of the wetness on her stomach before my shirt falls down and covers it. Angel begins to move but wrapping my fingers around her wrist I stop her. "I want to see."

"See what?" She asks.

"You, covered in my cum." Releasing her wrist I bunch up the fabric of my shirt, slowly lifting it to reveal the remnants of my cum coating her skin. "Fuck," I hiss, smoothing my hand across her stomach, rubbing my cum into her perfect flesh, branding her.

She silently watches me, her teeth biting at her bottom lip, her eyes hooded and filled with desire. "Come here and kiss me," I order gently.

She falls into my chest and eagerly kisses me while my fingers slide down her back and over her ass. Who knew white cotton panties could be so sexy? Pushing my fingers underneath the fabric I start to slide around to the perfect wet pussy that's hidden inside. My Angel couldn't look any more perfect than she does right now. My fingertip slides into her heat and Angel moans as I skim over her clit.

Knock, knock, knock.

Groaning in protest, I reluctantly pull my hand from Angel's panties, just as there's another rap on the door. "Go jump in the shower, baby, and I'll see who's here."

Angel nods and silently slides off me, dashing into the bathroom. My cock's rock hard again, despite me only coming a few minutes ago. Flinching, I drag the fabric of my boxers over the sensitive head, roll off the bed and pad to the door to open it.

Grits smiles at me. "Good morning, sunshine. Where's my Little Dove?"

"She's in the shower," I grumble.

"Okay, well I need to help her pick out an outfit, so go put some fucking clothes on and then go away while I help her get dressed," Grits says with an annoying wink.

"I can help her get dressed," I say, aggravated that I'm being told to leave, when I just want to stay holed up in my room with my girl.

"That girl is eighteen and about as innocent as they come, Daisy. You might have claimed her but you need to keep your dick in your pants."

I growl a low angry noise. "Grits, I get that you like Angel and I'm grateful that you're being a friend to her. But I'm only gonna tell you this once. She is my old lady. I would never, ever, do anything to hurt her or try to get her to do something she isn't ready for. What we are or are not doing is none of your fucking business and we're gonna have a huge fucking problem if you try to make it your business. You get me?"

Grits jaw hardens for a second, then she relaxes and nods. "Yeah, I get you. I also know that she doesn't know anything about the club or the world we live in and she won't if you keep her all to yourself. I only want to help her, and right now she needs to look the part."

Blowing out a breath I nod, knowing that Grits is right. Angel needs to learn how to navigate the Sinner lifestyle and I can't help her with that. "Yeah, okay, fine. Give me five."

Grits nods and then turns and walks away. Closing the door, I turn toward the bathroom, my cock literally straining towards the room where Angel is naked and wet. Groaning loudly, I yank open the drawers of my dresser and pull out clean clothes. I change quickly, knowing if I stay in here for too long, the temptation to go help Angel shower will be too much and all my good intentions of taking things slow will be shot to hell.

I'm fully dressed and pulling on my boots when the bathroom door opens, and a pink skinned Angel emerges from a cloud of steam. Her hair is wet and hanging around her bare shoulders and the only thing hiding her body from me is a small white towel.

"Oh, hi," she says and pads around the bed to where her backpack is leaning against the wall. She grips the towel tightly with one hand as she other roots around the backpack, pulling out another pair of those sensible cotton panties.

When she turns to face me, my eyes are riveted to the hint of her cleavage that's on show as the towel slips down her damp body. I force myself to look back at my boots and my fingers fumble with the laces. Eventually I manage to get them on and stand up quickly, looking from Angel to the door and then back again. "I should go so you can get dressed."

"Oh, err, yeah. Or you could stay, I mean if you want to," she mumbles, her eyes firmly fixed on her feet.

I'm not sure if I heard her right. "What?"

She doesn't say anything for a long moment, then her eyes drift up to meet mine. "I mean you don't have to leave while I get dressed. Oh God, what I'm trying to say is that, err, I don't mind if you stay."

I take slow steps toward her. "You want me to stay here, in this room, while you get dressed?" I clarify and try to tone down the hope in my voice.

She looks at me, then her gaze falls to her hands and she

fidgets, twisting the fabric of her towel. "I. You don't have to. It's just that I've seen you naked and I thought, that maybe, you know…"

"Come here, baby," I coo, and she quickly closes the space between us. Sinking down onto the edge of the bed I pull her between my legs. "This isn't tit-for-tat, Angel. Do I want to see you naked? Hell fucking yes, I do. I like touching you, I really like you touching me, but I don't have an ulterior motive. I'm in deep so it doesn't matter how long it takes for us to take these steps because we have all the time in the world."

"I'm making such a mess of this," Angel says lifting her hands to cover her face.

"What are you talking about, baby?"

"I just, I want to be brave enough to just drop this towel and stand here, but I'm not."

Her eyes look a little lost and my stomach drops. Reaching forward I pull her hands from her face and cup her chin, tilting her so our eyes lock. "You're so fucking brave, Angel, never doubt that. I don't expect you to start walking around the room naked, but if you want to share your beautiful body with me I'm not gonna lie and say I don't want to see you."

"Will you help me?" she asks, her eyes burning into mine.

I nod and lift my hands up to the edges of the towel. My eyes stay on hers as I slowly loosen the towel and let it slide down her body. Resting my hands on her hips, the towel pools across my arms so only her breasts are exposed.

I don't fucking know how I do it, but I keep my eyes on her face. Her chest expands as she pulls in a breath and then exhales. She closes her eyes, then opens them again, offering me a half smile and I pull her forward and kiss her gently.

Angel pulls back first, and her eyes fall to her breasts. My gaze drops, and I gasp at the perfection that's six inches from my mouth. Her breasts are small, but perky and high; her nipples are a rosy pink color and forgetting myself for a minute, I lean forward and lick the tip with my tongue. Her inhale of air is loud, and I quickly check she's okay with the change of direction, from show and tell, to interactive display.

One of her hands lifts to my head and when I cautiously lean forward and lick the other nipple, she tangles her fingers in my hair and holds me to her. I don't want to drop the towel around her waist so only touching her with my tongue, I draw patterns around her nipple and then suck the whole thing into my mouth.

Angel moans loudly and her head tips back in pleasure. Releasing her nipple from my mouth with a pop I move to the other side, repeating the same action. Dropping small kisses along her skin I trace the swell of her breasts while she watches me with hooded eyes.

"Perfect," I whisper, pulling her closer. Her fingers are clenched tightly around her panties and reaching up I take them from her. Keeping my eyes locked on hers, I hold them by her feet and she steps into them. I slide them up her legs and over her tight ass until they're covering her pussy.

Dropping the towel, I let my eyes run the full length of her body. "You're fucking perfect, baby. Let's take things one step at a time. You shared those beautiful tits with me and that's enough for now. I don't need you to suddenly become an exhibitionist. I want to savor you and earn everything you give me. I'm all yours, baby, but I'm happy to take my time and wait for you to give yourself completely to me because when you do I'll never give you back."

The anxiety and fear settle in her eyes and she throws herself into my chest, hugging me tightly. I fucking love that she's starting to touch me more freely. I wouldn't have called myself a tactile person before I met Angel, but now I want her near me, touching me as much as possible. I've watched Echo with Liv and wondered why he was always pulling her into his lap or holding her against his chest. Honestly, I thought he was just marking his territory, but maybe, like me he just can't stand to have her near and not have his hands on her. I'm starting to crave Angel, even after spending all night holding her close, I don't want to leave her.

"Thank you," Angel says, pulling away from my chest but keeping her arms wrapped around my neck.

"What for?" I ask.

"Everything," she says, simply. "In the last week my life's imploded and outside of this room it's all chaos, but somehow when it's just me and you I forget all the bad stuff. I like you. I don't really understand how all of this happened, but I like you and I like the way you make me feel. When it's just me and you, I'm not scared anymore and for the first time in two years I don't want to hide."

My heart pounds as she speaks. Every hour we spend here in our little safe haven I can see her finding herself again and it makes me want to lock the door and bubble wrap her against the rest of the world.

The knock at the door forces me to release her and I curse the Prez's old lady and her desire to help. "Fucking Grits," I grumble under my breath.

Lifting Angel into the air I place her on the floor in front of me and grab one of my T-shirts from my drawer. I pull it over her head, hiding her perfect breasts from my view. My cock twitches in dismay and I silently promise it some relief later. Though the idea of jerking off in the shower, is nowhere near as appealing as having Angel's tiny hands wrapped around my cock again.

Striding over to the door, I pull it open with a scowl. Grits smiles widely at my expression and breezes past me and into the room.

"Bye, Daisy, she'll be ready in thirty minutes," Grits says dismissing me.

Throwing a glare at Grits, I turn to Angel. "Come here, baby."

She rushes across the room and as soon as she's close enough, I pull her closer and kiss her thoroughly. When I release her she sways slightly, a ghost of a smile across her lips.

"Have fun with Grits, I'll see you out there in a while," I say.

"Okay," she whispers and stands on her tiptoes to kiss me quickly before she bounces over to Grits who is busy laying out clothes on the bed.

Like a fucking pussy, I spend a minute just staring at her before I pull on my cut and finally force myself to walk away.

TWENTY-FOUR

Angel

I glance over my shoulder just as the bedroom door clicks shut. Sighing wistfully I turn my focus back to Grits.

"Okay, so I might have gone a little OTT," Grits says as we both stand in front of the bed which is now covered in clothes and shoes.

"Grits, look at all this stuff, this is too much. Is it all refundable?"

Grits laughs and throws her arm around my shoulder. "You need clothes. I hadn't exactly planned on filling your closet without you, but I'm not going to return anything."

"I don't have enough money for all of this," I say, panic starting to edge into my voice, as I silently calculate how much all these clothes cost.

"These are my gift—a welcome to the Sinners present. Plus, I like to shop, and Anders likes to indulge me. Next time we test out his credit card you're coming with me and then you can get anything else you need too."

Shaking my head, I twist my fingers together. "Grits, I can't accept all of these. Anders is already doing so much for me, I feel like I'm taking advantage."

"You listen here, Little Dove, it's my money just as much as it's Anders. So how bout you just say thank you and then we can play dress up," Grits winks at me and lifts a shirt from the bed, holding it out in front of me.

Tears well in my eyes and I realize how lucky I am to have met this woman. She's been so helpful and supportive to me—a complete stranger. I reach for her hand and she looks over her shoulder at me. "Thank you," I say. "Thank you for the clothes, but more than that, just thank you. Thank you for being so kind to me. Since I turned up here and got you all involved in my drama you've been so incredibly nice and supportive, and I can't begin to tell you how much that means to me. So, thank you."

"You're welcome, baby girl. You might have brought some drama, but fate delivered you to us and I'm positive this is exactly where you were meant to end up."

I squeeze Grits hand and she smiles, pulling me into a tight hug. When we separate, we both have tears in our eyes, but at least for me they're not sad tears and I start to think she might be right, I'm exactly where I'm meant to be.

"I like that," I say pointing to a denim skirt with buttons going down the front.

Grits wiggles her eyebrows at me and lifts the skirt up. Handing it to me she grabs a handful of other items, thrusting them at me and ushering me into the bathroom.

I emerge a few minutes later with a huge smile on my face. "I love this outfit," I gush.

Messing with the heap of clothes on the bed, she turns to look at me and her face splits into a grin. "That is so cute on you."

Spinning around I look at myself in the mirror. The denim skirt is mid-thigh and tight, but Grits has paired it with a loose white tank top tucked into the skirt and an oversized check print shirt left open over the top. The shirt hangs lower than the skirt at the back and covers the remaining bruises on my thighs. But the best part of the outfit is the amazing thigh-high, black suede boots, they have a chunky heel and the buttery soft suede fits like a glove.

"I love these boots," I say, smiling and reaching down to stroke at the soft material.

"You just need this to finish the look," Grits says, dropping a long silver rope chain over my head that settles between my breasts.

She pulls my hair up into a high ponytail and like yesterday only adds a slick of mascara to my lashes. "Perfect," she says, and then starts to collect up the clothes from the bed. "Come help me get these clothes hung up and then we can go find Daisy. I'm sure he's chomping at the bit to have you back already.

I watch her open the closet and start to hang the new clothes up. "Errmm, I'm not sure I should be filling Daisy's closet with all of these clothes without asking him."

She looks at me, her brow wrinkled in confusion. "Why?"

"Because this is his room and I can't just fill it with my stuff."

"Baby girl, this is your room now too, at least until you guys find a place of your own. Trust me, Daisy isn't gonna care if you hang up some clothes in his closet."

Freezing at her words, I slump down onto the bed. Am I ready to move in with Daisy? We really don't know each other that well. I like him a lot, in fact I'm pretty sure I'm starting to fall in love with him, but moving in together is a really big thing.

"What's happened, Dove, are you okay?" Grits asks, rushing across the room.

"I'm fine," I say, forcing the words past the lump in my throat.

"You're not fine, you're having a crisis. So, tell me what set you off."

I lift my head up so I can focus on Grits, her worried face is hovering above mine. "I can't move in with someone I've known for less than a week. It's not right. I'm only eighteen and don't people normally date for at least a year before they take a huge step like that? We haven't even had sex yet. What if I'm no good at it and Daisy dumps me? Who keeps the apartment? I want to go to school, I can't afford an apartment on my own."

"Okay, slow down, Dove. Let's look at this one thing at a time. Firstly, if you don't want to move in with him, then don't. I've already told you that you can come and live with me and Anders, and he agrees that we'd love to have you. Secondly, Daisy's your old man and regardless of sex he wants you enough to put a property patch on your chest. When you're ready for the physical side of things, Daisy will look after you. He'll show you what to do, until you figure out what makes you both feel good. Thirdly, that boy is in deep with you and he wants to make you happy. If that's going to school, then I'm willing to lay money on the fact that he'll do everything he can to support you. Until you came along he always seemed like he was just going through the motions, but with you he comes alive. He's one of the good ones, Dove, but if you're having second thoughts—if he's not the guy for you—then you need to call time on this. Our help is not dependent on you and Daisy being a couple. Okay?"

I jolt back in shock. "No. I'm not leaving. I don't want to call time on anything. Daisy is… Daisy's mine."

Grits tilts her head to the side and smiles. "Yes he is, baby girl, and you're his. Everything else will sort itself out with time."

I nod and my breathing starts to slow from its erratic pace. "What if we don't have endless time? I've lost the last two years of my life and my sister was dead before she turned twenty; we have no idea what tomorrow will bring."

Grits smile turns sad. "That's true, we don't know what's going to happen tomorrow or two years from now, so make the most of every moment you have. Let's start by going and finding our men, I'm hungry."

Laughing, my anxiety begins to recede. I have no idea what my future holds but if Grits is right, then fate brought me to Daisy and the Sinners for a reason. A wave of longing for Daisy cascades through me and I hop off the bed. "Let's go find the guys."

Grits arches her eyebrow and looks at me with a knowing smirk, then she grabs my hand and we walk out of mine and Daisy's room together. We enter the bar and my eyes immediately zero in on Daisy. He's sat at a table on the far side of the room with Blade; and Echo and Liv, the couple we had breakfast with yesterday.

Grits squeezes my hand and I turn my attention to her. "Anders is over here. You want me to walk with you to Daisy, or are you good on your own?"

I glance at Anders who is sat on a group of sofas in front of the TV and then to Daisy on the opposite side of the room. "No, you go find your man, I'll be fine."

"Okay, Little Dove. I'm gonna be here all day with Anders so come find me later."

Twenty steps brings me to Daisy's side. He's chatting with Echo, but as soon as he notices me he pushes back his chair and pulls me down into his lap. "Baby, you look hot. I love these boots," he drawls against my lips, kissing me quickly before pulling back and continuing to chat to his friend.

I don't listen to the conversation at the table; instead I bask in the sensation of being back in Daisy's arms. I've missed him. It's been less than an hour since Grits arrived and Daisy left but being held in his lap with his arms around me feels like I've come home.

My heart starts to pound. When did Daisy start to feel like home?

"You want me to go get you some breakfast, baby?" Daisy says.

"No, I'll go get something in a minute."

Strong fingers lift my chin and a second later I'm gazing into Daisy's eyes. "You okay, Angel?" he asks.

"Yeah, I am now." I don't say anymore and sliding off his lap I head for the breakfast buffet.

"Hey, wait up, I'll come with you," Echo's wife Liv calls. I wait for her and we walk together across the room. Grabbing a plate, I hand one to Liv and then take one for myself.

"I love the breakfast here. Echo and I live on the other side of town, but we ride in almost every morning just for the food. I swear the best thing about America is breakfast," Liv says as she piles her plate with pancakes and crispy bacon.

"Don't you have the same food in England?" I ask, grabbing a muffin and placing it on my plate.

"We do but it's just not the same. Our bacon tastes like pig, but the bacon you have over here seems so fake, but it tastes so good," Liv says.

Laughing, I add an apple to my plate, then follow Liv as she weaves her way through the room back to our table. She immediately sits back down in her husband's lap and starts to eagerly eat the pile of food.

"You got enough pancakes there, Sugar?" Echo asks his wife in a teasing tone.

"I'm hungry, leave me alone," Liv mumbles between mouthfuls. Echo's face morphs into a scowl and he reaches up to wrap his hand around Liv's throat and turns her face to his.

Stood by the side of the table I freeze. My muscles tense and I stare at Echo's hand around his wife's neck. I want to shout, to warn Liv that he'll hurt her, but there's a lump of fear lodged in my throat that stops the words from coming out.

The plate in my hand is suddenly gone and Daisy is in front of me, blocking Echo and Liv from my view. His eyes are full of concern and he stares at me and then over his shoulder to where his friends are. When he turns back to me he smiles and pulls me into his chest. "He worships the ground she walks on. He would never hurt her, not the way you're thinking."

Loud giggling pulls my attention and Daisy steps aside to reveal a laughing Liv. Echo's hand is still around her neck, but he's whispering into her ear and the smile on her face is radiant. Liv giggles again and Echo's hand falls from her neck and spreads across her stomach.

"Echo, I'm hungry," Liv admonishes him when he starts to kiss her neck. Echo emits a low growl and Liv swings her head around to face him. "Don't growl at me, it's your fault that I'm starving constantly. This baby is stealing all of my food, so leave me alone and let me eat."

"Baby?" Daisy asks.

Liv swings her head back to where Daisy and I are standing and slaps her hand across her mouth. "Oh fuck," she cries, turning wide-eyed back to Echo.

Echo leans back in his chair, a smug grin spreading across his face. "Yeah. Livvy's pregnant, only about eight weeks. We were supposed to be keeping it quiet until she's through the first trimester."

"Please don't tell anyone," Liv begs. "I haven't told Brandi or James yet and they'll kill me if they find out they weren't the first people we told."

"Congratulations," Daisy says smiling widely, reaching over to shake Echo's hand and drop a kiss on Liv's forehead.

"Congratulations," I offer with a small smile. I quietly sit down in a seat and start to pick at my muffin while Daisy chats animatedly with his friends.

I'm ashamed that I thought Echo was hurting his wife. They're both obviously overjoyed that they're expecting a baby. On both occasions that I've met this couple, Echo has been nothing but loving to his wife, holding her in his lap and finding ways to have his hands on her all the time. I'm a horrible person for thinking the worse of someone Daisy considers a friend.

A tattooed arm drapes across the back of my chair and I turn to see Blade has sat down next to me. "You okay, Little Dove? You look sad."

I'm a little surprised that Blade is engaging me in conversation, I think this might be the first time he's spoken to me directly. "I'm fine thanks."

"You don't look fine little one, you look like you're thinking about crying. Now I don't know what's got you so down, but I doubt it's worth crying over. This is a big scary world and you're holding your own better than most people in your situation would. So don't beat yourself up if you get a little overwhelmed, you're stronger than you think."

Blade's words are quietly spoken so only he and I can hear. Lifting my shirt back into place where it had fallen to the side, he squeezes my shoulder lightly. The gesture is kind and reassuring but when I glance over to Daisy his face is angry and his eyes are zeroed in on Blade's hand.

I don't know what to do with Daisy's anger. I feel like I should shrug Blades hand off me, but that seems rude and he's not being inappropriate. Blade winks at me, stands and steps over to Daisy. I can't hear their conversation, but Daisy's tense posture gradually relaxes and Blade leaves offering me a smile as he passes.

"You finished?" Daisy asks coolly.

Daisy follows me as I take my plate into the kitchen, piling it with the other dirty plates that are waiting to be loaded into the industrial dishwasher. "I'm trying hard not to be a dick about this, Angel, but I really don't fucking like seeing my brother's hands on you."

"I didn't do anything."

"I know. Still makes me crazy though. I've never had anyone I cared enough about to be jealous over until you and I don't fucking like how it feels. You want me or him?"

"You," I say.

"Good, now come over here and kiss me," he orders.

Complying, I cross the kitchen and straight into his arms. His kiss is possessive and consuming, and I melt into him. When he pulls back I'm breathless and ready to return to our bubble.

"Come on, baby. Prez wants to see us."

I groan and Daisy laughs. "I know, but we need to know what's going on with your dad."

At the mention of my father I sober immediately. How could I have forgotten about my father or the fact that I'm here at the Sinners clubhouse hiding from him? I shudder as the memory of my father negotiating my sale flashes through my mind. Closing my eyes, I try to force the memories away, but when I open them again my father's words are replaying in my head. *"You've seen her. She's worth way more than I owe you. She'll make you a hell of a lot of money."*

Reality crashes down on me and I struggle to breathe. Daisy

reaches for me, but I step away from him. I can't let him hold me up right now. I need to feel my father's betrayal and harden myself. It's the only way I'll survive. Moving past Daisy, I straighten my spine, lift my head up, and walk to Anders' office.

DOOMSDAY
SINNERS

ARCHER'S CREEK

TWENTY-FIVE

Daisy

Following two steps behind Angel as she makes her way to Prez's office, I don't know how to feel about her rejection. On the one hand I'm fucking proud of her inner strength, she's had to be strong to cope with her dad's abuse. But I can't help feeling a hollow sting that she doesn't want to let me carry some of her burden.

Until this moment I thought she understood how I felt about her, but maybe I've been blind. I'm not the type of man who will sit by and let his woman suffer alone when I can protect her, it's just not in my nature.

I don't need to be the one in charge standing at the front, but I sure as fuck plan to stand right fucking next to her and definitely not trailing behind like a useless spare part. She was doing really well until I mentioned her father and then it was like a switch flipped in her head and the mask she uses to protect herself jumped right back into place.

Angel's an enigma; she's so innocent and sheltered, but her will to survive is so prevalent that she can become whoever and whatever she needs to get her through life. Right now, she's hard and trying to stand alone without any help or support. From the little she's told me, it seems like she's been alone since her sister died. Our histories are similar; we both understand how it feels to have no one in your life. I was lucky, I found the Sinners; they saved me and then they led me to her.

I'm trying really hard to respect her need to stand tall on her own, but I can't. As she lifts her fist to knock on Prez's door I grab her hand and swing her around to face me. "You're not going in there like this, Angel."

A scowl crosses her face, but she clears her expression almost immediately "What are you talking about? I just want to find out what my father's doing."

"Bullshit, baby. I can see your mask and you need to take a minute to calm the fuck down and let it drop. You're not alone, do you hear me? You. Are. Not. Alone. We are not going to let him get near you. I am not going to let him take you. I'm so fucking proud of how strong you are, but you don't have to shoulder all of the burden anymore. You are mine and you need to hear this right now and understand it. When you need me, I'll stand in front of you and shelter you from the entire fucking world. The rest of the time I'll stand by your side and we'll face whatever comes our way together."

Angel stares at me and I stare back. I don't know what she's thinking but I know this isn't the moment to back down. Since she showed up two nights ago, her masks have been dissolving and I've seen the real Angel. That's the woman I'm falling for and I'm not prepared to lose even a moment of the real Angel because of her douchebag father.

She closes her eyes for a second and when they open they're filled with tears. I scoop her into my arms and fold her into me. Her chest shakes with silent sobs and I carry her to a quiet corner and sink down to the floor, cradling her against me as she cries.

"Don't let him take me, please don't let him take me." Her sobs muffle her words, but I can still hear them.

"Never. Never, you're mine," I whisper into her hair over and over until her sobs subside and her breathing calms.

"It doesn't matter what Prez tells us or what your dad does, you're an adult and there's no law that says that you can't leave his house. You're my woman and you're a sinner; we will keep you safe and the sooner your dad realizes that, the better."

She lifts her tearstained face and looks at me. "I'm scared," she whispers.

Cupping her face with my hands, I wipe the tears from her cheeks with my thumbs. "It's okay to be scared, baby. You don't have to be brave all the time, not anymore. You just have to tell me when you're struggling, and I'll be brave for you."

"I'm so glad I met you," she says, her voice thick with tears and emotion.

"Me too, Angel. But it wasn't random. I knew the moment I set eyes on you. You're what I didn't know I was waiting for."

Her eyes soften and rising onto her knees she kisses me. "Maybe we're each other's reward? Fates gift for making it this far."

"You're the best fucking present I've ever got, baby," I say with a wink.

Angel laughs, and I wipe the last of the tears from her cheeks. Standing, I pull her upright and take her hand. "Come on, let's go see what your dad's been up to and then we can hibernate in our room for the rest of the day."

Knocking on Prez's door, we wait for his shout, then enter his office hand in hand. Prez is sitting behind his desk and Blade is slouched in his usual chair. I take the chair next to him and when I refuse to release Angel's hand she sinks down into my lap.

"What's the latest?" I ask Prez before he gets a chance to speak.

He raises his eyebrows at me and then focuses on Angel. "I contacted the sheriff's department at nine this morning and informed them that you were here, living at the compound with Daisy. I explained that you're an adult and more than capable of choosing to leave your parents' home. Unfortunately, because your dad is telling people that you're not capable of looking after yourself, the sheriff wants to meet with you. He needs to see for himself that you're okay and not here against your will."

"My father is the sheriff's boss; he'll try to force me to go home." Angel says, her body rigid against mine.

Both Prez and Blade chuckle. "Dove, honey, the sheriff has been on the Sinners' payroll for the last fifteen years. Your dad might be the mayor, but Sheriff Matthews isn't stupid; we keep this town clean and safe and we have for a very long time. This is just a formality; he'll be here in a minute and then you'll no longer be a missing person. I doubt your dad will give up, but it'll knock the wind out of his sails for a while. There are only three more days until the exchange date. This will all be over soon."

A knock at the door ends all conversation. "Come in," Prez shouts and the door opens to reveal the sheriff, with Smoke lurking ominously behind him.

"Sheriff, come on in," Prez says, a bright smile on his face.

The sheriff, a middle-aged man with a gut and a combover, enters the room. He's a slimy, fucking weasel but he comes in useful on occasion and he makes sure that any of our less legal dealings are overlooked.

Prez stands up and offers his hand to the sheriff. They shake and the sheriff settles into the seat next to me and Angel.

Prez sits back down behind his desk. "Thanks for coming in, Bob. Like I said over the phone we don't really understand why such a fuss has been made over two kids moving in together.

This here is one of my boys, Daisy, and his Old Lady, Dove, though I suppose you'd know her better as Angelique Jefferies."

The sheriff turns his attention to Angel. "Angelique Jefferies," he says.

"Yes, Sir," Angel replies and leans forward to offer her hand to the sheriff. Outwardly she looks calm and happy, but I can feel how stiff her body is when the sheriff takes her hand. They shake briefly and Angel quickly pulls her hand away and places it against my thigh.

"You've caused a whole heap of trouble, young lady. Your parents are beside themselves, worried out of their minds. Would you mind explaining why you ran away?" the sheriff asks her.

"Sir, with all due respect, I'm an adult. I didn't run away. I wasn't happy living with my parents, so I made the decision to move in with my boyfriend. I don't have a particularly good relationship with my father and his resentment toward the Sinners is well known, which is why I chose not to tell him where I was. Honestly, I'm embarrassed that my father has blown this so far out of proportion. As you can see, I'm perfectly fine, but I have no intention of returning to my parents' home." Angel's voice is level and strong and only I can feel the tremors that are running through her body.

The sheriff stares at Angel for a moment and then with a sigh he turns back to Prez. "That's good enough for me. Sorry I had to come down here like this, but you know what a dick our fine mayor can be. I'll go break the news that his daughter's shacked up with a biker, that should make for a fun afternoon. I'll let him know that as she's over eighteen she can live wherever she pleases, but I can't guarantee he won't turn up here."

Prez nods his head, "Don't worry about it, Bob. I know how it is. We'll keep an eye out for him, but you might want to let him know that Dove is Daisy's old lady—she's a Sinner and we won't tolerate any bullshit."

The sheriff visibly swallows, then purses his lips and nods slowly. "I'll pass that along."

Prez rises from his seat and the sheriff hurries to follow suit. "Thanks again, Bob. Blade can show you out."

Blade crosses the room, holds open the door and the sheriff scurries through it. Blade turns smirking, before he follows, closing the door behind them.

"My father won't give up," Angel says.

"I know. I imagine he'll be here banging on the gate in a matter of hours. I wouldn't put it past him to try to get Carduccio to retrieve you. This isn't over, Little Dove, but don't worry, we haven't even started to play our hand yet," Prez says with an excited grin.

"What should we do now?" Angel asks.

Prez laughs. "Go enjoy the peace and quiet; this is the calm before the storm."

"Come on, baby, let's go hibernate," I suggest and hand in hand we walk back to our room. Closing the door behind us, Angel wanders across the room. "What do you want to do, baby? We could watch more of that show you picked? We can take a nap, talk? Whatever you want."

"I want to have sex," Angel says, her face expressionless.

"What?" I splutter.

"I want to have sex."

My eyebrows furrow in confusion and I sink down onto the bed. "Hold on, Angel. You want to have sex?"

"Yes."

"Where's this coming from?" I ask.

What the fuck is going on? My cock's been rock hard since the word sex came out of her beautiful mouth, but as much as I might want to, I'm not going to have sex with her right now. If she were any other woman I'd be naked and getting my cock sucked already, but this is Angel. She's innocent, a virgin. I don't want her first time to be a quick fuck while she's frightened and waiting for her psycho dad to try to kidnap her. As much as it makes me a huge fucking pussy I want her first sexual experience to be special, I want it to be about us, and not a desperate act shrouded in fear.

"Angel, I'm not gonna have sex with you today," I say simply.

"Why not?"

"Because that's not how I want our first time together to be. I don't want you to be thinking about all the bullshit that's going on at the minute, or your fucking dad. The first time I slide inside of you I want you to be one hundred percent focused on us."

Angel sighs and rolls her eyes.

"Angel, what the fuck is going on?"

"I just, want… need something to take my mind off it. He's coming, Daisy. The moment the sheriff tells him I'm here, he'll come and he'll try to take me. I'm going to drive myself crazy just sitting here and thinking."

She starts to pace backwards and forwards in front of me. Grabbing her hand, I stop her movement and pull her into me. "I'm not going to fuck you today, baby. I don't want your dad to be any part of that, but I can help you stop thinking if that's what you need."

Her huge doe eyes focus on me and I watch her think over my words. A few seconds pass and she still hasn't spoken. "Is that what you need, baby? If you want me to quiet that mind of yours, all you have to do is ask."

"Help me stop thinking. Please," she whispers.

Standing, I pull her close to me and kiss her. Her eyes fall closed and she lets out a moan of pleasure when my tongue starts to tangle with hers. When her body starts to relax into me I pull away from her lips and lift her into the air. She gasps and grips my shoulders tightly as I turn her, placing her on the bed. Her tiny body settles against the pillows and crawling between her legs I hold myself hovering above her.

"I want to kiss you, baby. I want to tease and lick and stroke you until you can't think about anything other than the sensation of my tongue."

"You just kissed me, Daisy," she giggles.

"I know, baby, and your lips are fucking delicious, but now I want to kiss you here." My hand slides up her thigh and I gently stroke one finger along the length of her pussy.

Her mouth forms an 'O' shape and her cheeks tinge pink. "I want your taste on my tongue. I want to lick where my fingers were last night. Do you want me to?"

Her eyes are wide, and I suddenly regret my words. "It's okay if you're not ready, I'll find some other way to distract you."

"I've never, no one's ever done that to me," she says, stumbling over her words.

"I know, baby, and I can't wait to be the first."

Pulling her bottom lip between her teeth, I watch as she thinks. "Okay," she whispers in a breathy voice.

All of the air in my lungs lurches out of me in a surprised exhale. I need to know that she really wants this and that she's not just doing it because I suggested it. "I want you to say it, Angel. Ask me to taste you."

I hold my breath, unsure what she'll do. My mouth waters. I want to eat her perfect pussy more than anything, the taste of her on my fingers last night has been haunting me. I want to run my tongue through her hot, wet sex, and give her orgasm after orgasm, until her only conscious thought is my name.

"Daisy," she says, her voice breathy and unsure. "I want

you to taste me."

I grin wickedly at her. "Baby, I'm gonna make you feel so good." Leaning down I take her lips in a consuming kiss. Forcing my tongue into her mouth, I rub it against hers, until her hands tangle into my hair, pulling at the short strands. A small moan escapes her and pulling back, I nip at her bottom lip before trailing kisses along her jaw and down her neck.

She watches me lick a hot, wet path along the swell of her breasts, moving down her body until I'm resting on my elbows between her thighs. I push her skirt upwards, slowing revealing her cotton covered pussy. There's a small, dark, wet spot on the fabric and I hold in the groan that tries to force its way from me. I drop a kiss against the pale skin of her inner thigh and she jumps. "You okay, Angel? If you want me to stop just say the word."

"No. No, don't stop," she rasps.

Kissing the soft skin right below her panties, the smell of her arousal fills my nose. "Fuck, Angel, you smell so good."

I run my finger up and down her sex, circling her clit through the damp fabric. Angel arches her back, tilting her pussy closer to my fingers. "Patience, baby," I coo, as I press my tongue against her panties, teasing her.

She whimpers, and her hands grip the quilt beneath her. Trailing my fingers up to the waist of her panties, I slowly start to peel them over her hips. Angel lifts her ass off the bed and I slide the fabric down her thighs, removing them completely.

Lifting them to my nose, I inhale deeply, before dropping them to the floor.

Settling myself between her legs, I push her thighs apart. Her pussy is all smooth, pale skin. "I like this, baby. I thought you'd have some hair down here, but I fucking love being able to see and taste every inch of you."

Using a single finger, I stroke over her clit and straight down the length of her sex. Dipping just the tip inside her, I stroke back up to her clit and circle gently. Angel gasps loudly and her hips lurch into the air. Pressing a hand to her hips I hold her still as I replace my finger with my tongue.

Pushing on the back of one of her thighs, I encourage her to lift her leg and bend it at the knee. Once she's fully open, I lean forward and lick from the top of her sex all the way down to her asshole. Her taste hits my tongue and I groan in pleasure, immediately wanting more.

I flick my tongue over her clit and Angel cries, her back arching off the bed. Licking a path between her hot, wet folds, I plunge my tongue inside her and start to fuck her tight pussy. Using my hands, I keep her legs apart, as her thighs try to clamp around my head. I alternate between licking her clit and fucking her with my tongue, until she's chanting indecipherable words, gasps, and moans.

Sliding a single finger inside her soaked pussy, I flick my tongue over her clit and start to pump my finger in and out of her slowly. Her hips flex and twitch as she writhes on the bed, forcing her pussy into my face.

I slide a second finger into her tight sex and speed up the movement of my tongue. Her pussy clamps down onto my fingers and her stomach clenches and tightens as her orgasm builds. Swirling my tongue in circles across her swollen clit, I feel the exact moment her orgasm peaks. Her pussy pulses, gripping my fingers, and her arousal fills my mouth. Her back lifts off the bed and she cries out in a scream of bliss.

Before her orgasm fades, I gently curl my fingers inside her and slowly massage against her swollen muscles. I flick my tongue across her sensitive clit and she cries out.

"Oh God, oh God. Daisy, oh my God." Her words are punctuated by her hips twisting and grinding into my tongue. Within moments another orgasm hits and her body jerks upwards, a keening cry falling from her parted lips.

I watch as her pleasure abates, and her body collapses back onto the quilt. Her chest rises and falls in ragged pants and her eyes are closed. Her muscles slowly relax, and she melts into the pillows, a contented sigh falling from her lips.

Reluctantly, I pull away from her pussy and stare at her pink swollen folds, glistening with a mixture of my saliva and her arousal. My cock's so fucking hard it hurts. Reaching down I adjust myself before dropping a final kiss to Angel's pussy and moving up the bed to lie down beside her.

She crawls into my arms and rests her head on my chest. "Thank you," she whispers reverently.

I chuckle. "You're welcome, baby."

Her erratic breaths gradually slow and when I think she's fallen asleep I curl her closer into my body and rest my head on top of hers.

"Daisy."

"Yeah, Angel."

"I think I'm falling in love with you."

"Is that 'cause I just gave you two orgasms?" I ask playfully.

Her finger digs into my ribs. "I take it back, I'm not falling in love with you."

Flipping her onto her back I lie on top of her, caging her in with my arms. "Say it again, Angel."

Huge doe eyes soften, and she lifts her head up and gently kisses my lips. "I'm falling in love with you, Daisy."

Cupping her cheek with my hand I stroke my thumb across her soft skin. "I'm falling in love with you too, Angel."

TWENTY-SIX

Angel

The weight of his body on top of mine is perfect and wrapping my arms around his neck I cling to him, holding him in place. My skirt is still pushed up around my hips, my panties forgotten on the floor and I can feel his hard erection pushing against my sex. I want to have sex with him. I'm scared of the inevitable pain but despite that I want him to make love to me.

It's only been a few days. My father would call me an idiot and a whore for giving myself to a man I really don't know that well. But I'm falling in love with him and I want to be his completely, in every possible way.

Our gazes are locked, and I can't look away. He's so beautiful but rugged at the same time. The look in his eyes is full of earnest emotion, he doesn't even need to speak for me to know what he's thinking, because I can see my own thoughts reflected back at me through his eyes.

"Daisy?" I whisper.

"Angel."

"I'm so glad we found each other."

His fingers stroke my hair. "Me too."

We fall silent again, our eyes never wavering, our bodies touching, our hearts beating in sync.

"Daisy?"

"Yeah?"

"Grits said that I could move in with her and Anders once this stuff with my father is over."

His eyes snap back into focus and his face twists into a scowl. "What?"

"I can't go home, and I didn't know if you'd want me to stay here with you."

"I swear you don't hear anything I say to you. I'm falling in love with you. I want us to be together, living together, growing together. You're mine and I'm yours, that's not a temporary thing Angel, that's forever. It took me twenty-one years to find you, I'm never gonna be stupid enough to let you go," he says, his voice a mix of exasperated and passionate.

"Daisy?"

"Angel," he says pensively.

"I filled up your closet with the clothes Grits brought me."

A laugh bursts from him and he smiles. "Good. I want your

stuff all mixed in with my stuff. I want my life full of you, and you can have the whole closet if you promise never to talk about moving in with Grits again."

"I might need the whole closet. She wants to take me shopping for even more stuff."

"If it's more clothes like the stuff you've worn the last couple of days, then the closet's yours, baby," he says with a wink.

Lifting my head from his chest I steal a quick kiss, then let my head fall back down again. "My father's going to come here and I'm going to have to see him, aren't I?"

Daisy nods. "Yeah, I think so. I wish I could deal with him for you but he's gonna need to see us together. We might need to put on a bit of a show for him, especially if he brings Carduccio or any of his henchmen with him. We need to send the message that you're not an innocent little virgin anymore."

I start to speak, but Daisy stops me.

"I know you're still a virgin, baby, but we need him to think that I've corrupted you and that we're fucking like we're auditioning for a porno. My guess is that you appealed to Carduccio and his kid because you were untouched. Once he sees or hears that you're my old lady, then you're just a beautiful girl. Beautiful girls are ten a penny, but beautiful virgins that look like you are a much rarer breed."

I nod. "I keep thinking this is all just a horrible nightmare, that I'm going to wake up and Nicole's still going to be alive.

My father's trying to sell me; I just don't understand how this has become my life."

Daisy pulls me on top of him, his arms wrap tightly around me, and he whispers into the top of my head. "It's all gonna be okay. I'm so sorry that this happened, but I promise it's all gonna be okay."

Snuggled against his firm chest I let myself believe him. We hibernate for the next few hours, basking in the happiness of our bubble and then the knock on the door comes and I already know what they're here to tell us.

My father is here.

I don't want to see him. I don't want to see his face or deal with the anger and rage that I know he will direct at me. I'm scared of him and I want to hide in our room and pretend he's just a bad dream. But I can't. Climbing off the bed, I pull on my discarded panties and head to the bathroom to wash my face and redo my hair.

Staring at myself in the mirror, I blanch at the terror that's already visible in my eyes. The urge to hide behind the mask of indifference I usually use to survive my father is strong, but I don't want Daisy or Anders or any of these amazing people to see me cower to my father. I need to fight back, so I let all of the feelings of repressed rage, pain, and humiliation bubble up to the surface. All of the emotions I've tamped down in hopes of not aggravating my abuser pulse through me. Stuffing the sleeve of my shirt into my mouth I scream into the fabric. I scream and scream until my chest is heaving and my hands are shaking so violently, I can't hold the shirt against my mouth any longer.

Closing my eyes, I pull in gasping lungfuls of air. Looking up into the mirror I stare at my appearance. My eyes are sparkling, and my cheeks are streaked with red. I look alive, I look strong, and for the first time in two years, I look determined.

Letting my arms fall to my sides, I stand up straight, pulling back my shoulders and stretching to my full height. "Fuck you, Father." I say aloud. It's not a word I'm used to saying, but I feel a surge of power just by uttering it out loud.

Eyeing myself in the mirror I say it again. "Fuck you." My tongue wraps around the words and a smile spreads across my lips. "Fuck you, you evil, twisted monster." A laugh bursts from me and I watch how it changes my appearance. I look young and happy, so incredibly different from the terrified mouse I'd seen in my bedroom mirror just a few days ago.

Meeting Daisy has changed everything, and I refuse to go back to the broken mess I was. I'm not sure I'll ever be fixed but since Daisy came into my life the pieces of me are slowly moving together again. I won't ever be the perfect version of me, but I'll be whole.

"You okay, Angel? We need to go deal with him," Daisy says through the bathroom door.

"Yeah, I'm ready," I shout, allowing myself a final glance at the strong woman staring back at me in the mirror.

Pulling open the bathroom door, I find Daisy hovering by

the bed. "Let's go," I say and move toward the bedroom door.

"Hold up, baby. I've got something for you."

I stop and turn to face him.

Uncertainty crosses his face before he steps over to me and slides the shirt I'm wearing off my shoulders. He pulls it down my arms and drops it to the bed behind him. I glance down at the loose tank I'm wearing and then back to him.

"I know we already talked about this, but before we go out there I wanted to talk to you again," Daisy says, seeming to stumble over his words. "I'm falling in love with you, Angel. I want you in my life and in my bed. You make me feel and I'd forgotten what that was like. My life is so much better with you in it and I want everyone to know that you belong to me and I belong to you."

Watching his face, I can see all of the emotions that are swirling inside him. I've never seen him shutter his feelings and a sadness builds in my heart that this beautiful, kind man might shut himself off from people. I try to imagine what he would have looked like as a child and my heart twists as I think about him moving from home to home, never wanted, and refusing to make friends because he feared losing them.

He clears his throat and his piercing gaze focuses solely on me. "I want you to be my old lady and I want you to wear my property patch. I want to claim you and show the world that I'm lucky enough to call you mine."

He turns to the bed and picks up a small black leather vest.

It's a miniature version of the one he's wearing, except on the left-hand side is a beautifully embroidered patch that reads 'Property of Daisy'.

I reach for it and Daisy chuckles; the low sound makes a tremble of awareness pulse through me. "Is that a yes then, Angel?" he asks.

Taking a step closer, I stand up onto my tiptoes and kiss him. "Yes," I whisper against his lips.

My heels barely hit the ground before Daisy scoops me into his arms and swings me around. A giggle escapes me, but his lips catch it as he crashes against me, devouring me in a passionate kiss. Our tongues duel frantically against one another as our lips explore. The kiss gradually slows to a sensual embrace. When he lowers me to the ground my eyes flutter open and I'm overwhelmed by the love I feel for the man standing in front of me.

Daisy holds out the vest and I spin around, sliding my arms into it. Reverently, he lifts it over my shoulders and then turns me so I'm facing him again. He strokes a single fingertip across the words and silently mouths "Property of Daisy." His fingers tangle with mine and he leads us out of our room and toward an inevitable confrontation with my father.

Hand in hand we walk outside into the warm Texas sunshine. My eyes squint, shocked at the brightness, but we continue to walk until we reach the group of people standing in front of the compound's large metal gates.

"I want my daughter."

I hear my father before I see him. Daisy and I quickly reach the group of Sinners and as if it had been rehearsed the group parts and we walk straight to the front, stopping next to Anders and Blade.

The group of bikers close in around us and although I don't look, I can feel the presence of the guys looming behind me. Daisy releases my hand and pulls me tightly against his body. Eagerly clinging to his strong chest, I lift my head to look at the hoard of people that are congregated on the other side of the gate.

I try to scan the crowd and identify who they are, but apart from seeing the familiar brown uniform of the sheriff's department, the only people my eyes can focus on are my father and Senator Carduccio who is standing next to him.

I know the moment my father sees me. Even through the heavy metal barrier I can feel the weight of anger and hatred his gaze contains.

"Angelique, here. Now," my father barks, as though I were a disobedient dog being called to heel.

Every muscle in my body tenses and Daisy strokes a reassuring hand up and down my back as he tries to soothe me.

"Who the fuck do you think you're talking to?" Daisy growls.

"*My* daughter, that's who. Angelique, get here now," my father shouts, his face turning redder and angrier.

Daisy laughs. "Your daughter's fine right here thanks."

"I'm not talking to you. I don't deal with biker scum. So I suggest you release my daughter or I'll have the sheriff come in there and collect her," my father says haughtily.

The Sinners collectively grow restless as my father insults Daisy. A ripple of apprehension flows through me; these people have taken me in and sheltered me when I needed them. Right now, my father is insulting them. My arms drop away from Daisy's chest and I feel myself taking a step forward. Daisy crowds behind me, his body pushing against my back, literally holding me up as I find the strength to speak to my father.

"No," I shout.

Everyone goes silent and all eyes turn to me. My father's gaze narrows, as I look from him to Carduccio and back again.

"Angelique, this is your last warning, get out here right now," my father hisses between clenched teeth. His hands are balled into fists at his sides and I can see the rage building within him.

"No," I say, my voice loud and clear. "I'm not going anywhere with you. I'm Eighteen. I'm not a child, and I've decided to move in with Daisy."

My father's eyes bulge and his face reddens even more. "Angelique, you are *my* daughter and you will do what I tell you to."

"No I won't," I say. My body is shaking so violently that Daisy has to wrap his arm around my waist to keep me upright.

"Angelique, I'm warning you," my father says, his voice low and full of sinister warning.

"What are you going to do, hit me? Because the bruises are still here from the last time. Or are you going to pull off your leather belt with the big metal buckle and try to make me do what you want with that?" I turn to Senator Carduccio. "Did he tell you that the merchandise was damaged? Did you offer him a lower price for me when he told you that I'm covered in scars from where he's punished me with his belt? Did you get a discount because my back, legs, and ass are covered in lines from where he hit me so hard the buckle broke my skin?"

Senator Carduccio scowls at me and then turns to my father. "What happened to the mousy virgin?"

"She's untouched, she just needs to be brought back into line. I can deliver her subdued and knowing her place," my father says to Carduccio.

"Fuck you," Daisy shouts. "This is my old lady and my property. You don't get to speak to her or look at her unless I say so. You might be the mayor, but I don't give a crap. I suggest you get your pathetic woman-beating ass back home. You're not welcome anywhere near my woman."

My father starts to vibrate with rage. "No child of mine will ever be a biker's whore, get your filthy hands off her before I have you arrested."

"See this patch, old man?" Daisy says pulling my property patch forward. "That says 'property of Daisy'. She's mine."

The last two words come out as a roar, before he lifts me into the air. I wrap my legs around his waist and my hands around his neck and kiss him like it's the last time I'll ever get the chance. He slides his hands up my thighs and warm air caresses my ass when he lifts my skirt higher. I know that my panties are on display and that Daisy's hand is sliding between my legs. I know we have an audience and that this is all part of a show for my father and Carduccio, but I don't care. I want him to push his finger inside of me. I want him to stroke me and make me orgasm and I don't care who's watching.

"Enough," my father screams.

Sliding down Daisy's firm body, my skirt rides even higher. My ass is on display, but I don't pull it down. Instead I glance over my shoulder and smirk at both my father and Senator Carduccio.

Carduccio's mouth twists into a displeased line and he turns to my father. "Deals off, she no longer has any value to me. Biker sluts I can get for free. Please make sure that you bring the full amount to the usual place in time for your deadline. No need to contact me directly again; you can speak to Santos, you know the number."

Carduccio addresses Anders, who is stood next to us. "Anders, I've no business with the Sinners. I was not made aware that she was one of yours." Then he nods and walks away. When he reaches a large black SUV, a driver opens the door for him. Once the Senator is seated inside, the driver climbs into the front seat and the car pulls away.

"You little cunt," my father screams.

Pulling down my skirt, Daisy moves me to the side of the group. A hand grasps mine and I turn to see Grits has moved next to me. Sighing in relief I squeeze her hand back.

"It's almost over, baby girl. Just get through the next few minutes, that's all you've got to do," she coos quietly.

"Just who the fuck do you think you're talking to?" Daisy sneers taking a step closer to the gate. Anders, Blade, Echo, and another man, move as one to stand shoulder to shoulder with Daisy. This is a show of solidarity and my heart lurches at the wonderful family Daisy has made for himself.

"You. You're nothing but a disgusting, filthy piece of biker shit. Mark my words, I will have my daughter returned to me. The stupid little cunt belongs to me and I won't let my name be sullied by her spreading her legs for the likes of you," my father spits out.

Daisy laughs a humorless laugh. "How the hell did you get voted into office? You're a fucking idiot."

A quiet rumble of laughter burbles through the Sinners. "Prez, who owns this town?" Daisy asks Anders.

"The Sinners own Archer's Creek," Anders says with a smirk.

"And who runs this town?" Daisy asks Blade.

"The Sinners run Archer's Creek," Blade says throwing his arm around Daisy's shoulder.

Daisy glances at me and offers me a salacious grin. "Who owns you, baby?" he asks me.

I smile back. "You do." Then I pointedly look at my father. My legs are shaking but I force them to stay still. I need my father to see me stand tall and brave. I need him to know that I won't cower from him anymore.

"So, *Mayor* Jefferies," Daisy says accentuating the word mayor in a mocking tone. "The Sinners own this town, we run this town, and I own your daughter. You have no power here. You're nothing but an annoying little pussy who likes to beat up girls. You can't do shit to us, so why don't you crawl back into your hole and leave Angel the fuck alone."

My father purses his lips and breathes heavily in and out, rage pouring from him. Protected by the big metal gate and surrounded by Daisy and his biker brothers, I almost feel brave enough to laugh at the spectacle he's making of himself. He looks behind him at the two deputies from the sheriff's department and points at them. "Officers, my daughter is a danger to herself, please retrieve her."

The officers shuffle uncomfortably looking from my father to the Sinners compound.

"I'm the mayor. I pay your wages. I insist you go get my daughter," my father screams.

Anders starts to chuckle; the sound is low and sinister, and he takes a menacing step closer to the gate. Glancing to someone on his right, the gates slowly start to slide open. I grip

Grits' hand tightly and my heart starts to race.

"It's okay, don't worry, Dove. Just watch." Grits assures me.

My father looks unsure now, like he never expected them to just open the gates. Anders takes several steps forward and crosses the threshold of the compound and onto the road. We all silently watch as he spreads his arms wide and says. "Officers, feel free to come and collect Angelique if we've broken any laws."

The officers smirk to one another and saunter over to Anders. My heart's beating so loudly I swear I can hear it. I watch as the officers reach Anders, expecting them to stride past him and toward me, but instead they stop and the men exchange handshakes and warm smiles.

"Officer Perez, how are Molly and the kids? Officer Smith, that truck of yours is coming along nicely," Anders says cordially.

A bubble of laughter escapes me, and I slap my hand across my mouth to stifle it. Anders turns to me and winks. "Dove, sweetheart, come on over here and say hello to Archer's Creeks finest law enforcement."

Grits pushes me forward and I take unsteady steps over to the group of men. Daisy's arm folds over my shoulders as I walk past him and together we take the final few steps until we reach the police officers. "Officers," I say shakily.

I eye my father warily. He's only a few feet from me, he could be on me in a second; his mean grip in my hair, his hard fists against my skin. I move closer to Daisy and that's when I realize that Daisy, Anders, and the two police officers, have effectively formed a barrier around me. To get at me my father would have to go through four huge men. I look at each man in turn and all of them reassure me in some way that they won't let him hurt me. Anders squeezes my shoulder; the officers Perez and Smith smile at me and dip their chins in greeting, and then there's Daisy.

He wouldn't let my father hurt me, he'd keep me safe. There's not a moment of doubt in my mind that he wouldn't do absolutely everything in his power to protect me. I melt into his side and wrap my arms around him tightly.

"Miss Jefferies," Officer Perez says. I turn to look at him. "Are you okay?" he asks simply.

"Better than I have been in about two years." I reply.

The officer's eyes shutter for a moment and when he opens them I know he's taking in the faded bruises on my face. He offers me a single nod.

Glancing at my father again, I watch as he takes several steps closer to our group, a triumphant smile etched across his face. I gasp, and all four men direct their attention at me and then to my father. Daisy kisses the top of my head, then moves me behind him and closer to Blade. Blade shelters me until I'm within the main group of Sinners, and Grits who holds me closely at her side.

My eyes jump from my father to the group of Daisy, Anders,

Perez, and Smith. The officers turn as one and stand between my father and the rest of the Sinners. "Mayor, the girl's eighteen and she's living with her boyfriend, there's nothing against the law here. The only thing of concern I can see in this situation are the bruises all over that young lady's face. They're not fresh bruises and she didn't go missing until two days ago." Officer Perez says.

The color starts to drain from my father's face.

"Anders, did Miss Jefferies have those bruises on her face when she got here?" Perez asks.

"Why yes, she did, real beat up she was. Perhaps you'd like to come back later on and speak to her about that in more depth?" Anders says, his tone conciliatory.

"This is ridiculous," my father shouts. "These inbred criminals hurt her. Look at her, she's incapable of making rational decisions. As her parent I demand you return her to her home, so we can get her the help she so obviously needs."

"Well now, Mr. Mayor, I'm starting to take offense at all these ugly names you're calling us. As I'm sure the officers here will confirm, The Doomsday Sinners are simply a law-abiding group of citizens with a mutual interest in motorcycles. We own numerous businesses and contribute greatly to the town's prosperity. Hell, you yourself have attended more than one gathering right here at the clubhouse. Your daughter's the old lady of one of our members, she's a Sinner and we take very good care of our members. I'd think you'd be happy knowing that your daughter's going to be safe and well cared for within the compounds walls," Anders says. His words are pleasant, but his undertone is threatening and full of authority.

Both of the officers reach out and shake first Anders' and then Daisy's hands and then they start to make their way back to the police cruiser that's parked a little ways down the road.

"Where are you going?" my father shouts.

The officers ignore him and we all watch as they get into their car and drive away. My father's hands clench into fists and he starts to walk toward me. "You stupid bitch, look at all the trouble you're causing me. I won't tolerate this level of disobedience."

His angry words spew at me, but for once they don't hit their target. I don't withdraw into myself, I don't flinch at each step closer to me he gets. Instead I look to Daisy and find his warm, loving gaze trained on me. He smiles at me, then steps directly into my father's path.

TWENTY-SEVEN

Daisy

Mayor fucking Jefferies bounces straight off my chest, stumbling back a step before he stops and looks up at me.

"Move," he barks.

I chuckle. "Sorry, but this here is private property and we have a strict no woman-beaters rule for guests. Looks like your shit out of luck for an invite."

His piggy eyes narrow further and I smirk at him. How the fucking hell did my perfect Angel come from this evil little man? Pricks like him are the worst kind of snakes, smiling and shaking the right hands, all the while beating the shit out of his kids back home.

I fucking hate people like him and I've met enough of them. Most foster parents aren't in it because they love kids—in fact most of them hate fucking kids, but love the checks they get every month for looking after them. I was in so many homes, I've seen every kind of person: the do-gooders, the perverts, the sadists, and the ones like Angel's dad. He's the type that needs to beat his wife and kids to make himself feel like more of a man. Mayor fucking Jefferies gets off on exerting power over people and the wife that I've no doubt is so downtrodden she doesn't have it in her to fight anymore, making his daughters the perfect next targets. Nicole, Angel's sister, fought back and escaped, but I wonder if she knew that by leaving she was condemning Angel to take her place?

"Move out of my way you piece of crap. I'm taking my daughter and leaving, and neither you, nor any of your ingrate friends are going to stop me," he sneers.

Placing my hand in the middle of his chest I push him back a step. "See the problem we have here, Mayor, is that your daughter is my woman and she isn't going anywhere. Now why don't you run along and forget that you ever had a daughter, that's something you should be familiar with doing. You won't come near her again and then we won't have a problem. But I promise if you try to take her from me, I will hunt you down and I. Will. Kill. You."

The mayor huffs and looks at me like I'm dirt beneath his shoe. "My daughter owes me. She cost me a lot of money today, so one way or another I will retrieve what's mine. But perhaps if she means that much to you, then we could come to some kind of agreement?"

I fist my hands in his shirt. "Are you fucking serious? Are you suggesting that I pay you for your daughter?"

A shrewd look flashes across his face. "You took my daughter's virginity, valued at one hundred thousand dollars. That wasn't yours to take and as such I'm merely suggesting that you compensate me for that loss. I'll tell you what, as a sweetener you can keep the girl as a gift."

I see red, this asshole is taking about my beautiful angel like she's an animal. Everything around me disappears and all I can see is the man standing in front of me and all I can think is that he doesn't deserve to breathe. Pulling my fist back, I punch him in the face. He drops like a stone. Leaning down I grab his shirt, pulling him upright enough to punch him in the face again and again.

My arms move robotically. I want him to cower. I want him to beg me to stop and I want the pain to be so bad that he yearns to pass out just for a break from it. I want him to feel everything he inflicted on Angel, only I want him to suffer ten times worse.

"Daisy," the scream pulls me from my frenzy and I drop her father's prone body to the floor. I turn and find Angel in a ball on the floor, her knees are pulled into her chest and she's rocking back and forth humming that tune. I feel sick. I did this, I made her fall so far into herself that she's practically catatonic.

Her father's whimpers grow louder and change into threats of police and arrest, but all I care about is Angel. Pulling off my blood splattered shirt I rush to her and lift her into my arms. She calms the moment her skin touches mine and the humming stops.

"Angel, I'm sorry. Come back to me. I'm so sorry. Please, please come back to me," I whisper against her hair. Walking from the crowd, I hear people calling my name, but I need to take her back to our bubble and try to bring her back to me. I kick the door to our room open with my foot and stride straight over to the bed.

Climbing on with her still in my arms, I curl my body around hers, surrounding her. Stroking her hair, I kiss her cheek, her nose, her lips. I kiss her closed eyelids and her forehead. "Angel, I'm sorry, I'm sorry. I love you, I love you so fucking much."

A single tear rolls down her cheek and I kiss it away. "Don't cry, baby. I know I shouldn't have hit him. I know you don't want to see I'm capable of that, but it's him. He hurt you and I wanted him to know what that felt like. What it felt like to be scared and small and helpless. I love you, you're mine and he wants to take you from me."

"I love you too," she whispers.

A relieved breath escapes from me. "Fuck, baby, you scared the shit out of me." Her eyelids flutter open and I gasp, her huge doe eyes are full of anguish, fear and love.

"Wait, what did you say?" I ask.

"I love you too, Daisy," she says and I see it, right there in her eyes. She loves me.

"God, baby, I love you. I'm sorry, I lost it, baby. I'm not sorry I fucking hit him, but I'm sorry that you saw. You were so brave, I'm so fucking proud. You stood up to him, Angel, you stood tall and strong."

"I thought he was going to hurt you," she whispers, her eyes pooling with tears.

A laugh escapes me, and I cup her cheek with my hand. "Baby, your dad is a fucking coward who gets off on hitting women that won't hit him back. He can't physically hurt me, but it cuts me deep when he talks about you like you're an animal. I love you. I couldn't stand there and let him talk about you that way."

A sigh escapes from her and she closes her eyes. "Is it over? Senator Carduccio left. He called me a whore," she chuckles and a small smile twitches at her lips.

"I don't know. Carduccio seems to be out. He might be playing us, but I don't think so. He knows who we are and how we feel about the women we claim. If he tries to take you, he's essentially declaring war on the Doomsday Sinners and nobody wants that. At the moment we co-exist and don't encroach on each other's turf but that would all stop. He might have some powerful connections, but the Sinners have some hefty allies too. We need to speak to Prez. I think your dad is gonna be more of a problem. He's a fucking asshole and he's not gonna take you being with a Sinner with any grace. He just tried to coerce money from me; he's desperate, and a desperate man is a dangerous man."

Angel buries her head against my chest and my arms instinctively wrap around her, pulling her closer. "We'll get through this. I won't let your dad come between us. He's just an insignificant road bump on the path that brought us together. All the shit we've gone through was just to make sure we'd recognize how fucking perfect we are for each other. You've changed everything for me, Angel."

Lifting her head from my chest she raises her hand and runs her fingers through my hair. "I'm so broken, Daisy. Look at me today, I hid again, and I promised myself I was better than that. I thought I could be strong; you deserve someone strong, and I'm trying, I promise I am. Every day since I met you, my shattered pieces have started to fit back together. You're bringing me back to life and you're fixing me."

"You're fixing me too. We belong together," I say, shaking my head. "Fuck me, Angel. I'm turning into such a fucking pussy. This is your fault, baby. I fell in love with you and you made me feel something, apparently it was my sappy, sentimental side. I need to do something to make me feel like I didn't just grow a fucking vagina. Get your ass up here and kiss me. I need to make sure my dick still works."

Angel's tinkling laugh breaks the tension. Crawling up my body she straddles my thighs, her pussy pressed against my cock. Her denim skirt has ridden up her legs and I can see those innocent cotton panties of hers. Running my palms over her thighs I push her skirt higher, until it bunches around her waist. I want to see all of her, so I reach for the buttons on the skirt and start to undo them. Glancing up, I look at her face. She's watching me, nibbling on her bottom lip. The anguish has gone from her eyes and a heady lust has replaced it. "This okay, Angel?" I ask, undoing another button.

"Yes," she says breathily.

Making quick work of the buttons I push the last one through the hole and her skirt falls open. Her panties are white and modest, but on her they're the sexiest damn panties I've even seen. My eyes devour her, she has no idea how sexy she is and I fucking love that about her. Angel is effortless.

"I love seeing you wear my name," I growl and run my fingers over the 'Property of Daisy' patch on her chest. Never taking my eyes from her, I slide her skirt from beneath her and drop it to the floor. Reaching up, I start to push the leather cut off her shoulders. It easily slides down her arms and rests against my legs. "I wanna see you just in these panties and my name. I don't mean right now, I'll wait until you're ready, but when you are would you do that for me, Angel?"

Her eyes widen for a moment, then she leans forward and drops a fleeting kiss against my lips. "I love you."

Fisting her tank top, she slowly pulls it over her head. If it were anyone but her I'd think she was putting on a show, but she's not. This isn't her trying to be sexy, Angel has no idea just how beautiful she is.

She drops her tank to the bed and then pauses. I watch her take a deep breath, then reach behind her and unclasp her bra. The fabric falls forward and her perfect breasts are revealed. Her small pink nipples are pebbled and my mouth waters. I want to taste them, bite them, and suck them until she's writhing around desperate for more.

"Jesus," I hiss as she drops her bra to the bed. Her hands are clenched at her sides, like she's fighting the urge to cover herself. She's uncomfortable and that's not what I want. I want everything we do to be good for her. "We don't have to do this."

"No. I want to, this is just a little weird for me. I've never been naked in front of a man before and my boobs are small."

Reaching up, I cup one of her breasts in my hand. "They're not small, Angel, they're a handful and you've got the most perfect nipples I've ever fucking seen."

A beautiful pink flush covers her face and I smirk at her. The urge to suck on those pink peaks is too heady and I start to lift my head when she twists to the side. She picks up her property cut, sliding it back up her arms and all of the air leaves my lungs.

"Perfect," I whisper, my voice raspy. Her tits are playing a naughty game of peek-a-boo behind the cut, and the black leather against her pale skin is the perfect contrast.

My cock's pushing so hard against my jeans, my stomach twists. "Jesus, Angel you look… God you look… I fucking love you." I ramble.

"Is this what you wanted?" she asks shyly.

"Fuck, Angel. if I die right now then I'm good. That's the sexiest thing I've ever seen."

She looks down at herself and then back to me. "I'm not sexy, Daisy. I'm wearing ugly cotton panties from Target."

"I don't give a fuck where your panties are from. It's you. You make them sexy and wearing nothing but those panties and my name on you, that's the holy fucking grail, baby." Wrapping my hands around her waist, I roll her under me. Her cut falls open and I get the full view of her perky tits again.

Sitting up, I take in the full image of *my Angel* spread out for me to admire. Her arms are resting on the pillows on either side of her head and her white hair is spread around her like a halo. "All this perfection and just for me," I coo quietly.

"Why are you looking at me like that?" she asks nervously.

"I'm just memorizing this, baby, and trying to figure out how I got so fucking lucky."

She starts to fidget under my appraisal and I can't wait any longer, so I lean forward, bracing myself above her and take her nipple into my mouth. Lifting my eyes, I watch her mouth fall open and a silent moan escape her lips. Her neck arches and she eagerly curves her body closer to my mouth.

I swirl my tongue around her nipple, laving at the tip and then sucking it all into my mouth, nipping at her with my teeth. Her silent moans gradually become audible and when I bite down on her sensitive peak she hisses between her teeth.

"Daisy," she moans.

"What, baby?" I ask, pulling her other nipple into my mouth and starting to worship it with my tongue.

"Sex... I want... I want to have sex with you," she says breathlessly, between gasps and moans.

Releasing her nipple with a pop I look up at her. Her huge eyes are staring back at me, full of desire and lust. "Baby, you just need me to make you come. I'm gonna peel off your panties and lick your sweet pussy until you scream."

"No, no, no. I want you, Daisy. I want to be with you. I love you and I want to have sex with you. Please, please," she begs.

"Don't beg, Angel, never beg. I want you so much. I love you too, but I want you to be sure. Nothing between us should ever be a regret. I don't want to do this unless you're absolutely ready."

"I'm ready. I love you and I want you. I promise I won't regret this, I could never regret this with you." Her eyes are earnest and so full of love.

"It'll hurt you, baby, I don't want to hurt you. I'll be so gentle, I want to make this good for you but I'm not gonna lie, this first time it's gonna be more pain than pleasure," I say.

"Okay," she whispers.

I nod, scanning my eyes over her face to reassure myself that she's ready. Reaching up I cup her cheek. "I love you, Angel."

"I love you too."

My lips meet hers and the kiss is sweet and slow. Our tongues push against one another, but this isn't a race to the finish line, it's a moment of surrender for both of us. Neither pushes the other to deepen the kiss, we simply luxuriate in the bliss of being together.

Sliding my hand from her face I caress the smooth skin along her neck, moving lower until my fingers cover her breast, squeezing gently. My thumb glides over her already sensitized nipple, teasing her until she's gasping through our kiss.

Releasing her breast, I brush my hand along her flat stomach and push beneath the waist of her panties. My fingers slide easily through her wet heat and into her soaked sex. Pushing a single finger inside, her muscles clamp down on me and I groan as I imagine her strangling my cock when I'm deep inside her.

Angel's giving me her virginity. We both know I'm going to have to hurt her and just the thought of making her bleed sickens me. I want her so fucking much, but I want her to enjoy this too. I can't have her remembering her first time, our first time together, as something painful and unpleasant.

I need her desperate and panting, so crazy with want that her mind will forget the pain, as she searches for release. Her pussy is greedy, and she gets wetter and wetter as her hips start to rise and fall in time with my finger's movements. I push a second finger into her—fuck she's so tight—and her muscles clamp around me as I try to pump in and out.

Releasing her mouth, I kiss a path down her neck and move

to worship her breasts again. I lick a circle around the base of her nipple then tease the tip with my tongue. Kissing the underside of her breast I scrape my teeth along her skin, then gently bite down. Her moans change to keening cries as the mix of pleasure and pain pushes her closer to release.

My fingers continue to move in and out and her arousal soaks my hands. She's so fucking wet. Sliding a third finger into her pussy I try to stretch her, preparing her for my cock. I move my thumb up to glide over her clit and at the first touch she moans loud and long.

Pulling my hand from her sex, I sit up, dragging her panties down her legs and throwing them over my shoulder. "Fuck, Angel, you're soaked. I need to see your perfect pussy all glistening, covered in arousal. I know how sweet you taste and I can't deny myself." Her perfect pussy is shiny and wet and mesmerized I stare at her. She fidgets under my scrutiny and her legs start to close. "No," I command, and she pauses.

"You're staring at me."

I chuckle. "I know, baby, but your pussy wet and begging is the perfect fucking sight."

I glance up at her and laugh. Her hands are covering her face, hiding her obvious embarrassment. Lying between her legs, I look up, watching her as I run my tongue straight down the center of her sex.

Her hands fall away, her back arches and a low moan escapes her. "Jesus, Angel. I love making you moan."

Opening her folds with my fingers, I lick from her sex to her clit, circling it gently with the tip of my tongue. Her hips lift from the bed and I thrust my tongue deep inside her. Her sweet taste fills my mouth and I withdraw, flicking her clit again.

Her breathing is ragged and small moans escapes from her lips. I want to drag this out and tease her, make her wait for her orgasm but I can't. I want to see her fall apart again. I want her to scream my name and then I want to sink my cock deep inside her and make her mine completely.

Concentrating on her clit, I suck it into my mouth, scraping my teeth across the top of the sensitive bundle of nerves. She cries out in pleasure; her hips lift from the bed and she pushes her pussy into my face. I pump my fingers quicker, curling upwards and pressing against the sensitive spot inside of her. Her fingers tangle into my hair and she scrapes my scalp with her nails as she frantically holds me down and pulls at my hair.

"Oh God, oh, oh. Daisy, Daisy, oh God," she cries, her voice breathy and filled with desire.

Her legs tense and squeeze around my shoulders, she writhes beneath me and I know she's close. Sucking her clit into my mouth, I swirl my tongue back and forth until her back lifts off the bed and she explodes, her sweet cum filling my mouth.

I push my tongue into her sex, feeling her pussy pulse and clench around me. I want to make her come again and again but I can't wait a moment longer. Sitting up, I rip off my T-shirt and push down my jeans and boxers. I look down at my perfect

Angel; her tits are bouncing as her chest moves up and down with her ragged breaths. "You okay?" I ask.

"Yes, oh my God, yes. Please, Daisy, I want you in me, please," she gasps, her eyes locked on mine. I can't resist. Grabbing a condom from the dresser I rip open the foil and slide it over my rock-hard cock. Climbing over her I brace myself above her. My arms fall beside her head and I lean down and kiss her.

"I love you, Angel."

TWENTY-EIGHT

Angel

My body's still tingling from the orgasm Daisy just gave me, but I need more. I need to feel him inside me. My skin is literally itching for more of him. I need him to touch me, to kiss me and to make love to me.

I love him, and he loves me. I never thought I'd have this. I never considered that Daisy was out there, and I just needed to find him. My rational side is warning me that it's too much, too quick, but I don't care.

Daisy makes me feel loved and protected. He's become my safe haven and when I'm with him I don't feel so broken. I love him, and I want to have sex with him. I want to give myself to him and take a part of him in return.

His body is braced above me, so I bend my knees and cradle

him further between my legs. "Daisy, please," I beg.

"Are you sure? I want you so fucking bad, but I'll wait, I want you to be ready," he says, his eyes earnest and full of love.

"I'm sure. What else would I wait for? I love you and I want to have sex. I'm ready."

He kisses me, and I wrap my arms around his back, pulling him closer to me. I want to feel his weight on top of me. I want to be surrounded by him. Daisy's hand slides between us and his fingers push back inside of me. I love the feeling of fullness; my eyes fall closed and I moan quietly.

"Fuck, baby, you're so wet." His fingers leave me and are replaced by his cock probing at my entrance. I feel my sex stretch, as inch by inch he pushes his way inside me. The sensation is strange, my sex burns as his huge dick enters me. I feel pressure in my stomach, and the feeling of fullness his fingers gave me is a distant memory, as a painful burn overwhelms me.

"Are you okay?" he asks, his fingers stroking my cheek.

I nod. I know my face must show the pain I'm feeling, because his eyebrows are furrowed together. "We can stop, if it's too much," he says.

"No, no don't stop," I cry.

Leaning down he kisses me, then pulls back. "I'm gonna do this quick baby and then I'll give you some time to get used to me inside you."

I nod quickly and wrap my hands around his neck. He leans down and kisses me again, then I feel him pull out of me until only the tip of his cock is inside, and the burning lessens. In one quick thrust he pushes all of the way inside of me. I scream. His mouth on mine swallows the sound but the pain is like nothing I've felt before. Tears pool in my eyes and I fight not to let them fall, but my sex burns and my stomach is tight. Daisy's cock feels huge and I'm uncomfortably full. He flexes his hips and I hiss as the burn pulses through me again.

"I'm sorry, I'm trying to keep still, but baby you're gripping my dick so fucking hard."

"It hurts, I just, I just need a minute. I'll be okay in a minute." I say trying to sound confident.

Daisy nods and then squeezes his eyes closed tightly and drops his forehead to my chest. I wonder if this hurts for him too.

I pull in several deep breaths and the pain starts to recede. "I'm okay, you can move. Just. Just be gentle, please."

He lifts his head from my chest and his eyes find mine. "I promise. I love you so fucking much."

"I love you too."

The pain comes back full force when Daisy slowly starts to pull out of me. Gasping, I swallow down my cry and try not to tell him to stop. The slow push and pull is painful, but the uncomfortable feeling recedes and I watch the muscles in his back tense and release with his movements.

Daisy rests on one elbow and pushes my leg up further with the other. The movement pushes him deeper and a hiss of pain bursts from me.

"I'm sorry, Angel. Next time, I promise I'll make it so good for you. I hate that I'm hurting you, but in a minute I'm gonna lick you until you scream. I promise. I'm gonna make up for this pain with pleasure."

He pushes into me and then pulls back and pushes into me again. The pain is almost gone, but it's not replaced by pleasure the way romance books said it would be. His hand moves from my leg to my breast and he starts to play with my nipple. He squeezes and pinches and suddenly a wave of pleasure pulses through me.

His thrusts get faster, and the burning morphs into tingling. The sensation is a painful pleasure; it hurts but I don't want it to stop. The feeling of fullness has changed. My body begins to accept him and a warm feeling pools in my stomach.

"Jesus, baby, I'm close," Daisy gasps. His lips find mine and he kisses me. His tongue moves against mine in rhythm with his thrusts and every time he pushes back into me a burst of something sparks. The feeling is intense and painful, but addictive, and I find myself moving with him, searching for it.

"I'm gonna come, Angel. Your pussy's strangling my cock and I can't hold back anymore," Daisy groans against my lips. He pulls back and then pushes into me deeper than before. His back clenches beneath my hands and he moans loudly into my ear. His movements become frantic, his hips plunge back and forth, and his cock impales me again and again. After one final thrust he cries out, his moan guttural and tortured, then his muscles relax and he exhales a contented sigh against my cheek.

His cock is still buried deep within me, his weight rests on me and I run my hands up and down his back, caressing his muscles.

"I love you," he whispers.

"I love you."

I hiss when he pulls out of me, my sex protesting painfully. Daisy sits up between my legs and I can see the red blood coating the condom.

"Come on, baby, let's get you in the shower, then I'm gonna make up for you not coming. I promise you, Angel, this is the one and only time we'll ever have sex without you coming. Next time I'm gonna make you scream my name and come over and over with my cock buried deep inside you."

I watch as he pulls the condom off and drops it into the wastebasket. He strips my property cut from my shoulders, lifting me from the bed and carrying me to the shower. Silently, I watch him test the water and when he holds out his hand to me I take it.

The warm water runs over my skin and my tense muscles ease. Closing my eyes, I luxuriate under the cascade of the shower, jumping when a hand runs across my stomach. Forcing my eyes open I look down to watch Daisy's soapy fingers leave a line of bubbles across my skin. He washes me with reverence; his hands touch me everywhere, carefully removing all of the blood from my sex and thighs. He washes my hair and then I do the same for him. We don't talk, we don't need to.

My first sexual experience wasn't what I was expecting, but it was with him and that alone made it perfect.

Daisy turns off the shower and then steps out first, holding a towel open for me to step into. He wraps it around me and then grabs another for himself. He dries his skin quickly and then does the same for me.

I giggle when he drops the towel to the floor and lifts me into the air.

"Come on, Angel, time to make you come."

Lowering me to the bed he drops a small kiss against my lips. His naked body is beautiful and his cock is hard again. I wait for him to climb above me, but he doesn't; instead his eyes rake over my body, taking in my nakedness.

"I'm a fucking lucky man," he drawls.

Lifting one of my legs he kisses my foot, then my ankle. His tongue trails a hot wet path up my shin and another featherlight kiss is pressed against my knee. He lowers my leg to the bed and then lifts the other and follows the same pattern, tiny kisses and warm caresses. When he's finished, he lowers that leg to the bed and finally crawls beside me onto the mattress.

I squirm in anticipation, waiting for his talented tongue to find its way to my sex. He places a fingertip on each of my legs, just above my knee and then he draws patterns on my skin. Circles and swirls leave a path of tingling sensation behind them as they decorate every inch of my thighs with an invisible mural.

I wait for his fingers to pass over my sex, but every time the swirling patterns reach the apex of my thighs, the pattern turns and swirls in the opposite direction. Closing my eyes, I indulge in the sensation of his touch and my breathing becomes ragged, as he edges closer and closer to where I need him to be, only to move away again.

I hold my breath as his fingers brush against the folds of my sex. I wait for his touch but instead of him finally circling my clit, he swirls upwards and across my hips, onto my stomach.

The swirling stops and is replaced by his tongue gently winding its way along my ribs. Air hits the wet trail and my skin instantly cools, leaving me feeling like his touch is actually marking me. I shudder when his mouth pauses over my breast and I can feel the heat of his breath.

I need him to touch me; my skin feels hypersensitive, and the anticipation builds when I see his pink tongue dip out of his mouth and pause mere millimeters from the tip of my nipple.

Tipping my head back, I try to move my breast up to greet his tongue but as if he is expecting me to do it, Daisy's head is gone before my skin makes contact with his mouth. Daisy starts at my ribs on the other side of my body and his tongue follows the same path. When his hot breath heats my nipple this time I gasp, hoping, desperate, that he'll touch me properly.

His chuckle is low and laced with unrepentant amusement. His mouth doesn't close around my heaving breast, instead he pulls back and his fingers take over again. One hand lifts to the side of my face. His fingers comb back my hair, pushing it behind my ear and then trail down my jaw until they reach my chin. A finger lifts and Daisy's lips meet mine, the kiss is languid and slow.

His tongue pushes gently into my mouth and when he strokes my tongue with his, a fingertip drags across the underside of my breast and across the tip of my nipple. I gasp into Daisy's mouth, but the kiss continues, slow and deep and sensual.

His finger disappears from my breast only to scrape across the inside of my thigh a moment later. A touch swirls along the length of my arm only to disappear and then reappear at the base of my neck.

Daisy's featherlight touch is teasing me, a trail of tingles are left in the wake of his barely there caresses and with every stroke, swirl or sweep of his fingers or tongue I'm left desperate for more.

My body sways into his touch, willing him to move to the places I need him. When a single fingertip strokes across my nipple I cry out. Daisy's lips swallow the sound, and the noise dies in my throat when he starts a pattern of lines, crisscrossing back and forth over my sensitized peak.

Daisy pulls back from our kiss and when our eyes meet, his are full of mischief and lust. My limbs tingle and ache with the need for more, all of the pain between my legs forgotten. His teasing is pushing me closer and closer to desperation and begging him to do something, anything, to make me come.

He moves to my other breast and the pattern of back and forth across my nipple starts again. I can't take any more, my body is writhing, and I feel like I'll go mad if he doesn't do something. "Daisy, please. God, please touch me. Please," I beg.

A single finger runs across my mound and I cry out, pushing my needy pussy into his hand. His fingers leave my breast and he moves down the bed until his face is level with my sex. I can feel his hot breath against my skin and a trail of goose bumps surface. My hips start to writhe of their own volition and my fingers twist into the sheets beneath me.

Small kisses feather my thighs. Tiny touches that only heighten the frenzy of lust, never staying in one place long enough to satisfy my desire. I twist, moving away from him, then closer to him again as my clouded brain tries to process what I need. A sharp pain snaps at my thigh and I cry out from the heat and pleasure that flows from the spot where he bit me.

"Easy, baby," he coos.

Squeezing my eyes tightly shut, I wait for his touch. My brain whirls with expectation, hoping his fingers will finally move to my aching desperate sex. Cool air wafts across my stomach and moves down between my legs. Instinctively parting my thighs, Daisy blows across my clit. Crying out, everything happens at once. His tongue hits my clit as his fingertip squeezes my nipple. My body explodes with sensation, white light flashes behind my closed eyes and my entire body arches from the bed.

His tongue rapidly licks at my sex, my clit, and then pushes into me briefly only to quickly move back to my clit again. Pressure pools in my stomach and a fire lights up my body as I detonate and an orgasm cascades from me.

A keening cry escapes from my mouth and I start to shudder. My orgasm begins to fade but Daisy's tongue moves faster and faster against my clit and the sensations rise again. Sparks and tingles start in my toes and speed upwards, my stomach muscles tense and I feel my limbs try to fold into the sensation.

Moaning loudly, I squeeze my legs together. The pleasure is too much, and I can't stand it anymore. "No more, I can't, oh God, I can't." I cry.

"I could watch you come all day. You're so fucking beautiful." Daisy nips at my thigh playfully then climbs across me, pulling me into his side.

My muscles are lax and I melt into Daisy's side. Lethargy washes over me and my eyes fall closed . "I love you," I slur into his chest.

He chuckles lightly. "I love you too, Angel. Sleep now, I'll wake you up in a couple of hours."

I try to nod, but I'm not sure if it works or not. Unconsciousness takes me quickly and I fall asleep in the arms of the man I love.

DOOMSDAY SINNERS

ARCHER'S CREEK

TWENTY-NINE

Daisy

Angel's naked body is pressed close against mine and I can feel her chest rising and falling as she sleeps peacefully. I love her. I knew what I was feeling, but I hadn't planned to blurt it out the way I had last night, and I really hadn't expected her to tell me she loved me too.

She's so innocent—too perfect, too pure. She's been *my* Angel since that very first time I saw her, and I'll do whatever I have to do, to keep her safe and protected. Fate might have given us a fucked-up path to each other, but now I have her I don't ever want to be without her again.

She gave me her virginity. No woman has ever offered me that before. Probably because the women I've been fucking weren't sweet and untouched; in fact most of them were wild and unrestrained. Angel wanted *me* to be her first. I'm the first man to ever slide into her perfect fucking pussy and I'll be the last, she's one hundred percent only mine.

That's a heady fucking feeling, I'm the only person who'll ever know what she looks like when she comes. I'm the only person who'll ever know what her pussy feels like when it's clamped around my fingers or my cock. I'm the only person who'll ever get to sleep with her naked body curled up next to them.

I don't deserve her, but I want her anyway.

A white halo of her hair's spread out across my arms, and she truly looks like an angel. Being inside her was better than anything I've ever felt before, she was so tight I could barely move. I need to ask her to get on some birth control because I want to feel her without a condom between us.

I've always been careful. The idea of going in any pussy bareback just seemed stupid, especially with the women I've fucked in the past. They were just a way to pass the time, only using each other to scratch an itch. I never dated, I never wanted to. Until I found Angel, I've never wanted to get to know a woman, why would I?

But she's changed everything.

Dealing with her dad today had been a shit storm. I knew it would be bad but fuck he's a serious piece of work. He spoke to Angel like she was a dog needing to be brought to heel. I never knew my parents, but I know that's not how you speak to your kid. If Angel and I had a child, I'd love that baby more than anything else, I wouldn't treat it like a commodity.

Her dad isn't going to go away quietly. Carduccio's gone and I don't think he's coming back, but if Angel's dad can't repay his loan, things are about to get uglier. I'll do anything I can to make sure that his shit doesn't blow back on Angel again. She's my old lady and a Sinner now, and the Sinners look after their own. I know Anders and Blade and the rest of the club will do everything they can to protect her, but she's my responsibility.

I've never loved anyone, or had anything worth keeping safe before, but I'll never let anything happen to her. In such a short amount of time she's become vital to me, she's everything.

I don't know how long I lie watching her sleep, but when her eyes start to flutter open, the warm sun has faded and a quiet darkness has taken its place.

"Hi," she says, her voice sleepy.

"Hi."

"Have you been watching me sleep?"

I chuckle lightly. "Yeah."

"That's weird."

"I know. I love you though, so I think it's okay," I reply.

Her face breaks into a glorious smile. "I love you too."

"You want to get dressed and go get a drink or you want to hide out in our bubble tonight? Either way I need to feed you so it's up to you."

She thinks about it for a minute. "What would you be doing if I wasn't here?"

"I'd either be over at Beavers or I'd be playing some pool and having a few drinks."

"What's Beavers?" she asks.

"Err, I work security over at the titty bar that Grits runs a few days a week," I say, cautious of her reaction at knowing I spend my time watching strippers.

"Oh. Should you have been there the last couple of days while you've been with me?"

I smile at her. I don't know if the naked woman thing hasn't sunk in with her yet or if she just isn't bothered. "Yeah, but it's okay. Smoke's been covering my days."

"I don't want you to get in trouble because of me," she replies earnestly.

"So you don't mind that I work in a strip club?" I ask.

Her brow wrinkles. "I can't tell you what to do, Daisy."

"Sure you can. You're my old lady," I say.

"Daisy, do you love me? Are we together, as in me, you, and no one else?"

"Of course we are. You're mine and I'm yours, no one else gets to touch you and I don't want anyone but you." I growl.

A small blush covers her cheeks. "Okay then."

I start to speak but I can't find any words. She just left me dumbstruck and in awe of her faith in me. I try to speak again, then close my mouth. She's right, there's nothing left to say.

I love her, she loves me and that's enough. She doesn't need to worry about me being around other women, because now I know she exists, why the fuck would I want anyone else? I'm not worthy of her, but I'll fucking fight tooth and nail to keep her. She's what I've been waiting my whole life for, she's my future.

"I don't want to keep you away from all of your friends, let's get up and go have a drink," she says sweetly.

Quickly rolling her beneath me I kiss her. "I don't like any of them as much I do you. Plus, you're naked. I'm a big fan of naked."

She giggles and wraps her arms around my neck.

"You sore?" I ask.

She looks away from me and the blush that had faded, blooms back into her cheeks. "A little."

"Then, yeah, we need to get out of this room. I want to fuck you again, baby, but you're sore and I don't want to hurt you. Next time I take that pussy of yours I want you to come. I hate that you didn't today, and I don't plan on that ever happening again. I want you seeing stars and screaming my name every time my cock's inside of you."

Her eyes widen in shock. I normally try to tone down the dirty talk around her, but I took her virginity tonight, she's not so innocent anymore. I want to tell my girl all the dirty things I plan to do to her. I want to make her cheeks turn pink, then get her so riled up she's squirming and needy. But tonight she's sore, so I need to get her out of bed and into some clothes before her naked body becomes a temptation I can't resist.

"Come on, Angel, get that sexy ass into some clothes and let's go play some pool," I say climbing out of bed, then lifting her up and swatting her on the ass. The moment she's standing naked in front of me, I watch as she tries to cover herself from me with her arms. "Angel, I've seen you naked. I've licked or kissed almost every inch of you."

"Hmm, I know, but that's different. I can't just wander around with no clothes on," she says fighting to hide her discomfort.

I laugh. "I want you to wander around with no clothes on. In fact, I think that our room should be a clothes free zone, and you should be naked all of the time."

"Daisy," she says with an amused gasp.

Rolling my eyes, I grab my T-shirt from the floor. Pulling it over her head, I drag her close to me and cup her ass with both of my hands. "Is that better?"

She nods and stands on her tiptoes, kissing me lightly. "I'll get dressed."

Reluctantly, I release her and watch as she pads over to the closet and pulls open the door. My cock twitches and I will it to calm the fuck down. Grabbing jeans and a clean shirt from the dresser, I pull them on quickly not bothering with underwear. I slide on my cut and then settle back onto the bed to watch Angel.

She pulls down a shirt and some shorts, then she seems to pause. "What's up, baby?" I ask.

Spinning around to face me, her eyes are wide and she's gripping something in her hands. "Er, Grits got me some underwear, and it's not exactly what I'm used to wearing. I need to do laundry, all of mine I brought with me are dirty."

Smirking, I raise an eyebrow at her. "Put them on, let me see."

She bites her bottom lip, then steps into the panties and pulls them up her legs. My shirt hides them from view, so I crook a finger at her and beckon her over. Turning quickly, she grabs the outfit she's chosen and then slowly walks to me.

Taking the clothes from her, I drop them onto the bed and pull her between my legs. I slide my palms under the hem of my shirt and slowly lift it, so I can get a look at her. The panties are a pale pink and made of satin, they're pretty but fairly modest. "What's up with them? You don't like the satiny fabric?"

"Err, no, the fabric is soft and lovely, it's just that…" Her voice fades off and I still don't know what the problem is. Dropping my shirt, I reach around her and cup her ass.

My palms hit warm, soft skin. Smiling widely, I spin her around so she's facing the other way, lift my shirt again and get the most amazing view of Angel's ass, perfectly displayed in a G-string. "Oh, fuck me. Remind me to kiss Grits next time I see her. Your ass in this thong is a thing of fucking beauty."

"Daisy," Angel admonishes.

My smile fades when I stop staring at her ass, and see the full extent of the yellowing bruises, scabbed over cuts and faded scars from the punishments she's endured in the past. Old silvering scars are mixed with fresh pale pink ones that scatter from her thighs all the way up to the base of her spine. He did this to her, he marked her, and these scars won't ever go away. He did this, but she'll have to live with them for the rest of her life.

Guiding her forward a step, I sink to the floor at her feet. Starting at the lowest scar, I kiss each one in turn. I can't take them away or make her forget the anger and pain that she felt while they were made, but I can love them because they're a part of her.

When I've finished, she turns to face me, tears running down her cheeks. Wrapping my arms around her waist I bury my face against her stomach, and her arms hold me to her. Neither of us say anything, we don't need to.

Both of us were broken, but piece by piece we're putting each other back together, that's all that matters.

Angel pulls away and wipes the tears from her cheeks. "God, I'm sorry. I've cried more in the last couple of days than I have in years."

"You can cry as much as you want, baby. Hopefully once all this shit with your dad is over you won't have any reason for tears."

She looks at me and I want to carry her to the bed and stay locked in our bubble for the rest of the night. I don't want to share her with anyone else, she's too special. She's *my* Angel, and she makes all kinds of possessive feelings swell up within me.

"Do you just want to stay holed up in here tonight, I don't feel like sharing you," I say, taking a step toward her.

Smiling indulgently at me she shakes her head. "We can't hide in here forever. You need to get back to your normal life and that'd be you spending time with your friends. I don't want to be the reason you don't see them."

"I don't give a fuck about them. Why would I want to be out there with a bunch of hairy bikers when I could be in here with you. Naked."

I try to step closer to her, but she lifts her hand and places her palm against my chest, halting me. "Daisy, let's go spend time with your friends, then we can come back and hide in our bubble for the rest of the night."

"Naked," I say.

"Naked," she agrees, her cheeks flushing pink.

Begrudgingly, I get dressed, then sit on the bed and watch her. She slides on her shorts, then turns her back to me before she pulls my shirt over her head, replacing it with a white Sinners tank.

Walking back over to the closet, she roots around then pulls out a black pair of cowboy boots and slides them on. When she turns to face me, I almost swallow my tongue. The shorts are short, the boots make her legs look fucking amazing and even though the tank she's wearing is fairly modest, knowing that she's not wearing a bra underneath makes it seem indecent. Her hair is loose and flowing down her back and I want to throw her on the bed and bury my cock in her.

"Do I need to wear my 'I belong to Daisy' vest?"

"It's a property cut, Angel, and hell fucking yes. I want every single one of those fuckers to know you're not available. I don't care if I sound like a caveman, you look fucking gorgeous and if I didn't already have you, I'd be panting for you."

She scoffs at me but retrieves her cut and slides it on. I groan. "Baby, let's just stay in here."

Her eyes dim, and she scans her appearance. "Do I look stupid? Because Grits picked out these clothes for me. I don't know how to dress to fit in with your friends, I thought this would be okay, but I can change."

"Angel," I say interrupting her. "You look hot as fuck, I already told you that. I'm being a jealous idiot and I don't want all my brothers checking you out. Just ignore me. Come on, let's go play some pool."

I take her hand and open the door, pulling her behind me as I move into the corridor. "Just do one thing for me, okay?"

"What?"

"I need you to sit on my lap."

"Okay, but why?" she asks, her brow wrinkled in confusion.

"Because I've got such a hard on looking at you dressed like that. I need you sit on my lap, so my brothers don't see."

"Daisy," she cries, laughing loudly.

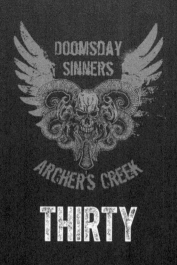

THIRTY

Angel

As we enter the bar I'm surprised at the number of people that are here. Nearly every table is full, with more standing in groups around the bar and pool table. Daisy drapes his arms over my shoulder and leads us across the room, to a group of sofas that are filled with people, some I recognize some I don't.

Spotting us, the people move around to make space and Daisy sits, pulling me into his lap.

Echo's wife, Liv, smiles warmly at me and waves. "Hi, Daisy. Nice to see you again, Dove."

I smile back and offer her a small wave. For the first time I notice that she's wearing a leather cut like mine, I'm assuming hers says 'Property of Echo' on it and like me she's sat in her husband's lap.

"What do you want to drink?" Daisy asks.

"Erm, I don't know. What are you having?"

He shrugs. "A beer. You want one?"

"I've never tried a beer," I admit.

"Then let's get you a beer. After all today's the day for doing new things," he says with a wink.

Blushing, I fight the urge to cover my face with my hands. Daisy asks the rest of the group if anyone needs a drink and a few of the guys stand to go to the bar.

Daisy lifts me from his lap. "Go sit with Liv until I get back."

Nodding, I shuffle to the end of the sofa where Liv is sat with another woman wearing a property cut.

"Hey, Dove," Liv calls. "Have you met Brandi yet?" she asks pointing to the other woman.

I shake my head.

"Brandi, this is Dove. She's Daisy's old lady," Liv says to the woman. "Dove, this is Brandi. She's Sleaze's old lady, but I'm not sure if you've met him yet either."

Brandi waves at me. "Well, hello, sweetie, I'd heard a rumor that Daisy had found himself a keeper, but I didn't know if it was true or not. Hell, girl, you're gorgeous and that boy's not stupid, no wonder he got you in that patch so fast."

I don't really know what to say. I take a moment to think of a response, but Brandi starts talking again, before I even get a chance to speak. "Wait, have we met before? Do you live in town, you seem really familiar?"

Do I admit who I am? I don't suppose it really matters who knows now, especially seeing that my father knows I'm here after today's showdown with him at the gates. "Err. I've lived in Archer's Creek for a few years now. I don't think we've met before though."

She looks at me quizzically for a moment, then she snaps her fingers. "You've been on the TV. You're the mayor's daughter."

I force a smile and nod slowly. "Yeah that's me. My father didn't appreciate me moving out."

Brandi's eyes narrow in suspicion. "On the TV it said you were missing."

"Not missing. I've been here with Daisy the whole time," I say.

The suspicion dissolves from Brandi and she wiggles her eyebrows at me and laughs. "Oh, I know how it is, girl."

Liv shakes her head good naturedly at Brandi, then leans into me. "Ignore her, she's only teasing. I don't want to pry but is everything okay with your dad now?"

How the hell do I answer that? I can't tell a complete stranger that my father tried to sell me, so I ran away. She'd think I was insane. So instead I shrug and say. "I don't have a good relationship with my father. Moving out was the best thing for me to do. He's not a nice person."

The sofa bounces when someone sits next to me and a soft arm curls around me. "Hey, baby girl, how you doing?" Grits asks.

Exhaling in relief, I melt against her. "Hi, Grits. I'm good thanks."

Grits glances at Liv and Brandi, who have started chatting quietly to each other, then she turns back to me. "I've been so worried about you. Last time I saw you, you were catatonic in a ball and Daisy was running off with you in his arms. What happened?"

"I'm so sorry," I say, looking around me hoping no one can hear our conversation.

"You don't need to be sorry, I was just worried. I wanted to come see you, but Anders wouldn't let me. He said Daisy would look after you. Did he? Are you okay?"

"I saw Daisy hitting my father and, well, sometimes it's just safer to stay inside my head. But I'm fine and yes Daisy looked after me, you don't need to worry. I'm fine now, I promise."

Her arms wrap around me and she pulls me into a tight hug. "Dove, your daddy is an asshole."

I burst out in laughter. Grits gapes at me for a moment, then starts to laugh too. "God, he really is," I say.

"Anders thinks that Daisy giving your dad a beating will make him back off. So maybe we could go shopping and have some lunch tomorrow?" Grits says.

Daisy appears in front of me, hands me two beers then lifts me into the air and sits back down, settling me into his lap. Taking one of the beers back from me, he leans across to Grits and kisses her on the cheek.

"Thank you, Grits," Daisy says with a smirk.

"What for?" she asks smiling at him.

"G-Strings," Daisy says smugly.

My face burns with embarrassment and I cover my cheeks with my hands as Daisy and Grits laugh at me teasingly.

"Tell Dove that she needs to come shopping and to lunch with me tomorrow," Grits says to Daisy.

"Hell no. Not until after the deadline date. She's not safe until Jefferies has paid up," he scowls at her.

She glares at him, annoyed, but Daisy talks before she gets a chance to respond. "It's only a couple more days, then you can have all the girly lunch dates you want. Until then she stays in the compound where we can keep her safe."

Grits reluctantly agrees, kisses me on the cheek and leaves.

Warm lips hit the back of my neck and I smile. Daisy's arm is wrapped around my waist and the other rests on the arm of the sofa holding his beer. Relaxed against his chest I sip at my drink, wrinkling my nose at the bitter taste.

"Do you want me to get you something else?" he asks, amused.

Turning to him, I shake my head. "No, it's fine, it's just not what I was expecting it to taste like. I thought it would be sweeter."

"Do you want to play pool?" he asks.

"I've never played before."

His eyes twinkle mischievously. "I'll teach you."

Daisy boosts me up from his lap, then takes my hand and leads me across to the pool table. A couple of guys are just finishing a game and when they see us approach, they greet Daisy and tell us the table is ours.

Handing me a pool cue, he walks around the table and sets the balls into a triangle shape. Rolling a white ball across the red fabric, he carefully lines it up with a spot that's directly opposite from the triangle of balls at the other end. "Come here, Angel, I'll teach you how to break."

I walk over to him and he reaches out and pulls me into his body. His lips crash down onto mine and he kisses me until I'm breathless and panting. Ignoring the soreness I'm feeling, I push myself closer into him. "Daisy," I whisper.

"Baby, don't get me started. You're sore and no matter how much I want you, I'm not gonna take you again tonight. So be a good girl and spin around so I can teach you how to break. Okay?"

Reluctantly, I spin around, ultra-aware of Daisy's hard cock pressing up against my butt, as he positions me bent over the pool table.

"Here, like this," he says and moves my hands to create a rest for the cue to sit on.

"Now pull back your arm and hit the white ball, right here." He points to a spot in the center of the ball and I pull back the cue and then push it forward. The white ball rolls forward six inches, then stops.

Daisy's body vibrates with laughter behind me and I spin round scowling and point my finger at him. "Don't laugh at me."

"I'm not, baby," he says trying to stifle his chuckles. "Just try again, okay, and this time hit the ball a bit harder."

Nodding, I turn around and place the white ball back onto the spot. Repositioning the cue on my hand where Daisy had shown me, I pull back my arm and push it forward harder. The ball rolls forward quickly, hitting the triangle of balls at the other end of the table with a satisfying thwack.

Spinning round I smile brightly at Daisy, who grins back at me. "I did it," I cry.

"Good job, baby. Now it's my turn."

He walks to the table and proceeds to get ball after ball into the pockets. I stare at him in shock as the last ball with a circle on it disappears, and he turns, his gaze locking with mine, and winks. "Black ball, top right-hand pocket." Then he spins around, leans over the table, giving me the perfect view of his butt in his jeans and pots the black ball.

"I win," he drawls.

"I think you might have had an unfair advantage."

He feigns outrage. "I won fair and square baby, now I want my prize."

My heart races, as his eyes darken. "Come here, Angel."

I take a step towards him and he hauls me into his arms and kisses me. His tongue invades my mouth. He tastes like beer and

Daisy. A moan escapes me, and his arms wrap around me tighter pressing his hard cock into my stomach.

Pulling away, he moves his lips to my neck and I tip my head back to give him better access. Butterflies dance in my stomach and my eyes fall closed. I feel his hot breath on my ear a second before he speaks.

"I want you so much, Angel. I can't fuck you with my cock, but I want to taste your pussy again and watch you come. Will you let me play with you? I need to touch you."

"Yes," I rush out with a gasp.

Instantly I'm airborne and I wrap my arms around his neck and my legs around his waist while he carries me to our room. Kicking the door open, his lips find mine the moment we step over the threshold of the bedroom.

The door shuts and I hear the lock turning, all while his lips devour mine. I feel the movement as he walks us across the room and the soft quilt beneath me, as he lowers me to the bed.

Our kisses become frantic as his hands fumble to unbutton my shorts and push them down my legs. Daisy pulls away from me, so he can remove my boots and slide my shorts and panties off my feet.

"Shirt off, baby, I want to see all of you," he orders. I comply quickly and seconds later I'm completely naked and Daisy's head is between my legs.

His tongue, lips, and fingers tease, stroke, and caress me, until my breathing turns ragged and a mind-blowing orgasm explodes within me.

Lying on the bed, my chest pounds as I drag in gulps of air and my skin vibrates with sensation. A smug looking Daisy appears above me and I try to pull him to me, but my muscles are so languid I can't muster the energy.

Daisy chuckles softly. "Angel, you look fucking perfect. All soft and sleepy from the orgasm I just gave you."

I try to smile but I'm too tired to move, my eyes fall closed and I try to force them open. The bed moves behind me and Daisy's warm body wraps around me, pulling me against his hard chest and his harder cock.

My eyes snap open when his cock prods me in the back. "Daisy?" I ask uncertainly.

"Yeah, baby?"

"Do you? Are you? You're..." I say, struggling to find the words.

"Spit it out, Angel."

"Your penis is poking me in the back," I rush out.

Daisy's body vibrates with laughter behind me. "Fuck baby, call it my cock. I just licked your pussy and watched you come, of course I'm fucking hard. My cock just hasn't got the memo that I'm not fucking you again tonight, baby, that's all. Go to sleep, it'll get on board with the plan soon, don't worry about it."

I should help him with that right? He's given me so many orgasms today and he only got one, so the polite thing to do would be to offer to give him something in return. Wouldn't it? I squeeze my eyes shut and then force them open again. "Do you want…? I mean, do you need me to…? Err, shall I help?"

"How you planning on helping me?" he rasps into my neck.

"I don't know. I could maybe touch you, like you did to me."

I'm rolled to my back, Daisy above me a second later. "You want to suck my cock?" he asks, shocked.

"What! No." I shout. Then I pause, did I want to do that? No, I didn't. But the idea of seeing what the hard, smooth skin tasted like intrigued me. "Maybe," I say, my voice small.

Daisy's eyes go wide, and he disappears from above me. The bed beside me bounces as he collapses next to me. Sitting up I turn to look at Daisy. His hands are over his face and his voice is low and chanting. "Mrs. Myers naked, lady boys, genital warts, Anders naked."

"I don't understand what's happening," I say confused.

The chanting stops, and Daisy drops his hands. "I want you to suck my cock, so fucking bad. But after I see your lips spread around my dick, I'm gonna want to fuck you. Scratch that I'm going to fuck you. But you're sore and you were a virgin until a few hours ago and I don't want to scare the shit out of you on the first day you decide to have sex."

I stare at him, stunned and unsure what to say. The butterflies in my stomach have started dancing and my overused vagina is eagerly pulsing and clenching. I open my mouth intending to speak but Daisy stops me.

Leaning over the side of the bed he grabs his shirt and shakes it at me. "Put this on and get over here, Angel. We're gonna go to sleep, so my dick can realize that your pussy is a no-go zone until tomorrow."

Silently, I pull the shirt over my head and Daisy hauls me into his arms, pulling the covers over us. His dick is still hard and pushing against my back, but as he doesn't say anything neither do I.

Sleep finds me quickly and before I know it my eyes are fluttering open and the room is full of cheerful daylight. At some point during the night, Daisy rolled onto his back and I'm using his arm as a pillow. The sheets have fallen to his waist and my eyes rake over his exposed chest. His face is peaceful in sleep and he looks young and innocent. Trying not to move, I enjoy the quiet moment to take everything in.

In just four short days my life has changed beyond recognition. I've run away, met a guy, faced down my father, and lost my virginity all in less than a week. I don't feel like the same person. I'm not the same person. Daisy was the catalyst for all of this; meeting him that day at the wedding literally changed my life.

My heart flutters as I watch him sleep, I love him. I can't explain the feeling, but I know it's there and that I've only ever felt this way about him. We had sex. I internally check my body for aches and pains and find none. I feel good. I feel excited and even though there's still a huge black cloud of unknown surrounding my father there's a smile on my face.

"Quit staring at me," Daisy croaks out, his voice full of sleep.

"No, you're pretty," I quip back.

I barely see him move, then he's on top of me, his arms caging my head on either side and his hard cock pushed against my stomach. Biting my lip, I arch my back and push myself against his hardness.

"Angel," he warns.

I freeze, unsure if he's actually annoyed with me or just being playful.

Dropping his head, he kisses me. "I love you," he whispers against my lips, then he kisses me until I'm panting and squirming beneath him.

Lifting his mouth, he rests his forehead against mine and we both gasp for breath. His hand slides down my body and between my legs. I part them eagerly for him. "Fuck, Angel, you're soaking wet. How sore are you? I want you so bad, but I don't want to hurt you."

"I'm not sore," I rush out.

His finger slides easily inside me and he begins to pump in and out of me slowly. A moan escapes and my hips roll into the movement of his fingers, pushing him deeper.

"Do you need more, Angel?" he drawls.

I nod, but I don't know if he sees, as my eyes are closed,

and my head is tipped back. I hear his soft chuckle as he pushes a second finger into me. Sparks of sensation tingle as he slides in and out of my sex and I lift my knees up, spreading wider, needing more.

"God, Angel, your cunt's greedy for my fingers. You okay? Tell me if it hurts," he drawls.

"It doesn't hurt. Oh, wow it feels really good," I cry.

As his fingers move, a warm sensation builds in my stomach. The tingling spreads along my limbs, until I'm moaning and gasping every time his fingers hit that spot deep inside of me. He pushes me closer and closer until the heat consumes me and my body tenses, exploding as an orgasm pulses from me.

Daisy's weight moves from above me. My skin is still trembling with the aftershocks of my orgasm when he pulls me into a sitting position and rips his shirt over my head.

"I want to watch you ride me, Angel. I want to see that greedy pussy of yours swallow my cock."

His dirty talk kickstarts my sex, it flutters in delight at the idea of another orgasm. Daisy lies on the bed, his head and shoulders propped against the pillows and he lifts me to straddle his legs.

I watch, fascinated, as he grabs a condom from the dresser and slides it over his hard cock. My fingers itch to touch him, to explore his hardness and watch him as I drive him to release. I start to reach forward but Daisy's hands on my hips stop me.

"Lift up onto your knees baby, I need to be inside you."

Doing as he asks I move until I'm above him, then he guides his cock into my entrance.

"Sink down onto me, nice and slow. It's gonna feel bigger in this position."

My mouth falls open as inch by inch I lower myself onto his huge, hard cock. Daisy's hands on my hips guide my movements and he lifts me up and down, slowly working himself further inside of me. The fullness is overwhelming, and I grab Daisy's arms. "I can't, it's too much," I cry.

"I'm only about halfway in, baby, you're so fucking tight."

His words make me want to cry. There's no way the rest of him is fitting inside of me. I start to lift myself off him, but he stops me.

"I'll fit, baby. I did yesterday, and I will today. Ride my dick. Roll your hips and lift up and down. Each time you'll take a bit more of my cock and by the time I'm filling you completely, you'll be screaming my name."

I try to roll my hips, but I can't and instead I feel uncoordinated and a little silly. Sensing my unease, Daisy grips my hips again and rocks me back and forth, as he slowly slides me up and down his cock.

Each time I sink down his length, a pleasurable pain bursts in my sex. My hips start to feel the rhythm and as Daisy moves me up and down, I grind back and forth, searching for the pain that feels so delicious. Daisy's thumb moves to circle my clit and I moan long and loud when the pain in my sex morphs into a burning pleasure that pools deep within me.

"Oh fuck, baby, yeah. Your cunt full of my cock is the most perfect sight I've ever fucking seen." Daisy rasps out.

Rocking back and forth while he teases my clit, I feel another orgasm swirling inside of me. Each thrust adds another layer of pleasure that will soon topple over, and I can feel the scream building in the back of my throat.

The pain has gone and all that remains is overwhelming pleasure. All I need is a little more to push me over the edge and without realizing I push down onto him harder. One thrust, then another and my breath turns ragged as I gasp, moving quicker, searching for release. Daisy bucks his hips up to meet me at the same time as his thumb quickly rubs across my clit and I scream.

Drowning in sensation, another orgasm barrels through me and throwing back my head I bask in the unimaginable pleasure.

THIRTY-ONE

Daisy

Fucking hell.

Angel's riding my dick, her tits bouncing and she's screaming as she comes like a fucking train. I can't help feeling a bit smug, but that quickly disappears when her tight as hell pussy clamps down on my dick as she orgasms again.

My balls hurt. I've needed to come since yesterday, but as much as I like her hands on my cock, I wanted to be buried balls deep in her. I've never felt so lucky in my life and I don't ever want this to end. I've never craved a woman like I do Angel. Hell, I'm still fucking her and I already want her again.

I can feel my own release building in my gut, but I'm not ready for this to be over yet. She's gonna need a few hours to recover and I want to keep her wet and screaming all day.

Closing my eyes for a second, I hold her hips and work her up and down my length, teasing myself with short, shallow thrusts that will hopefully make this last a bit longer.

Her fingers wrap around my wrists and I open my eyes to find hers, lust-filled and sated, staring back at me. Her hair is tousled, and her lips are pink and swollen. All thoughts of making this last fly out the window, my balls pull tight and I pull her down hard onto me. Two more thrusts and I explode. Hot spurts of cum fill the condom and I wish more than anything that I could feel her skin to skin.

A groan bubbles from the back of my throat, as more cum bursts from me. Slowing her movements, I work myself down, emptying my balls and letting the trembling in my arms settle to an invisible vibration beneath my skin.

Our movements slow to a stop and I push up to a sitting position, pulling her legs around my waist and wrapping her in my arms. "I love you so fucking much," I growl against her hair.

"I love you too," she whispers in reply.

I don't know how long I hold her in my arms. I don't want to let her go. I don't want this to end. I've had a lot of sex, but it's never been as good as this. I've fucked women with moves like a porn star and I'd take Angel's perfect inexperience every fucking time.

Reluctantly I lift her off me and she groans as my still hard cock slides from her wet pussy. Quickly disposing of the condom, I pull her back into my arms and lean back against the pillows, her naked body stretched out on top of me.

"What do you want to do today?" I ask.

"Stay here with you."

I laugh. "Okay, baby, I like that idea."

So that's what we do, we shower together and then get back into bed. I throw on sweats and get us food but other than that we spend the entire day in our bubble. Just me and her, young, free, and in love.

When the bright daylight turns to dusk I slide back into her and this time we take it slow. I worship her body and bask in the feeling of her. Unhurriedly I make love to her and for the first time in my life I see what the difference is. When she orgasms, I swallow her cries and when I come a few minutes later she tells me she loves me.

....

I wake up the next morning filled with a sense of impending doom. Today's the fifth day. Today's the day that Angel's dad has to pay up what he owes to Carduccio. This is the day he was supposed to hand her over to be married off or pimped out to Carduccio's son, or whoever the fuck else the illustrious senator decided to give her to.

In theory, after today it's all over. Angel should be safe. As far as we know Carduccio no longer sees Angel's value as equal to her father's debt, so the mayor's going to have to settle what he owes in cold, hard cash.

Tomorrow Angel can walk away and not fear her father

using her as collateral. She could walk away from me. Running away and starting over somewhere new was always her plan. The only reason she's still here is because we convinced her that this was the safest place for her until this was all over.

I don't know if I can let her go. She's told me she loves me, and I love her, but is that enough to keep her in a place so close to people who abused her and tried to sell her? If she leaves, can I turn my back on the club and the people I see as my family to go with her?

Watching her sleep in my arms, I try to imagine what my life would be like without her. I can't. Even after such a short time she feels intrinsically linked to what happiness feels like. I've never considered myself a caveman when it comes to women, but then I've never had anyone like Angel in my life. She's mine and I just don't think I can let her go.

She starts to stir, and I watch as she stretches out her arms and legs like a sleepy kitten. She seems so young and I feel like even more of a bastard for wanting to keep her. She deserves a fresh start, a chance to find out who she is without the shadow of the last few years hanging over her, in a town that her father doesn't run. But the possessive, selfish part of me isn't prepared to set her free, even if it might be what's best for her.

"Hey," she says her voice full of sleep.

"Good morning, beautiful."

A knock on the door interrupts us and I climb out of the bed, dropping a quick kiss on Angel's head as I grab some sweats, pull them on and open the door.

"Hey," Smoke says.

"What's up?" I ask.

"Prez wants to speak to you and Dove," Smoke says with a wry smile.

I nod. "Okay, tell him we'll be out soon. Dove's only just woken up."

He taps the door frame with his knuckles, nods and leaves. Closing the door behind him I turn to find Angel sitting up in bed, the sheet pulled up to cover her breasts. "Sorry, baby. We can't hide out today. Prez wants to talk to us."

She groans and I chuckle, amused at her defiant attitude. I fucking love that she's starting to lose the frightened rabbit look from her eyes. I'd like to think that I've got something to do with her feeling safe enough to show some of her personality, but truth be told her strength and determination is all her. All I've done is give her somewhere safe to stay, where her dad can't beat the shit out of her.

Pulling her from the bed, I carry her to the bathroom and she watches as I turn the shower on. I pull her with me under the warm spray and we wash quickly. After I've wrapped her in a towel, she follows me out to the bedroom. I get dressed while she brushes out her wet hair and braids it back into two fancy braids, then I watch as she opens the closet and decides on an outfit.

The towel is wrapped tightly round her while she lifts

clothes from hangers and pulls underwear from the drawers. I half expect her to run into the bathroom to get changed, but instead she drops the towel and I get a fucking perfect view of her naked ass. She slides on another one of the silky G-strings and I groan and fight the urge to go bite her round, smooth ass cheeks.

A tiny white summer dress with black dots on falls down her back, obscuring my view of her ass, then she bends over to pull on black boots. Straightening, she slides her arms into a fitted black leather jacket and then spins to face me. Her nipples are pushing against the fabric of the dress and I hiss under my breath.

"Baby, you need to put a fucking bra on, your nipples are showing."

"I can't. I only brought one bra with me and it broke the day before yesterday. Grits only brought me these stringy panties that are sticking up my butt," she says self-consciously looking down at her chest.

I step closer to her and run my hands underneath her dress until I'm cupping her ass. "I fucking love these panties. I'll take you to go get some bras tomorrow or you can go with Grits if you'd rather not get fucked in a changing room."

"What?" she gasps.

I chuckle. "Angel, if I have to watch you try on underwear, I'm gonna end up fucking you. I just saw you pull on a pair of panties and I'm ready to bend you over the bed and take you right now."

Her eyes widen in shock, but it quickly turns to lust. She likes the idea of me fucking her like that and so do I. God the image of her ass in the air while I fuck her from behind, has my cock pushing against my jeans and my hands itching to push her down and flip up that tiny dress of hers.

"Later," I say, taking her hand and pulling her toward the door before I change my mind.

Walking over to the breakfast spread I make us a plate to share, then with the plate in one hand and Angel's hand held tightly in the other, I lead us the short distance to Anders office. Angel knocks on the door and Anders shouts for us to enter. Releasing her hand, I hold the door open for her. She brushes against my body as she passes me, and I take the chance to glance at her ass in that dress again.

We both slide into the seats in front of Prez's desk that are starting to feel like *our* seats and I hand Angel the plate. "Eat," I say tipping my chin at the muffins and biscuits.

Blade sits to our left and I nod at him in greeting "Brother," then I turn to Anders, "Prez."

He nods at me and then his gaze moves to Angel. His expression instantly gentles, and he smiles at her. "Good morning, my Little Dove, how you doing?"

Angel smiles brightly. "Good morning, Anders. I'm good thank you. How are you?"

"Well, I'm fine, thank you, sweetheart," Anders coos at her.

I watch the interaction between my club president and my girl and I fight back the smile that threatens to overtake my face. Anders is a scary fucking bastard. He's hard and uncompromising and before Angel came into my life I'm not ashamed to admit that I had a healthy fear of him. But seeing him melt at my sweet girl's words and smiles has kind of ruined his hard ass persona.

"Good morning, Blade," Angel turns to Blade and smiles at him.

"Morning, Dove. Life as an old lady seems to be suiting you. You look beautiful today, honey," Blade says, his eyes taking in her tiny white dress and bare legs.

I growl in warning and Blade laughs. "I'm just paying the lady a compliment, brother," he says, his voice laced with amusement.

Prez settles himself behind his desk and we all fall silent, waiting for him to break whatever news he called us in here to tell us. "We've had word from Carduccio's people that Dove is no longer an 'asset' that they're interested in."

Dove's sigh of relief is audible, and I reach over and squeeze her knee reassuringly.

Prez continues speaking. "Dove's daddy's debt is due today in cold hard cash, so by this time tomorrow this should all be over. Unless Mayor Jefferies chooses not to pay up, but either way Carduccio has no further interest in Dove. As far as they're concerned Dove belongs to the Sinners and any value she might have had previously is no longer valid."

"What will happen if my father doesn't pay?" Angel asks.

Blade speaks up and we all turn to look at him. "Carduccio normally sends his goons in to collect. But a hundred grand isn't chump change. My guess would be that Carduccio will take the house."

"Our house?" Angel cries.

Blade shrugs. "Does your father have anything else that's worth a hundred K?"

"I don't know. I don't think so," she says, her hands twisted together in her lap.

"We can't, and we won't step in to help him, little one," Anders tells her, his voice soft but unyielding.

Angel sits straighter in her chair. "I know. I would never expect you to. He's not worthy of anyone's help. But my mama, well she doesn't deserve any of this."

"I'm sorry, sweetheart," Anders says, his face solemn.

She nods, pulls in a deep breath and then smiles. "Don't be sorry. Maybe if my father loses the house, my mama will come to her senses and leave him. That's all I want for her. To realize that she doesn't need to stay with him."

Reaching over, I take her hand in mine and pull it to my lips. As much as I want to there's nothing I can say to make her feel better. I can't force her mom to leave her asshole of a father and I don't want to give her false hope by talking about it.

The room falls silent and I wait for Prez to tell us we can go.

Instead he smiles at Angel. "Dove, sweetheart, why don't you go find Grits? She's clambering at the bit to see you. Take your breakfast with you and go finish it, you're too skinny."

She nods and stands. I jump from my chair and drop a quick kiss on her lips. Handing her the plate I pull open the door to the office and say quietly. "I'll come find you, okay?"

I watch her sashay into the bar and keep my eyes on her until I see Grits pulling her into a hug. Closing the door, I turn back around and steel myself for whatever Prez didn't want to say in front of Angel.

"What's going on?" I ask, settling myself back into my chair.

"Nothing yet. I had Puck take a look at Jefferies finances and like Dove said he's cash poor. He's been living it up, trying to play with the big boys and get himself elected as Governor, but he ran out of money and that's how he ended up getting mixed up with Carduccio. The house is mortgaged up to the hilt, and he's got no assets to sell or barter with," Prez says.

"So, is Angel still on the table? I thought you said Carduccio had lost interest," I ask.

"According to our sources, Carduccio has no interest in Dove. But that doesn't mean that her father hasn't been throwing around her photo to anyone who might have an interest in the girl trade."

My breathing starts to labor. Anger builds in my chest and my fingers clench into fists. "That fucking bastard has a death wish. What the hell is wrong with him? She's his daughter, his kin."

"Calm down," Anders orders. "No one's interested in a teenager whose face has been splashed over every TV network in the state. He's fucked, and he knows it, but that makes him stupid and reckless."

"This idiot is starting to piss me off. Dove's a sweet girl, although I don't know how the fuck she's ended up that way with that asshat for a father. We need to get rid of him," Blade says, his voice low and menacing.

I swing my head to Blade and smile. Since Angel turned up he's been surprisingly quiet and I was starting to think he was pissed that her arrival had dragged us into her dad's mess.

Anders glares at Blade. "We're not murderers. That might have been the way they handled things back in the desert, but we don't run things like that here."

"I can make an exception. I'll even throw my Nevada cut on that day if that'll put your mind at ease, Prez," Blade says condescendingly.

"You came here to get away from all that," Prez snaps.

Blade sits up straighter in his seat. "Yeah, well that was until an eighteen-year-old girl ended up on our doorstep covered in bruises and running from her daddy. Some people don't deserve to walk God's good earth and men who try to sell their daughters are at the top of that list."

Prez sighs, drops his head and rubs at the skin between his

eyebrows. "I know."

My head flits between the prez and vice prez like I'm watching a tennis match. They're talking about killing Angel's dad. I'll admit I've wished him dead a few times in the last four days, but to actually do it, to take a life, that's some serious shit. The Sinners aren't walking the straight and narrow in terms of the law but growing weed and a bit of distribution is a hell of a long way from cold-blooded murder.

At this moment I feel like a fish out of water. I already knew that other Sinners chapters were into heavier shit than we are. Hell, Prez only told me a few days ago about the whorehouses his old chapter ran, but Blade, my V.P., talking about coming out of retirement to kill Jefferies is still a fucking shocker.

I don't want to look like a fucking pansy, so I keep my mouth shut and watch as Anders and Blade work through their silent standoff.

"It'll be a last resort," Anders finally says.

Blade nods. "Fair enough."

My breathing gets shallow and my heart races. I wait for the punchline, for them to tell me they're joking. but they don't. Instead an intensity descends over the room as they lock eyes and nod.

"What the fuck is going on?" I rasp out. "Did you just agree to kill him?"

Blade turns hard eyes on me. "She's your woman, Daisy. Do you want to spend the next however many years thinking that he's trying to pimp her out to cover his debts? Do you want to always wonder if he's planning to try to take her back? He sees her as property, and when she ran she cost him a hundred grand. Men like that don't move on from that shit. Is it fair to her to be cooped up in the compound because she'll never be one hundred percent safe? She's eighteen and she's been a virtual prisoner for the last five years. She's already coming out of her shell; she's smiling and speaking and yeah she still flinches, but that haunted, dead look is starting to fade from her eyes. Are you prepared to lock her up until he dies of old age just to keep her safe?"

Staring at him, I let his words sink in. I don't want her to live like that, she deserves to be happy. "No," I say firmly.

Blade looks proudly at me. "Exactly. I did this kind of shit for years. I walked away from that life because my soul had gotten so black I couldn't do it anymore. But Dove is a bright light and I'll happily do this for her, for you."

I hold out my hand and Blade takes it. We shake and in that moment, I know I'll owe him a debt for the rest of my life. "Thank you," I say, my voice thick.

"You got yourself a good woman, brother," Blade offers quietly.

"This is a last resort," Prez says loudly, and we all nod, silently wondering what else could happen to resolve this peacefully.

After the revelations and agreements are done with, I make

my way back to Angel and lose myself in her soft curves and her tight pussy. We don't talk about her father. I think we've somehow come to a silent agreement that here in our bubble he doesn't exist, so we don't acknowledge him.

That night we venture into the bar and sit with my brothers, drinking and chatting like we're a normal couple and this is a normal night. We crawl into bed well after midnight and I pull her into my arms, holding her body close against mine. "I love you, baby," I whisper into her neck.

THIRTY-TWO

Angel

Three days pass and my father doesn't come to the clubhouse again. Daisy and I exist in our little bubble, pretending the threat has gone and I'm safe now. Only neither of us truly believes that I am.

I'm starting to feel like I exchanged one prison for another. It's been eight days since I fled from my parents' home and ended up here at the Doomsday Sinners clubhouse. In eight days I've only been outside once, on the day my father came to try to retrieve me.

I'm not unhappy, quite the contrary. I love Daisy and I love being with him, but I want to be free to come and go as I please. I watch with envy as Grits and Daisy leave the compound while I stay here, hiding, protected in a gilded cage.

I hear the shower switch off and sit up in bed holding the sheet around my chest to cover my naked breasts. Daisy emerges from the bathroom with a towel hanging low around his hips, his skin flushed and glistening with water. Gulping, my eyes roam his body and even though we only had sex a few hours ago I start to feel the stirrings of want again.

Daisy's eyes land on me and instantly darken with lust. He pauses at the end of the bed and heatedly looks me over. Only his eyes are taking me in, but I feel caressed and my skin tingles. His knee hits the bed and I know unless I say something I'll be beneath him and coming in a couple of minutes. "I want to go out today," I blurt.

He stills, then pushes back upright until he's standing by the side of the mattress. "What?"

"I want to go out. It's been eight days, Daisy. I can't stay hidden in here forever."

Shaking his head, he starts to speak, but I interrupt him. "I just want to go out with Grits for lunch, just for an hour, and then we'll come straight back."

"We don't know if your dad paid Carduccio, baby. It's not safe."

"I don't want to live like a prisoner," I say, my tone pleading.

He flinches, and I instantly wish I could take the words back. Rolling onto my knees I take the sheet with me, wrapping it around me until I'm knelt on the bed in front of him. "I love you," I say. "You make me the happiest I've ever been, but

I don't want to hide anymore. I want to start living this new, wonderful life you've given me and the first step to doing that is leaving the compound."

I watch Daisy consider my words. "I just want you to be safe. We don't know what your asshole of a dad is planning; he isn't gonna just accept you being here and move on. I'd lose my mind if anything happened to you, baby."

Shuffling forward to the edge of the bed I reach out and grab his wrist, pulling him closer to me. "Nothing's going to happen to me. Someone can drop us off and pick us up if that will set your mind at ease. I just need to get out and start living again."

Daisy's hands reach out to cup my face. "I'll take you. We can have a nice lunch and then you can see Grits later."

Smiling, I roll my eyes at him. "I haven't had a friend in a really long time, Daisy. I've never been invited out on a lunch date with a girlfriend ever. I would love for you to take me on a date, but not today, okay? You need to work, and I want to act like a normal person, at least for an hour or so."

His arms wrap around me and he pulls me into his chest, his lips dipping to reach mine. Kissing me thoroughly he pulls back. "Okay. You take a cell phone with you. One of the guys drops you off at the restaurant and picks you up an hour later. Neither you nor Grits leaves the building until someone comes to get you. No risks. You get your girl time and I get to keep my damn mind."

Dropping the sheet, I jump into his arms. "I love you."

"I love you too, baby," he whispers.

Three hours later, Grits and I are seated at a beautiful table on the patio of Portofino's, a gorgeous Italian restaurant that has a pretty outdoor seating area filled with scented flowers. Slow, the creepy guy who manhandled me when I first arrived at the Sinners and now the only remaining prospect since Daisy was made a full member, drove us into town with strict instructions from both Daisy and Anders to collect us in exactly one hour's time.

Both men had looked nervous when Grits and I had waved them goodbye. Anders had pulled me in for a gentle hug and kissed me on the top of my head, before he passed me over to Daisy who handed me a brand new iPhone and kissed me senseless. A little dazed, Daisy had whispered in my ear. "Don't go out, baby. I want to lick that pretty of pussy of yours until you're shaking and screaming my name. I want you so bad, I want to feed my cock to your greedy cunt. I know you love it when I fill you up and fuck you nice and slow. Then I'll put you on your stomach and fuck you hard from behind until you've come so many times you won't ever want to leave our bed."

His words had made me tremble, my nipples had hardened, and I'd been on the verge of letting him take my hand and guide me back to bed. Grits' hand on my arm had shook me from my lust filled haze. "You ready, baby girl?"

Now sitting with her on the patio, drinking a cocktail Grits had ordered for me, I'm glad I hadn't let Daisy persuade me to stay at the compound. The warm sun is beating down from overhead and even though the patio is quiet, a couple of patrons are seated on the opposite corner quietly eating.

"Cheers," Grits says, holding up her glass for me to clink mine against.

"Cheers," I say and take a quick sip of the drink. "Ummm, what is this?" I ask.

"It's a Strawberry Daiquiri. Do you like it? I can order you something else…"

"It's delicious," I say taking another long sip.

Grits laughs. "So how did you convince that man of yours to let you out?"

"It was time. I can't keep hiding in his room forever."

Nodding, she sets down her drink and picks up the menu. "The food here is amazing, but I can never choose what to have. They do a taster platter with little plates of a selection of dishes, do you feel like sharing that?"

I glance at the huge menu and quickly agree. "Yes, that sounds great. My mama makes great pasta, but I've never even heard of most of the stuff on this menu."

The waiter appears, and we give him our order and ask for another round of drinks. "Grits, you do know I'm not actually old enough to drink alcohol, right?"

She laughs. "I know, honey, but we're celebrating."

"Oh, okay. What exactly are we celebrating?"

"Our first girls lunch, your first time out of the compound, your daddy slinking away and leaving you alone. Lots of things, Dove, and the best way to celebrate is with a cocktail," she says raising her glass to me again.

I think about her words for a minute and she's right, I do have a lot to celebrate. "This is a pretty special occasion isn't it?"

We clink glasses again just as the waiter arrives with our drinks and the food quickly follows. Several small dishes are placed in front of us, all filled with different pastas. A bowl full of olives and a plate of buttery garlic bread fills our table and I slowly start to spoon out a little of each onto my plate to try.

"So, you and Daisy…" Grits says a few minutes later.

"Huh?" I grunt, my mouth full of delicious creamy pasta.

"You all good? Have you talked about the future, how you're gonna work once you don't have to be on lockdown anymore?"

I finish chewing and place my fork onto my plate. "I love him, and he told me he loves me too. We've been so focused on all this stuff with my father that we haven't really gotten any further than that. I know I want to be with him. He makes me happy, happier than I ever thought I'd be and he makes me hope that I can move on with my life. I don't want to be scared anymore and Daisy makes me feel brave."

Leaning forward she places her hand over mine and squeezes. "You are brave, honey, and I'm real happy for you and Daisy. You're good for each other."

She squeezes my hand again, then releases me to pick up

her fork and carry on eating. We chat about this and that while we finish our lunch and then Grits insists that we need dessert when the waiter appears to clear our plates.

We laugh and joke, and I smile so much I know my cheeks will be hurting later on. Grits is so warm and caring and I'm thoroughly enjoying this time together. I order a rich crème brûlée for dessert and I'm scraping the last dregs from the dish when I hear her.

"Angelique."

I spin around to find my mama standing on the far side of the patio. "Mama?" I say, unsure that it's actually her. I rake my eyes over her and take in her disheveled appearance: her hair is pulled back into a messy bun, she's not wearing any makeup and the skin around her eyes is dark and haggard. She looks like she hasn't slept in days. Her plain cotton skirt and blouse are wrinkled and seem to be hanging off her petite frame. She looks awful.

Standing, I start to move toward her, but Grits' hand on my wrist stops me. "Dove, baby, I don't think you should go over there."

"It's my mama," I say my voice cracking.

"I know it is, honey, but you need to be smart about this. Your dad could be here too."

I shake my head. "No, my mama helped me get away from him, she knew what he'd planned, and she helped me escape. She wouldn't hurt me, she's my mama."

Grits nods briefly and releases me. She doesn't look happy when I start to move away from our table and towards where Mama is standing. "Mama, are you okay?" I say once I'm in front of her.

Close up she looks even worse. The dark circles around her eyes are actually the fading bruises of two black eyes. "Oh my God," I cry. "Oh, Mama, did he do that to you?"

She shakes her head. "No, sweetie. You know how clumsy I am. I took a fall down the stairs; it looks much worse than it is."

I flinch at the lie that falls from her lips. If I didn't know what an evil twisted person my father was, I might believe her story.

"Are you okay?" she asks.

"Yes, Mama, I'm fine. I'm more than okay, I'm real good and happy."

Her eyes scan my face and I smile, trying to reassure her that I'm safe and content. Her fingers twist together in the fabric of her skirt and I'm struck by how nervous she looks. "What's going on? Why are you here? How did you know where I was?"

She tries to smile but her lips barely move. "Could we, could we go somewhere and talk?"

Glancing over my shoulder, Grits is watching us intently, a phone held to her ear. "Why don't we sit at a table and I'll order us some drinks," I say pointing to a table a few feet from where we're standing.

"No," Mama snaps. "Not here. Can we go somewhere more

private?"

Shaking my head, I fidget with the soft leather of the property cut Daisy insisted I wear. "I can't, I'm sorry. Did my father tell you that I have a boyfriend now? His name's Daisy, and he's waiting on me. Why don't you come with me, you could meet him? You'd like him, Mama, he's real good to me. I'm happy. He's from a real big family, that's what the Sinners are, Mama, they're a family and they all look out for each other. You could come with me and they'd look after you too. They protect me. They protected me from my father when he came for me. Did you know he came? He brought Senator Carduccio with him and father planned to sell me to him. I know he's your husband and my father, but he's not a good person. Come with me, we can go right now, and we can both be safe."

Tears fill her eyes and she reaches out and grabs my wrist. "This was all a mistake, sweetie. I miss you. Your daddy's real sorry, and he wants you to come home; we both just really want you to come home where you belong."

Pulling at her, I try to free myself from her grip, but she holds me firmly. "Mama, let me go." I say.

The restaurant's patio overlooks a dirt road that all of the store owners use to access the backs of their properties. A low ornate metal fence and an archway covered in trailing vines and flowers divides the patio from the road. I hear the vehicle before I see it. Mama's grip on my arm tightens as she walks backwards, pulling me along with her.

My father's fancy SUV screeches to a halt right outside the exit to the patio and he throws open the door and runs in my direction. "Grits," I cry, thrashing my arm around frantically, trying to release myself from my mama's grip.

"Get her over here now," my father shouts and Mama drags me toward him.

"Mama, what are you doing? Let go of me. I'm not going with him," I shout.

"Shut up, you little cunt," my father screams, only a step away from me now.

Fear flows through me and I see my life flash before my eyes. If I let him get close to me I'll never see Daisy again and my father will kill me or sell me to someone. Doubling my efforts, I rip my arm from my mama's grip and stumble backwards. "Why are you doing this?" I shout.

"He's your father and my husband. We need to do as we're told," she answers.

Right here in this moment, I realize that Mama's so far gone I can't save her anymore.

"Dove, get over here behind me," Grits shouts, her heels clacking on the tiles as she rushes toward me. I turn, ready to run, just as my father grabs for me wrapping one arm around my chest and the other across my mouth.

Grits is standing a foot away from us, her legs spread wide and her arms held out in front of her. The gun in her hands is pointed directly at my father's head and the gleam in her angry eyes tells me, she'd be more than happy to shoot him. "I suggest you let her go right now," Grits snarls.

"I'm the mayor, you won't shoot me. This is my daughter, my property. She's coming with me and there's nothing you can do about it," he screams.

"Think again, jackass, there's a whole lot of pissed off bikers heading this way right now. I reckon they'll be here in a minute or so, and they won't take kindly to you manhandling Daisy's old lady."

Captive in his arms, I'm frozen with terror. Grits is in front of me, fearless and fighting and I'm just motionless allowing this to happen to me. NO, I won't let this happen. He's not taking me. I won't be his victim anymore. I'm not alone, I have a new family who will do whatever they can to keep me safe. I have a wonderful friend who even now is facing down my father with a gun in her hands.

Allowing all the anger, hurt, and fear to bubble to the surface, I buck and thrash against his grip. I scratch at his skin and try to kick at his legs. Twisting in his arms I turn so my chest is against his and forcing my hands between us I try to pry my way out of his grip. His hold loosens, and I kick at his leg, but he raises his fist and punches me in the face. I stumble back but he fists my shirt and pulls me back to him. His hands wrap around my throat and tighten in a choke hold. Gasping for air, I claw at his arms. I can hear my mama's anguished cries as she pulls at his shoulders, frantically trying to get him to release me.

The sound of the gunshot cracks around us and my father's hands fall from my neck. Gulping air, I scramble backwards away from him, jumping when a hand touches my shoulder and Grits pulls me next to her, the gun still pointed at my father.

The howl of pain that escapes him is one of the most gratifying sounds I've ever heard as he clutches at his arm, blood pooling around the bullet wound. Grits helps me to my feet, dizziness whooshes through me and I tighten my grip on her arm. Breathing in and out through my nose I lift my hand to my neck and gently touch the tender skin. I stare at my parents and an overwhelming sense of fury consumes me. "What the hell is wrong with you?" I shout at them. "You're my parents, you're supposed to love me and protect me. Mama, why did you do this? Do you know what he wants to do to me? He wants to sell me to the highest bidder. He doesn't care what happens to me, or what they do to me, he just wants the money they might give him for me."

My father steps forward.

"I suggest you stay right there, Mr. Mayor. I'm a fucking good shot and I'd like nothing more right now than to put a bullet hole right between your eyes." Grits growls in warning.

"Mama," I shout, needing her to answer me. "Do you know what he plans to do with me, if I get in that car with you?"

Her eyes fall to the ground. "They'll kill him if he doesn't get them the money."

Her words make me stumble backwards. "So you're

prepared to sacrifice me, to save him?"

"They'll kill him," Mama says again.

A single tear falls from my eyes, right before I close them. I can't look at her.

"Back the fuck up," Grits shouts as my father tries to take another step closer. "How did you know where we were?"

Opening my eyes, I glance around the patio expecting to see staff or the other patrons, but we're completely alone. I'm thankful that there's no one here to witness the abomination that are my parents, but there's also no one here to help.

Another gunshot cracks out and I jump, swinging my eyes to where Grits just fired a warning shot at my father's feet. "Let's try this again, shall we? How did you know where we were?" she demands, her gun pointed back at my father's head.

"One of your disgusting bikers told me. He asked me how much a chance to get Angelique alone was worth," he sneers.

"Who was it?" Grits asks.

"I don't know. They're all trash and look the same to me," he says with a smirk.

"Try again, asshat, or I'll remove one of your balls and shove it down your throat," Grits says with a smile, as she moves the gun to aim between my father's legs.

"Slow. He told me his name was Slow," he blurts out, turning to the side, his hands dropping to his groin.

"Stupid, little rat," Grits seethes.

A roar of motorcycle engines fills the air. They're here.

Moments later the door from the restaurant to the patio bursts open, the glass smashing loudly as it crashes against the wall of the building. I spin around to see Daisy, Anders, Blade, Echo, and Smoke, stomp onto the patio. Daisy's eyes frantically scan until he sees me. A pained cry of relief escapes me, and I rush across the tiles and throw myself into his arms.

Mama's scream pierces the air as my father drags her across the patio. Blade pulls out a gun and shoots at my father while Daisy and Echo run to the SUV. The bullet misses by an inch, hitting the car door just as my father pulls it closed. Mama climbs into the rear seat and her eyes find mine just as she pulls the door shut. Daisy's hand grips the door handle, trying to yank it open as the tires spin and the car careens away.

"Echo, Smoke, go." Anders barks and the two men rush from the restaurant, their bikes roaring to life a moment later.

"Fuck," Daisy roars.

Grits hand lands on my shoulder and I jump. "I should have shot him in the leg," she snaps.

I laugh "I wish you had."

Daisy pulls me into his arms and I melt into his safe embrace.

"It was Slow," Grits says.

Anders' head turns slowly between me and Grits. "What?"

"Jefferies said that Slow had contacted him and asked how much a chance to pick Dove up was worth. That's why they knew where we were. Dove's mom came straight up to the patio and tried to get Dove to go with her," Grits explains.

Daisy's hands run across my shoulders and down my arms, his eyes rake over me. His thumb runs over my cheek and around my neck. "I'm fine," I assure him. "Grits shot him, and I had a chance to get away."

Daisy growls. "He hit you. I can see the finger marks on your neck, Angel. He tried to fucking kill you."

He looks up and something passes between him, Anders, and Blade. It's like they silently discuss and agree on something. "Come on, let's get you back to the compound. We need to see if Echo and Smoke caught up with your dad, and then I need to hunt down Slow and kick his ass," Daisy says, his arm wrapped around me as he leads me from the patio.

"Slow's the club's problem now, Daisy. We don't accept betrayal. You'll get your chance, but the club needs to deal with this," Ander's says, his tone lethal.

THIRTY-THREE

Daisy

My heart doesn't settle until Angel is wrapped around me on the back of my bike. I almost lost her again today; her asshole of a father tried to take her and he almost succeeded. Fucking Slow deserves to die; he betrayed us, he betrayed the club. His dad is a Sinner, so Slow must know what this will mean for him. I don't understand why he'd do this, but whatever his reasoning, he's out and he'll never be forgiven. Things would have been worse for him if he'd been a fully patched-in member, but even as a prospect he's gonna be eating through a straw for a long ass time.

Once we reach the clubhouse, Angel and Grits head to our room and Anders, Blade, and I, silently make our way to Prez's office.

Anders cell buzzes and he listens for a minute then shoves it back into his pocket. "Echo and Smoke lost him. They circled the town, but Jefferies has gone to ground. My guess is he's either stupid enough to go home, or he's running."

Reaching the office, we settle into our seats but remain silent. We know what we're here to discuss, but I don't think I can be the one to start the conversation.

Blade breaks the silence. "You want to be there when it happens?"

I stare at him, my mouth dropping open in shock. Do I? Do I want to watch the man who would have been my father-in-law die? I feel myself nodding without even being aware that my head's moving.

"Come on then, if Jefferies has any sense at all he'll be heading out of town. I don't want to waste time," Blade says, his face a mask of indifference.

He stands, and I follow him out of the office and across the compound to our bikes. My head buzzes and even though I know a hundred and one thoughts must be fighting to be heard, everything remains surprisingly quiet. The lack of remorse is disconcerting; shouldn't I be justifying our actions? Shouldn't I be trying to talk myself out of this?

Anders' hand rests on my shoulder. I know it's him without looking. "You don't have to go, son."

Looking over my shoulder, I lock eyes with him. "Yes. I do."

He nods. "I understand. I'd want to see too. To watch as the life drains from his eyes."

In this moment, I wonder if he was the one who killed the man that hurt Grits, and then I see it, the confirmation he did and that he doesn't regret it. I hadn't realized that I'd needed his approval, until I see that he doesn't judge me for wanting this to be over. If there was another way I'd take it, but this is the only way to make sure she's safe.

Anders' hand slides from my shoulder. I take the final step and climb onto my bike. Blade is stoic and silent. I don't know for sure, but he seems to be fighting his own demons. His bike roars to life and I turn the key so mine follows suit. My eyes lock with Anders' briefly before Blade pushes his bike forward and we fly out of the compound.

The hunt is on.

Side by side, we ride the few minutes journey to Angel's parents' home. It's been less than two weeks since I was dropping her off here and wondering how I was going to get to see her again. Only a few days before that, I didn't even know she existed. My gut twists at the thought that there was a time when I didn't know Angel. Now I know I wouldn't make it through even a single day without her. She's everything, she's my life. I love her.

The Jefferies' car is missing, and the house is empty when we get there. Blade grabs his cell from his pocket and quickly makes a call.

"Puck. Yeah, they're gone. Yeah, that's what I figure. Okay, we'll head out of town. If they're not too far ahead we might catch them up. Keep an eye on their cards; if they buy anything we can find them that way. Okay, yeah, thanks."

I watch Blade as he has a one-sided conversation and once he ends the call, he turns to me. "Puck's looking into their cards, see if they've been buying anything to skip town. There's only one main road out, so let's head that way and maybe we'll be lucky."

I nod and we push forward heading to the highway. Ten minutes later the wind is in my face and the familiar sense of freedom pulses through me. Following Blade, we weave in and out of the cars that are leaving Archer's Creek, headed for Houston and the other towns and cities that lie beyond the small town we live in.

About twenty miles out of town, I spot a familiar looking silver SUV. Signaling to Blade, we speed up, moving through the stream of traffic. Edging closer we pause about five cars behind Jefferies obnoxious MayorAC registration plate.

The large, black SUV comes out of nowhere.

Swerving across the highway, the SUV darts into the stream of traffic directly ahead of Jefferies. The mayor's car lurches across the road, narrowly avoiding the black SUV, only for a second black SUV to cross onto the wrong side of the road again, heading directly for Jefferies vehicle.

Time slows, and we watch the accident almost in slow

motion. Jefferies tries to avoid the second vehicle. He skids to the left, then tries to correct the skid by turning to the right. His silver vehicle slides across the road, his tires hit the gravel at the roadside and the wheels lift. The SUV spins in the air, rolling over and hitting the scrub at the side of the road. Rotating again I hear the crunch of metal against gravel and wood as it travels down the slight incline, finally coming to a stop against a tree.

The black SUV's never pause, driving away as if nothing happened. Red taillights fill the road ahead of us and Blade signals for us to pull over to the side. Jumping off my bike, I rush to Angel's parents' SUV. The vehicle landed on its wheels, but one look into the front seats has me spinning around and gulping in deep lungfuls of air.

Blood. So much blood. Jefferies and his wife are in the front seats, along with the remains of the tree that killed them both. Angel's mom's eyes are wide, her mouth still open, silently screaming in death. Jefferies' head has fallen to the side, the angle unnatural. His eyes are open and full of surprise, like even in death he was shocked to have been beaten.

Blade wraps his hand around the back of my neck, pulling me away from the car and the bodies of Angel's parents. "Must have been Carduccio," he says.

"What?"

"Carduccio. Two black SUV's, tinted windows and no plates. This was a message that ended as an execution," Blade says, his eyes lifeless.

I nod, because he's right. This was a warning that went wrong. Carduccio isn't the type of man you don't pay, and Jefferies found that out the hard way. The police and EMT's arrive quickly. They take statements and tape off the scene so that the bodies can be removed. Blade and I watch until Angel's parents are placed in black body bags and taken away.

Eventually I follow Blade back to the compound. We'd planned to kill her father, but until I'm off my bike and walking toward the clubhouse I hadn't considered how I would tell Angel that he was dead.

Covering the distance from my bike to my room seems to take an eternity. Pushing open the door, my eyes land on Angel. She's curled on her side watching TV and she looks so young and innocent. I close the door behind me. She looks up from the bed and a glorious grin spreads across her face. She jumps up and rushes across the room , leaping into my arms. "Hey, I missed you."

Lowering my head, I kiss her, then hold her away from me.

"What's the matter?" she asks, her head tipped to the side in question.

The words stick in my throat. How do you tell someone that both of their parents are dead? Even though her parents were horrible excuses for human beings, they were still her parents.

I swallow. "Baby. I have to tell you something."

Her eyes go guarded and I want to tell her it's nothing, and that it's all going to be fine, but that would be a lie.

"There was an accident. It's your parents. They were in their car. They're dead, Angel; they're both dead. I'm so sorry, baby."

Her legs give way and she collapses to the floor. Her face goes blank, like she's not entirely sure how to react. When the sobs start, they consume her whole body. Sinking to the floor, I pull her into my arms, but she thrashes and pushes away from me.

"No, no, no." Her voice is hoarse and so filled with anguish that my heart actually hurts just at hearing the sound.

Scooting away from me, she buries her head into her knees and wails. The sound is inhuman, like an animal caught in a trap. I don't know what to do, or what to say, so I just sit next to her and watch the woman I love fall apart.

I don't know how I expected her to react. Did I think she would somehow be relieved that both of her parents were dead? Eventually her sobs quiet and she just rocks back and forth, lost to her grief. Pulling her into my arms, I try to comfort her, to offer her my love and support, but she pushes away from me and scrambles across the floor, climbing onto the bed and curling into a ball.

Crouching at the side of the bed, I watch as she stares unseeing into space, tears streaming down her face. "Talk to me, Angel. What can I do? I hate seeing you like this, just tell me what you need me to do."

"Nothing. You can't do anything for me. My parents are dead. I wanted him to die, I prayed for it, begged for it, again and again. Daisy, I did this. I asked God to take his life. I didn't understand how God could let him keep hurting me and my mom so I begged him to take him away. I'm a terrible person and because I wanted him to die, my mama was taken too. She suffered so much. He'd brainwashed her, but she was a good person deep down. She helped me escape and because of me, she's dead too. What kind of person wishes for another person to die? Their deaths are my penance for leaving. I could have saved them. If I had just stayed put and let him sell me, then they would both still be alive. I did this. I did this."

"No," I cry. Kneeling up I cradle her face in my hands. "No. You didn't do this. I wished for him to die too. I didn't cause their deaths, and neither did you. It's a tragedy, but it's not your fault."

Closing her eyes, she twists her head to the side and blocks me out. I let my hands fall from her face and sink back down to the floor next to the bed. I've never dealt with grief before, never mourned the loss of anyone, especially not the death of a parent. I don't know what to do, so I just sit next to her, silently offering her my love and support.

We stay like this, me on the floor, her curled into a ball on the bed, for the next two hours. She doesn't speak and neither do I, any words I could offer her seem inconsequential. A knock on the door finally breaks the solitude and rising from the floor I cross the room to open it. A grim looking Smoke is on the other side. He glances past me to look at Angel before his eyes return to mine. "Cops are here. They need Dove to formally identify the bodies."

I finch. "Someone else needs to do it. She's not in any fit state."

"I'm fine. I can do it," Angel says, her voice monotone and lifeless.

Spinning around, I look over my beautiful broken girl. Her face is puffy from all the tears she's cried. She looks so fucking young, and all I want to do is pull her into my arms and smother her with all the love I have. Instead, I move to the side as she pulls on her boots and walks past me, straight out of the door.

Smoke and I share a look as I close my bedroom door behind me and follow after my girl. She walks purposely to Prez's office and knocks, before opening the door and entering the room. I follow her, quietly closing the door behind me.

Grits, Prez, and two uniformed officers are in the office. Grits pulls Angel into her arms, but she doesn't react; instead she stands rigid and unyielding as her friend tries to offer her comfort and support.

The cops speak, but I can't focus on what they're saying. My eyes don't move from Angel. I watch her, waiting for the chink in her impenetrable armor to show, but she never falters. She's emotionless as the police inform her that her parents were both involved in a fatal car accident. She's detached as we climb into the police cruiser and head to the hospital. Her expression is impassive as the mortician draws back the curtain that reveals the bodies of both her parents.

She finally loses it when her eyes fall to her mother's lifeless body. She twists her face into my chest and a strangled cry escapes from her. I nod to the officers and the curtain is quickly drawn, hiding her parents from us once again.

Angel's limbs give way and I lift her into the air, carrying her from the room. She clings to me, hot tears running silently onto my shoulders. I hold her in my lap the whole drive back to the compound and then carry her back to our room where I hold her in my arms for the rest of the night. She alternates between inconsolable wails and silent, body wracking sobs. By the time the sun starts to filter through the blinds, we've barely slept at all.

I don't know what to do. I fetch us food, but she refuses to eat. She hasn't spoken in hours and her eyes are dead. I want to kiss her, hold her, and surround her with all my love. I want to tell her over and over that I love her and that she's not alone, but right now I'm not sure that's enough. Anything I can offer her seems insignificant in the face of her loss.

THIRTY-FOUR

Angel

My parents are dead.

Every bruise, cut, and injury, my father caused me seems to have reopened in the face of his death. The pain is overwhelming. When I close my eyes, I see all of the anger and hatred he had for me replay over and over in my mind.

I hated him and I'm glad he's dead—and that makes me a terrible person.

The feeling of grief engulfs me when I allow the reality of my parents' death to permeate my mind. The little girl inside of me is terrified at being all alone in the world, the sole surviving member of my family. But the downtrodden teenager who suffered at the hands of my father, who wasn't protected by my mother, keeps reminding me that they hurt me, that they betrayed me and deceived me.

My mama loved my father, that love was the reason she chose him over me. That love is what caused her to accept his abuse and defend him. My sister fell in love and that love caused her to leave me behind, that love meant she chose her freedom over her family. I don't blame her, but that love ultimately led to her death.

I love Daisy.

I don't want to die. I don't want Daisy to die, and so far, all love has brought me and the people around me, is pain and death.

I don't want to be alone. Daisy saved me, and I know I'll never love anyone the way that I love him, but I don't want to be the reason he's hurt. I don't want to be the reason he dies.

Thoughts swirl around inside my head, Daisy, my parents, my sister, all of them warring for the last word in the spiral of depression that seems to be consuming me.

I'm hungry, but when I try to eat my hands won't move. I'm tired, but when I close my eyes all I see are their cold, dead faces turned and staring at me. I want Daisy, but I don't want to hurt him more with my guilt and grief.

I find solace in the void within my mind. Retreating to the familiar peace, I let the silence overwhelm me and I block out everything else.

Someone organizes a funeral. I stand at the front of the church while Daisy guides me. I don't remember the service. I don't speak, I don't eat, I don't cry. All of my tears have dried up, all grief I felt for my father has gone. I'm glad he's dead. My heart aches for my mama, her love was ultimately the architect of her death. She would still be alive if she had found the strength to walk away from him, if she would have acknowledged that he was hurting her, that he was hurting all of us. But she couldn't.

Daisy told me that my parents' death wasn't an accident, that they think it was Carduccio's men who forced my parent's car off the road. It was meant to be a warning, a threat to force them to pay the money they owed, but in the end the money killed them.

Grief is a fickle beast. The only thing keeping me sane is Daisy. His constant and enduring love is the only thing keeping my head above water, the only reason I manage to drag myself out of my own head each day.

My hate for my father and his responsibility for my mama's death consumes me. I want to shout it from the rooftops, that he killed them. He killed my sister, he killed my mama and he was the only one that deserved to die.

Because of him I'm eighteen and alone, that shouldn't happen. My mama won't be there on my wedding day, she won't know my children, she won't get to see me happy and loved.

"I love you," Daisy whispers, as he pulls me into his arms.

He's told me dozens of times already today that he loves me, that we will get through this, that I'm not alone.

It takes seven days for him to permeate my depression, when

finally his words start to be louder than the pain and anguish in my mind.

I'm not alone.

Because I have a man whom I love, who loves me in return.

I have a family, who in the short time I've known them, have shown me more support and affection than my father did in my entire life.

I have friends. Grits has visited me every day. She's consoled me, brought me brochures for the community college, and talked at me when I couldn't fight my way to speak back. Anders and Blade have taken all of Daisy's shifts so he didn't have to leave my side. The Sinners have accepted me and taken me under their wing.

I wake up and it takes me a few minutes to remember that my father's gone. I feel grateful that he can't hurt me anymore, that I'm safe and free. But then I remember that she's gone too and that it's his fault.

I'm angry. I'm angry that my mama didn't leave him, that she didn't see how evil he was. I think she must have known deep down, but she was just so frightened of him. Her spirit was so beaten down that she lost her fight.

I miss my mama. I miss Nicole. I miss the history and despite my father there were good times and good memories.

But I'm not alone.

Even in the darkest depths of my grief, anger and loss I have Daisy, the light at the end of the tunnel. It might take some time, but he will help me pull all of my broken and shattered pieces back together again.

Two random meetings, nine emails, and four days, led me to the beautiful boy with the silly name. He brought me back to life and I'll never be alone again, because that beautiful man loves me and he taught me how to love him back.

THIRTY-FIVE

Daisy

I thought that seeing her bruised was the worst thing I'd ever see. I was wrong.

Watching Angel struggle with this loss is impossible. I don't know how to help her. I've never had parents to lose, I don't know what to do.

We planned a simple funeral and Angel went, but I don't think she really knew what was happening. For a few days she was so lost inside her own head, she just stared into space. I've never felt so helpless. Watching the woman you love retreat so far inside herself that she struggles to function is heartbreaking.

I tried to care for her myself. I thought that I could love her enough to keep her afloat, but after a few days Grits insisted we have a doctor see her. Doc said she was grieving so hard, her brain wasn't allowing her to focus on anything else and that she needed time, love, and patience.

So that's what I've given her. I tell her repeatedly that I love her and that she's not alone, that we'll get through this.

Grits visits with her every day and spends hours talking to her. Even when Angel didn't speak back, Grits talked enough for the both of them. From the moment she got here, Angel has impacted all of our lives. I fell in love with her, but she managed to charm Anders and Blade, two of the hardest men I've ever met. The entire club has rallied round us because Angel's a Sinner now and Sinners take care of their own.

Echo finally tracked down Slow two weeks after he betrayed us, selling Angel out to her dad for a pathetic thousand dollars. A thousand dollars to turn his back on his family and his legacy. The spineless bastard cried when his dad stripped him of his prospect cut in front of every member of the club. Then he sobbed as every man in turn stepped up to avenge the Sinner's. When it was my turn I poured every bit of anger into my fists and rained down blow after blow until he was nothing but a sniveling disgrace. The asshole will be okay once he gets out of the hospital, but he won't ever be welcomed into this town or this family again. Her voice pulls me from my thoughts.

"I love you," she says. The sound of her voice is so fucking sweet, especially when for a moment I wondered if I'd ever hear it again.

She crawls into my arms and I wrap myself around her.

She's even more tiny than before but she's slowly regaining her appetite and the light is gradually returning to her eyes.

"I hate him," she whispers. This isn't the first time she's said these words and I agree. I hate him too.

"I know, baby."

"He took them both away from me. Why was he so awful? He's part of me, his blood runs in my veins. I don't want to hurt you. I love you. I don't want you to die and the people I love all die."

"Shhhh," I soothe. "You loving me brought me back to life; you couldn't hurt me, you're everything." She quiets and slowly her breathing calms and she falls asleep.

Days pass and little by little she starts to come back to me. She talks about her mom and her sister, she tells me the good memories instead of the bad. She talks about her mom's cooking and her sister's passion for life and how she would sneak out by climbing through Angel's window.

We don't talk about her father. I hate the man and I'm fucking glad he's dead. I'm grateful but aggravated that I didn't get a chance to kill him myself. I would have, if it would have kept her safe, but I'm selfish enough to admit that I'm pleased the burden of his death isn't resting on my soul.

Angel and I talk about the future and she tells me that she wants to go to college and get a proper education. I grab the brochures Grits left and hand them to her. "So pick a course and do it," I tell her. I'm rewarded with the brightest smile I've seen since before her parent's death.

The next day I pull out my phone and show her the apartment I've found. "Move in with me properly, Angel. Wake up next to me every day and come home to me after college every night." She doesn't say anything for several long moments, then she throws herself into my arms and kisses me senseless.

It's been a month and my Angel is almost back to life. She speaks and eats. She smiles and laughs. The woman I love is so brave and so fucking strong and I tell her every day how fucking perfect she is and how fucking lucky I am to have her.

In return, she tells me how much she loves me and how I saved her. She's fucking clueless. I didn't save her, she saved herself, and together we make each other whole.

I'm the luckiest man alive.

Two random meetings, nine emails, and four days brought me my perfectly broken Angel and she changed everything.

EPILOGUE

Angel

It's been six weeks since my parents' death. I fell apart, but with the help of Daisy and my new family, I'm slowly putting myself back together. I won't ever be a normal, carefree teenager, but that's okay. The things I've been through all make me who I am.

"Come on, baby. As perfect as you are naked, you need to get some clothes on so we can go get the keys for the apartment. Tonight we can get naked and start christening every room, but right now we need to get going."

I laugh and walk over to the closet pulling out the tiny denim shorts and ripped Sinners vest I know he loves me to wear. He groans when I slide my feet into my peep-toe wedge sandals and pull my hair up into a messy bun on top of my head.

"Seriously, Angel, I know you have at least ten bras. Why

can't you wear one with that shirt?"

"Daisy, my breasts are tiny, I don't need to wear a bra," I say smiling at him. I walk toward the door and his arms wrap around my waist pulling me back into him.

His lips nuzzle into my neck before he bites me playfully. "I love your tits, baby, but they're mine and I don't want anyone else to see them. Where's your cut?"

Rolling my eyes, I spin in his arms until I'm facing him. "There's not a single person in this club that doesn't know I'm yours."

"I don't care. I like seeing my name on you, so go put your cut on."

I'm smiling as I slide on the soft leather cut. I know he loves seeing the 'Property of Daisy' patch embroidered across my chest and I love the way he looks at me when I'm wearing it.

We walk out of our room hand in hand. The bar is full and I smile to myself as we walk across the room, to the table full of our friends. Liv is sat in Echo's lap, his hand protectively placed over her stomach where their baby is growing. Blade is nursing a coffee and looking a little worse for wear. Anders and Grits are sitting close to each other, smiling and chatting. Smoke and a couple of the other guys are eating breakfast and laughing.

Daisy pulls out a chair for me and I slide down into it. He kisses me on the forehead and then goes to grab breakfast for us both.

He places a plate full of fruit and muffins in front of me and then sinks down into the chair next to me.

"Do you get the keys today?" Grits asks.

I nod. "Yes. I'm so excited."

"Does that mean we can go shopping for house stuff for you then?" she asks.

Daisy and Anders groan in unison. I laugh. "Yes, we have nothing, so I need to get the essentials at least."

Grits and I start to chat about where we can get a sofa from when Dino the new prospect comes running into the room. "Prez, err, Sir. Err, she barged her way in, and I don't know what to do."

Anders stands up and sighs. "Dino, what the hell are you talking about? Who barged in?"

Dino shuffles his feet nervously. "Err, I don't know who she is, she just, she insisted."

"What the hell? Who?" Anders shouts.

"Hey, you little wimp, get back here. Where is she?" a female voice screams.

We all fall silent and watch as the doors to the bar fly open. The bright sunlight plows into the room and a silhouetted figure appears.

"Where is she? Angelique. Angelique," she hollers loudly.

Slowly, I rise from my seat, my legs shaking. The figure moves further into the room, heels clacking loudly against the floor.

"Angelique. Angelique."

My mouth falls open and I stare at the woman that's just entered the room. At the bright red heels, dark skintight jeans, fitted shirt, colorful tattoos covering both arms, bright red lipstick, and equally bright red hair twisted into sleek pin-up victory rolls.

Her eyes reach mine and she gasps. "Angelique." The word falls from her lips and she freezes.

"Nicole!"

I feel Daisy step up behind me, his warm, reassuring and protective presence silently supporting me.

"Who the hell are you?" Anders asks the woman.

I don't wait for her to speak.

"This is Nicole. My sister," I say.

"You told us your sister was dead," Anders questions.

"I thought she was," I reply quietly. "Nicole?" I say again.

Nicole moves forward until she's in front of me. "Hey, Sissy," she whispers, a tear rolling down her cheek as she pulls me into her arms.

The End... for now.

ACKNOWLEDGEMENTS

Holy crap I wrote a second book!!

To my lovely friend and beta reader number one, Sarah. You have lived and breathed Daisy with me and I can't thank you enough for letting me talk through every scene that wasn't working and character I wasn't sure about. I'm fairly sure I've harassed you every day for the past six months and you haven't complained once. Even though you'd already read it, you still pre-ordered Daisy from iBooks the moment I told you the pre-order was live. I'm so grateful for all your support and I apologise in advance because the harassing will start all over again once I start writing book three.

To my husband, Martin. I think we were all a little shocked when Echo first released and did better than any of us expected. Thank you for assuming that this second book would be as good as Echo, if not better, and allowing me to write seven nights a week, and never moaning about it. I love you so much for supporting me while I'm living my dream.

Kelly, Joanne, Carrie and Stace – my book besties, my life is richer for having you guys in it and I just wanted to say thank you for all your unending support.

To my babies Sophie, Eddie, and Myles, I love that you tell people mommy is an author. I don't really feel like one yet, but you make me feel like a superstar when you tell people that your mommy writes books and that they should buy a copy.

Lastly to you the reader. Thank you so much for taking a chance on my stories. I hope you enjoyed Daisy and I promise there's more to come from the world of Archer's Creek.

To keep up to date on the next book in the series, pop over to Facebook and like my author page. https://www.facebook.com/GemmaWeirAuthor/

Echo (Archer's Creek #1) is available on Amazon, iBooks, Kobo & Nook

ABOUT THE AUTHOR

Gemma Weir is a half crazed stay at home mom to three kids, one man child and a hell hound. She has lived in the midlands, in the UK her whole life and has wanted to write a book since she was a child. Gemma has a ridiculously dirty mind and loves her book boyfriends to be big, tattooed alpha males. She's a reader first and foremost and she loves her romance to come with a happy ending and lots of sexy sex.

For updates on future releases check out my social media links.

ALSO BY GEMMA WEIR

The Archers Creek Series
Echo (Archer's Creek #1)

Daisy (Archer's Creek #2)

Blade (Archer's Creek #3)

Echo & Liv (Archer's Creek #3.5)

Park (Archer's Creek #4)

Smoke (Archer's Creek #5)

The Scions Series
Hidden (The Scions #1)

Found (The Scions #2)

Wings & Roots (The Scions #3)

The Kings & Queens of St Augustus Series
The Spare - Part One

(The Kings & Queens of St Augustus #1)

The Spare - Part Two

(The Kings & Queens of St Augustus #2)

The Heir - Part One

(The Kings & Queens of St Augustus #3)

The Heir - Part Two

(The Kings & Queens of St Augustus #4)

OTHER WORKS FROM HUDSON INDIE INK

Paranormal Romance/Urban Fantasy

Stephanie Hudson

Sloane Murphy

Xen Randell

Sci-Fi/Fantasy

Brandon Ellis

Devin Hanson

Crime/Action

Blake Hudson

Mike Gomes

Contemporary Romance

Eve L. Mitchell

Elodie Colt

Daisy

CPSIA information can be obtained
at www.ICGtesting.com
Printed in the USA
LVHW111952060422
715482LV00029B/88